Praise for Love and Other Unknown Variables

"A quirky and heartbreaking coming-of-age novel. Fans of The Fault In Our Stars *will fall in love with Charlie and Charlotte's story!"*

—International bestselling author Julie Cross

"It took me 1.00749 seconds to fall in love with this book. Love and Other Unknown Variables *shines with the light of a thousand stars, and Shannon Lee Alexander's smart and emotive storytelling creates a chemical reaction called: Love At First Sentence."*

—Regina at Mel, Erin, & Regina Read-A-Lot

"Heartbreaking and real, Love and Other Unknown Variables *will have readers experiencing the soaring heights of first-time love with whip-smart characters reminiscent of a John Green novel."*

—Swoony Boys Podcast

"Brilliantly poetic and touching, this book ripped the heart out of my chest, stomped on it, and then fluffed it back up and stuffed it back inside me. An utterly fantastic read!"

—A TiffyFit's Reading Corner

"(Humor + Snark) x (Love + Strength) / Tears = a book that I couldn't put down. Shannon Lee Alexander has written a story that will stay with me for a very long time."

—Flutters and Flails

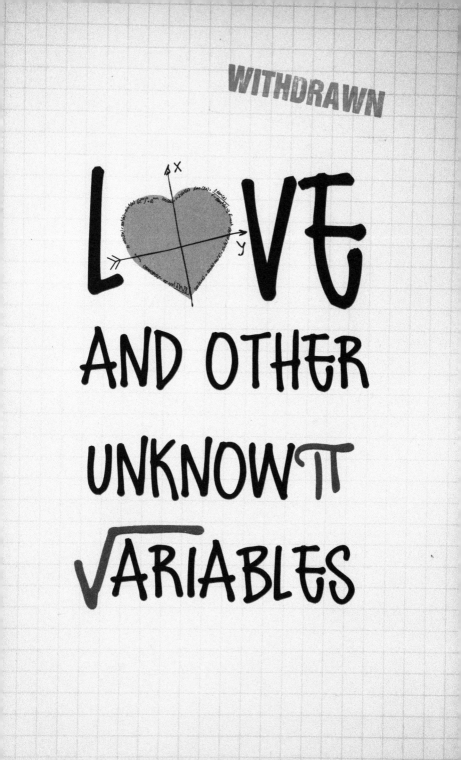

L♥VE AND OTHER UNKNOWπ √ARIABLES

SHANNON LEE ALEXANDER

Entangled Publishing, LLC
2614 South Timberline Road
Suite 109
Fort Collins, CO 80525

Visit our website at www.entangledpublishing.com.

Edited by Heather Howland and Kari Olson
Cover design by Kelley York
Interior design by Jeremy Howland

Print ISBN 978-1-62266-467-2
Ebook ISBN 978-1-62266-468-9

Manufactured in the United States of America

First Edition October 2014

10 9 8 7 6 5 4 3 2 1

for my Em

"How on earth are you ever going to explain in terms of chemistry and physics so important a biological phenomenon as first love?"

—Albert Einstein

1.0

Beginnings are tricky things. I've been staring at this blank page for forty-seven minutes. It is infinite with possibilities. Once I begin, they diminish.

Scientifically, I know beginnings don't exist. The world is made of energy, which is neither created nor destroyed. Everything she is was here before me. Everything she was will always remain. Her existence touches both my past and my future at one point—infinity.

Lifelines aren't lines at all. They're more like circles.

It's safe to start anywhere and the story will curve its way back to the starting point. Eventually.

In other words, it doesn't matter where I begin. It doesn't change the end.

1.1

*G*eeks are popular these days. At least, popular culture says geeks are popular. If nerds are hip, then it shouldn't be hard for me to meet a girl.

Results from my personal experimentation in this realm would suggest pop culture is stupid. Or it could be that my methodology is flawed. When an experiment's results are unexpected, the scientist must go back and look at the methods to determine the point at which an error occurred. I'm pretty sure I'm the error in each failed attempt at getting a girl's attention. Scientifically, I should have removed myself from the equation, but instead, I kept changing the girl.

Each experiment has led to similar conclusions.

1. **Subject**: Sara Lewis, fifth grade,

   Method: Hold her hand under the table during social studies,

   Result: Punched in the thigh.

2. **Subject**: Cara Whetherby, fifth grade, second semester,

   Method: Yawn and extend arm over her shoulder during Honor Roll Movie Night,

Result: Elbowed in the gut.

3. **Subject**: Maria Castillo, sixth grade,
   Method: Kiss her after exiting the bus,
   Result: Kneed in the balls.

After Maria, I decided my scientific genius was needed for other, better, experiments. Experiments that would write me a first-class ticket to MIT.

I'm tall and ropey with sandy blond hair so fine it's like dandelion fluff—the kind of dork that no amount of pop culture can help. Which is how I already know how this experiment will end, even as my hand reaches out to touch the girl standing in front of me at Krispy Kreme donuts.

There was a long line when I walked in this morning, so I'd been passing the time by counting the ceiling tiles (320) and figuring the ratio of large cups to small cups stacked next to the coffee (3:2). I'd been counting the donuts in the racks (>480) when I noticed the small tattoo on the neck of the girl in front of me.

It's a symbol—infinity. There's a cursive word included in the bottom of one of the loops, but I can't read it because one of the girl's short curls is in the way.

Before I realize what I'm doing, I sweep away the hair at the nape of her neck. She shudders and spins around so fast that my hand is still midair. Flames of embarrassment lick at my earlobes, and I wonder if I should be shielding my man parts from inevitable physical brutality.

"What's your problem?" Her hand cups her neck, covering the tattoo. Her pale skin flushes and her pupils are black holes in the middle of wild blue seas, but since I'm not coughing up my nuts, I'm already doing better with this girl than any before.

She's waiting for me to explain.

It takes too long to find words. She's too beautiful with that raven-hued hair and those eyes. "I wanted to see your tattoo."

"So, ask next time."

I nod. She turns back around.

The curl has shifted.

The word is "hope."

"**R**apido, Chuck. J's pissing his pants because we're going to be 'tardy,'" Greta says, using her shoulders to wedge the door open so she can make air quotes around James's favorite word. "God, it smells good in here."

Greta McCaulley has been my best friend since our freshman year at Brighton. On the first day of Algebra II, Mr. Toppler held a math contest, like a spelling bee only better. I came in second, one question behind Greta. Since then, her red hair, opinions, and chewed-up cuticles have been a daily part of my life. She has a way of ignoring the stuff about me that makes others want to punch me. And she's equal parts tenacity and loyalty—like a Labrador/honey badger mutt.

She'd also beat the crap out of me if she knew I'd just thought of her as a hybridized breed of animal.

Outside, her boyfriend James unfolds himself from the cramped backseat of my car, and rips open the heavy doors. "People of Krispy Kreme, I will not be made tar—" He takes a quick breath and loses his concentration. Krispy Kreme's sugary good smell remains invincible.

Greta stands beside me in line, while James drifts toward a little window to watch the donuts being born in the kitchen. Greta and James have been together since the second quarter of ninth grade. If I wanted to continue to hang out with Greta, her Great Dane of a boyfriend would have to become part of my small circle of friends.

Actually, it's not a circle. It's a triangle. I'd need more friends to have a circle.

The girl with the tattoo steps up and orders a glazed and a coffee. She's about our age, but I don't know her, which means she must go to my sister's high school, Sandstone. It's for the regular kids. I go to Brighton School of Math and Science. It's for the nerds.

Greta leans into my shoulder, and I know I'm not supposed to notice because a) we've been friends for a long time, b) James is four feet away, and c) I just fondled a stranger's neck, but Greta's left breast brushes against my arm.

"So what's with the girl?" she asks. "I saw her turn and—"

My ears feel warm. "Shhh."

Mercifully, Greta whispers, "I thought she was going to punch you."

"Me, too."

"What'd you do?"

"She has a tattoo," I say, shrugging.

"And?"

"And, I may have touched it."

Greta's mouth hangs open, a perfect donut.

"Fine. I touched it."

"Where?" Greta quickly turns and scans the girl. "Oh, thank God," she breathes, touching the correlating spot on her own bare neck. "I thought maybe it was a tramp stamp."

I must look blank because Greta points to her lower back, just below the waistline of her khaki uniform skirt.

"God, no," I say, too loudly. The girl with the hope tattoo glances over her shoulder. Greta and I both look at our shoes.

James steps in front of us, and for once I'm thankful that the width of 1 James = 2 Charlies + 1 Greta. His large frame blocks us from the girl's glare. James taps the face of his watch.

"I know," I say. "Look, both of you go back to the car. I'll be right there. We have plenty of time to make it before the first bell."

They turn to leave just as the girl is stepping away from the counter, coffee in one hand and donut in the other. I should let her walk away and be thankful she didn't punch me, but without thinking, I touch her arm as she goes by. I can feel the muscle of her bicep tighten under my fingertips.

I'm locked in place, like when an electric shock seizes all the muscles in your body so that the only thing that can save you—letting go of the electrical source—is the only thing you can't do.

"Yes?" she asks, her jaw looking as tight as her bicep feels.

"I wanted to apologize."

"Oh," she says. Her muscles relax. "Thanks."

She smells amazing. At least, I think it's her and not the warm donut in her hand. Either way, I have to force myself to focus on what I was about to say.

"So, I'm sorry." *Now, walk away. Go, Hanson.* "But I'm afraid you're mistaken about infinity. Infinity is quantifiable. *Hope* is immeasurable."

Her expression shifts, like Tony Stark slipping into his Iron Man mask. She shakes her arm free from my slack grip. "So if it can't be measured, I shouldn't count on it? That's bleak, man. Very bleak."

She turns and pushes through the door.

Subject: Girl with the hope tattoo, first day of senior year,

Method: Grope her neck. Follow with a lecture on topics in advanced mathematics,

Result: No physical harm, but left doubting whether I'll ever figure this relationship stuff out.

1.2

I pull into the school parking lot as James finishes the last of his donuts. He ate all six. He also ate one of mine. Greta hasn't touched hers yet. She'd been fixated on the scenery of the suburbs dying off and the city rising up, the same scenery we've seen every day for three years. The early morning sun winks through the haze of southern humidity clinging to the buildings like a wet blanket. I guess it is hard to believe this is our last first day of school at Brighton. Only 179 more morning drives like this one.

I spent the time wondering what someone would do with boundless hope. I mean, that's a lot of hope.

"What'd you think of that tattoo, Gret?"

Greta turns away from the window, one ginger brow arched. "I think it's none of our business."

"Yeah, but don't you think that's maybe an excessive amount of hope?"

"Depends what you're hoping for. Why do you care? And what was with that stellar display of social ineptitude back there?"

"I *don't* care." Except, why hope? And why can't I stop thinking about the way the soft skin of her neck felt under my fingertips? And why did she look so sad just before she stormed away? I need more data. "Let's just call it an experiment."

James laughs, leaning forward between the front seats. "Thought you'd agreed to let the big boys do that research," he says, flexing the thick muscles of his forearms.

Greta snorts, but I catch her watching the muscles dance.

"I'd offer to get y'all a room, but I wouldn't want James to be tardy." They both blush. "Oh, but look at that," I say, pulling into an open spot, "three whole minutes to spare. Maybe I should have stopped?"

And the punch I've been waiting for all morning finally lands on my shoulder, solid enough to rock me sideways a bit.

"Oh, shut up, idiot," Greta says, shaking out her fist, "or I'll destroy that proof you've been working on in seven seconds flat."

"You can't disprove shit," I say, but a sliver of doubt wedges in my mind.

That proof is my ticket to winning over Dr. Martin K. Bell, god of mathematics, who will take me under his wing at MIT next year and mentor me, until one day he'll proclaim, *There is nothing more for me to teach you. The student has outshone the teacher.* Shortly after, I'll receive the Nobel Prize.

I've got a lot riding on this proof.

"*I* only need six seconds," James counters, a wide, white smile lighting his dark brown face.

They bicker about who can dismantle three years of my work the fastest as we climb out of the car. Eager to change the subject, I point at Greta's uneaten donut.

"Ungrateful much, Gret? 'Take me to donuts,' you said. So I did." I fold my arms across my chest in mock protest.

James swoops in and tries to pluck it from her hands. "I'll eat it. I'm still hungry."

Greta's attention is diverted. "How can you be hungry, J? You've eaten more calories than a cheerleader eats in a week."

"What cheerleader?" James says, pretending to look around

for one. Brighton doesn't have cheerleaders. We'd need sports teams to justify them. Mathletes don't count, even if they think they do. "Show me the cheerleader?"

They're a teenage version of a middle-aged married couple. She shoulders her large bag, and sighs. "Why do I put up with him?"

I shrug. "Beats me, but someone may as well enjoy that donut. I almost got beaten up by a girl getting it for you."

"If it means that much to you…" She shoves the entire donut in her mouth at once, and smiles at me, her freckled cheeks full of donut.

"Did you see that?" James asks as she walks away, his voice soft, maybe even reverent. James thinks most everything Greta does is amazing—even the gross stuff—which gives me hope for a positive experiment result in the future.

Not infinitely hopeful, of course. That's just nonsense.

1.3

At lunch, we eat under an apple tree in the courtyard. There is a plaque dedicating the tree to a former principal with her favorite quote, "Millions saw the apple fall, but Newton asked why."

James leans against the plaque as he compares our schedules for this year. He and I had a class together this morning. I've got advanced physics with Greta after lunch, and we'll all meet up again at the end of the day for senior English.

"Wonder who the new target is this year," James muses, cramming his schedule card back in his pocket.

The target in question would be the English teacher. Brighton goes through English teachers like Hogwarts devours Defense Against the Dark Arts teachers.

"We can deduce it's a female," I point out, tapping the name on my schedule card. Ms. Finch—Senior English.

"Hope she's not like *Ms.* Kelly the fem-bot," James says with a shudder.

Greta is busy finding something in her bag. "Not this already," she says. Her face is mostly buried in there, but the part of it I can see looks annoyed. "Promise me you dorks will stay focused on what's important."

"I am always focused," I say.

Greta looks up. "True," she says, a flicker of her fierce protectiveness crossing her face. Two years ago, I took on too much—too many classes, mathletes team captain, a junior internship with the university physics department, and a shot at the national science fair. I failed an assignment in chemistry. I'd never failed before. My mind went a little berserk.

I only remember pieces (which Dr. McCaulley, Greta's psychologist mom, says is normal), but I was convinced I could work out the glitch in my chemistry experiment if I could give it one more try. Of course, in order to do that, I needed to break into Dr. Stormwhiler's lab. It was one a.m., and I may have triggered an alarm when picking the lock on the disused gym door.

Alone inside the school, I panicked and called Greta. Her mom called the police and met them here. Greta found me, catatonic by that time, in the storage room off one of the labs.

If Greta hadn't been there to pull me back from the edge, and tell me to stop being a whiny quitter, I'd have left school and given up on all my ambitions.

Turning her attention toward James, Greta says, "*You* promise to stay focused." She punctuates the sentence by poking him in the arm with a pencil she's just pulled from her bag.

"Hey, I'm focused."

Greta scoffs. James scowls at the apple he's about to bite into. "Whatever."

Satisfied, Greta starts scribbling computations in her notebook while James rubs a bruise on his apple and mumbles loud enough for me to hear, "I'm focused. Focused on carrying out a proud high school tradition."

Brighton is a STEM academy. The mission statement, emblazoned on another plaque by the front office, states our time here is meant to prepare us for futures in fields related to science, technology, engineering, and mathematics. Our motto (yep, another plaque) is *Aut viam inveniam aut faciam.* Meaning, "I'll either find a way or make one."

So, we've *found* a way to reduce the time we have to spend on things like poetry and literature by *making* the English teachers hate their jobs here. It's not hard either. It only takes a little shove to start a ball rolling before inertia takes over. The constant tide of teachers means that little learning goes on in the English classroom.

It's a simple equation. No teacher = no English. No English = more time for things that matter. Like math.

We take seats near the back of the English room. I study the bookshelves lining all four walls and crammed full of books. I don't recognize any of the titles, which isn't saying much. Above the bookshelves are paintings. Big ones of trees with people laughing as they hang in the branches. Small ones of books stacked neatly. Tall paintings with stacks of books in the act of tumbling over. Forty-two paintings. They are all different, but the same.

Forty-two paintings, but zero teachers.

At Brighton, class starts on time. In fact, the advanced physics teacher, Mrs. Bellinger, will write you up for tardiness for being on time. She says "on time" is late. James is in love with Mrs. Bellinger.

"This does not bode well," James says, preparing to launch into an assault on the English teacher's lack of respect for timeliness. Greta shushes him by pinching his arm.

And then, walking in, grimacing while wiping one hand on her skirt and carrying a spilling cup of coffee in the other hand, is this year's target, Ms. Finch. She's got long black hair and is wearing a knee-length black skirt and a white shirt open at the neck to reveal the creamy complexion of her throat. Let's just say she doesn't look like any of the other teachers here.

"Sorry for being tardy," the woman says. James chokes a little on his superiority.

Ms. Finch swears under her breath as the coffee sloshes from the overfilled cup onto the hand clutching it. She switches hands and wipes the other hand on her skirt. Looking up at the twenty-two sets of eyes staring at her, she blushes.

"I've been so…let's just say I haven't been sleeping well lately," she says raising the coffee cup and spilling more. "Guess I was a little overexcited when I refilled."

Déjà vu sweeps over me. Where have I seen her before?

No. Not her *exactly*.

The girl with the hope tattoo.

"Let's get started. Better late than never," she says. She pulls a stool over to her podium, picks up a small paperback novel and begins to read.

I can't tell you what she reads to us because I'm too busy finding all the similarities and differences between our new teacher and the girl in the donut shop. It becomes a puzzle, like the "Find the Difference" puzzles in *Highlights* when I was little.

They have the same eyes and jet-black hair. This one is taller and older, but not by much. I wonder if she has a tattoo, and what it might say.

When she finishes reading, Ms. Finch closes the book and looks out over us. "I'd like to begin," she says, "by letting you all in on a little secret."

Students shift closer in their seats.

"I know all about you." She pauses to let that sink in. "I know you think your precious math and sciences have all the answers and what I have to offer"—she waves the paperback in her hand—"is useless. But you're wrong."

There's a faint hiss in the room.

"There are some things in life that cannot be explained with logic. They cannot be understood through dissection. They are what they are—good, bad, or epically crappy. Sometimes they are all those things at once." She walks up the center aisle as she speaks. Like lambs to the slaughter, our eyes follow her.

"I know what you all do with English teachers here at Brighton. I know," she says, turning at the back of the classroom to be sure she has our attention. "And I say: Bring. It. On."

1.4

I toss my keys onto the counter as I walk into the kitchen. Someone is rummaging behind the refrigerator door for the good stuff Mom hides in the back.

I assume it's my younger sister, Becca. She's a sophomore at Sandstone, although how she got that far, I'm not sure. She's wicked smart, but getting good grades doesn't motivate her. Mom swears Becca has an eidetic memory. There's no conclusive evidence eidetic memory exists, according to scientific research, but Becca can recite almost word for word every book she's read since she was nine. And she has seven overflowing bookcases in her room alone.

"Dibs on the last Milky Way, Bec."

I hear a soft curse from inside the fridge. Becca doesn't curse.

"Possession *is* nine-tenths of the law." The girl with the tattoo closes the refrigerator door, then winces when she recognizes me, the doofus who manhandled her from the donut place.

"You?" I glance around. Yep. In my kitchen. Did she follow me? No. That's dumb. It was hours ago that we were at Krispy Kreme, even if it was only moments ago that I was thinking of her in English. I take in her simple purple T-shirt and the way her skinny jeans hug her calves. "What are you doing here?"

"Getting a snack," she says, her inflection sounds like she's choosing her tone with each word. She grins, deciding to play it cool. "Becca said I should help myself, and we don't have any good stuff at my house." She waves the candy bar like a magic wand.

"Becca Hanson?" Becca doesn't have friends. In fifteen years, she's had three. One moved away when she was eight. The other two were imaginary. I am calculating the statistical improbability of Becca choosing this girl—of all the girls in our town, this beautiful, tattooed girl—to be her friend when Becca comes flying down the stairs.

"Charlie! You're home." Her face floods with relief.

"You have to meet Charlotte. She's my partner for this project I have to do, even though I told Mr. Bunting I'm not good at group projects, because they include other people, and other people don't like me."

Becca twists her brown hair around her index finger as she carries on. "He didn't listen, and because she's new in school and doesn't know about the whole me and people thing, Charlotte said she'd *love* to work with me." Becca's voice wavers a little.

It's not that people dislike Becca. Rather, people make Becca anxious, and the anxiety makes her build these impregnable walls around herself. It also causes babbling spells that make mere mortals cringe. I haven't seen her this upset since the Harry Potter series came to an end.

She's still rambling. "She said I should call her Charley instead of Charlotte, and I said, 'No, because, my brother's name is Charlie and it would be weird.' And she said, 'Okay.' So, I'm just calling her Charlotte." Becca runs out of breath and stops.

I take a second to drink in this other Charley, from her glossy curls down to her once-white Converse sneakers, covered in Sharpie doodles of what appear to be feathers. That stupid déjà vu feeling steals over me again.

Charlotte interrupts my inspection of her. "I like the idea of a new town and a new me. Charlotte is perfect. Back home I didn't get a choice, you know? Charley is what my older sister calls me, so everyone followed suit."

Sister? It's the last piece of evidence I needed to prove my theory. Forty-two paintings. The English teacher. Matching sets of blue eyes. This isn't a doppelgänger coincidence. They must be related.

"You look like my English teacher."

Charlotte's smile tightens as she studies me. "You must go to Brighton, then. Impressive. And possibly useful." She tosses the candy bar from hand to hand and says, "I'm Charlotte Finch."

Our eyes meet and she fumbles the candy bar. When she bends to retrieve it, I catch a glimpse of the tattoo.

"Why useful?"

"*Possibly* useful." Her ink-stained fingers flit across the back of her neck. "Like you said, I can't count on things I can't *measure*." The acidic inflection she loads onto the statement makes me cringe.

"I just meant hope isn't part of any infinite set."

One of Charlotte's thin, dark eyebrows disappears under the fringe of hair on her forehead.

I sigh. "Most people don't understand infinity. It bugs me."

Charlotte nods. "Busybodies. That's my pet-peeve." She smiles. "Oh, and pets named Peeve."

Becca guffaws beside me. I'd forgotten about her. "This is my pet, Peeve," she mumbles to herself. I notice that her finger is so twisted in her hair that she has to yank to get it out. Before she can do any damage, I help her unwind it.

I can feel Charlotte watching me. It is both satisfying and horrifying.

Once Becca's free, Charlotte suggests they get back to work. Becca is just about to start with the hair thing again when Charlotte adds, "I'm in desperate need of something to read, and I couldn't help but notice you have some great books."

"Sure," Becca says, smiling. She doesn't smile much, so it's easy to forget, but when Becca smiles she looks like a whole new person.

Charlotte flicks the candy bar at me with the warning, "Think fast."

I grab for it, but the Milky Way smacks me in the center of the chest and falls to the floor. Charlotte laughs, and it sounds like fingers dancing up piano keys.

I know I should pick it up, but I'm frozen to my spot. When she laughed, something inside my chest shifted. I don't know what it means, but it feels like I've got more room inside myself.

It takes a few minutes after she leaves before I realize that she never told me how I might be useful to her.

1.5

I've spent today deflecting James's repeated pleas for me to join forces with him to start the war against the English teacher.

In computer programming, he gave a moving speech about brotherhood and camaraderie. He spoke of the oncoming tide of literature, and how we could stand by and be crushed by it or rise up and defeat it. He even tossed in a "Semper Fi."

At lunch, he tries to make me his superhero sidekick.

"You have to help me pull off at least a few stunts. What would Batman be without his Robin? Superman without Lois Lane?"

"I'm a Marvel fan, dumbass. And did you just call me a girl?"

He's quiet the rest of lunch until I cave and ask, "Why do you care?"

His eyes kind of light up like coals burning low. "It's a chance to leave a legacy."

"But I've already got a legacy. It's called being the valedictorian."

Greta scoffs. "You wish, Chuck. I'll be the one delivering that speech, thank you very much."

James sighs and traces the letters of the "why" on the apple tree plaque. He's not in the top ten of our class. He's number eleven, and not because he isn't brilliant, but because he has other priorities that Greta and I don't, like spending time with his sisters. I sometimes feel like I only think about my sister when she's right in front of me, but James is always thinking about his—whether they are safe, did they eat their lunches at school, what they got on spelling tests…

"Fine, then," James says. "It's not about the legacy. It's about us doing something together this last year before we all go to college."

Greta's smirk falls away.

James's father passed away six years ago when James was eleven. Greta has explained to me that James's frustration over people leaving him (both actual and hypothetical) can leak out in strange and surprising ways—like, if he could trap us all in a biodome to keep us together forever, he would. I guess this need of his for us to band together against the English teacher is another of those ways.

Greta squeezes his knee. "We've still got all year together."

"Yeah, man. A year is a long time," I say, trying to be encouraging. "Twelve months, fifty-two weeks, three hundred sixty-five days, eight thousand seven hundred sixty hours—"

James holds up a hand to stop me. "But this would be something that when we're old we could look back on and laugh about. Together."

Greta's eyes soften. "I'd make a pretty kickass Batwoman, don't you think?"

James's face brightens with the smile he gives her.

I snort, and Greta raises a brow at me, daring me, as always, to challenge her. I stuff my trash in my lunch sack and mutter, "I'm no Boy Wonder."

1.6

I take my seat beside Greta in English and glance at my phone: 2:59:21 p.m. I've got bigger worries than James now that I'm about to face Ms. Finch. I'm afraid of what Charlotte may have told her about me.

Hey, I met one of your students yesterday, sis.

Oh, which one?

Charlie Hanson molested my neck in the Krispy Kreme and then told me hope doesn't exist.

I don't want to give Ms. Finch the chance to engage in some parameter-setting discussion involving Charlotte. A discussion like, "Don't ever touch my little sister again."

That's why I timed my arrival for thirty-nine seconds before the bell.

I shouldn't have worried about a lecture though, because Ms. Finch isn't even here yet.

2:59:45 p.m. and James hasn't showed up, either. James is fifteen seconds from being tardy.

At 3:00:52 p.m., Greta looks at me like I've done something wrong. "Where is he?"

Just then, the English teacher walks in, cup of coffee in one hand and a paperback in the other. Technically, she's late, but not as late as James.

Ms. Finch takes in the room with one long, sweeping glance and instructs us to, "Shut your traps and listen up."

Greta looks stunned for a second before Ms. Finch smiles.

"It's what my dad used to say each night before he'd read a bedtime story to my sister and me." She opens the paperback as I try to ignore the unbidden vision of Charlotte in lingerie looming in my mind's eye. I calculate square roots to squelch the boner threatening to embarrass me in the middle of English class.

3:01:14 p.m. and still no James. This is remarkable. For a millisecond, I think maybe he's hurt. Maybe he went to the restroom between classes, slipped on someone's misdirected piss, and knocked himself unconscious on the lip of the urinal. It could happen.

3:03:32 p.m. He's three minutes and thirty-two seconds late. James is dead in a boys' restroom.

Greta grasps my arm and squeezes, hard. I look up from the phone and see James strolling into the classroom at 3:03:36 p.m.

He's smiling at us, but as he enters his face shifts, jutting out his chin and cocking one eyebrow into an impressively high arch. Greta groans. "Oh. Dear. Lord."

James's normal gait disappears, too. He is now walking like his left hip is dislocated and swinging his right arm at an awkward angle. He swaggers past Ms. Finch's podium and comes down the center aisle, nodding greetings at the gaping students all around him, even holding his hand up for Tobias Quartell to slap him five. I've never seen anything like it. Neither has Tobias, whose mouth is as wide as Jupiter's Great Red Spot.

I can't help noticing, too, that everyone's eyes travel back and forth like a tennis match from James's strange display to me. Like I'm somehow in control of him. Like if I think it's cool that he's acting like a wannabe thug from the suburbs, then we should all support him in his stupidity.

Throughout this bizarre scene, Ms. Finch doesn't stop reading. James makes a huge production of scraping the legs of his chair across the floor and dropping his textbook-laden bag on the desk with a thud. Still no response from Ms. Finch.

Defeated, James flops into his chair. Moments later, Ms. Finch finishes the passage she's reading. I glance at my phone. 3:05:06 p.m.

"Mr. Hanson?"

I freeze. Twenty-two sets of eyes burn into me.

"Please be sure your phone is on silent and put away. I believe that is the policy at Brighton?"

I look up in shock. *This* is the issue she's choosing to address? I catch Tobias's curious expression and think I've found an ally until he gives me a sly grin and a nod. What the hell?

I shove my phone in my bag and mumble a "yes, ma'am." Heat pulses through my ears like a heartbeat.

James drops his head into his hands like he's disappointed his stunt didn't get a reaction, but the rumbling chuckles that follow tell another story.

After class, I walk silently beside Greta as she shreds James for his "asinine, embarrassing, culturally deplorable display of stupidity."

"Maybe if some*one* had helped." James gives me a light shove, toppling me into a locker.

"Easy, man." I rub my elbow and jog to catch up, but Greta stops mid-step and I have to sidestep to avoid crashing into her, essentially throwing myself into another locker. James grins.

"I'm still not convinced this is the best way for us to spend our senior year, J," Greta says, ignoring me as I rub my elbow *and* shoulder. She places one of her small hands on James's enormous bicep and looks him in the eye. "There are plenty of other ways to spend quality time together."

I clear my throat. Without turning to look at me, Greta snaps, "Don't be a perv, Chuck."

I shake my head and stalk off. I don't need this aggravation. "What I can't figure is why his stunt got no reaction, but I get busted for checking the time." I glance at my phone, 4:01 p.m.

Greta and James catch up, flanking me. "She's showing us her A-game," Greta says. "Nothing's going to get past her. She may teach English, but she's no dummy."

I laugh, but the look on Greta's face tells me that wasn't a joke.

Tobias closes his locker and steps in front of us. "So this is on, right?" He looks from me to James. "Time for a little mayhem?"

Greta crosses her arms over her chest, and I instinctually lean away from her.

James is about to answer, when I hold up a hand. "I don't know what you're talking about, man."

Tobias studies my face, which I try to hold perfectly still, but he somehow manages to read something there that he likes. I see it the moment his brows jump up and his pupils dilate. "Got it," he says, nodding as he backs away, holding a finger up to his lips.

"Seriously," I call out, but the crowd has already swallowed him.

1.7

Dinner is at James's house. He informed us at lunch that he'd put a pot roast in the slow cooker this morning. Who does that?

Before I left for his place, I got a text from him asking if I'd pick up a fresh loaf of "nice, crusty bread—maybe sourdough?" I don't know what that means, so I'm wandering the bread aisle of the grocery store, reading the packaging. I'm about to give up and grab a package of hot dog buns when I glimpse a familiar head of black curls walking perpendicular to the aisle.

Is it the girl with the tattoo? My whole body feels jittery as I speed walk toward the end of the aisle and peek around the corner, just in time to see her turn down aisle twelve. It's her. It's Charlotte.

Now what? Do I find her and say hello? Did she see me? Do I pretend to bump into her and act like I'm surprised to see her?

Just knowing she's two aisles over is messing with my body's cooling system. I'm sweating even though the air conditioning is going full blast. I'm just about to make a dash for the front door when someone taps my shoulder.

I whirl around to face Charlotte, smiling in this crooked way. "Thought that was you," she says. "Charlie, right?"

"Other Charlie," I mumble, shoving my hands in my pockets.

"Nah, just Charlie. I'm Charlotte now, remember?" She pushes a curl off her forehead. "Are you shopping?"

"Uh, bread."

Looking around us at the shelves full of bread, she laughs. "You're getting warmer."

What does this mean? Charlotte went out of her way to say hello to me and is now standing here bantering with me like we're old friends. Maybe she's just really nice. Maybe it doesn't mean anything and I need to get over myself.

"James—my, uh, friend—needs bread. He's making me dinner."

Charlotte's eyes widen a fraction. "That's nice of him."

"I guess. It's pot roast." Why am I telling her this? I pull out my phone for lack of anything better to say and show her the text.

She smiles as she reads it. "I was wrong. You're ice cold." She takes my forearm and drags me down the aisle. There is green paint under her fingernails. "You should be in the bakery."

I follow her past the cheese and yogurts along the back wall, to the corner where the bakery sits with its glass cases full of colorful cakes. There are racks and racks of fresh baked breads too. A delicious, warm scent wraps around my senses as Charlotte deposits me in front of a wooden rack and points toward the bottom. "Sourdough," she declares.

"Thanks." I stoop to grab one and when I stand, she's examining me like I'm a specimen in a Petri dish.

"How long have you known James?"

"Since freshman year."

"What's he like?"

I shrug. "I dunno. Tall, dark, and handsome, I suppose."

"Handsome?"

"That's what I hear."

"Tall like you?"

"About the same, but broader." I squeeze the bread in my hand, wondering if it's supposed to be so hard. "You saw him at the Krispy Kreme." I touch the back of my neck in the spot that corresponds with her tattoo.

"The guy with the little redhead?" Her whole face lights up as she makes the connection.

"Yeah, that's my friend Greta. They've been dating for years."

"Dating?" Her thin, black brows are so high up they're hidden behind the curls on her forehead.

"Yeah?"

Charlotte's cheeks puff out when she exhales. "I thought—no, never mind what I thought." She points at the bread I'm holding. "You're so hot, you're on fire."

"Wait, did you think—"

"Nope," she says, turning away, her cheeks going hot pink.

"You thought he was *my* boyfriend." My voice cracks with surprise.

Charlotte has reached the produce section and grabs a few lemons from a teetering pile. "If it helps, I hoped I was wrong." She smells one before beginning to juggle them.

It does help. Well, it would help if it'd bothered me to begin with. "How are you doing that?" I point at the lemons orbiting her head.

Charlotte shrugs. "I've had a lot of free time in the past."

I set the bread down and grab my own lemons. "Teach me?"

She grins. "So you can impress your boyfriend?"

"So I can impress *you*. I'm not James's type, which is a shame because Greta says he's a great boyfriend. Very giving."

Charlotte snorts and drops one of her lemons.

By the time I leave the grocery store, I can juggle three lemons for over a minute. Of course, that's only if I turn away from Charlotte because one look at her face and I lose my concentration—and my lemons.

At James's, I hand him his crusty loaf of bread and grab Greta's elbow. "I've got a question."

"It's called a nocturnal emission and it's completely normal, Chucky."

"Grow up, Gret."

"*You* grow up," she says, her smile so wide it's smooshing up the freckles on her cheeks.

James is busy plating dinner as his little sisters, Melody and Ella, dance around the table setting out the silverware. I tug Greta into the front hallway.

"How do I know if a girl is interested in me?"

"What girl?"

"Any girl."

"Are you going to ask someone out? Is it Jenna?"

"No, now answer the question."

"Okay, okay," she says, shaking me off her elbow. "First, let me say that I think this is a great idea. Having a girlfriend will help you gain perspective, see that there is more to life than school and MIT and the future."

I roll my hand to get her to move along.

"Fine," she snaps. "If a girl is interested in you she might find little ways to touch you, like your arm or shoulder. She may compliment you, sometimes indirectly."

"Would it be complimentary if she looked a little upset when she thought maybe I had a boyfriend?"

Greta begins to nod and then her brow furrows. "I'm sorry. What?" I can see she's biting back laughter.

"Never mind."

"Boyfriend?" A snicker escapes. "Who's your boyfriend?"

James calls for us from the kitchen and my ears go bright red at the sound of his voice.

"Oh, shit, no," Greta squeals. "James, you are never going to believe this." She takes off down the hallway.

"Greta don't—" Judging by the howling coming from James, I'd say I'm too late. I make a mental note to try to figure this stuff out on my own next time. Or maybe since James is supposed to be so *giving*, I'll ask him first.

1.8

James makes an ass of himself in English on each of the remaining days of the week, making me think I'm definitely on my own when it comes to figuring out relationships. He says he's starting small, laying the foundation for the skyscraper of hell he will erect around Ms. Finch. I say he's sniffed one too many chemicals in the lab, and his brain is starting to short-circuit.

On Wednesday, he "forgot" his textbook. He may get an Oscar for his performance as Genius Suffering a Nervous Breakdown. I caught Greta's attention during the climax of his performance to ask, "Did I look like this?" She snorted and shook her head. It took 7.27 minutes of class before Ms. Finch could regain control.

On Thursday, he sneezed every time she said the word, "story." She was lecturing on the structure of the short story. Fifty-three sneezes. Tobias even got up to get him the box of tissues from the bookcase in the back.

I do my best to keep my head down in class and never make eye contact with my classmates. I don't want anyone thinking I've got anything to do with this crap.

Today, James's plan A had been to fall out of his chair and fake a head injury, but Ms. Finch declared we all needed a special Friday treat (her words, not mine). We grab our bags and follow her to the grassy courtyard, where we sit cross-legged in a circle.

Thwarted, James reverts to plan B.

"Buzzzzzzzzzzz."

The buzzing noise is coming from my left, where James is sitting, looking overly interested in a wrinkle in his pants. On my right, Greta groans. Across the circle, Ms. Finch is reading to us from the paperback book.

"Buzzzzz. Buzzzzzzzzzzzz."

This time Greta leans behind me and smacks James on the back of his head, denting his kinky black curls. James gives her a devilish grin and, looking right at her, he barely parts his lips and goes, "Buzzzzzzzzzz."

Two people over, Debbie French's blond ponytail starts swinging around as she whips her head from side to side looking for the phantom insect. Once Debbie starts flinching, the movement moves around the circle like a ripple, until it stops at Ms. Finch. She continues to read.

"Buzzzzzzzzz."

Debbie looks at me, and I curse inside for letting her catch my attention. She mouths, "Is that you?"

I give my head one solid shake.

With my response, she hops up. "Um, excuse me? Ms. Finch. There is a bee somewhere. I don't, um, like bees."

Ms. Finch looks up from her book. "I'm sure we'll be fine," she says, a soothing smile lining her face. Debbie's eyes are wild, but she nods and sits back down.

James stifles a laugh on one side of me, while Greta grinds her teeth. James's being pretty stupid, but the pandemonium is cool from a sociological perspective. James gives me an elbow nudge, a silent plea to join him. Greta kicks my foot.

"Buzzzzzzzzzz," James hums more loudly.

A breeze blows through the courtyard. Small vortexes of trash swirl in the corners. One bit of paper escapes and drifts our way, brushing Debbie's neck as it makes its way around the back of our circle.

Debbie screams, jumping to her feet and swatting her neck with both hands. She takes off running for the doors to the school. Her panic spreads out behind her like the tail of a comet. Justin sprints after her. He's allergic to bee stings. Half the girls and a good handful of the guys jump to their feet and alternate between scanning the area for the illusory insect and shooting me questioning looks. I remain still, arms crossed over my chest, staring at a spot in the grass straight ahead.

James stands, his hands up like a ninja ready to kick the bee's ass. Greta jumps up and starts swatting at James, which others misinterpret. They think Greta is rescuing him from the bee, but she's just pissed. Mob mentality takes over and everyone is standing and ducking and swatting the air.

Ms. Finch and I are the only two people left sitting in the circle. She closes her book, and watches me from across the grass. I want to look away, but her eyes are so similar to Charlotte's. I'm trapped in them.

A flash of heat burns my ears as I realize Ms. Finch thinks I've orchestrated this. I'm the only one not reacting to the attack of the invisible bees.

Greta wallops James in the chest with both her hands and he falls backward over me. I'm swept up in a cascade of limbs. When I right myself again, Ms. Finch is no longer studying me. Instead, she's motioning for everyone not swept away in the wave of panic to follow her back inside.

James breaks free from Greta and surreptitiously pumps the air with a victorious fist. It's only a small victory, but he looks elated. Too bad Ms. Finch looks more amused than pissed.

When we get back to the classroom, she apologizes for the

disturbance, saying, "Well, that did not go the way I'd planned, but then, you all, as scientists and mathematicians, must know how that feels. At least I've learned something from it. How about you?"

The grin on James's face slips into a grimace. She's not pissed. Not even a little. And she turned it back around on us and made it like she's some sort of scientist, too. Something like admiration tickles the back of my mind.

1.9

Besides James's antics in English, the rest of the week went by in a blur of physics labs and multivariate equations. It's good to be back in school, where I know what to expect.

Home is a different story. Becca's new project partner has been over almost every afternoon. Mostly they stay holed up in Becca's room, but just knowing Charlotte is here shorts the electrical impulses in my brain.

Back when Greta and James began to date, Greta went through this annoying phase where she was very un-Greta-like. James would join us at lunch and she'd stop eating, twirl her hair like Becca, and blush whenever either she or James said anything. I did a lot of talking back then. It was the only way to keep Greta from looking like she was about to overheat. Even when James wasn't around, it felt like he was because Greta never shut up about him.

I couldn't understand what was happening, so I did some research to figure out what was short-circuiting Greta. Turns out, other scientists had the same questions and conducted studies to understand what makes us act like assholes when we fall in love.

The answer is chemistry—brain chemistry. These scientists discovered three phases in relationships: lust (all hormones, all the time), attraction, and attachment. Greta and James are in the attachment phase now, which means Greta can eat again and doesn't obsessively talk about James. But back during the attraction phase her neurotransmitters were all out of whack.

I'd like to think my brain is more advanced than most humans, but whenever I think about Charlotte, which is more than I'd like to admit, I feel completely adrift in a chemical bath.

I'm at the kitchen table making quadratic equations with the alphabet cereal Mom buys because I said I liked it when I was five. As far as I can tell, Becca and Charlotte's group project today is an experiment to determine at what decibel a bass line can fracture plaster. The entire kitchen ceiling rumbles like an aftershock.

"What is that?" Mom asks.

I look up from my cereal. "That," I say, pointing toward the ceiling, "is Charlotte."

"Becca's...friend?" Mom says it like she's test-driving the word.

I shrug and go back to my cereal. Charlotte's coming over on a Sunday feels like a friendly visit, not a schoolwork thing. She walked in with a sketchpad and a fistful of charcoal pencils, but no textbooks. I'm not sure what's more disconcerting—Becca having a friend, or the friend being the girl with the infinity tattoo that I can't stop obsessing about.

Mom drops the armful of files she's carrying on the kitchen table and papers scatter. She's an elementary school principal (spelled with a p-a-l because she's your pal!), so the beginning of a school year means tons of paperwork.

She pushes her glasses up on her head, pinning her blond hair back. "Please go tell them to turn it down," she says, scrabbling to put the wayward pages back in order and mumbling about noise ordinances and buying Dad a new weed whacker. His is whining just outside Mom's office window.

"Don't make me do that, Mom." I carry my bowl to the sink and face off with her. I get my height from Mom's side of the family.

Last year, I finally overtook her in height. She always jokes that she's 5 feet, 12 inches tall. I'm 6'4". Still, she's far more imposing than Dad's 5'9".

"Charlie, please. I'm buried. What's the big deal?"

"Nothing," I say heading for the stairs. I don't tell her "the big deal" is that for every moment I spend with Charlotte, my mind must then spend many, many more moments analyzing each aspect of our brief interaction. I fail to mention that I think her eyes look like a clear day at the ocean when it feels like the horizon is at your fingertips. And I definitely don't let on how much all of this bothers the hell out of me.

The music is louder upstairs. I bang on the door and holler, "Mom says to turn it down."

I'm hoping to retreat to my room, but—

"What?" Becca asks as she whips open the door. Her shoulder length brown hair is falling out of its usual ponytail and her cheeks are pink. "Charlotte's teaching me a funny dance. I couldn't hear you."

Behind her, I catch Charlotte shimmying to the thick bass. Her slim hips move in a sweet, slow circle. She's singing along with the music. I'm shocked by how effortless her song is, like a bird in flight.

Since I'm still not moving, Becca asks, "Did you want to learn?"

"God, no," I say, but just as I say it the song ends, so my voice is extra loud in the hallway, crowding us all. "Mom just wants you to turn down the music."

"Oh, sure," Becca says as she's closing the door. I tell myself not to, but before the door clicks shut, I crane my neck to catch one more glimpse of Charlotte swaying with the melody of the next song.

2.0

12:38:17 a.m. I want to sleep, but my normally obedient brain will not shut up. I keep imagining myself striding into Becca's room and sweeping Charlotte in my arms in some elaborate, yet terribly manly, dance move.

2:09:52 a.m. When Charlotte smiles you can see a small chip on the bottom corner of her central incisor. I wonder how it got chipped. It makes her smile even more appealing. She has a smile with a story.

I'm getting stupid with sleep deprivation.

3:14:15 a.m. Pi. It's pi time. Is there pie leftover? What kind of pie does Charlotte like, I wonder? It'd be some unique flavor, like fig. Fig pie would taste like butt.

4:57:04 a.m. OhmyGodIamsotired.

6:00:00 a.m. I rouse myself from half-sleep to a zombie-like state that passes for awake.

6:20:15 a.m. I must have fallen asleep in the shower. Moving too slowly. I stare at my shaggy, sand-colored hair and decide it would take too much energy to comb it.

6:29:53 a.m. I'm leaning on the counter with Mom waiting for the coffee to finish brewing. She's eyeing me, but not questioning me. When Mr. Coffee stops, she pours herself a cup and one for me.

She drinks hers black. I give it a try and gag.

"That's terrible."

Mom laughs. "You'll get used to it," she says, adding lots of cream to mine.

I try another sip and grimace. "Seriously, how do you drink this?"

Mom shrugs and finishes her mug. "Sometimes, we do what we have to do to get by." She fills her mug again and holds the carafe out to me for a refill. I shake my head and take one last sip. Blarg.

6:32:22 a.m. I'll just have to kick James in the sac if he whines about being tardy today.

6:41:01 a.m. "You look like crap," Greta says as I pull out of her driveway.

James snorts from the backseat.

I'm too tired to care.

Greta fiddles with the radio and tunes into a familiar song. My vision is flooded with a replay of Charlotte's hips moving, pulling me into a chaotic world I have no chance of controlling—the world of hormones. I exhale like a gorilla just punched me in the stomach and reach for the dial to turn the station.

"Hands off, Chuck. I like that one." Greta swats at me, defending her tune. I try darting around her, but she's lead to my gamma rays.

I'm obviously not paying attention to the road. Which is how I end up driving into a garden.

In my defense, the road curves right in front of old Mrs. Dunwitty's house. The road curved, and I did not.

"Chuck," Greta screams, half in my lap trying to grab the wheel. My car has bumped up the small curb and laid tracks through the green grass, through a small decorative fence, and over some orange flowers.

I crush the brakes and fishtail in the mulch, spraying it all over the yard and ripping up a few more bushes of flowers. Once I manage to stop the car, it's in the middle of Mrs. Dunwitty's garden. There's part of a rose bush on the hood.

"Everyone okay?" I ask turning to Greta and then James.

James's eyes are wide, but his lips are set in a grim way. Greta's hands are a little shaky, but she manages a sympathetic smile, until she notices the carnage. "Oh, Chuck," she says on an exhale. "Look what you've done."

I look at the yard. My stomach sinks to the threadbare floorboards. I've totally screwed up Mrs. Dunwitty's garden — the same garden that has won her the coveted Yard of the Year award seven years in a row. It's the only thing on this earth Dimwit loves. She loves her garden more than I love MIT.

Greta shoves at my shoulder, saying, "Go! Go tell Mrs. Dunwitty you're sorry."

"But we'll be late," I say, jabbing my finger at the digital clock on the dash. 6:42 a.m. The lines in the middle of the six and four don't show up anymore so it looks like hieroglyphics. "I'll stop by after school."

"She'll have called the cops. You'll be in way more trouble. Do it now."

I look at James for backup.

His muscles are clenched so that his square jaw looks like it's made of rock, not flesh. Instead of agreeing with me, he nods at Greta who doubles her effort to shove me out of my own car.

"Fine. But when this old lady turns me into compost, I'm coming back to haunt both of your asses." I can hear the final strains of Charlotte's song still playing on the radio as I slam the car door.

Mrs. Dunwitty's front door is painted a sickly shade of pink. The only reason she gets away with exterior pink paint (total neighborhood no-no) is she's been here longer than anyone else. And she's way meaner.

Dad grew up with her son. He's witnessed her wrath. Once,

her son neglected raking the leaves to go to a movie with Dad and some girls. She made her son pick up every leaf. One by one. By hand. Dad says she sat on the porch overseeing her sentence, calling out whenever he missed a leaf.

My hand hesitates by the doorbell. I peek over my shoulder and see James glaring at me. One false move and he'll be out of the car and ringing the bell himself. I take a deep breath and press the button.

I hear the lock *click*. Before I can blink, Mrs. Dunwitty whips open the door, and stares out at me with hawkish eyes and a too-wide mouth that seems to stretch from ear to ear. She's rail thin and about a foot shorter than me, so I try to stand in front of her so she can't see the wreckage behind me. No use. She sees past me to her war zone-esque garden and starts shrieking.

"What happened? Did you see what happened?" She's breathing fast and clutching her chest, her brown weathered skin turning ashen.

Oh, crap. She's not going to kill me. I've killed her. I hadn't seen that one coming.

"Charlie?" Her voice shakes.

"Um…" I stumble. My brain is telling me to lie. Lie real good. *Tell the woman you were on your way to school and you noticed some vandals had torn up her garden. Charles Mortimer Hanson = Good Samaritan.* "See, what happened was—"

"*You*," she says, jabbing a bony finger at me. "You did this, didn't you, you little shit?"

Too late. I blink away my surprise. My parents work with young kids so their vocabularies are pretty PG. I've never had an adult speak to me like Dimwit.

Mrs. Dunwitty pushes past me. "My beautiful garden. My roses." The sagging skin on her arm flaps as she gesticulates and hollers. "My statuary. Dammit, Charlie, what kind of a jackass drives over an angel?"

I look over the garden and notice a small stone angel tipped over by my front bumper. One of her wings is lying in the dirt beside her. Bet God doesn't like you to rip the wings off his angels. Now I'm dead *and* damned. "Yeah, see, I'm real sorry. I was driving and got, um, distracted and lost control." My voice fizzles out.

Mrs. Dunwitty's whole face is pinched in deep thought, like she's seeing something I can't. She mutters to herself. What I catch sounds like, "… won't like this at all. Just the excuse he's looking for." I think she's talking about her son. I know he checks in on her every so often, although why he'd care about her garden, I can't figure. I'm sure she'll fix it. The woman lives to garden.

When she looks back, I fight the urge to dodge the daggers in her glare. "I can't do this alone." I flinch away from the sharp edge of her tone. "You'll fix this. Starting this afternoon. You'll make this right." She nods once before shutting the door in my face.

James is still grumbling at me as we pull into Brighton's student parking lot. The bulk of his bitching is out of his system though. For the last half mile, he's been having an angry conversation all by himself.

"Don't know why we put up with his shit," he says.

"Cuz he's got a car," alter ego James replies.

"We don't know anyone else with a car?" James v1.0 asks in a desperate whisper.

Back and forth he goes. Greta laughs, which snaps James out of his psychotic rambling. He flushes and runs a hand across the stubble on his cheek. "What? You know it's a valid question."

"True," she says, her eyebrows pulling down low as she studies me.

"I said I was sorry," I say, pulling into the first open spot in the lot.

Greta laughs again, but it doesn't sound so nice anymore, like she's laughing to cover her urge to punch me in the face. "No, you didn't," she says.

"He reckons he doesn't need to," James says. "God of numbers shouldn't have to apologize to anyone." He does a little mock bow with his head.

The god of numbers wouldn't have crashed in the first place because the god of numbers wouldn't have been trying to block out visions of a certain long-legged girl's hips and how the skin there might feel under his fingertips. I scrub at my burning eyes, wiping away my exhaustion.

Screw James and his whiny bullshit. It was an accident. No one intends to drive over a foul-mouthed octogenarian's prize-winning rose garden. No one *wants* to spend time sweating his balls off under the glaring eye of a demented grandmother, no matter what those Hallmark Channel movies say. Frustrated, I snarl, "Shut up, James. You think you're Mr. Perfect? You can't even piss off an English teacher."

"My stuff *is* working." James leans forward between the seats. "You couldn't do any better."

"Can too."

"Can not."

"Can—"

The car shakes with the force of the door slamming. "I'm the god of numbers, and *I* demand an apology!" Red hair dull against the morning light, Greta storms through the parking lot saluting us with both middle fingers.

James swears under his breath, grabbing his bag and following.

"James," I call out after him, but he doesn't turn around.

2.1

"Mr. Hanson?" The sound is muffled, like I'm swimming. "Mr. Hanson, can you rank these acids from strongest to weakest?"

I blink and shake my head vigorously to wake myself. "Uh, twelve?"

"Mr. Hanson, what class do you think you're in?"

I squint at the teacher. "Um…yours?" The class chuckles, and I smile at them like I know what they're laughing about.

"I'll see you for lunch detention, young man," the teacher says.

"But, sir," I give my head another shake to clear it, "uh, Mr. Browning, I already have lunch detention for Mrs. Keele."

"Hanson, what is wrong with you today?"

Sleep deprivation brought on by the hypnotic dancing of the English teacher's sister. I shrug instead of answering.

"Tomorrow. Lunch. Here." He points at my desk before moving back to his.

Two lunch detentions? Who the hell am I today? This is all Charlotte's fault. My brain is fried, and I blame the girl who's taken up residence there. Serotonin is such a pain in the ass. Maybe if I help James, Ms. Finch will quit and move herself and her sister far, far away. But as soon as I have that thought, my traitorous brain riots.

I'm exhausted.

Before lunch, Greta catches up to me in the hall on my way to Mrs. Keele's.

"Hey, derelict."

"Huh?" I look at her, rubbing my eyes to clear them, balancing my Styrofoam lunch tray in one hand.

"Heard you got detention."

I nod. "Look, Gret. About this morning, I didn't sleep well last night and—"

"Wait," Greta says, reaching in her pocket for her phone. "I want to record this."

"What?"

"Well, aren't you about to apologize? They're such a rare species, your apologies. I'd like to have it on record."

My ears instantly burn and my jaw locks. I've got no way to unlock it and let the words come out.

Greta notices. "Maybe next time," she says, putting her phone away.

"I have apologized for stuff before. Remember the squid?" In freshman biology, I accidentally pierced the ink sack of the squid we were dissecting and sprayed Greta in the face. I'm trying not to laugh at the memory. "I said I was sorry then, didn't I?"

Greta raises a brow.

"Didn't I?" I thought I had. At least, I thought I had after I'd laughed my ass off. Greta's lips are pressed into a firm line. "Look, I'm just not usually wrong about things," I say with a grin, hoping she'll smile back.

With a huff, she rolls her eyes and finally allows for a small smile. "Anyway," she drawls, "I know it was an accident, and I felt a little bad about being kind of bitchy, so I brought you something." She reaches into her Mary Poppins bag and pulls out two cans of Mountain Dew. "These are to show you that I'm sorry for overreacting," she says, carefully depositing them on the tray in my hands.

Mountain Dew: defibrillator in a can. "Thanks, Gret."

She nods. "See, how easy that was?"

I look blankly at her.

"I apologized and yet the universe didn't implode."

"Right. Sorry."

She pretends to catch her balance. "Whoa, did you feel that? No? Me neither," she says, looking unimpressed. "Now, you'd better get going. You don't want to be 'tardy.'" She makes her usual air quotes around James's favorite word.

On my way to detention, I pound back both sodas and feel revived...and twitchy. I make it through advanced physics with Greta and molecular biology, but by the time I get to English class, I'm feeling a Dew crash of epic proportions.

I'm nauseated and sweaty, can't stop bouncing my knee, and Greta has smacked me twice now to stop my fingers from drumming the table.

As soon as Ms. Finch walks in, everything goes into hyperdrive. It's like I'm seeing into the future. Given a decade, this is what Charlotte may look like.

My brain starts screaming at itself to shut up. I don't care what Charlotte will look like in ten years. I don't care what Charlotte looks like now. Charlotte's appearance will not get me into MIT. Her full lips will not get me a spot as one of Dr. Bell's research interns. Her long, lean legs will not win me a Nobel Prize.

A wave of nausea crashes over me. I lean forward and put my head on the cool desktop. Closing my eyes, I let the waves roll over me, waves the color of Charlotte's eyes.

"You okay, Chuck?" Greta whispers.

"Is there something wrong with Mr. Hanson?" Ms. Finch asks from the front of the room.

I sit up. "No. I'm fine," I manage to say, but the room is spinning, which doubles the vomit-y feeling. I make fists and worm my knuckles into the muscles of my thighs, hoping to distract myself.

"In that case, shut your traps—"

Oh, how I wish I could. Just then, I feel the horrible burning sensation of Mountain Dew going the wrong way in my esophagus. There's not much I can do. It's coming up. It knows it, and I know it.

I spring from my seat and sprint up the aisle with one hand clamped over my mouth. *Please don't let me barf in front of everyone.* I'm almost to the hallway. Jenna, sitting in the front row, pales as she watches me. Something about the terror in her eyes, like a mirror of my own, distracts me, and I trip over her bag in the aisle. Flailing through the air, I take my hands away from my mouth to brace for a fall, and all hell breaks loose. Mountain Dew and cafeteria corn dog go flying in every direction as I tumble to the ground.

The class erupts into a chorus of disgust. I roll myself up and notice I've landed right next to a pair of black pointy-toed heels. Well, they were black. My eyes run up the long legs attached and stop at Ms. Finch's face, contorted with revulsion.

"Well," she says, "that's one way to get out of a pop quiz." She bends over and offers me a hand. My braced arm slips in some puke and I crumple at her feet.

"Mr. Thomas. Please come help Mr. Hanson to the bathroom." Ms. Finch steps away from me as James tries to figure out the best way to help me up without getting covered in nastiness.

"We're finally doing this," James whispers as he drags me out the door, "together."

"I didn't do it on purpose," I say, but my voice is too loud in my head, so I shut up.

"There's no recovering from that. It'll take the custodian the rest of class to clean up your mess. Everyone is all shaken up. And Ms. Finch is covered in your gastrointestinal fluids. I knew you'd come through for me." James finishes with a fist pump. The motion shakes me. I feel my stomach twist again and for a second, consider letting loose right on James. The thought exhausts me, though. I hang my head and allow myself to be led away.

2.2

That afternoon, Dimwit takes one look at me and swears, "Jesus, Mary, and Joseph, Charles. How are you supposed to work if you can't even stand up straight?"

I shrug, regaining my balance by clinging to the porch railing.

"Go the hell home."

So I do.

I climb into bed fully clothed. Everything about me feels thick like wool. I want to slip away and sleep, but the strange sense that I'm not alone is holding me back.

I prop myself up on one elbow, blinking in the dim light, and see someone silhouetted in the doorway. It's Charlotte.

"What are you doing here?"

"Congratulating you," Charlotte says, maneuvering around piles of clothes, papers, and miscellaneous crap. She moves a stack of science journals and pulls my desk chair closer.

"Oh." I'm confused by her presence, the smell of her skin, and whatever it is she just said. "For what?"

She laughs, and I relax into the sound of it. "You annihilated my sister." She shows me a text with a picture of Ms. Finch's boots. "Those were her favorite shoes. Can you make yourself puke on command, or did you just decide to take advantage of a great situation?"

"I didn't do it on purpose."

"But it did happen." Charlotte digs the toe of her shoe into the carpet between us.

"Is there a universe in which anything you say makes sense?" I ask, rubbing the back of my hand across my mouth to get rid of any drool.

"She knew what she was getting into when she took the job. Everyone warned her, said Brighton kids are a pain in the ass. Said y'all wouldn't listen to her." Charlotte is leaning forward on her knees, a gleeful look in her eyes. "I had the best summer in, like, six years because she was so intent on creating lesson plans that would intrigue you guys and make her some freaking local hero. The English teacher that tamed the dorks or something."

My head feels like it's being stretched between opposing forces, and I'm struggling to pull it back into shape. "Why does she care?" I lie back on my bed and cover my face with my pillow.

"She likes being the best. At her last school there was weeping in the streets when she left."

I lift the pillow so I can see her. "Weeping?"

Charlotte fakes big sniffles, grabbing my pillow and pretending to use the corner of it as a tissue. Her charcoal pencil-stained fingers leave tiny fingerprints.

"Why'd she leave then?"

She tosses my pillow back to me. "Small town. Better opportunities here, ones she feels we can't pass up."

I try to ignore the inviting smell of Charlotte's perfume all over my pillow. "Like?"

"Well," Charlotte draws the word out. "Better pay, cultural diversity, proximity to the university," she declares in a voice that sounds like a recording of Ms. Finch.

"That where you want to go?"

Charlotte wrinkles her nose. "No, I'll be taking a year off from school when I graduate."

True sign of a geek: my heart just stuttered at the idea of taking time away from school. My face must have blanched as well because Charlotte chuckles.

"You going to be sick again?"

I shake my head. Charlotte sits back in the chair, propping her feet up on the side of my bed. "Haven't you ever just wanted to take time off from your life? There's so much clutter. I'd like time to live *my* way—with no interruptions."

"What would you do?"

Charlotte shrugs. "See stuff. There's plenty I haven't seen yet, like the Grand Canyon."

"The Grand Canyon isn't going anywhere."

"No," Charlotte says, her voice dark like the shadows in the corners of my room. "It isn't."

So this is what it means to be *possibly useful.* "You *want* us to drive your sister nuts so that she quits her job at Brighton and you can go see a giant hole in the ground?"

She shakes her head and bites on the bottom corner of her lip. "No, not so she quits, but some stuff has come up, and Jo's turning more and more of her attention back to me. I want all her attention on you."

"What kind of stuff?"

Charlotte arches a brow. "Personal stuff. Trust me, a distraction would be good."

She's a mystery to me. Why would I trust her? "Distractions are bad, Charlotte."

She sits forward. "Depends on your perspective. The more she's focused on you geniuses, the less she worries about me. It'd be a kindness to give her a break from me. I mean, she's my sister, not my mother."

I didn't think it was possible, but I'm more confused than ever. This girl's universe operates under an entirely different set of rules.

I have so many questions for her, and end up surprising myself by asking, "Why didn't you tell her that you know me?"

"You're the only person I've met so far that goes to Brighton and has access to her. Plus, I've got a certain kind of feeling about you."

"Nausea?"

Charlotte laughs. The sound relaxes my busy mind. "What?" she asks.

"I've been told that before. You know, by girls."

"When? In the third grade, back when boys had cooties? I think you may want to take a look at yourself sometime, Longshanks. A girl would be lucky to go out with a smart guy like you." She stands behind the chair, her long fingers tracing the frayed stitching. When she looks up at me again, the iron mask is back in place. "Get some sleep, Charlie," she says, business-like. "And thanks."

Charlotte fades to shadow as the dim light from the hallway engulfs her.

Thanks? Thanks for ruining her sister's favorite pair of boots? And did Charlotte just hint that I was hot? Well, maybe not hot. But she did say I don't have cooties. And I have long shanks. Whatever that means.

I can't take on too much. Asking Charlotte out would open up a whole new world of worries—worries that would distract me from my work, and not in a good way. I can't risk another breakdown this close to the finish line. When I close my eyes and imagine it, I can almost feel my MIT acceptance letter in my hands. My hands are replaced though by a second pair with charcoal-smudged fingers that press against my chest as I pull Charlotte closer to me.

I need to get it together.

2.3

Ms. Finch is already in the classroom when I arrive the next day. I fuss with the strap on my bag to avoid looking at her as I walk down the aisle to my desk. Next to my seat sits one of the jumbo cafeteria trashcans, the kind on wheels. I drop my bag at my feet, my ears instantly flushing. Greta and James are looking like they may explode with laughter.

I punch James's shoulder. "Idiot," I say under my breath.

James doubles over snickering. "Man, it wasn't me."

"Don't even go there," Greta says when I look at her.

Ms. Finch, standing with one hand on the trashcan, says, "I can only afford so many pairs of boots on my teacher's salary." I peek at her feet to see if she's wearing slippers or something because how the heck did she sneak up on me? She nudges the can in-between us, its wheels squeaking.

Striding back up the aisle, she tells us to shut our traps and begins the day's reading. Seated, I can't see over the giant trashcan.

When she's finished reading, Ms. Finch grabs a marker and writes on the white board behind her.

Pure mathematics is, in its way, the poetry of logical ideas.

"Anyone know who said this?" she asks, capping the pen and tapping it on her right palm. No one has an answer. "Really? After all I've heard about the intellectual superiority of Brighton students, I thought someone would be able to answer."

I'm sure she's looking right at me.

"I'm guessing, then, most of you are unaware of the ways in which mathematics and literature intersect."

More silence.

"Here's your first big assignment from me," Ms. Finch says amidst the sound of shuffling papers. I lean sideways and see the class passing back packets of papers. Waiting for them to reach me feels like standing rooted to one place while a tsunami approaches.

"This quarter, you'll work in groups and research one mathematical or scientific idea represented in literature."

I glance around and almost laugh at the expressions on the faces around me. Shock, horror, and physical pain are predominant.

"For example, you could look into the ways in which the meter of some poetry can be found in Pascal's Triangle, or similarities between mathematical and literary paradoxes, or even the ways in which Lewis Carroll wove algebraic formulas into his greatest works. Oh! And, did you know one of the inventors of computer programming was the daughter of a famous poet?"

Ms. Finch's smile is so big it crinkles her eyes at the corners. She thinks we're going to be excited about this. Obviously, she isn't as smart as she thinks. Or, we aren't. I'm not sure which, but I know what I'm going to choose to believe.

"Why even Einstein," she says, pointing to the quote on the board, "had an appreciation for literature."

Einstein has forsaken us.

Ms. Finch ignores the hushed disbelief building around her and draws two intersecting circles on the board, labeling one "Math/Science" and the other "Literature." With the rest of the class time, we're expected to fill in the Venn diagram. It becomes plain when the literature side stays blank that we've got a lot to learn. Judging by the satisfied look on Ms. Finch's face, she's ticking this off as a victory for her, proving we need her more than she needs us.

When I arrive at Dimwit's house, she's rocking on her porch while a tall glass of iced tea perspires on the table beside her, and staring out at the garbage heap of her garden. The garden used to be a kidney-shaped island of color in the midst of her immaculately trimmed lawn. The rose bushes varied from miniature versions to tall, climbing vines, and everything in-between. Now the tall vines hang limply from a smashed trellis and the miniature red rose bushes look like roadkill.

I stop at the bottom step and shift my weight from foot to foot. Sweat runs down my spine, pooling at my waistband. I clear my throat.

"I know you're there. I see you."

"Oh. Well…what should I do?"

Mrs. Dunwitty fixes me with what can only be described as an evil-ass stare. "Fix the mess you've made." She takes a swig of tea, making the ice cubes clink against the glass.

When she stands, her rocker smacks into the siding of the house. Not proud of this, but the sound makes me jump. "It's too damn hot out here for me," she says, holding her cool tea glass up to her cheek. She's stood too fast and steadies herself by holding onto the doorframe. Once she's regained her composure, she steps inside and slams her pink door in my face.

I wait for more detailed instructions, but the door stays shut. How the hell am I supposed to fix this mess? I scan the yard and notice tools upright in a garbage bin next to the garage door.

Heaving a big sigh, I grab a shovel and start pulling out the

broken stalks of roses to stuff into the garbage, trying—and failing—to avoid the thorns. I don't think it's a coincidence Dimwit
didn't leave gardening gloves for me.

As the sun is setting, Mrs. Dunwitty comes outside to inspect
my work. "Tell me, son," she says, plucking a damaged rose from
the garbage, rubbing one of the petals with her desert dry fingers.
"How did this happen?"

My hands are blistered and the skin on my forearms looks like
I got into a brawl with Greta's cat. I'm in no mood to explain the
suckdom of my life to the ornery old bag. "Well, see, the car was
moving at a velocity of—"

"You think you're some kind of smarty britches."

"No," I sigh, wiping my dirt-stained hands on my T-shirt. "It's
Greta's fault."

"She was driving?"

"No, but—"

"Then how do you figure it's her fault?" Mrs. Dunwitty looks at
me like I'm a garden pest.

I shrug. It wasn't Greta's fault. It was Charlotte's—Charlotte
and those stupid sexy hips of hers.

"Know what you need to do?"

I shake my head.

"Man up." Dunwitty slaps me on the back like my little league
coach after he told me to stop crying and hit the stupid ball. I only
had to play one season before my parents decided "socialization"
was not the answer. For the record, I wasn't crying.

"Same time tomorrow," Mrs. Dunwitty calls as she walks back
to her porch, the remains of a fat orange rose in her withered fingers. "Oh, and take that broken angel away. I can't stand to see her
all busted like that."

I heft the small angel into the trunk of my car and slam the lid.

2.4

The footsteps bounding down the stairs can only belong to Charlotte. Becca does not bound. Becca drifts.

I run my fingers through my fine hair, still wet from my shower, willing it to look all casual messy-like. There was a bed-headed guy in one of the movies Becca and Charlotte watched over the weekend, and Charlotte kept saying she'd love to run her fingers through his mane. I'm not sure I can achieve his look, though, since my hair feels more like yellow duckling feathers.

Giving up, I grab my pencil and hunch over my notebook. I'd probably pass out and split my skull on the hardwood floor if her fingers were tangled in my hair anyway. I hate Hollywood.

"There you are," Charlotte says, leaping from the bottom step into the kitchen.

"Me?"

Charlotte's smile is teasing, and even though I know I'm alone in the kitchen, I glance over my shoulder to be sure she wasn't talking to someone else.

"Yes, you." She comes closer and plops down in the chair beside me. "Becca says you have a compass."

I narrow my eyes at her.

"You know. The stabby-end thing I can make perfect circles

with. It's called a compass, right?"

I nod, eyes still narrow.

Charlotte squints back at me, her face a mirrored mockery of mine. "Don't look so skeptical. I need to borrow it."

"For math?"

She wrinkles her nose and her bow-shaped lips pucker with the movement. "Not for math. Obviously, I'm planning on murdering someone with it." I snort, and the sound seems to delight Charlotte, even though my ears are now volcanic. She chuckles and smacks at my shoulder. "I'm drawing something and my circles are seriously shitty."

I erase a stray mark on the page, trying to keep my mind on the numbers before me, not the image that just flashed through my mind of me running my fingers through Charlotte's wild curls and pulling those bow lips toward mine, teasing them open with my tongue.

Holy crap. Numbers.

Numbers = good. Hard-on in front of Charlotte = bad.

Charlotte leans closer, her shoulder pressing against mine, her perfume of sweet vanilla making the math in front of me blur. "What're you working on so intently that you're just going to ignore me?" My breathing has gone shallow and I may pass out when she breathes the word, "Dude," along my neck. "What the hell is this?"

"Calculus."

"Nuh-uh. I've seen calculus. I'm *in* calculus. This is—I don't know what this is."

"Really advanced calculus."

Charlotte studies the formula I'm working with. I allow my eyes to flick toward her face for just a fraction of a second, taking in the way her brow pinches together making brackets along her forehead.

"It's kind of beautiful, isn't it?" she asks.

"Yes."

She smiles at me, a sunrise.

"You understand it?"

"Hell no." She does the nose wrinkle thing again and I have to turn back to the page in front of me. "But I don't have to get it to *get it*. You know?"

I shift away from her, running a sweaty palm down the thigh of my pants. "No."

Charlotte holds one finger up, a gesture for me to wait, before she scurries up the stairs. I copy a new problem into my notebook. I could work solely on the computer, but I like the way the paper feels under my palm as I work through the numbers, finding the solutions I need. I'm a quarter of the way through when she reappears, clutching her sketchpad.

She opens it and holds it out for me. "Do you understand this?"

The page is covered with oranges, reds, greens, and yellows. It's like smudges of each color, bleeding together in a multitude of shapes. It doesn't look like anything at all.

"What's to understand?"

Charlotte doesn't respond. She simply holds the picture steady for me to study. The more I look at it, the more I can see, though. Suddenly, it isn't just colors, but fall leaves in the mountains.

"Is it leaves?"

One of her brows lifts and she tilts the page to examine it. "Perhaps."

But when she shows it to me again, it's no longer leaves, but fish in a pond, like the Koi in the lobby of that hotel I stayed in once. When I blink, I see Mrs. Dunwitty's rose garden at its peak.

And suddenly, I get it.

It's a million problems all in one, and every way I work it I get a new solution. It's beautiful.

"May I?" I ask, reaching for the sketchpad.

She captures the corner of her bottom lip between her teeth as she considers. After handing it to me, she sits and begins fidgeting, her fingers tapping softly against the underside of the table as I turn through the pages. Without thinking, I grab her restless fingers, tangling them with mine like the colors in her sketch. Her hands relax, but her whole body goes rigid beside me.

"Sorry," I say letting go of her hand, ignoring the stuttering of my pulse. What was I doing? I've spoken to this girl a handful of times and here I am trying to hold her damn hand in my kitchen.

Now that I've let go, she starts to wriggle again.

"Am I making you nervous?" I meant looking at her sketchbook, but the way she blinks like I've snapped at her makes me wonder what she thinks I could have meant.

Charlotte takes a deep breath that hitches as it travels up her spine like it's catching on snags along the way. "I'm not used to sharing. It's always been easiest to keep things close."

I want to know what things she's keeping so close. I want her to unpack them from inside herself, perhaps making room for…what? For me? This is ludicrous. I should hand her back her sketches and walk away.

I push my own notebook toward her instead. "It's only fair."

She chuckles and glances down at the open page. "What's this?" Her voice is soft beside me. She's pointing at the problem I was working on moments ago. In it, I've had to use the symbol for infinity, but I drew her tattoo instead. I didn't even realize I'd done it.

"Trying to figure me out, Mr. Hanson? Think you'll get extra credit?"

"I—" I've got nothing to say. I stare at the symbol I've drawn with the word hope bound up in its endlessness. There are many ideas in mathematics that we know are true, even if we'll never be able to solve them. Too many. They're the paradoxes that make math so beautiful.

Charlotte feels like that. Like a problem I'll never really figure out, but that I know is just right for me.

She leans her shoulder into mine. "You and me, Charlie, we're on the same team—both artists. We just work with different mediums."

Now it's my fingers that can't be still. Charlotte eyes them as I drag one hand up and down the metal spiral binding of her sketchbook and simultaneously tap a rhythm against my thigh with the other hand. She reaches for the one tapping between us, clasping it lightly in her own. Without another word, she begins flipping through my notebook, her eyes skimming the formulas. I wonder what kinds of things she's seeing in them.

I wonder what she sees in me.

2.5

Ms. Finch is on time the next day. She leans against the blackboard and waits for the tardy bell, flinching when it finally pierces our ears.

"Shut your traps and listen up." She sets down her coffee, opens up the book, and reads. When she's finished, she turns on the projector and today's notes appear on the screen behind her.

Paradox is...

She's about to launch into her lecture when a hand juts into the air near the front of the class. Jenna Barker has a question.

Ms. Finch nods at her, and Jenna's reedy voice whispers, "Should we be taking notes while you're reading?"

"Why?" asks Ms. Finch.

Jenna's tiny hands flutter by her sides. She turns to look at Misty sitting beside her, and I can see her face flushing. Jenna isn't so good at speaking in public, but man, she can race through a genome project like lightning.

Misty takes over in her brash voice. "Don't we need to have notes for the test?"

Ms. Finch's brow pulls forward for a second before she smiles.

"Oh, no, this novel is just to enjoy. There's no test."

A snort escapes from me. "No test?" It's the craziest thing I've ever heard a teacher say. There's always a test. Too late, I notice all eyes are on me.

"Something funny, Mr. Hanson?"

I look down at my hands and shake my head.

"Wait. Wait," Greta says in a panicked whine as her face drains of color. "We're not being graded on this?" She indicates the pages of notes from the last week. "I mean, wait." It's like listening to one of my dad's vinyl record albums. Every so often the needle gets stuck in a groove and skips so that a word repeats over and over.

James surveys the chaos in the room and turns to me with one of his giant toothy grins. He mumbles, "My mom will not care for this. Not one bit." But it is one of those loud mumbles meant to carry. And from there it grows and grows into a chorus of whining voices, many of them aimed at me, pleading, "Say something, Charlie."

Ms. Finch is watching us, mystified. I can't help but realize how insane our complaints are because there couldn't be an easier assignment than to shut our traps and listen up.

The noise around me is peaking. James is looking victorious. The class is a united front on this issue, and they want me to join, sign my name on the Declaration of English Sucks. Shit, even Charlotte's John Hancock is all over this thing—well, not the English sucks part, but she's definitely signed off on the annoy Ms. Finch clause.

Charlotte cannot be my sole reason for joining this fight. I fight for math and the Brighton way. I am Mathman, able to solve tall problems in a single, well-calculated bound.

God, that's lame.

If I lead my classmates, will Charlotte come to my room again to congratulate me?

I grit my jaw to banish the idea of Charlotte anywhere near my room before I can stand at my desk. The class turns in unison to look at me, their pleas falling silent on their lips. Ms. Finch watches me with interest. I want to apologize to her for some reason. Instead, I clear my throat and stuff my hands in my pockets.

"Ms. Finch, why waste our time with the novel if there is no test?"

There. I've signed my name. Happy?

The class nods and begins to murmur again. All eyes are on Ms. Finch. She takes out the novel in question and leans on her podium. "You think experiencing a brilliant piece of literature is a waste of time?"

I shift my weight from foot to foot. "Um…yes, ma'am. I guess I do."

Ms. Finch's face pulls into a look of disgust.

Stupid libido thinking it's so smart. This is so going to blow up in my face. Everyone is quiet as we wait. My palms begin to sweat and my knees wobble.

Or maybe this has nothing to do with my southern hemisphere. Maybe my standing up today is the result of the way Charlotte looked at me, in the dimness of my room last week, like I'd be some kind of hero if I helped distract her sister. And the way her fingers, cool and soft, felt in mine as we sat in silence at the kitchen table last night, thumbing silently through the pages of each other's minds.

Ms. Finch studies the book in her hand, running her fingers over the cover. Looking up at the whole class, she asks, "So you *want* a test on this novel?"

There's a wave of nodding across the classroom.

"If we listen to the story, then we should be fairly compensated through a corresponding grade." I sound like some ridiculous cartoon using every fifty-cent vocabulary word I've ever learned, but I can't stop myself. "On the first day of class, you said that you knew all about us. If you want to motivate us, you've got to grade us."

James snorts.

Greta exhales, a small sound like, *ohhhhh*.

I cross my arms across my chest to keep my hands from shaking as my ears burn. Ms. Finch's forehead wrinkles, and she nods a few times. And for a fleeting moment, my chest seizes, thinking I've convinced her.

"No. No test," she says. Without another word on the subject, she begins her lecture for the day.

I slowly take my seat. On the one hand, I'm glad there's no test because I haven't been paying attention to the novel. On the other, Ms. Finch has demonstrated once again that she is the one with the power in this classroom. We're at her mercy.

I'd forgotten about the whole Revolutionary War that followed the signing of the Declaration. I'd forgotten that signing was only the first step. It's not like John signed his name all huge and the king handed over the keys to the country saying, "Right then, you win."

We'll have to *earn* our independence.

Through some sick twist of fate, my locker is on the humanities hall, right beside Ms. Finch's office. She sings when she works. Toneless and nearly tuneless songs seep out around the closed door into the hall. I would laugh, but there's something earnest about this private singing.

Suddenly, the song ends, and Ms. Finch steps out of her office. She slings her red bag over her shoulder and sets her empty coffee mug on top of the lockers while she locks the office door. Turning to leave, she spies me as I'm willing my locker to devour me.

"Afternoon, Mr. Hanson."

I drop my *Advanced Theories in Physics* book (a good eight pounds) on my foot and swear involuntarily. Jedi mind trick: *You heard nothing.*

I bend to retrieve the book, and when I stand I notice that she's looking at me like she's trying to see inside me.

"So, it's you this year, eh?"

"Me?"

"Big man on campus. Top dog. King of the class. Crowned head of the seniors." She rattles off a list of titles. I look at her stupidly. Ms. Finch stops listing and looks surprised. "Wow. You don't even know, do you?"

"Know?"

"You've been chosen."

"For what?"

"Greatness," she says, hiking her red bag up on her shoulder and stepping closer. Her scent is all around me, but something is missing. Charlotte's is full of so much more.

"They want *you*," Ms. Finch says pointing her car key at my chest to accent the last word, "to take me on."

It hits me. I don't give a crap what "they" want. High school is a holding pattern. All I've ever cared about is the future. "They" can piss off.

Charlotte has chosen me, though. Hell if I know why, but she said as much the other night. I stood up to be counted for Charlotte.

Ms. Finch sizes me up one more time. "I'm glad it's you."

I flush like a star-struck tween, trying to knit together the threads of our conversation so my mind stops wandering toward Charlotte. "Why?"

"You're a smart boy. I can see that. I bet you'll make this interesting. Just remember," she says solemnly, "'with great power comes great responsibility.'"

I'm frozen like a jerk.

"The great Stan Lee. Spiderman? You must know it." She grins and the flash in her eyes stops my heart. A challenge? Charlotte did say she was all about being some sort of Superteacher. I guess it's a bigger victory to take down a fighting bull than to tip a sleeping cow.

While I stammer for a reply she heads down the hall and leans on the double doors, opening them to the afternoon light.

"See you tomorrow," she calls before she dissolves into the glare from the autumn sun.

2.6

There's a pallet of new stones to rebuild the small retaining wall around the garden bed at Dimwit's today. They aren't evenly shaped, so stacking them is a pain. They keep toppling and I keep shoving them back in place, grumbling things like, "Quote Spiderman to me, will she?" and "I'd like to hang her from the flag pole with a web." Real intelligent crap.

I'm rebuilding the same section of wall for the third time when Mrs. Dunwitty's shadow falls over me. "Hey, Sisyphus," she says. "Ever think of, oh, I don't know, thinking?"

I look up at her, the sun behind her making her skin darker than usual so that her eyes are lost like black holes. "Did you just call me a sissy?"

Dimwit tilts her head back and holds her sun hat as she cackles. "You may not be smart, but you sure are good for a laugh." She rumples my hair, which totally weirds me out. "I called you Sisyphus."

I look at her blankly, and shove a tilting rock back in place.

"It's a myth. Sisyphus was an ancient king. He was punished by the gods and spent eternity pushing the same rock up a hill only to have it roll down again."

"That sucks."

"Guess ya'll haven't studied it at your smarty pants school."

I shrug and reach for another rock. I fit it into place and it rolls back into me. I peek at Dimwit to see if she's noticed.

"Answers a lot of my questions, like how you can be so smart and yet stupid at the same time."

"I'm not stupid," I mutter and shove the toppling stone back in place again. Not that she's buying the load of manure I'm selling.

"Prove it," says Mrs. Dunwitty. "Use your super-knowledge to engineer me a proper wall."

Engineer? I stare at her a second longer before looking at my pitiful wall. Of course it's falling down. I'm just grabbing at stones and stacking them, but if I were to apply some geometry and basic physics, adjust the angle of the stack, and add some drainage to reduce internal pressure...

My brain starts to race as I pull down the bit of wall I've already built. I run to the car for paper and a pencil to sketch a plan.

I've sorted the rocks and dug a trench for the foundation by the time the sky darkens. I'm laying the base stones when Mrs. Dunwitty shuffles over. I peek at her face as I reach for another stone. She looks pleased as she studies the plan I've drawn out, holding it at a shaky arm's length and squinting at it. I'm surprised to feel pride swelling in my chest.

"Looks good, son," she says. "Why don't you clean up for tonight?"

I sit back and brush my hands off on my gym shorts.

"You've got potential," Mrs. Dunwitty says as she hands me back my plan. Coming from Dimwit, that's like winning the lottery.

When I walk into my house, I hear singing coming from the family room. It's a man's voice, but Charlotte's buoys it as she sings along. I follow the sound to find Charlotte and Becca watching some old musical. Well, Charlotte is watching, and Becca is reading in the recliner.

I go up to shower and then work on my MIT application. Last thing Greta said to me this afternoon was, "Grow a pair and finish it, Chuck. MIT is waiting." And while I think the pair I have is just fine, she is right about MIT. There are fifty-four days until the early application deadline.

I spend ten minutes tinkering with my short answers. I have seven versions of *"What has been the most significant challenge you've faced?"* Every last one of them reeks of bullshit.

I read the next short answer question.

We know you stay busy with many school and extra-curricular activities. Tell us about something you do for fun.

Algebra.

Probably not the answer they were looking for. These questions are meant to show what a well-rounded individual I am. The thing is, I'm not round. I'm straight, like an arrow.

I doodle a straight line on a scrap of paper. I put an arrow tip at one end. Now my line will go on and on in that direction. I put an arrow tip on the other end. I have no limits in either direction. I am infinite.

My stomach grumbles. I'm not infinite. I'm hungry. Frustrated, I close my laptop and head to the kitchen.

I pull a box of cereal from the pantry, trying—and failing—to ignore the flickering light from the TV in the family room. But then Charlotte laughs, and I'm done for. Attracted to her laughter like a moth drawn to the TV's soft light, I drift into the family room.

Becca is stretched out on the recliner now. She's fallen asleep with her mouth slightly agape. I'm pretty sure she was up most of last night reading. I notice she's nearly done with the giant book resting in her lap. The sound of her light snoring is like the last traces of thunder in a distant storm.

Charlotte is curled up on one end of the couch. Her sketchbook and a handful of charcoal pencils are on the end table beside her. I crane my neck to see what she's working on. I can't make out any shapes from here, just darkly smudged lines.

"You're freaking me out," Charlotte says, not looking away from the TV. "In or out?"

At the sound of her voice, I jump and crush my box of cereal. I hear the unmistakable sound of the contents being pulverized and spy a crooked smile on Charlotte's lips.

"Sorry," I say, stepping closer. "I needed a break from MIT."

"I thought you *loved* MIT."

"Yes, but I don't *love* writing application essays."

The men on screen are singing some nonsense song. The words are meaningless. Sort of like my answers to MIT's questions. I sigh. "I've got to finish, though. Greta won't quit bugging me until I hit send."

"So you're doing it for Greta?"

The tension built up inside my chest leaks out between my pursed lips with a sound like air hissing from a tire. "No. MIT is for me."

She pats the seat next to her on the couch and thankfully changes the subject. "Ever seen *Singing in the Rain*?"

I grimace.

She mimics me. "It's a classic. You'll like it. Plus, you can pick up some dance moves."

I chuckle. "Oh, I've got moves."

"If you've got moves, then I want to see them." She laughs and then offers to share her blanket with me, but I'm suddenly sweating.

I set my smashed cereal box on the table by her sketchpad, and steal a closer look. It's a picture of a girl standing in a downpour, her face tilted upward. Her mouth is open and her eyes are shut. I can't tell if she's laughing or screaming. Maybe something in-between.

I trace the taut charcoal line of the girl's jaw before moving to sit down. I feel the way that sketched girl looks, caught between desire and fear, and I'm amazed that it took a drawing—Charlotte's drawing—to help me understand why I keep avoiding my application. MIT may be what I want, but it terrifies me, too.

I just can't figure out exactly why I'm afraid.

I settle on the far side of the couch, and Charlotte catches me up on what I've missed. The movie depicts the change Hollywood went through as silent movies were replaced by talkies. That part is pretty interesting, but then out of nowhere, people break into song and dance, which makes me squirm in my seat because who does that?

Charlotte sings along with the actors. Her voice has a rich texture in the semi-darkness. I'd like to wrap myself in the silkiness of her song. Where did this girl come from, and what am I to do now that she's here? I study her profile in the flickering light of the TV.

"You'll miss my favorite scene staring at me like that." She doesn't look at me when she says it, but points toward the TV. "You don't want to miss this."

The man in a fedora (Don) kisses the lady in the strange purple hat (Kathy). They're standing under an umbrella. Kathy tells Don to stay out of the rain.

Charlotte leans forward, grabbing my knee. Her fingertips are blackened from smudging the charcoal lines of her sketch. She recites Don's next line along with him.

"From where I stand, the sun is shining all over the place."

She squeezes my knee and then clasps her hands at her chest, like she's trying to hold herself all together. She sings along with Don as he sings and dances in the rain, her eyes big and glassy in the light from the TV.

The guy's soaking wet, splashing around in puddles, and probably going to lose his voice, the one thing he needs to make his new movie, for what? "It makes no sense," I mutter to myself as Don tap dances through puddles.

"He's in love. It makes him happy. What doesn't make sense?"

"But why's he singing and dancing around in the rain? Can't he just be happy somewhere dry?"

Charlotte shakes her head. "Please don't confuse love and logic, Charlie. They aren't even remotely related."

Don keeps dancing, his movements exploding with wild joy, until he runs into a cop who is also out strolling in the rain for no reason I can see. I wonder if he's in love, too. I still don't get it, but I do have to admit that by the time Don walks off, humming the tune, I do feel lighter.

"Have you ever sung in the rain, Charlie?" Charlotte asks when the scene's over.

"No."

"It's a romantic notion, but highly overrated. Reality can really suck." She tucks her blanket around her more tightly. "I read that Gene Kelly had a fever of 103 degrees when they shot this scene. It's all an act."

"It *is* a movie, Charlotte. It's not supposed to be real." I smile, but what she's said has struck a nerve. *That's* why I'm stalling on my MIT application. Reality. What if MIT isn't everything I've made it out to be?

"For one thing," Charlotte says, bringing me back from my thoughts, "you get wet when you sing in the rain. Very wet."

"You don't say," I deadpan.

Charlotte kicks one foot out at me. It lands in the palm of my hand and, without thinking, I tickle it. She gasps and bites back a peal of laughter.

"You're a dead man, Hanson," she cackles, yanking her foot away, and pursing her lips. God, I'd love to kiss those lips. Just once.

She maneuvers so she's kneeling on the cushion between us wiggling her fingers in my direction in a prepare-to-be-tickled sort of way. Her eyes roam over my body to find her target. Every inch of me pleads to be chosen.

When Becca stirs in her sleep, Charlotte's fingers freeze. Her eyes widen. I grit my teeth in a startled expression, which makes Charlotte snort, which makes me laugh. Actually, it may be fair to say I guffaw. I don't know that I've ever guffawed before. It feels pretty good.

The old recliner squeals in protest as Becca sits up. "What did I miss?" She's looking toward the TV, so I'm guessing she means the movie, but I'm suddenly all too aware that I was just about to get into a tickle war with her best friend. Her only friend.

Bad form, Chuck, the Greta in my head snipes.

I stand and straighten out my rumpled shirt. "I'd better get back to work."

Charlotte sits back and pulls the blanket over her again. She runs her smudged fingers—the ones enticing me just moments ago—through her inky hair.

My insides ache. "Thanks for the movie, Charlotte," I call out as I turn to leave. I need to go. I need to do some wicked math to get this girl out of my system.

"Anytime, Charlie."

Settling in front of my computer again, I pull up the proof I'm working on for the *Young Mathematicians* online journal, the one I'm hoping will catch Dr. Bell's eye. Working through the numbers usually calms me down. Instead, I keep imagining Charlotte, standing alone on an empty street, singing in the rain.

When she tilts her head back to sing, I see the girl in the picture Charlotte drew. The girl lost somewhere between a song and a scream.

Nope. I can't work on this proof if I'm distracted like this. I'll screw something up.

I pull out my scrap paper, noticing the infinite line I'd drawn earlier. I mark off a section, assigning each point a value. Behind the line, I draw an X- and Y-axis and begin solving for the slope. It's a simple problem. I've solved hundreds of them. It's like breathing. Isolate the variable. Stick to the plan. Solve the equation.

It's as easy as 3.14159265.

I scribble more problems, increasing the difficulty, until I'm finally staring down an equation worthy of my skills. But even working through this behemoth does nothing to erase the memory of Charlotte's eyes on me in the dark.

I jab my pencil at the paper, pressing the tip so hard it snaps. Closing my eyes, all I see is the nape of her neck, a black curl draped along the soft line of her spine, and her tattoo. There is a physical pulling in my gut, tugging at me in all sorts of places, aching to reach out and trace the lines of the indelible infinity symbol there.

Math isn't working. How can math not be working? Is this the beginning of another psychotic break? If it is, why do I suddenly feel so calm, like I've broken through the eye wall of a hurricane and into the tranquil heart of the storm?

I open my eyes and focus on the first straight line I drew. When I stood up in class to be counted on Charlotte's side, I changed the direction of my life. I deviated from my safe course. I could go back and erase the point at which I turned, but I don't want to. I don't want to erase Charlotte from my life.

Looking at my page of solved problems, the inkling of a plan wheedles its way into my mind. It's there on the sheet in front of me—over and over again. Have a problem to solve? Isolate the variable.

If Ms. Finch can refuse to give us feedback in the form of a grade on that stupid novel, then we'll withhold our feedback, too. All of it. Every last word.

2.7

"So we're really doing this, eh, Chuck?" Greta asks Monday morning on our way into school.

"It's what the people want." I grab the heavy exterior door before it closes in my face. "As the valedictorian, it's my duty to lead."

"In your dreams," Greta hisses, squeezing through the door before me. "This moves forward because I made it so. Without me, you'd be the only jerk-off in class playing this little game."

James chuckles. I scratch my nose with my middle finger. He grins even wider.

"You're right. We're a team."

James tosses his meaty arms around our shoulders. "The A-Team."

Greta and I both groan.

By lunch, Greta confirms every student in our English class is committed to my plan. If this is going to work, we have to be all in.

Class starts as usual. We're in our seats as Ms. Finch rushes in sipping coffee seconds after the bell. She sets her coffee down on her podium, picks up the novel she's reading to us, and tells us to shut our traps. Thing is, no one's trap is open. Everyone is silent, with hands folded on their desks, looking anywhere but at Ms. Finch. The lecture begins and we take notes, but no one asks questions or makes any unnecessary noise.

The silence is eerie. And awesome.

Ms. Finch pauses at one point during the lecture and gazes out over the class, a crease in her brow. "Any questions?"

Silence.

"Oh-kay," she continues. "Kinda weird, but okay." The way she's biting her bottom lip lets on how un-okay today's class has been. "I tell you what," she says. "I'll give ten extra credit points to the first person who can tell me the difference between an epic and an ode."

Nothing. Which she realizes may mean we weren't listening when she went over that crap earlier, so she tries again. "Too hard? Twenty points to the student who can tell me who wrote Shakespeare's sonnets."

She looks triumphant, like surely even lit-illiterates like us can figure out that one. Still, no one answers. I know it's killing them. It's killing me. Twenty free points going to waste.

"It's Shakespeare, guys. Shakespeare wrote *Shakespeare's* sonnets."

We look through her.

She sighs, "Right. Um…so use the rest of class to work in your project groups. Anyone need a pass for the library?"

A few people look at me. They've already forfeited extra credit points, and using this time to do research on our stupid projects would save valuable after-school time for research we care about. I shake my head once and look at my hands.

I steal a glance around and notice everyone has his or her back turned away from the front of the room where Ms. Finch watches us with a furled brow.

And that, ladies and gentlemen, is how you isolate a variable.

If Ms. Finch has a compulsion to be the best, then our ignoring her should get so far under her skin, she'll want to peel it off layer by layer to get to us. And while she's peeling away, Charlotte should be able to enjoy her life for a little while with no interruptions. Perhaps she'll enjoy some of that free time with me, in my room, in the dark—

It started raining during English, so I'm free from my indentured servitude for the day. Charlotte's car is parked in its normal spot on the curb when I get home. The joke around the house these days is that Charlotte hangs out all the time because Mom loads the pantry with junk food. Mom says as long as Charlotte stays, she'll keep buying the good stuff. That's how thrilled my parents are about Becca socializing for once. They are willing to slowly poison us with artificial flavors and preservatives. I say hurray for junk food, but sometimes it feels more like Charlotte is hiding out at our place, like we've taken in a refugee.

Inside, Charlotte's melodic voice is everywhere all at once. It makes my pulse stutter.

She's in front of the microwave, a bag of popcorn turning inside, singing a tune that's upbeat and sad at the same time.

I drop my keys on the counter, and Charlotte turns to see me. She's not embarrassed that I came home to find her singing in my kitchen. Instead, she smiles, wide and warm, and reaches for a wooden spoon from the jar by the stove. Using it like a microphone, she switches to a familiar refrain from *Singing in the Rain*.

She stops inches from me. The last note trails off, washing away my senses.

She laughs, her breath soft against my face. "Any requests, Charlie?" She grins up at me. Part of me wishes she'd take a few steps back so my heart can slow a little, but another part of me wants to pull her even closer.

"N-n-no."

"Jo had a bad day at school today," she says, her smile brighter than a supernova.

Joe? "Is Joe your boyfriend?"

Charlotte steps away from me, her head cocked to the side like a bird. "My wha—Jo is my sister." She leans back on the counter. "Seems the kids were being mean to her last period."

"We weren't mean," I say, feeling heat rising to the tips of my ears. "I solved your problem with algebra."

Charlotte squinches her nose at me. "I don't care what you did. She's madder than a hatter."

I want to understand her. I do. "That's good, right?"

Charlotte taps out a rhythm on the palm of her hand with her wooden spoon microphone. "Yes, that's good. So good that she'll be working late on new lesson plans for the geniuses. Currently, I am not her top concern. I'm even on my own for dinner tonight."

Becca has come downstairs to hear this last bit. "You can have dinner here. Right Charlie?" Charlotte stops mid-drum and arches a brow at me. My heart ratchets up again.

Dad comes in from the garage, shaking water from his coat. Becca asks, "Charlotte? Dinner? Yes?"

Dad nods. "Food. Good." His brown curls are sagging into his eyes and his mustache looks like a wet dog hanging out under his nose. Dad likes to point out that he's had a mustache since before the hipster douches decided they were cool. "Cool" being a relative term. He notices he's dripping everywhere and heads for the mudroom.

"That's settled," Becca says as she plunks one of my science journals on the counter.

I thought my heart was flying before, but the thought of Becca sifting through my magazines has launched it into supersonic speed. "Where'd you get that?"

"I didn't go anywhere near your stash of girlie magazines."

"Becca—"

"Research, Mr. Hanson?" Charlotte's face is a replica of Ms. Finch's teacher-y look.

I try to act cool, as if that's possible after my little sister has sunk me like a battleship. "Whatever," I say, coughing on the word.

"Actually," Charlotte says, laying the journal on the counter so I can see the page, "I could use that super brain of yours."

I don't step any closer. I'm not getting sunk twice.

"I need you to explain this Austrian cat thing."

"Austrian cat what?"

"Schrödinger," Becca says.

I groan, "God, not Schrödinger again? That theory is so played these days."

Charlotte giggles. "I'm sorry. Did you just say that some obscure Austrian scientist is *played*?"

I cross my arms over my chest, trying to stand my ground, even though the look in her eyes is threatening to make it impossible for me to stand at all. My voice falters, only an angstrom, "I'm just tired of the stupid cat. Is it dead? Is it alive?"

"Yes." Charlotte waves one finger in the air "That is the question. So which is it?"

"Well, it isn't anything, really. It's just a thought experiment to illustrate the concept of quantum states. Until we look in the box, the cat is in a superposition of being both dead and alive. But, once we look, we force the dumb cat into one state or the other. It's called a collapsing reality."

"Which is the real reality?"

"I don't care. It's a cat."

"Let's suppose it isn't a cat," Charlotte says, her voice tinged with a current of electricity. "Let's suppose it's something else."

"Like what?"

"I dunno—me."

Shit.

Charlotte continues. "So if I die, but no one is there to see it, am I still alive until the moment someone notices?" I exchange a look with Becca. *What the hell?* Becca shrugs and looks like she may say something until Charlotte says, "Or, if I'm alive, but no one notices, does that mean that I'm already dead?"

"Where is this coming from?"

Charlotte's smile is mysterious, but it doesn't reach her eyes. "Let's call it scientific curiosity."

Becca leans on the counter beside Charlotte, shoulder to shoulder. "I've read another interpretation—reality splits instead of collapsing. So the cat is alive in one reality and dead in the other, right Charlie?"

I nod, watching Charlotte's face as she digests this new possibility. "In this instance, the observer becomes entangled in the cat's state. So to those on the outside of the box, the cat is either dead or alive when they peer in, but the cat kind of gets to decide."

Becca rolls her eyes at me. My interpretation is loose, at best. I don't care though because Charlotte is smiling, a close-lipped curve to her bow lips directed solely at me. I've made her happy and, in turn, I can feel a rush of pleasant neurochemicals flooding my brain.

"Well," Charlotte says, "that's nice for the cat, then, isn't it?"

2.8

It's quiet enough in the English classroom to hear the soft rattle of Ming's asthmatic breathing, and he sits three rows over from me. The controlling Mrs. Bellinger would keel over in ecstasy if her class were this well behaved.

At first, I felt squeamish whenever one of Ms. Finch's questions went unanswered, but now, just one week into my plan, I'm used to the odd feeling of not performing to my potential. Plus, I've noticed Ms. Finch is asking fewer questions. Better not to ask than to leave unanswered questions cluttering the classroom.

I'll admit the plan isn't bold, but sometimes simplicity is best. I hope that's true. I'm not sure I've got it in me to be a true agitator.

When I walk into class today, Ms. Finch is standing at her podium, staring into a half-empty coffee cup with unfocused eyes. I hide a smile. She looks deeply distracted.

The bell rings and she doesn't bother telling us to shut our traps and listen up before reading to us. About mid-way into today's pages, she loses herself in the story and becomes animated again. But when she finishes and sees us, her good mood slips away. This looks like more than distraction.

There's a strange little tug in my chest, but I ignore it. My allegiance is with Charlotte (and algebra), but I wish I knew more about why Ms. Finch is smothering Charlotte. What's the cause to that effect? The action behind that reaction? Charlotte seems convinced that by distracting Ms. Finch, we're actually doing her some sort of favor, but I don't see how.

A small anxiety purrs in my stomach like Schrödinger's damn cat. There's a piece to this problem I haven't accounted for, and I need to know what it is.

"None of you care," Ms. Finch says, closing her novel and sipping her coffee, "but today we are going to talk about circles."

Ms. Finch projects a poem onto the board—a poem so poem-y it makes me seriously consider puking on her again. The kind of poem that's full of words like "thy," "thou," "whilst," "wilt," "hearkens," and a few "doths." Oh, and one "erect."

In the poem, a guy is going on a trip and has to say good-bye to his girlfriend. He's not cool with PDA and wants her to remember they are like a compass (the stabby-end thing for drawing perfect circles).

"I'm kind of in love with the idea that kindred spirits stay connected no matter the distance between them," Ms. Finch says. "We're safe within the boundaries of the shared circle our lives create." Since she's facing the board when she speaks, we're not sure she's even talking to us. I can tell no one would know what to say even if responding to the teacher were allowed.

I don't want to think about who I'd like to draw close in my circle. Or maybe I do want to think about her, but whenever I do, everything else fades, which scares me more than finishing my MIT application.

"**S**pecial treat today," Dimwit says as I get out of the car. She's leaning on her porch railing with a wicked grin stretched across her weathered face, her wide, white dentures gleaming at me.

This can't be good.

Dimwit meets me by the garden. I haven't been back since I finished the wall last week because of all the rain. It's holding up fine against the heavily saturated ground.

"Today, you're going to add life to the soil."

I look at her like she's speaking Wookie.

"Come on," says Dimwit, grabbing a cane from beside her rocking chair and walking toward her backyard. The cane is new. I mean, it looks old, but I've never seen her use one before. I'm a little worried she's only carrying it so she can beat me in the head if I do something wrong. "Bring the wheelbarrow and shovel," she calls back to me.

More shoveling? At least I'll have something to defend myself with.

I follow her to the back where she shows me to a neat pile of, well, garbage. It's her compost pile, and from it I can tell she had eggs and a banana for breakfast this morning.

Dimwit smiles. "Black gold," she says, grabbing a handful of the decomposing nastiness. "Mix this up real well and fill the wheelbarrow full of the good stuff from the bottom. Bring it around front to add to the garden soil."

"You're just making up gross stuff to torture me longer, aren't you? Mom made a flower bed last spring in less than an hour."

"How are those flowers looking?" Mrs. Dunwitty asks.

Dead. I grimace and thrust my shovel into the pile of compost.

Dimwit chuckles. "That's what I thought. It's the circle of life. From all this decaying matter, my new roses will grow taller and stronger. Respect the circle." She hobbles back around to her porch, humming.

"Sick of circles," I grumble and immediately feel guilty. I love circles. They're amazing. It's not the circles' fault I'm stuck here mixing the new ick with the old ick and chopping up bigger pieces of ick with the point on the shovel. When I'm done, I bring the full wheelbarrow around to the garden and freeze.

You'd think in a neighborhood as huge and sprawling as mine, I could play servant boy to the pissy octogenarian without everyone I know finding out. The theorem would read: If the neighborhood is huge, then the chance of being seen is small.

In my experience, though, a more accurate representation might be: If the neighborhood is huge, then everyone will still be all up in your business because this is the South, man, and being nosey is what we do.

I shouldn't be surprised to find Charlotte walking some monstrosity of a dog past Dimwit's house, but I'm shocked enough to freeze in plain sight rather than hide.

"Charlie?" She gives a gentle tug on the leash and the ginormous dog heels.

"Uh, hey."

The hellhound positions itself between us, eyeing me like I'm a feast. A low growl is rumbling in its throat.

"Nice doggie," I whisper. It growls louder in response. Charlotte laughs, and the sound, if possible, is more unsettling than Satan's growl.

"Sit, Luna," Charlotte commands. The dog sits, but doesn't take its eyes off of me. "I never figured you for the do-gooder type," she says, surveying my work.

"I'm not. This is penance."

"For what?"

"Preoccupation."

"Oh-kay? I'll bite. What is that supposed to mean, great genius?"

Dimwit's voice, harsh like the caw of a crow, swoops down at me from the porch. "Now don't go getting all distracted by a pretty face. You've got work to do." Both Charlotte and the dog skitter back a few steps at the hollering.

"Just give me a second," I snap at Dimwit, which surprises us both.

We're staring each other down across the beat-up garden when Charlotte says, "I can help. Maybe it'll go faster."

Dimwit switches her focus, glaring at Charlotte now. To Charlotte's credit, she doesn't flinch away again. "Get her a shovel," Dimwit says before lowering herself back down into her rocking chair. "Let's see what she can do."

I retrieve a shovel for Charlotte. As she takes it from me, I say, "You don't have to do this."

She smiles. "But I can, and I will."

Charlotte bends to scratch her hellhound behind the ears. She whispers, "Stay," and then gives it a kiss on the top of its ferocious head. A pang of jealousy whaps me in the face.

"Let's do this," she says, grinning her crooked grin at me.

I eye the dog, but it doesn't move. Course, if Charlotte told me to stay, I'd probably do the same. Especially if I thought I might get another kiss.

I shake my head and turn back to the wheelbarrow of ick. Together, Charlotte and I work shovelfuls of the compost into the garden.

I break the comfortable silence to ask, "How's your sister?"

Charlotte breaks up a chunk of mud with the tip of her shovel. "When I left she was scratching away in her lesson planner. I'm not even sure she noticed me leaving."

"And that's good?"

"Very good."

"Sometimes I wonder if we're being mean. I wonder if we

should just drop it."

"No." The word is a projectile and it hits me at point blank range. Even the dog, who was lying in the grass watching us, sits up. From the porch, I notice the absence of the wooden squeal of Dimwit's rocker.

Charlotte wipes a bead of sweat from her pink cheeks. "I mean, why would you stop? I thought Brighton kids did this every year— the whole 'English sucks' thing? Isn't that the motto?" She raises her shovel like a sword, "All hail King Math."

My smile feels sickly as I nod. "Yeah," I say, turning away from her to heft another shovelful of ick into the garden, "you're right."

Dimwit's rocker starts squeaking again as we return to work. The soil is wet from all the rain, and it's hard to move around. We're both grunting and sweating and slipping in the muck.

I hear Charlotte's shovel cut through the sloppy mud behind me, followed by a shrieky, "Whoop." When I turn around, she's on her butt.

I try to maintain my cool, but before I can stop myself, I'm laughing.

"Thanks for the concern, assbag," Charlotte mutters trying to stand, but slipping again. I laugh harder, closing my eyes as my face tilts toward the sun. This is why I don't see Charlotte grabbing a handful of mud and hurling it at me.

Thwump!

I look down, bewildered by the glob of mud running down my chest, my brain scrambling to figure out what just happened.

Charlotte's got an arm on her because that hurt like hell.

No one's thrown mud at me since I was four.

Payback's a bit—

Thwump!

I'd stooped to make my own mud ball when Charlotte hurled a second one.

"This means war!" I throw a huge wad of mud at Charlotte, who dodges it by rolling to one side, but her supporting arm slips and she goes down on her face.

"Aaarrrgh," Charlotte screams and stumbles to her feet, blindly throwing another handful of mud. This one catches me in the nuts.

I gasp and crumple in the mud. Charlotte presses both her muddy hands over her mouth. "Oh, man. I'm sorry. Total accident." She drops to her knees so she's eye to eye with me.

"S'all right," I groan, biting back the tears. Thankfully, she only nicked my junk so I can still make words. "Not broken."

She dissolves into the mud in a fit of giggles.

"Un-cool, Charlotte. Very un-cool laughing in the face of my pain. Now you must pay." I dive in the mud and start lobbing it at her as fast I can.

She retaliates by rubbing mud into my hair like it's shampoo. She's laughing so hard that tears are rolling down her cheeks, making muddy rivers flow down her neck and empty into the neck of her shirt.

"The hell're you doing?"

We freeze and look up at the shadow falling over us. Dimwit. She's leaning on her cane, her brown knuckles white against it, and a look in her eye darker than any black hole. On the other side of us, the wolf dog is whining, shaking with the desire to either comfort Charlotte or tear me apart.

Charlotte goes silent and focuses on the mud covering her clothes like it's the Mona Lisa.

I stand and help Charlotte to her feet. Her left foot slips out from under her, but I manage to grab her under the arms and pull her toward me for balance. We're face to muddy face, and I know I'm surrounded by the twin threats of a pissed off Dimwit and an overprotective pooch, but I can't seem to disentangle my arms from hers.

Mrs. Dunwitty clears her throat. "Asked you a question, son. What do you think you're doing?"

Charlotte pulls away, cooing at her dog to calm it down. I shrug at Dimwit and grab our shovels. "Shoveling?"

"Do I look like a dumbass?"

"Uh, no?"

Dimwit turns to Charlotte. "Sweetheart, I know you're trying to help, but this just won't work. Can't say we didn't try."

Charlotte's face flushes so pink I can see it even through the dirt.

Dimwit gently takes Charlotte's shovel. "I'd like to see my garden fixed before I expire. No one lives forever." Dimwit smiles at her, her lips stretching tight. "You can go."

Charlotte looks at me, but I'm as stunned as her. Then, she gets the giggles.

"Later, Charlie," she says punching me in the arm. The sound of her punch landing makes a squishy noise—mud on mud. She gives a whistle to her beast and leaves me with one more smile.

I watch her walk away. The familiar tang of anxiety coats my throat. What am I doing with this girl? I'm standing in a busted garden, covered in mud, with my heart racing so fast, it's leaving all logical thoughts in the dust.

"Back to work," Mrs. Dunwitty says, but before she can teeter away on her cane, she leans in to get a better look at my muddy face. "You all right, son?"

My eyes feel swollen. I can't go back to the paralyzing black hole of fear I slipped into two years ago. That was over a chemistry problem I couldn't figure out. This—this is way bigger. This is Charlotte Finch.

"Girl's got you confused."

"I'm not confused." But that's a lie, and we both know it. I look at the wheelbarrow of rotten compost and blink my giant eyes, hoping they don't start crying giant tears in front of Dimwit. Oh, she'd never let that go.

Having a girlfriend has never been something I had the bandwidth to take on. Not that I don't think about girls. I do. A lot. But, one thing I've learned is theoretical mathematics is a vastly different creature from applied math.

I'm a theoretical mathematician, thus I will never get laid.

Shit.

"You afraid?" Dunwitty asks, her tone teasing, but her face serious.

"Of what?"

The smile on her face shrinks, and I realize with a sick pang she's about to impart some sort of old-lady knowledge. "Know why I love a garden?"

I shake my head.

"It's always changing."

Dimwit's garden has definitely changed. It went from beautiful to smashed and now it's, well, in progress. How this relates to me, I have no idea.

"Don't you nod your head at me like you understand."

"But it's only a garden."

"You've never heard of a metaphor?"

She pulls her sun hat off her head and shoos me off with it saying, "Get back to work."

I open my mouth to say something, but end up closing it again, like some deranged fish.

How's that for a metaphor, you old hag?

2.9

I have to shower twice. The first time I don't get all the mud out of my hair. I find some in my ear when I dry off. Shower v2.0 is much more successful.

Mud-free, I clear the steam from the bathroom mirror, double-checking my reflection before opening the door, my towel hanging low on my hips.

"Oh." It's the faintest of sounds, an inhalation more than a word, but it pounds in my ears like a gong. Charlotte halts on the top step, one hand over her open mouth. Her eyes roam over my torso, as one brow twitches upward.

I clutch at the towel wrapped around my waist with one hand, hitching it up and securing it in place, and try to casually drape my other arm across my chest.

"Sorry. I mean, don't mind me," Charlotte says, the words tumbling over one another in a rush to get out of her mouth.

"No. I mean. Why would I mind? I, uh…" I drift off and stare at her feet. I'm an idiot. I should have guessed Charlotte would be here. She spends most of her time at our house.

Mom and Dad love her. They love the way she makes Becca more like a normal teenage girl rather than the paper doll she used to be. I get the feeling they'd like some of that normalcy to wear off on me, but Charlotte's different around me. We juggle lemons in a grocery store, hold hands in my kitchen, and argue over the logic of old movies…and then she shows up at Dimwit's and lobs mud at my balls? What the hell? How am I supposed to know how to act around her?

It's like I'm being tested somehow. I'd easily pass the test, if only I understood what she wants.

Charlotte chuckles and says, "I had to shampoo my hair four times to get all the mud out. I even had mud between my teeth. Why didn't you tell me I had something in my teeth?" I peek up at her and see that she's smiling, but her eyes are darting around like she's looking for a safe place to rest them. Her gaze settles on her own feet.

"So, listen," Charlotte continues without waiting for my response, "Becca and I are making pizza for dinner. We just picked up the ingredients. You want to help?"

I glance at her face for a second, but my own is so red I look back at my bare feet. "Can't," I say, "I have to be somewhere." I take a few sideways steps toward my door.

"Right," she says. "Of course."

I peek at her again. She's smiling this crooked smile with her full lips closed and hiked up to the left. I'd love to close the gap between us, just one step now, and kiss those lips. The thought hits me so hard that I begin to worry about the flimsiness of the towel currently hiding my growing interest in Charlotte Finch.

Don't mind me, Charlotte, just pitching my tent here in the hallway. You know the motto: thrifty, clean, brave, uh, I don't know—I totally flunked out of Cub Scouts.

Once she turns back down the stairs, I fall into my room and close the door. Leaning my back on it, I thump my head softly against the wood. I'm in over my head. Trouble is that I'm not sure I want to surface again.

When I get to James's, Greta is already there. I can hear his deep laugh, and when I peek through the sidelights, I see them in the kitchen tossing bits of bread at each other, trying to catch them in their mouths. Greta lunges to catch one, and they both cheer.

I don't want to intrude, and I know that's weird because we're all friends and I'm invited and—I don't know. But James is looking at Greta like her athletic display of bread-in-mouth catching is the coolest thing he's ever seen anyone do, and I don't want to be the third vertex tonight. Without me, there's no triangle. They get to be something entirely different. Adjacent points.

When I get home, I text a lame excuse.

I'm just in time for pizza.

Charlotte hands me a plate with a large wedge of pizza, the steam still rising from the cheese. She and Becca are at the table. Mom and Dad are perched on the stools around the kitchen island. Charlotte pats the chair next to her. We begin to eat in comfortable silence.

I take a bite of my pizza, immediately spitting it back onto the plate. "Hooooot," I breathe, my upper palate cauterized.

"You okay, honey?" Mom asks, holding out a napkin for me, like a paper napkin is any kind of salve for fried flesh. I'm afraid talking would slough off the tender layer of skin I've singed, so I give her a thumbs up before waving away the napkin.

Charlotte hands me her water, saying, "This'll help." Our fingers overlap around the glass. Adjacent points.

The heat between our fingers is more intense than the molten cheese that just laid waste to my mouth. Dear god of numbers, help me, but I want to be burned alive right now.

3.0

*G*reta and I are lab partners. As soon as Dr. Hale sets us loose to run our lab experiments the next morning, Greta says, "We need to talk."

I freeze with my head in the storage cupboard, wondering, if I stabbed myself in the eye with this test tube, would I still "need to talk?" Probably.

I grab our supplies and set them on the lab table between us. "I'd love to talk about how we're going to test Hooke's Law on this rubber band." I pull one of the rubber bands taut and let it loose. It flies across the room and lands in Misty's hair. She doesn't notice.

Greta gives me a why-are-you-so-dense look before pulling the equipment toward her on our table. She moves with speed and grace setting up the experiment. Once it is ready, she crosses her arms over her chest and snaps, "Happy? Now listen."

"How'd you do that?" I nod at the elaborate set-up before me.

Greta shrugs. "About last night—"

"Yeah, sorry to bail, but I got home from Dimwit's and was too tired to go out. I didn't think you guys would mind."

"I saw you. At the window. I saw you leave."

I've wrapped a rubber band around my finger so that the tip is turning purplish. "I didn't want to be in the way."

"That's stupid. You know that, right?"

"Of course I know that." I release my finger from bondage. I can feel my heartbeat throb under the nail.

Greta grabs a rubber band from the pile on the table and aims it at me. "I mean it. Chances of me killing James are much less if he's got a witness around. You're doing him a favor."

"Sure."

"You don't believe me?" She pulls the rubber band tauter.

I hold my hands up in surrender. "I totally believe you."

Dr. Hale walks by checking experiments. "At ease, soldier," he says to Greta. He rushes to help Jacob and Rashaad shouting, "Nonononono! Not like that, boys!"

We turn back to our own work. I appreciate what Greta is saying. It's not like she and James throw their relationship in my face. They're discreet.

But three is an odd number.

I want to tell her about Charlotte. I want to explain that I couldn't hang out with James and her last night because for the first time ever I want what they have. Maybe. At least, I think I want what they have. I don't know. I do know I want to kiss Charlotte.

That I know.

By the time I reach Mrs. Dunwitty's house, my nerves are as knotted as the gray clouds looming over the pines. She's waiting for me, as usual, on her front porch. When I get out of the car, she motions for me to follow her around to the back of the house.

"You've got to get busy if you're planning on staying dry," she's saying as we walk to a small outbuilding made of windows.

"What's this?"

"Greenhouse. My Darryl built it for me years ago." She opens the door and we duck inside. "I keep my babies in here."

The heat in the greenhouse hits me like a fist in my chest. The idea of Dimwit as the old witch in the candy house cooking up children feels about right.

Mrs. Dunwitty picks up a tray of young plants. "Harvest Moon roses. My own breed."

I can tell she thinks I should be impressed from the way her eyes are lit from behind, but they look like plain old roses to me.

Dimwit purses her lips and shoves the tray at me. "Plant the roses, and don't screw it up." She waits for me to leave then turns back to the other plants.

Kneeling in the soil I tilled yesterday, I snatch a plant from the tray and wince as its tiny thorns bite into my fingers. I stare at the rose in my hand for a second and cram it in the hole I've dug.

"Christ, Charlie, a turkey could do a better job than you."

I mumble to myself, "I'd like to see your ancient butt do a better job."

She may be old, but her hearing is seriously intact. From three yards away, she hears me and counters, "My ancient ass had planted perfectly good roses before you drove over them."

Should have said ass. Your ancient ass is some sweet alliteration. Or is it assonance? Crap. Ms. Finch is a bad influence.

I roll my eyes and attempt to push dirt around the prickly rose. The thorns lash out at me once again, drawing fresh blood. Frustrated, I swat at the beastly plant with the trowel.

"There you go again," she says. "Messing it all up."

Exasperated, I snarl, "Show me then. Teach me, Obi Wan."

Mrs. Dunwitty snatches the trowel out of my hand and waggles it in my face. "All right, jackass. Let's get to work."

Kneeling next to me in the dirt, she lovingly lifts the rose out of the hole I'd shoved it in. Her nimble fingers brush the dirt off the roots. "These right here are the life of the plant. The soul." She checks to see that I'm paying attention. "These hold the power to regenerate life year after year. This here is the beginning."

She prepares the hole with compost and gently places the plant inside. She covers the roots with more dirt and soft, black compost. The plant is spindly now, but it has one big-faced flower open on it, a deep orange rose with petals smooth as velvet. Mrs. Dunwitty breathes in the scent of the rose and sighs.

"Nothing like it. Reminds me of my momma and her garden. Of late summer and fireflies and big orange moons hanging in the sky. That's what a rose smells like to me."

She rocks back on her heels, her face grimacing like something hurts. Getting old does not look fun.

"Funny how it works," she says. "The scent of this rose is made from one chemical compound, but it smells differently to each of us." She pulls off her garden gloves, stretching her long, dark fingers out to touch the rose. "It's a rose, plain as day, but what I smell is so much more. Perception is a powerful tool."

My mouth is hanging open out of pure shock. I know about plants and roots and growth patterns from botany classes, but this is something different. Something alive. This is poetry. Dimwit is a poet.

"Close your mouth, son. You'll swallow a fly." She stands, her joints sounding like a bowl of Rice Krispies. "How about you perceive yourself planting the rest of these?"

I watch her back as she shuffles to her rocking chair. She closes her eyes, and I guess she is remembering the smell of her youth and the big orange moon.

3.1

The clouds let loose as I pull into the driveway. I jog into the mud room, shaking off my wet jacket, and see Charlotte leaning on the kitchen counter thumbing through an MIT course catalogue that I had left out. I was inspired to finish my short answers after watching the movie with her (forty-seven days to spare), and am just waiting for all my transcripts, scores, and recommendations to come in before I double-check that everything is in order and hit send. Greta says she's proud of me, but every time I think about it, I feel like I'll puke or crap my pants or maybe both at the same time.

I push the application and MIT from my mind.

"Hey," Charlotte says, smiling and closing the booklet. Her face looks pale with dark circles under her ocean eyes. "We need to talk."

"Ugh," I groan as I toss my keys on the counter. "I'm no good at talks."

The half-smile on her lips makes my blood rush audibly past my eardrums. "Regardless," she says, pulling me toward the table. "We need to talk."

Charlotte sits at the kitchen table, her knees facing me with her ankles crossed and fingers intertwined in her lap. It reminds me of Mrs. Web, my third-grade teacher; nothing good ever came out of her mouth when she assumed this position.

I flump into a hard wooden chair beside her and fight the urge to put my head down on the table. "Okay. Talk."

"I appreciate whatever it is you've been doing to drive my sister crazy."

"You're welcome."

"But—"

I can no longer hold my head up. It thuds to the table.

"I was wondering if you could maybe do something else."

"But this is working. You said this was working."

"It was, but—"

"She's miserable at school." I lift my head.

Charlotte bites her lip and turns her face to look out the window. "I think that has less to do with you and more to do with me."

She pauses, taking a deep breath and forcing a weak smile. "Look, Jo's been acting as surrogate mom to me since our mother died fourteen years ago." She shushes the condolences on my lips. "I don't remember my mother." Charlotte covers my hand with hers. "I'm only telling you to illustrate the depth of experience I have in the field of Jo-isms. She's not going to give up on you because you ignore her. I've tried. She has ways of getting in."

I'm looking at my dry, cracked fingers under hers as she continues to speak. Her fingernails are painted a pinkish orange, like the roses in Mrs. Dunwitty's garden. I envision the tips of her rosy fingers tracing circles down the back of my neck just before I kiss her. Obviously, I'm not listening anymore.

Charlotte removes her hand and snaps her fingers in my face to awaken me. I feel my ears flame up. An apology tumbles off my lips. "Sorry." Why am I always apologizing to this girl? Greta'd have a fit if she saw how easy it is for me.

"Me, too," Charlotte says, her voice full of disappointment. She pushes away from the table and stands with her hands in fists on her hips. I can tell I've missed something during my daydream.

I stand to face her, even risk putting my hand on her shoulder. "Look, Charlotte, I want to help you. I think I mean that."

She shrugs away from me. "But?"

I don't want to hurt her, but I need her to understand I'm doing the best I can. "You don't know me. You don't know that I feel like I'm constantly teetering on a fine edge of madness and the only thing that keeps me balanced is focusing on a steady horizon. My carefully planned future is what keeps me sane—a future I've been working toward since well before I met you."

Charlotte's lips part as a breath hisses past her teeth.

"This is my future." I pick up the MIT catalogue. "This is who I am."

"Some ass puppet on the front of a brochure?"

A hybrid scream/groan gurgles up from my chest. "Why do you need my help?"

Charlotte looks away, her breathing ragged. "I need more time—"

"For what?"

Charlotte practically spits her answer in my face. "To figure my shit out."

"See? I don't know what that means." Frustration, fueled by anxiety, is crawling up my spine. I don't even try to keep my voice low. "We've all got shit to figure out!"

My outburst surprises us both. We're inches from each other, too close. In the aftershock of my yelling, we each take a step apart.

"You're right," she says before she turns and walks away, rubbing at her eyes with the heels of her hands. "Just forget it. Forget the whole thing."

The front door slams right about the same time the adrenaline washes over me with a wave of jitters so violent my skin crawls.

Now that she's gone, I feel like my entire future may hinge on the girl I've driven away.

Sighing, I follow her outside.

Charlotte's legs extend from the top step of our porch into the rain. Rivers of water are running down those long legs and pooling in her sneakers.

"I shouldn't have shouted," I say, as I close the door behind me. She looks up at me with dull eyes, but doesn't answer. I try again. "Will you be okay?"

She looks out at the gray rain and chokes on a bitter laugh.

I'm not sure if that was an answer. Should I leave her alone? Offer her a ride home? Stand here and recite pi to the thirty-fourth decimal?

"Sit with me?" she asks, her eyes still on the rain.

I lower myself onto the step next to her, trying to tuck my legs under me in some strange yoga pose to keep them from sticking out into the rain. It's no use though. I end up losing my balance and toppling into Charlotte. I jut my legs onto the steps below and watch as the rain splatters on my pants, dark pinpricks that spread into thumbprint sized splotches.

Charlotte groans next to me. "Oh, God, Charlie," she exhales. "I'm sorry, too. I know what I'm asking you to do is insane. You should just forget you even know me."

"We both know that's not possible."

Charlotte's eyes seem so much older, full of things I can't understand. When she smiles, it doesn't reach them. She wraps her hands around my arm and shakes me as she pleads. "Okay, don't forget me, but please, don't make me go home. It's miserable."

She drops her head on my shoulder and looks up at me. "Did you know Jo doesn't allow sugar in the house? Has us on this horrible whole foods diet. It's all antioxidants all the time. How's a girl supposed to survive like that, Charlie?" She's trying to be funny. I think. It feels so sad though that I just stare at her.

She drops her hands back into her lap.

"You can stay for dinner," I offer.

The right side of her mouth pulls up a little. "You asking me to dinner?" Her shoulder nudges mine.

"No," I say too quickly.

More silence as the rain continues to kiss the ground.

"Why don't you and Ms. Finch get along?"

"Because I'm sick in the head."

I think she's joking, so I say, "Crazy teenager," but her laughter feels wrong. My body shivers with the sound of it. Or, perhaps, I'm just cold. My pants are soaked and the fabric is wicking the cold rainwater toward my crotch. "Charlotte, is there something I don't know?"

"Despite your IQ, I'm sure there's plenty you don't know."

"That's not what I mean."

Charlotte watches the rain instead of me. My ears are feeling hot. Why won't she just say what she means? Girls defy all logic. Or maybe I'm just incapable of understanding their brand of logic. I don't know. What I do know is that I can't sit here any longer, feeling the touch of her arm on mine and imagining her head resting on my shoulder. I hop up, wrenching myself from the closeness of her skin.

Charlotte grabs my calf. "Wait. I'm sorry. Again. Pay no attention to the foolish girl in the rain."

We chuckle, but it's hollow. I shift my weight from foot to foot and wish I'd been able to get Becca out here to help. I think I've only made Charlotte's mood worse.

Charlotte tugs on the leg of my pants. "Where ya headed?"

Crap. Uh, wherewherewherewhere? Somewhere she'd never want to go. "Comic book store."

"Take me?"

It's a simple question. She wants me to take her to the comic book store. Right? Simple question = simple answer. Except what I say isn't simple.

"Love to."

Charlotte may be beautiful and cool, but as soon as I get her into Comic Place, her true colors are out. Charlotte is a nerd.

She's in love with every comic and graphic novel she touches. I'm surprised once again by the things we share—the things that move us both. We pour over the racks as she devours the colors, action, and shapes that move for her across the pages.

"Look at the lines in this one, Charlie," she says, shoving another *Avengers* in my face. "Look at the expression on Hulk's face."

"Well, it's hard being Dr. Banner," I say, looking up from my book. She stops flipping through pages and looks at me with her brows pulled together. "He's hiding a monster inside himself. Never sure when it'll erupt and tear down, like, a city block."

She looks back at the illustration. "I totally get that."

I reach over and pull out a *Fantastic Four*, pointing to The Thing on the cover. "It'd be worse to be Ben though. All everyone sees is the monster."

Her expression gets serious, lip clenched between teeth, eyes narrow, as she studies Ben.

"I feel his pain," I say.

"Why?"

"Well, look at me," I pause, frozen in her eyes as she looks at me. I swallow. "I'm a geek, right?"

"If you say so."

"No. Everyone says so."

There's a half-smile pulling at her lips. "So, what you're saying is that you are a geek on the outside, but a muscle head on the inside?"

"Sure," I say, drawing the word out. We laugh. "I'm just saying, it's hard to be anything but a monster, when that's what everyone expects of you. Plus, we can't all be gorgeous like—"

"This guy," Charlotte says, pulling Thor off the rack and shoving his blond, muscleyness in my face.

I laugh. "I hate that guy."

Charlotte puts Thor away, and takes the comic with The Thing. "I'd like these," she says, handing the cashier an *Avengers* and my *Fantastic Four*. When we leave, she touches my arm. "Thanks."

"For what?"

"For making me feel like less of a monster."

On the drive home, I consider her from every angle. But any way I look, she's beautiful.

3.2

It continues to rain. Not gentle rain, but wake-you-too-early-with-thunder-and-wind-slamming-against-the-windowpane rain. When we get to English on Monday, Ms. Finch is sitting by the windows in the back of the classroom. The syllabus on the board is a unit on short stories, which will be painful, I'm sure, but at least they're short.

A streak of lightning reaches for the ground outside, making her flinch. Forgetting we aren't speaking to her, she asks, "Does it rain like this often here?"

The class stares back at her, careful not to shake or nod our heads.

She sighs, her chest rising as she fills her lungs with the silence. "Right."

Another flash draws her attention back to the window. "Anyone familiar with the poet Robert Frost?" She doesn't pause for an answer, but continues, "Normally, kids learn about him in American Lit. However, since you're *obviously* not normal kids, you may have no idea to whom I'm referring."

She places a hand against the windowpane. "'Something there is that doesn't love a wall.'" She turns and assesses our faces, her lips pressing together. "It's from 'Mending Wall,'" she says in exasperation. "In the poem, two neighbors meet each year to mend the gaps in the fence between their properties."

We look uninterested, but sweat prickles along my brow. Too much talk of walls and barriers. When are we going to get to the short stories? I can't believe the lesser of two evils at this juncture is a short story.

Ms. Finch strolls up the center aisle toward her podium. "Literature is different from math and science because we don't always have one correct answer. So I ask not what are you keeping out," she says, turning to face us, "but what are you holding in? The answer will be different for each of you."

This time it's impossible for most of the class to keep up the disinterested façade. Every one of us is searching for the answer to her question. Ms. Finch's keen eyes are on me. She's made a gap in the wall. She's made her way in, just like Charlotte predicted.

And she knows it.

*G*reta grabs my arm above the elbow as we leave Ms. Finch's classroom. She steers me past my locker, which is far too close to Finch's office, and around a corner before letting go.

"Something's going on."

"What?" I swallow a chunk of anxiety wedged in my throat. I still haven't said anything about Charlotte, and with each day it gets harder to keep it to myself, but equally as difficult to find the words to explain her.

"Finch is acting weird."

Yes. In my experience, this is true.

James leans against a locker beside me. "Naw. She's just worn down. Teachers like to make an impression and all that crap." He shrugs his massive shoulders. "She's just bummed she's not making a difference in our lives."

I nearly pass out from the exertion of holding up all the irony. Ms. Finch just so happens to be making an enormous impact on my life.

Because Ms. Finch couldn't pass up some stupid opportunities, she moved herself and her little sister here. As a result, said little sister (and her tempting long legs) have practically moved into my house, making it impossible for me to go a day without discovering something new that intrigues me—things that I must study more in depth. God help me, I love a problem to solve.

Greta's shaking her head though. "No. It's something else. I'm not the only one. Some of us were talking about it in—"

"Mr. Hanson," Dr. Whiting, our principal, interrupts, his loud voice cutting through the chaos of the busy halls. "Just the young man I was looking for. A word?" He nods in the direction of his office and takes off without waiting for me.

Greta and James exchange a look, but before either of them says anything, Dr. Whiting turns around. "Actually, Miss McCaulley, please join us." He nods once at James before spinning on his heel again.

James turns a deep mahogany, but he rolls his eyes and grins. "Later, suck-ups."

Greta swats at him before grabbing one of the straps of my backpack and pulling me after her.

"Have a seat," Dr. Whiting says, pointing to a set of uncomfortable-looking red chairs in front of his massive desk. He runs a hand down his tie, straightening it along his barrel chest. I keep my backpack on, perching myself on the edge of my seat.

"I asked you here because I wanted to discuss a pertinent matter with you both." He gives us what I'm sure he thinks is a soothing smile, but since his canines are prominent, it looks more like a snarl. "As our top students, you two are paragons at Brighton.

The other students look to you for guidance."

I try not to snort because they aren't looking for guidance. They're looking for weak spots to exploit so they can be top of the class—chinks in my armor like Charlotte Finch.

Dr. Whiting leans back in his chair, his hands behind his head; his elbows jut out, reminiscent of less than and greater than symbols. "We on the staff are all aware that Brighton has a reputation where the humanities are concerned, chiefly our literature classes." He pauses to let that sink in, still reclined like a sleeping puma ready to shred our skin when we least expect it. Greta and I steal glances at each other. Her face has gone so pale even her freckles have disappeared. "Unfortunately, that reputation is starting to spread into the STEM community. I will not be a laughing stock. I'm expecting both of you to be the kind of leaders Brighton deserves. The kind of leaders I can feel good about standing behind when universities come calling."

He drops his arms and leans forward to turn a picture frame around on his desk. "Mr. Hanson, this may interest you." It's a picture of a young man and a younger Dr. Whiting at a graduation. MIT banners are unmistakable in the background. "That's Devon, my son. Graduated a few years ago. And let's see…" He turns to the bookshelves along one wall and points to another picture. "My daughter Annabelle is there now. In fact, she's one of Dr. Bell's research interns. You're a fan of Dr. Bell's research, if I'm remembering correctly?"

My ears are on fire and the heat has dried out my mouth. I'd choke if I tried to answer.

"You must be proud," Greta says beside me.

He looks her straight in the eye. "As proud as a Stanford man can be."

Holy mother of batshit. He's passive aggressively threatening us. Greta's number one university choice next year is Stanford.

And MIT has been a plot point on my straight arrow lifeline since I was ten. The fire in my ears spreads to my whole body, scorching my insides so that I fight the urge to scream and run away.

Greta is cool, though. She just smiles and nods. "You needn't worry, Dr. Whiting. Charlie and I are committed to our studies. Just the other day, we were commenting on how much more agreeable English is this year because Ms. Finch is trying her hardest to help us relate it to math and science." She nudges my knee with her own. "Right, Charlie?"

"Uh," I cough to clear my baked throat. "Yes. Books are fun."

Greta groans imperceptibly.

Dr. Whiting smiles as he stands and comes around his desk, his arms open. We stand and he takes each of us by a shoulder. "That's just what I expected to hear. You should also know that I have other, particular, reasons for wanting Ms. Finch to have a smooth year here." He walks, tucking us under his arms, to the door of his office. With a final squeeze he pushes us gently out the door. "I'm glad we're all on the same team."

*G*reta rages the whole way home. She pulls strings of curses out of her mind like she's unraveling the universe's favorite sweater. James is in freak-out mode.

"How does he know? Who ratted?" He's dented the kinky curls on both sides of his head, squeezing it tightly between giant palms, so his head now looks oblong, like an egg.

"He doesn't know dick," Greta says. The sound of her voice is a fierce growl in her throat. "How dare that pompous, meddling…" She continues to unwind another mile-long thread of swear words.

I agree with Greta. Dr. Whiting doesn't know we're actively doing anything to harass Ms. Finch. Probably because we're passively harassing her. In the past, seniors were a bit more up front about their distaste for literature. And the thing is that Dr. Whiting didn't do much to stop them.

Brighton recruits students from all over the state. The facilities are immaculate, the teachers are top in their fields (at least math and science), and the students are indulged like rock stars. Normally, our more displeasing attributes are overlooked in the name of status quo. That status being that Brighton produces some of the brightest minds in the southeast and therefore has very generous donors. I'm not sure why this year is different, but something is going on.

"What're we going to do, guys?" James is rolling his head from side to side on the back of the seat. "I'm the one who dragged you into this, but I had no idea Whiting would—" He smooshes his hair again. "What do we do?"

Greta looks at me and I'm reminded of a story her father loves to tell about her great-great-great-grandfather who was a street fighter in Ireland. He saved every penny from his fights and bought two tickets to America on the earliest steamer. Then he went to his favorite girl's house and proposed. I've even seen a picture of him, his arm thrown around Greta's great[3]-grandmother.

Greta gets her looks from granny, short and curvy with fair, freckled skin and fiery hair the color of a bonfire at full blaze, but the fierceness in her eyes that burns brighter than the fire of her hair is from her impetuous, street fighting great[3]-grandpa.

"No one threatens Greta Lynn McCaulley," she says through gritted teeth. "We carry on."

"But—"

"We. Carry. On."

3.3

Charlotte is curled up on the couch in my living room with a single light on when I get home. The steady rain has begun to rumble with thunder like Smaug waking from his sleep.

"Don't you ever go home?" I ask, flopping down on the chair adjacent the couch.

She closes the book in her hands and I can see Shakespeare's face peering out from the cover. Yes, I know who Shakespeare is. No, I haven't actually read any of his plays.

"Who wadded up your panties and shoved them down your throat?" she asks, sitting up.

I mentally gag on that unpleasant image. "Ew, Charlotte. Just. Ew."

A smile snakes across her face.

"Seriously, why are you always here?"

She hugs the book to her chest and picks at the binding. "I like it here. Gotta problem with that?"

I shrug. "Are you fighting with your sister? Something is up with her and I don't think it has to do with a bunch of math geeks ignoring her. Is she sick or something?"

Charlotte sits up straighter. "She's not sick."

"Okay, then what?"

"I don't want to talk about Jo."

"Well, neither do I, but my principal felt the need to drag me into his office this afternoon and threaten me if I mess with her."

Charlotte sinks back into the cushions, curling in on herself like smoke in a vacuum.

"Spill. Why not go home, Charlotte?"

"What home?" Charlotte's voice drowns under a roll of thunder. "My sister's house? My stupid, selfish father's house full of sad memories and empty bottles?" She stands, clutching her book. "What home, Charlie?" Her cheeks are flushed and I have to look away to ignore the way her ragged breathing is rattling her very bones.

I stand, too, but I'm afraid to move closer to her, afraid she'll move farther away, like an electron repelled by one of its own kind, which strikes me instantly as strange because Charlotte and I seem so different. How can we be made of the same stuff? I pitch my voice low, in yet another attempt to keep her from skittering away. "I don't understand."

"Neither do I. I can't explain what I don't even understand in my own head. I just know that when I'm here," she gestures to the space between us, her hand fluttering like a flame about to be guttered, "I *am* home."

I unintentionally take a step away from her, surprised by her admission. It's what I thought I wanted, but it scares me, too. Charlotte looks away, swiping at her eyes with the back of one hand.

When a beautiful girl says you are like a home to her, you should swoop in and kiss her or something. Not leap away. I try to bridge the fissure opening again between us. "Am I like home?"

"I don't know, Charlie. Are you going to let me in?" Her glare is a paradox in itself. It freezes my heart, but ignites other parts. It's like I'm constantly being torn in two whenever I'm around her. It's inevitable. I snap.

"Me?" My voice cracks on the word. "You're the mystery woman, asking about theoretical cats and refusing to explain what's going on with you and your sister. You lay all this shit out at my feet, but don't bother to explain any of it. What am I supposed to do?"

There is a tiny moment where I can see past the seething anger in her eyes. One tiny moment when I can see something else—fear, confusion, hunger, maybe even hope. But then it's hidden again, deep below Charlotte's surface.

She spits the words, "Figure it out, genius," at me before turning to leave, but I step in front of her.

"I'm trying to, but you need to let me in, too."

"Don't tell me what I need to do, Charlie." Her voice wavers, sad and angry tones tearing each other apart in her throat. "I've got enough people telling me what to do."

"I'm not telling you what to do. I'm asking you to let me in."

"What if I can't do that?"

"Then why should I care?" This I ask as much for myself as her.

Charlotte's intake of breath is quick and sharp, like I've plunged a syringe of adrenaline into her chest.

"I thought we were friends," she says, her voice breathless.

"If we were friends, you'd trust me enough to tell me the truth."

Her eyes waver, and I think I've done it. I think I've cracked her code. But then she shakes her head, crossing her arms over her chest, a universal sign she's done talking.

I want in. Why won't she let me in? I'm helping her. I'm—tired.

"I don't need this," I say, and every atom in my body feels how wrong it is, but I turn away from her.

3.4

The next day, school was pretty uneventful, which was good because I can't handle much more. The only problem is that the crack in the wall Ms. Finch made is growing. Today we read a science fiction story about time travel. Afterward she asked if anyone had an opinion about the probability of the author's time machine actually working. Three people's hands sprang up before they realized what they'd done. Charlotte was right. We're going to need a new plan.

On top of that, I kept thinking I heard Dr. Whiting's loud whistle out in the hallway during English, but I never caught a glimpse of him through the small window in the door, so I can't be sure.

When I arrive at Mrs. Dunwitty's to do my penance, she calls me up to the porch and motions for me to sit in the other rocking chair. "Sit your bony ass down, Jack."

I want to ask who Jack is, but decide to do as I'm told. I remind myself this is the last day I'll have to put up with her. I'd have bailed on her weeks ago, but she wouldn't think twice about narc-ing on me to Dad.

"Tools can get you to powerful places," Mrs. Dunwitty says, turning the fraying brim of her sunhat in her hand.

We've been rocking along in silence for a few minutes when

she hits me with the crap about the tools. I raise my eyebrows and she finishes, "But having the tools doesn't mean you know how to use them properly. Understand, son?"

No, you insane bat, I have no idea what you mean. But I nod and mumble, "Yes, ma'am."

Mrs. Dunwitty is no dimwit. "Don't lie to me, Jack."

"My name's Charlie," I say, but I can't make myself say it loudly and it comes out like a question.

Dimwit rolls her big eyes at me. "Short for jackass."

"Oh, well. Okay…" I look down at my hands gripping the arms of the chair. The white paint is worn.

"Today, *Jack*"—she puts great emphasis on my new nickname— "you'll clean and store the garden tools. Winter's coming and the tools will be put away."

"Easy," I say, standing. "I'll get right to it."

"You do that then," she says in a tone that indicates I've made a fatal mistake. I pause and glance back at her. She looks expectant, but seriously, how hard can it be to shove some tools in a shed? I shrug and walk around to the shed at the back of the house. She's still rocking when I come back ten minutes later.

Wiping muddy hands on my stained T-shirt, I declare, "It's all done."

She gets up from her chair, reaching for her cane, and follows me to the back yard. She's slower than usual and I have to stop and wait for her to catch up a few times. Must be all the rainy weather affecting her joints. My grandma used to complain about that.

Mrs. Dunwitty nods toward the door of the shed, which I open obediently only to have a rake handle crack me viciously on the forehead.

"Ow! Crap."

"Yep. Crap job. Do it again," Mrs. Dunwitty says as she begins walking away.

I stand rubbing my forehead. She won't let me go until I get it right. She'll keep me here cleaning tools until spring arrives.

"Wait," I call. "Aren't you going to tell me how you want it done?"

"I want it done correctly," she says, still walking away from me.

"But—"

She stops.

"I don't know how. Can you teach me?" I ask, defeated.

She turns around with a wide smile, "Yes, Charles. I can."

When we're finished, we walk back to the front. "One last thing. Would you please put the new angel in the garden for me?"

I'd laugh, but I've just swallowed my tongue. Mrs. Dunwitty just said please. The world must be coming to an end. She laughs at my expression and shakes her head as she walks up to the porch, "She's in the garage. Don't break her."

I find the new angel where Mrs. Dunwitty said, but this angel is twice as big as the old angel and probably weighs as much as me. I'm not sure how to move her. I can't even heft her into the wheelbarrow myself. I need help. Crafty old biddy is testing me. The angel's wisp of a smile agrees with me.

I walk back out to admit that I can't move her alone and see Mrs. Dunwitty scratching the pointy ears of a familiar hellhound. She looks up at me with a knowing expression in that wrinkly face. "Problem?"

"I need help." I peek at Charlotte, her cheeks pink from walking her dog. "The angel's too heavy."

"Don't look at me," Mrs. Dunwitty chuckles. "That's why I've got you around. I'm too damn old for lifting angels."

Charlotte pushes a curl behind her ear. She holds my gaze prisoner with her own. "I'll help, if it's okay."

"Well, aren't you lucky? Looks like you've got a personal savior." Mrs. Dunwitty leads Luna up to her porch for some water.

Charlotte and I stand like we're stuck in tar. My savior is looking hot today in a pair of running shorts that show off her long legs.
She catches me staring and bites back a grin. I motion for her to
follow me to the garage.

"Charlie," Charlotte says as soon as we're out of Mrs. Dunwitty's
sight.

I don't want to fight. Not now. Not where Mrs. Dunwitty will
inevitably butt in and spout out more metaphors about gardening
and life and crap. "Let's just move this thing," I say, positioning the
wheelbarrow by the angel.

Charlotte swallows whatever she was going to say. She nods and
follows my lead as we lift the new angel and settle her carefully in
the wheelbarrow without incident. It was so easy that I'm thinking
I could have lifted the stupid thing by myself after all.

I roll the angel out to the garden where I've prepared a spot
for her amongst the roses. "I think I can get this," I tell Charlotte,
stepping up to the angel. I bend my knees, take a deep breath, and
grip as hard as I can. Blowing all the air out of my lungs as I lift, I
manage to pick the angel up in one swoop. I open my eyes and yelp.
Charlotte is standing so close, just opposite the angel, her arms out
like she was about to offer to help. She laughs and between that
and the surprise and the actual weight of the angel, my grip slips.

"Whoa there." Charlotte steps in to help. Her hands meet mine
under the angel's wings and we clasp them together to make a
human safety net for the statue.

Protecting my machismo, I say, "I got it," and try to yank the
angel away, but Charlotte is freakishly strong and won't let go of
my hands.

"Let me help. Would it be so bad if you let me help?"

I sigh and study her face, soft and inviting, dissolving my residual
frustrations. If the angel didn't weigh so much, I may have lingered on
it longer, but the rough concrete begins to dig into my skin. Without

a word, I nod and we sidestep our way into the garden. Carefully, we tip the angel into place and step back to admire our work.

"See," says Charlotte, wiping her hands on her shirt. "We make a good team."

I snort. "Yeah. We make something." Her smile is crooked and an errant curl is looping across her temple.

Mrs. Dunwitty and the dog join us by the garden. It looks good with the new angel resting at its center. Which reminds me, the old one is still rolling around in the trunk of my car. *Must dispose of broken angel.*

My hands are calloused, my back is sore, and I've ruined all my gym clothes, but I also feel stronger somehow. I guess it's all the endorphins or whatever, but I feel good, better than I've felt in a while, so I give Mrs. Dunwitty a small smile.

She shakes her head slowly and says, "Don't get all sappy. You're done here. Next time, stay on the road."

My smile slips away. "Don't flatter yourself, old woman. If I never have to see this garden again it will be too soon."

"That's more like it," she chuckles. "Now please escort this young lady home."

I nod. "Yes ma'am." That's two pleases in one day.

Luna hops into the backseat of my car and begins drooling right where James sits. "Good girl," I say as I close the door. Charlotte and I are quiet on the drive back to her house.

"Turn here," she says. "Mine's the third one on the left. Jo's not home yet, so you can pull in the driveway."

"As opposed to slowing down and tossing you out as I drive by?"

"Something like that."

Before opening the door, Charlotte touches my arm. "Thanks, Charlie." She looks like she may say more, but bites down on her bottom lip. Her hand slips away from my arm, leaving a warm spot under the memory of her touch.

"I should be thanking you. I'd be crushed under an angel if it weren't for you."

She smiles. "I meant for trying to help with Jo." She looks out the window. "And for putting up with me."

"Charlotte—"

"Does it really bother you that I'm at your house so much?" She's rubbing a hand along the worn vinyl of the car door's interior, still not looking at me.

The answer is yes. Yes it bothers me. Everything about her, from her smile to her crazy doodled-on shoes unnerves me. She makes me want to step away from my straight-arrow life, if only so I can peer over her shoulder every once in a while and see how the world looks through her sketches.

I brush my fingertips over the back of her other hand. There's a current between us running faster than water over the falls. "Don't go anywhere, Charlotte."

She rewards me with a smile that crinkles the corners of her eyes. God help me, I want to kiss those lines, but I'm held back. Charlotte needs my help. She does not need to deal with my over exuberant, inexperienced hormonal urges. She needs a friend.

"I do want to let you in," she says, her smile softening. "But everyone's always known my business, and they thought knowing gave them the right to make decisions for me. I want to make the choices now, which means I have to keep everyone out until I know what I want." Her pupils are dilating with panic. "And I don't know. I don't know what I want." She pulls her trembling hand from under my fingertips.

I double my grip on the steering wheel. My fingers ache. "I'll do whatever it takes to help, Charlotte. That's a promise."

3.5

After showering, I head to James's to study. I'm falling behind in a few classes since I've been spending my afternoons gardening. Greta and James have agreed to help me catch up. Plus, Greta says we have to finish our topic presentation outline for Ms. Finch. Topics get approved this Friday.

James has made a cake. He leads me into the kitchen, steps aside and holds his arms out, like ta-freaking-da, showing off this lopsided monstrosity of a cake. Melody and Ella are posing next to the cake while Greta snaps a picture of it with her phone. She's laughing so hard she's wiping tears from her eyes.

"Isn't it wonderful?" She's practically cackling.

James leans against the fridge watching Greta laugh her ass off. "It's carrot cake." He winks at me, which is weird, and I hope never happens again. "Melody helped," he says, tickling his little sister who is standing beside him.

"Wow, Mel. It looks great," I say. She smiles her broadest smile.

"Jamie did the frosting," she says, pinching off her smile and wrinkling her nose. "I would have made it prettier."

"I don't doubt that for a second," Greta says lowering her phone and looking at the cake with new interest. "Carrot cake is my favorite."

"I know," James says with a satisfied smile on his face.

Greta's about to step into his ginormous gorilla arms for a kiss, but she stops, her eyes darting toward me. Redirecting, she grabs forks from the drawer and fans them out toward us.

"Do you think it tastes as bad as it looks?"

James does a valiant job straightening the disappointed slump in his shoulders. He wanted a kiss, but got forked. He stabs a chunk of cake the size of my fist. "Guess there's only one way to know."

My friends are acting like dumbasses around me. I should let them off the hook. Say something like, *Oh, go on and kiss the big lug!*

I should also close my door the next time Charlotte and Becca are watching their stupid old movies. Big lug? Who says that? I contemplate lobotomizing myself with my fork.

James cuts pieces for his sisters. They take them into the family room to finish a game of Pretty, Pretty Princess. I'm actually really good at that game. I always get the tiara.

Greta takes a bite of the lopsided cake and moans her approval. She and James tear into it like wolves over a fresh kill. I like carrot cake too, and I didn't get a chance to eat before I came over, but I've lost my appetite. Maybe I should go play the princess game with the girls.

"So listen," I blurt, determined to press on despite the weird-ness. "We have a problem with Finch. My plan is failing. I hate to admit this, but I need help with a new plan."

Greta takes another bite. "Let us have cake and figure it out, too."

I look at James. "I'm not hungry."

"Suit yourself," Greta says with another mouthful of cake. "I say the key to figuring out what's going wrong with our plan of attack lies in what's really bugging Ms. Finch. She's hiding something. Whiting knows what it is. We need to know, too. It's probably a weakness we can exploit."

That weakness is Charlotte. I don't know why Charlotte is the key, I'm just sure I'm right. Like Euler's Identity—I can't solve it, but I know it's true.

"Let's agree to keep our ears and eyes open, but we need a plan in the meantime."

Two-thirds of the way through the cake, we've rejected half a dozen ideas. James finally suggests something decent between giant mouthfuls of frosting. "Sometimes, when Mom is interviewing someone on the stand, she'll do this hot and cold act. She fluctuates from friendly and understanding to hostile and intimidating in the bat of an eye. Eventually, the dude gets so confused he accidentally admits stabbing the bouncer in the eye with his granny's knitting needle."

"Brilliant," says Greta. "Your mom is so my hero."

"So you're saying we need to act like we care?"

"Yes, particularly about poetry, because I think I'm developing a taste for it." James rolls his eyes and shoves me. "What I'm saying is that we feed her positive reinforcement for her efforts to literature-ize us, but just when she looks comfortable we toss in a little sabotage."

It's a brilliant idea. By showing an interest in her class, Ms. Finch will spend more time preparing lessons to keep challenging us. It's what she was trying to do in the beginning. When we first started ignoring her, she'd kept trying for a while, but as time wore on and the wall grew higher, she gave up. If she's busy with lesson plans, Charlotte said Ms. Finch pays her less attention. By sprinkling in some negative reinforcement, we send a clear message to Ms. Finch that no one truly likes her dumb poetry. We're all playing a game.

"Operant conditioning, eh? That could work." Greta stands and smacks her hands on the counter. "How do we start?"

James grimaces. "We have to do an excellent job on our outline for this project of hers."

"Got it. Academic suck-up mode," Greta says, opening her laptop and our project notes. "Can do. But what about the sabotage?"

"I may have an idea." I hop up from my stool and pull out my phone. "Ingrid's been working on a new contact adhesive in chemistry."

"Ingrid?" Greta sits up straighter, her fingers freeze over the keyboard. "And you've got her number on your phone?"

I pause mid-scroll. Her voice was a little too hopeful, like Becca's when she needs a ride to the library. "Maybe? What's it to you?"

"You and Ingrid…" James says, his fist extended for a bump.

"Are lab partners? Yes."

James sings, "Getting freaky in the lab, oh, oh, oh." He attempts to dance along with his impromptu song, but he looks like a rooster running in place.

"Stop, for the sake of our eyes and ears. Stop." Greta throws her napkin at James, who slows his movements, but keeps doing a miniature version of his rooster dance. Turning to me, she says, "You should ask her out—I mean if you like her—maybe we could double?"

Great, my underage adoptive parents are trying to set me up.

3.6

I can tell most of my English classmates have heard we're switching tactics. It's in the way they stare at me like I've walked into class naked. I don't know how Greta gets information out so efficiently, but I'm glad she's not my enemy.

Ms. Finch follows me into the classroom, her usual tanker-sized coffee mug in tow, coffee slurping over the sides. I give her a diminutive smile. "Good afternoon, Ms. Finch," I say with a nod. "I wanted to tell you that I've thoroughly enjoyed putting together our project outline."

Ms. Finch arches her eyebrows.

"The research has been enlightening. I had no idea poetry could be so mathematical. It almost makes it interesting." I pretend to chuckle at my own joke. Greta is staring at me like I am not only naked, but have also emerged from a pool of icy water.

Ms. Finch recovers by taking a huge swig of coffee before setting her mug down in its usual spot. "Right, well, Mr. Hanson, why doesn't your group present your outline first?"

I drop my backpack and bow in her direction. "We'd be honored." James snorts as Greta groans and fishes our outline from her bag. The three of us stride to the front and do our three-minute spiel on "The Infinite Nature of Poetry." The topic choice was Greta's. I'd never pick anything that has anything to do with poetry.

During the presentation, I watch Finch's face in my periphery. Deep worry lines angle upward from the bridge of her nose. Charlotte has the same lines, not so deeply ingrained.

When we finish, I hand her our written outline as Greta and James return to their seats. She takes it slowly, like it might be a trap. Glancing at it quickly and turning it over in her hand she wrinkles her nose and looks up at me quizzically. "Thank you, Mr. Hanson. I agree with you. This is…" She puts the outline away in her grade book without looking at it. "…very interesting."

She reaches to take a sip of coffee, but when she tries to lift her mug, it doesn't budge.

The beauty of Ingrid's adhesive is that it is colorless, odorless, and only adheres when moisture is present. Early this morning, we coated the corner of Ms. Finch's podium with it. Once the epoxy dried, it was undetectable, until Ms. Finch placed her over-full mug of coffee on it.

Bam! Instant bond.

Best part is, Ingrid hasn't found anything to dissolve the glue, yet.

I admit it was risky to depend on Ms. Finch to have sloshed some of her coffee over the edge of her mug on the way to class, but the probability was extremely high based on my observations of her routine behaviors.

Ms. Finch looks from the stuck coffee mug to me, where I'm trying my best to look shocked. "Wow. That sucks. How're you going to drink all that good coffee now?"

Her jaw clenches.

I pull a 10-milliliter pipette from my pocket. "Maybe this will help?"

Before she can say anything, I return to my seat. The class is frozen, waiting for Ms. Finch's reaction.

She looks from the pipette to the mug of coffee and up at us.

Her jaw muscles twitch as she composes them into a smile. "You're a class act, Mr. Hanson," she says, sucking up a sip of coffee in her pipette and squeezing it into her mouth. "Ahhh. That's just what I needed."

I try to savor my victory, but it feels hollow.

3.7

It's been a month of alternately kissing and kicking ass. Ms. Finch acts like most of the pranks are strange coincidences, like her response when walking into her office, adjacent to the classroom, and finding it overflowing with balloons. "It's not even my birthday. How thoughtful."

Ms. Finch isn't above throwing some punches of her own either. Our big English project presentation is due Monday—the day after Halloween. "The same day your MIT early application is due," Greta reminded me. "It's been done for over a month. Just click the little button, Chuck."

Ms. Finch was gracious enough to okay our topic, even if our presentation was a thin veil for the initial attack. Greta says Ms. Finch wasn't being nice, but that our topic is actually good. I think Greta's been sampling the mushrooms Jeremy Peters has been propagating in the bio lab for "research."

Driving home the Friday before Halloween, James announces, "It's slumber party night."

I look at Greta, whose wide-eyed expression mirrors my own. "I'd love to come, J," I say, "but my teddy bear is at the cleaners."

"No, idiot," James says, sitting back in his seat and crossing his arms over his chest. "Greta was saying earlier we need a place to meet to finish our project for Finch. I'm saying, unless we want to dodge a dozen screaming pre-adolescents, my house is out."

"Not it!" Both Greta and I shout at the same time.

"No, boys. Not my house," Greta continues. She arches one gingered eyebrow at me. "Mom and Dad are having a dinner party, so my house will be overflowing with shrinks."

"Scary." James shudders.

Greta nods. "There is one universal truth. You plus you," she says, indicating us each in turn, "plus a house of psychologists drinking wine, equals one cataclysmic disaster."

My palms are starting to get sticky, so I grip the steering wheel tighter.

"Charlie's house it is then," says James.

"No."

Greta graces me with another arched brow glare.

"Um, see, Becca's got a friend—"

"Really?" Greta interrupts.

"Uh, yeah."

James leans up between the seats, exchanging a grin with Greta. "Is her friend rabid? Are you worried about her biting us?"

"Is this friend wanted by the law for keeping human eye-cicles in her freezer?" Greta laughs.

"Was this friend sent back from the future in a time machine to warn us of our nation's impending invasion by wallabies?"

"Does her friend shoot lasers from her eyes like what's-his-face from the comic book you two are always talking about?"

"Cyclops!" James and I both shout. I cut in before James can launch his next theory. "She's none of those things, but she plays loud music and sings into wooden spoons, and is a huge—"

"Distraction?" I can feel Greta's cool green eyes watching me.

"Yes. I mean…it's hard to concentrate with all the noise. Let's meet somewhere else."

Greta and James nod and remain quiet. I assume they are thinking of a place to meet while I'm trying to convince my nervous system there isn't a need to attack every nerve ending at once.

Greta turns toward me until her seat belt catches her across the chest. "Nah. We'll meet at your house." She arches a brow at me one more time, but this time it isn't a why-are-you-so-stupid look so much as what-the-hell-are-you-hiding-and-don't-think-for-an-instant-I-won't-find-out look.

Charlotte's car is in its usual place outside. I was hoping she'd be somewhere else tonight. Hope is stupid.

When the pizzas arrive, I liberate one from the stack of warm boxes and a handful of sodas. I'm on my way to my room when Mom calls out, "Hey! Who stole my veggie special?"

Ew. I bring the box back to the kitchen. "You can have this back. James is allergic to vegetables." While there, I stack a bag of chips, three bananas, and a package of Oreos on top of the pepperoni pizza I snag. That'll keep everyone happy.

"Are James and Greta moving in?" Mom nods at my mountain of food.

"Yes. Greta's pregnant, and their parents tossed them out."

Mom's hazel eyes get huge for a second before she swats at me. "Not funny, Charles Hanson." But she starts to chuckle as she grabs a plate. "Be sure to leave some food for the girls, or they'll come busting down your door come dinner time."

I put the bananas back. I don't want Charlotte anywhere near my door tonight.

I figure if I can get Greta and James up to my room—fast—and keep them there, I may make it through the evening without the planets colliding. In other words, without Greta and James discovering Charlotte and asking me all sorts of questions that I don't have answers for.

I'm half way up the steps when I hear someone coming down. I peek around my tower of junk food. My brain hiccups when I see Charlotte. I trip and land hard, sprawling across six steps. Food goes flying. The only thing I manage to save is one soda that comes free of the plastic holder thingy. The others clank down the steps, each jolt shaking them into canned explosives.

"You okay?" Charlotte is at my elbow, helping me up.

"I'm fine," I say, rubbing my knee, already turning red from carpet burn. Is that blood on the carpet? Nope. It's pizza sauce. Pizza is all over the steps.

"You're sure you're okay?" Charlotte is still holding my elbow, her brows pulled together.

"Really, I'm fine."

"So I can laugh now?" She's pressing her lips together, fighting to keep a smile in check.

"Laugh?"

She nods, a small snort escapes.

I sigh. "If you must."

"Oh, thank you." Charlotte exhales a gale of laughter. Her eyes water and her knees buckle and she's babbling, "pizza flying," and "your face," and "ohdearlordthatssofreakingfunny."

The sound of her laughing echoes in the stairwell, multiplying her joy. It's a sound I could get used to.

"Har, har," I say, chuckling at myself as she chokes back more giggles. "We're going to need more pizza."

Sobering, she looks around. "This is totally salvageable. Five second rule, man."

"Yeah, but you've been laughing for like an hour."

"Sixty minute rule, man."

We both laugh, as she helps me pick up pizza slices and arrange them in the box so it looks as though they were never projectiles.

"For your friends?" Charlotte asks, balancing the chips back on the top of the pizza box. I nod and look down the stairs to the sodas I dropped. I want to invite Charlotte to join us, act like she's just any other girl and not the English teacher's sister, not the secret I've been hiding from my friends.

But then, Charlotte isn't just any other girl, so instead I say, "Well, thanks."

"Remember, it's one step at a time," she says, giving my arm a squeeze before stepping aside to let me pass.

3.8

As soon as they get out of Greta's mom's Volvo, I usher James and Greta straight to my room.

"Geez, Chuck," Greta grumps. "I didn't get to say hi to your mom."

"Pizza's getting cold," I say, motioning to the box in the center of my floor, praying no one notices the elliptical shape of the slices Charlotte and I shoved back together.

James flops down in front of the food. He's about to shove a piece of pizza in his mouth when he stops. "What's this?"

Is it carpet fuzz? It thought I got it all out.

James examines the pizza and grins. "Hell yeah, man," he says, pulling apart the crust, "stuffed crust."

I laugh, a stiff, strangled sound. I cover by stuffing a huge bite of pizza in my mouth.

We finish our project crap quickly. Ms. Finch wants us to demonstrate how our mathematical concept can be used in literature. We're showing how words can be combined in infinite combinations to make poems. Like the poetry magnets my dad gave Mom for Valentine's Day a few years ago. With the 50-word magnets in the box you could make 2,118,760 possible 5-word poems. Which isn't an infinite number of poems, but it is, in layman's terms, a butt load.

Since words are constantly being created, it can be assumed language is infinite. If you raise the power in the exponential equation to infinity, it equals a possible number of poems stretching from here to eternity. Not quantum physics, but not the worst topic ever either.

As soon as Greta puts her computer in her bag, I stand and step over the landmine of junk on my floor. "Well, guess that's it. I'll see you guys bright and early Monday." I'm reaching for the doorknob, but no one has moved.

James stuffs a handful of chips in his mouth. Greta grabs another soda, cracking it open and asking, "What's with the rushing?"

"Uh, no rush. I thought we were done."

James gets up on his knees and wraps both hands around the bag of chips in a prayer position. "Please don't make me go home. It's like an estrogen explosion over there." He scoots toward me on his knees, shaking his hands in supplication. "Don't send me to the front lines, general."

Greta laughs and tosses a cookie at him. It bounces off the tight curls on the back of his head. "God, you're an idiot," she giggles. "Seriously, Chuck. I'm not leaving either. By now the shrinks will be on bottle number who-knows-what. They'd analyze me into a catatonic state."

"Yeah, of course. Mi casa es su casa." Inside my head, I hear yelling. *Don't anyone leave this room.*

I fiddle around on the computer while Greta and James keep playing my-family's-crazier-than-yours. Before long, I can hear the familiar bass of Charlotte's music playing across the hall in Becca's room. James and Greta notice it too.

"Is Becca listening to music?" James asks, stopping mid-my-mom-is-so-crazy. Before Charlotte, Becca never made noise.

"No, idiot." Greta smacks him in the shoulder. "It's Becca's new friend's music."

He touches one finger to his forehead. "Oh, yeah. Cyclops." Laughing, he asks me, "So what's she like?"

I shrug and lean closer to the computer screen.

"Come on, man, is she hot? Or, is she weird, like Becca? No offense."

I shrug again. "I don't know. She's Becca's friend."

"So she's weird," he says to Greta, who tries to swallow her giggles. My stomach coils at their laughter. I make fists with my hands and dig my knuckles into my thighs to distract myself from the suffocating need to round on them and defend Charlotte.

"You like her, Chuck?"

I wiggle the mouse, making the little arrow on the screen move in the shape of infinity.

"You do. Our little Chuck has a crush." Greta hops up and spins my chair around so I'm facing them. "That's awesome. You should totally ask this new girl out. We could double."

"Uh, no." I spin back around to the computer. I'm sure my asking out the sister of the least popular teacher at Brighton would go over well. I'm sure Greta'd love to double with us—in a parallel universe where unicorns prance and everyone speaks in Dr. Seussical rhymes.

James puts down his pizza and stands, too. "C-man, you gotta man up. She has to be better than Ingrid. Ingrid's got the personality of an amoeba. Even if this one's weird, she's a girl, right? Ask her out." He kicks my chair so its spins around to face them again. "Shit, ask her out if she's a dude. We'll love you no matter what." They're standing together, arms around each other looking down on me like underage adoptive parents again.

This shit is getting old.

"Yeah, right." I try to spin myself back to the computer, but James's meaty paw stops my momentum. My ears are on code red, ready to burst into flames. "Look," I say. "Stop trying to set me up."

I push his hand away. "I can't ask Charlotte out."

"Why not?"

"It's complicated."

"Because she's Becca's friend?" Greta asks.

Yes, that's one of the many reasons, and the easiest to explain, so I hang on to it like a lifeline. "Yes. Exactly. Becca's never had a real friend before. I can't screw that up for her."

Greta nods as James scowls. "He's right," she says, looking up at him.

"Damn." James flops back down to the floor and grabs another slice of pizza.

Greta pats me on the shoulder before crossing to my door. I jump from my chair, sending it spinning in circles, and meet her there. "Where are you going?" My voice sounds like a guitar string pulled too tight, sharp and whining.

"To the bathroom?" Greta purses her lips in a funny snarl.

"Why?"

Her eyes widen in her round face. "Uh, three sodas is why." I'm leaning my back against the door, blocking her. She squirms from one foot to the other. "May I be excused, your lordship?"

I swallow a shallow breath and open the door for her. I follow and watch her walk the hallway of doom. As if on cue, Becca's door opens as the bathroom door closes.

"We've got to stop running into each other here." Charlotte laughs like a songbird as she bursts out into the hallway. I feel the heat ignite in my chest.

James is on his feet, tripping over the pizza box and spilling his soda down the leg of his pants to get a look at Becca's friend. "Hey," he says, jutting out his chin at Charlotte in a nod.

Charlotte parries with her nod. "Hey." She smiles, a bright and genuine smile, and sticks out her hand. "I'm Charlotte, Becca's friend," she adds, thumbing toward Becca's open door.

James shakes her hand, eyeing her in a way that makes me want to kick him in his balls. Instead, I clear my throat. "Yes, this is all nice," I say as I step between James and Charlotte. Looking at Charlotte, I ask, "Whatcha doing out here?"

Charlotte leans in conspiratorially and whispers, "I have to pee." She speaks slowly, dipping her chin with each word, so when she's finished, she peering at me from under her thin, black brows.

My hand shakes with the familiar need to tilt her chin back up so her full lips would be inches from mine.

Someone clears her throat.

For the love of Pythagorus. I've got no luck.

"Greta, this is Charlotte," James says from behind me.

Greta studies Charlotte like a scientist through her microscope. "You look familiar. Have we met?"

"Not formally. I look like my sister," says Charlotte.

Greta's eyes go wide.

"I don't mean to be rude, but—" Charlotte nods toward the bathroom.

"Sorry," Greta says, moving out of the way.

I look at Greta, whose face is scarlet, and cringe.

3.9

When most people think of explosions, they go for the Hollywood special effects version, with lots of noise and fire and people's limbs flying everywhere. In actuality, the silent ones are more devastating. An exploding supernova can create enough radiation to outshine every star in a galaxy, but no sound. Greta's fury unfolds like that.

Once the bathroom door closes, Greta remains still for a few seconds. Her chest rises and falls in measured breaths. With each inhale, the color from her face fades.

"Gret?"

She turns like she's in slow motion. "Your sister's new friend isn't Cyclops. She's a Finch."

"Yes."

"I notice she has a tattoo."

"Yes."

"And you didn't tell me you knew her?"

"Yes."

"Will she help us?" James asks.

"Sabotage her sister?" I ask, still looking at Greta. "Yes."

Greta's next question isn't a question at all. "You like her."

"No?"

"Liar."

I take a deep breath and hold it in.

"She likes you."

"You think?"

"I wouldn't say it otherwise," Greta says, folding her arms over her chest.

She seems to be fighting a silent war in that head of hers. I'm surprised when she laughs. It's a hollow sound, but still a laugh. "You're a real piece of work, Chuck." She retrieves her bag. "We're done here, right? So, I'll see you guys on Monday."

She brushes James's cheek with a kiss before turning to leave. At the top of the stairs she turns around and tosses out, "Don't forget to hit send, Chuck," before disappearing down the steps. I hear the front door open and my muscles tense up in anticipation of a shuddering slam, but it closes with a silent whoosh, like an exhale.

Leave it to Greta to be looking out for me even when she's pissed at me. I'll send the application. I just want to read over my short answers one last time.

James takes off after her, but returns within minutes. "She left me here," he says, slouching back into my room.

"I'll take you home," I say. I can't look at him any longer. Instead, I study his big feet standing in a pizza box.

"No. I'm not going back to Estro-pallooza." He takes a big breath and sits on my bed. "You should've told us. You could've told me."

"I know, but this girl, she messes with my brain functioning."

James cracks a smile. "Yeah, it's called testosterone, you horn-dog."

I roll my eyes and sit across from him in my desk chair. Actually, I'm well past testosterone. I'm into adrenaline, dopamine, and seratonin territory now. This is way worse than simple lust. "Now what?" I ask, and the question nearly swallows me.

"Get your coat," he says.

"Why?"

"We're going out," James says, grabbing his sweatshirt.

"Where?" I ask.

James stops in the middle of tugging his sweatshirt over his head. "Good question," he says, muffled from inside the fabric. Pulling his head out he asks, "Where do teenagers go, and why don't we know this?"

"Mall?" I suggest.

"Uncool after the age of twelve."

"Because you're the king of cool?"

"No, C-Man. That's your gig." James finishes messing with his sweatshirt and grabs his backpack. Looking at it, his face brightens. "I've got it," he says. He knocks on Becca's door.

"Hell're you doing?" I try to pull him away from the door, but it's like a rowboat trying to move an ocean liner.

"I've got a fantastic idea. It's going to make you happy, which will make Greta happy. And if Greta's happy, then she'll make me happy."

"Ew."

"Get your mind out of the gut—" Becca pops her head out her door. "Ladies."

Charlotte is lying on her back looking up at the ceiling conducting the music with two charcoal pencils. She rolls onto her stomach and pushes herself up to join Becca.

"Anyone interested in a little star gazing?"

The girls look at each other. Becca smiles. Charlotte opens the door wider. "We're in."

"Meet us out back. I know a spot on the greenway." James gives the girls one of his toothy smiles that can be seen from space before ducking down the back steps to the kitchen.

Charlotte leans against the doorjamb. "You mind if we join?"

"Yeah. I mean, no. It'll be great."

"C-man," James hollers from downstairs. "A little help?"

"James!" Dad shouts from the master bedroom. "A little quiet?"

"Sorry!" James shouts back before we hear him mock-whispering, "You won't hear a peep out of me again."

I grin at the girls like an idiot, feeling my ears burn, and then bolt down the stairs. When I reach James, he's rooting in the pantry. "You're seriously still hungry?"

"Nope, but I am thirsty," he says, pulling down a bottle of bourbon that's been there, untouched, for maybe two years. Dad can't metabolize alcohol well; he ends up completely smashed after three sips, so Mom hid the bottle.

"Uh, no," I say, trying to grab the bottle.

"Uh, yes," James retorts. "I'll be your wingman."

"Bad idea."

"No, it's a brilliant idea." He puts the bottle in his backpack.

"Midnight snack?"

I turn around as James drops his backpack and kicks it toward the back of the pantry. "Dad. Hey! Uh, we were—"

"Just going to bring these out to the greenway for some star gazing, if that'd be okay?" James is holding out a can of Pringles and a bag of cookies. "Star gazing makes me hungry."

"Hold on," Dad says, his face pulled in a stern grimace, but he's wearing an old Muppet Babies T-shirt so it's hard to take him too seriously. "Are those my cookies?"

I peek at the bag. "We can't take those, J," I say, grabbing the bag. "These are the gluten-free ones. They taste like cardboard hockey pucks."

"Hey," Dad says, grabbing his precious cookies. "It's all I've got."

James grins. "Sorry, Mr. H."

Dad wanders back to the bedroom with his cookies.

"Too damn close, man. This is not good."

"You're right," James says, and I let out a sigh. "This is great. Let's hit the greenway." He walks out the side door assuming that I'll follow.

I follow.

"This is a very bad idea," I whisper to James as we crash through the underbrush to get to the greenway with the girls a few feet behind us. James lets go of a branch too soon so it smacks me in the face. The trail winds throughout the whole neighborhood, but this section follows a creek and opens up in a glen with picnic tables less than a mile from my house.

I watch him unscrew the cap and take a swig. He swallows and makes a face like he's licked a dirty diaper.

Coughing, James shoves the bottle at me. "Drink."

I hold the bottle up and swirl the brown liquid. In the moonlight, it looks like molten amber.

"It'll do you good," James says quietly. "Guaranteed to grow you balls big enough to ask out a certain girl."

I sniff at the open lip of the bottle and feel the inside of my nose heat up from the fumes. "This stuff is toxic," I say, holding the bottle out.

Charlotte comes up behind me. "I believe that's the point." She takes the bottle and tips it up to her lips. She takes a sip, and I can tell she's trying to be cool, but as she swallows her eyes water and the muscles at the corners of her mouth pull into a frown. "Oh, God. That really is awful," she says, her voice sharp like razors.

I take a swig, and it's like ingesting fire. I spew the liquid out in my best impression of a sprinkler.

James jumps back laughing.

"You okay, Charlie?" Becca asks.

"Don't drink this, Bec. It's poison."

"You're not the boss of me."

"True," I say and take another drink. I force myself to hold the flames inside.

By the time we make it to the glen, we've all had a few big gulps of the stuff. My whole body is warm and my fingertips feel electric. Also, my teeth feel fuzzy.

James excuses himself to go water a tree, and I flump in the grass near the creek. The dew soaks through my clothes, cool against my hot skin. I set the bottle down in the grass beside me. I can hear the low whispering of the creek, the slight breeze in the tops of the trees, and a chorus of crickets.

Becca tosses pebbles in the creek. They go *plink, plink, ker-plonk.*

Charlotte stretches out beside me. There's maybe a single blade of grass separating our fingertips.

When I open my eyes to watch the branches sway above me, a feeling of complete contentment washes over me. Followed by a feeling of nausea. I close my eyes again.

"See, I thought you had to keep your eyes open for star gazing."

"I can see them just fine," I say, my voice a timpani in my head.

Charlotte's laugh crashes around me. "You look a little... unwell. You okay?"

I shake my head. It makes a soft, scratchy sound in the grass. Inside my head, it sounds like a landslide.

"You're kind of a cheap date, huh?"

"Wha—" I stupidly open my eyes and turn my head to look at her. The movement sends a ripple of panic down my spine. It wraps around my stomach and squeezes. I hold my breath.

"Close your eyes," she says, sitting up and moving so she can place my head in her lap.

I try to sit up, but my head feels both hollow *and* heavy. How is that possible?

Her cool fingers find my temples. "Don't yak."

"Okay," I say, laying my head back again. "No yakking. I promise."

"Good because these are Jo's shoes and she'd be pissed if you ruined another pair."

I peek up at her. Her cheeks are pink and the moonlight is tangled in her black hair like a halo. "You're so…" *Beautiful, funny, talented, smart, sexy…*my tongue sits like a weight in my mouth.

"Uh-huh. *You* are so drunk."

I manage a thumbs-up sign. Charlotte's fingers now curl through my hair, brushing it away from my forehead.

"You're a good guy, Charlie."

"Are you using me?"

Charlotte's cheeks pale a little, but her lips twist into a smile. "A little."

"It's okay if you are. I let Carmen cheat off me in organic chemistry last year. But she wasn't as pretty as you. Greta says we should double date."

"Oh, she does?"

"Yes."

"What do you say?"

"What do I say to what?"

Charlotte chuckles. "I'm going to give you a pass on that invitation." Her fingers massage my skull making my mind blank out. "Where is Greta?"

I can't even remember who Greta is for a second. When it comes to me, I manage to murmur, "Mad."

Charlotte's fingers freeze in my hair. "At whom?"

"Me. Always me. I'm kind of a huge disappointment as a best

friend. She kinda saved my life, or at least my future life, one time. I owe her a lot, but this year feels different. I haven't told her certain things."

"About me?"

I nod. "Which sucks because she's smart, not just about school stuff. She's people smart. She helps me figure out my next steps, you know. Without her help, I may end up stepping in a land mine."

"You should definitely talk to her if she's mad," she says, her fingers moving through my hair again, behind my ears, along my neck. It feels so damn good. "A sincere apology wouldn't hurt."

"She could finally get that video footage she wants."

Charlotte chuckles. "Yeah, I don't know what that means."

"We should definitely double," I say just as Becca yells for Charlotte to come see something.

Charlotte leans so her lips are just above my forehead. "Ask me when we're sober." She lays my head on the grass where I instantly pass out.

4.0

James smacks my shoulder. "Hey, we gotta go. I hear someone coming." He's trying to pull me to my feet. Either he's slurring or my ears are stuffed with cotton.

When I stand up, the trees around us do a funny jig. "Oh, God. Dancing trees are not good." Charlotte buoys me up from one side, while James holds the other. We all lean into each other for stability as a lone figure comes around the corner.

"What the hell's going on?"

Busted.

Greta stops five paces before us and puts her hands on her hips. Becca yelps and hides behind James.

"It's Greta! Hey, guys! It's Greta!" James shouts and barrels toward her. Charlotte catches me before I face plant. "I didn't know if you got my text, but you did! And you're here!"

Greta eyes the mostly empty bottle in James's hand. He holds out the bottle toward her. "I saved some just for you."

Greta grimaces, but it turns into a lopsided grin. "Um, wow, I'll pass on the alcoholic backwash, but thanks."

James nods. "You sure?"

She laughs. "Yep." When she looks at me, leaning on Charlotte, her expression gets grim. "You okay, Chuck?"

I don't answer. My brain feels like it's wrapped in a fur coat.

"He's fine," James says, wrapping an arm around Greta. "I did good, huh?"

"Good?"

"They look cute."

"They look wasted."

"We can hear you," Charlotte sings.

Greta glares at her.

I'm concentrating on keeping my feet under me. I must have Dad's sucky-alcohol-metabolism-disorder. James seems to be better off. He can walk and talk at the same time.

"No one's wasted," James says, demonstrating his amazing walking/talking skills.

Just then my legs buckle, and Charlotte can't hold me up. I sit down on my ass and end up pulling Charlotte down with me. Greta eyes us, folds her arms over her chest, and then glares at James.

"He's tired is all," James says.

I groan. Becca helps Charlotte up, but I just roll over on my face. The cool grass feels exquisite. Yes, I said exquisite.

I silently pray. *Please, lord of drunken night stupidity, let me get out of this with just a shred of my dignity.* I think I asked Charlotte on a date. Unfortunately, I don't remember her answer. Now Greta is here making her mean face. And I get why she's mad at me, but why's she looking at Charlotte like that? *And dear lord of drunken stupidity, also could I not puke on anyone right now? Thanks.*

"Oh-kay." Greta stomps over and pulls me to my feet. She leads me away from Charlotte. "Let's go. I came back to talk to Charlie, but I can see it'll have to wait."

"You can talk, G. We're listening," James says, pinning my other arm in his grip.

Greta searches my face and looks over her shoulder to where Becca and Charlotte are leaning on each other. "Nope. Let's go."

"Right," James says, lifting the bottle in a toast and finishing it off. "Homeward." He tosses the empty bottle into the creek. It makes a funny plunking sound.

Greta and James lead me off toward home with Becca and Charlotte trailing after us. I look over my shoulder once and catch Charlotte's eye. I hope my expression tells her how sorry I am that my underage adoptive parents are psychos and all, but I probably just look like I've got alcohol poisoning.

I wake to a distinct pounding. My mouth feels like I've spent all night sucking on James's ratty Adidas sneakers. And my head—oh my God, my head. I wriggle further under my covers to get away from the thudding in my head.

Except it isn't just in my head.

Thud! Thud! Thud! "Better be decent in there, boys. I'm coming in."

I peek from my covers. Greta promised she'd be back, first thing in the morning. Actually, she said, "I can't talk to you when you look like you're gonna puke. Sleep it off drunk-ass."

The door flies open, but gets stuck when it jams into James's body sprawled on the floor. It had to hurt, but he only moans and rolls over.

Greta stomps into the room and slams the door. My head erupts with another round of pounding, and I want to retreat, but I've been spotted.

"Get up," Greta yells. Maybe she isn't yelling, but it feels like it. She rips the pillow from under my head and whirls to smack James with it. "You, too, Sleeping Beauty." She hits him again. He snuffles and grabs the pillow from her mid-smackdown. Snuggling up to the pillow, he falls comatose again.

Greta rolls her eyes and turns back to me. "You sober?"

The room tilts like a gyroscope as I sit up. My throat feels raw. "Maybe. I honestly don't know."

"I barely got you home last night. How much did you drink?"

I squint in the dim light. "I don't know."

"What were you thinking?"

"You were gone. We don't do well without you."

Greta slumps into my desk chair, like all the angry wind holding her afloat has died away. "Jesus, Chuck. What are you going to do next year when we're at different schools?"

"Throw myself into my work?"

Greta's smirk is grim. "As long as that work doesn't involve the distillation of ingredients to produce C_2H_5OH."

"Alcohol. Very funny."

Using her foot, Greta rolls James onto his side. Watching him sleep, she looks so sad.

"I'm sorry, Gret." I pause, swallowing hard. "Did you want to get your phone to video this?" Her right eye twitches a little. "Sorry for that, too," I say, pointing at her eye. She smiles.

"I should've told you about Charlotte. It was stupid. I'm stupid. But, Charlotte's like—"

Like what? The answer? I thought I had my future settled until I met Charlotte. Now, it's all a blur.

Greta gnaws a fingernail. There are shadows under her eyes. Even her curls look tired.

"You're my best friend," I say. "I should've told you."

She nods. "You're not the only one with secrets." She frowns at James. I think she's going to chew on her fingernail again, but instead, she gives her finger a good lick before reaching down and jamming it in James's ear.

"Arragag," James sputters, sitting up and swatting at his ear. As soon as he's vertical, his spit-soaked ear is the least of his worries.

He grabs his head, smooshing his kinky curls. "Ohmygodmyhead hurtsIthinkI'mdying," he mumbles before flopping back down.

Greta chuckles. "Good. I hope your head hurts all the way to next week, you drunk." She nudges him again. "Stay awake. I'm about to confess some shit."

James groans, but he's paying attention.

Greta inhales, sitting up straighter in the chair. "We all know Chuck and baby Finch are buddies, and Chuck sucks for not telling us."

James and I grunt because nodding would hurt too damn much.

"Okay, before I go on, Chuck's got to be honest."

"I will."

"How much do you already know about Charlotte Finch?"

"Not much." I pick at a grass stain on my pant leg. "She likes old movies where people randomly break into song, but also has an appreciation for comics."

James gives a thumbs up. "Cool."

"She sketches constantly in this notebook she keeps. She does this amazing hip wiggle thing when she dances. She smells like a garden of sugar-cookies—"

I shut up, my ears suffering a sudden heat wave.

"Ohh-kay," Greta encourages me. "These are all super nice things, but what else?"

There are plenty of other things I can say, but they would all fall into the "super nice things" category, and Greta looks like she might punch me if I continue down that vein.

"I don't know, G. What do you want me to say?"

Greta looks away, watching the dust swirl in the gray light from the blinds.

The pounding in my head ratchets up a notch forcing me to yell over it, "Greta, What? She's a he? She's wanted for murder? She has thirty days to live?"

"Oh, Chuck."

I push myself up from the bed—too fast—the room sways, but I hold my ground. "Don't you, 'Oh, Chuck,' me. What do you know?"

Greta holds her hands up, surrendering. "When I met Charlotte here last night, I was shocked to be face to face with the girl whose secret I'd been hiding. When I bailed on you guys, it was mostly because I was mad at myself. I'm supposed to protect you, Chuck, and I failed."

"Secret?" I ask.

"Dr. Whiting called my mom a week ago."

"What did that assbag want?" James growls from his prone position on the floor. "To threaten you some more?"

Greta looks down at him. "I wish."

"What then?" I ask.

"I'm not supposed to know this. I overheard my mom's half of the conversation and some of Dr. Whiting's, too." Greta pauses to gnaw what's left of the fingernail on her index finger (not the one that was just in James's ear). "Ever noticed how loud he is? I always thought it was the school's loudspeaker system, but no, that man is loud."

"Fortissimo," says James, most of his face buried in his pillow.

"People," I say, my patience draining fast. "This tangent is not interesting me."

"Charlotte's sick." The words tumble out of Greta's mouth.

"Sick?" I see Charlotte in my mind's eye, staring out at the rain from my porch.

"Real sick, Chuck. Sick enough Dr. Whiting asked my mom to come meet Ms. Finch for a few therapy sessions."

"Whoa," James says. He sits up too fast and reels. "That's why Whiting was being all protective."

Greta nods. "He doesn't care about Ms. Finch any more than he does about any of us though. I heard him say he was counting on her to turn around the school's reputation. It's all about the prestige. He's worried Finch will let a little thing like her sister being sick get in the way of her performance at school." This last sentence is so laden with sarcasm I fear the floor joists can't hold its weight.

"This is stupid." I can feel anger ignite in my blood, like I'm an explosive ready to blow. Charlotte and sick do not go together. These are realities that cannot coexist.

"What kind of sick?" James asks.

"Cancer."

Monster.

"What kind?" I ask.

Greta shrugs.

I don't know why I asked. Charlotte already told me. *Because I'm sick in the head.*

My mind is racing. This can't be true. I'm still dreaming some messed up, alcohol-induced nightmare. The inside of my mouth feels like something vile has crawled in and died. I attempt to spit out whatever is decaying. "Fuck."

It doesn't help.

I pace my room and smash the remaining Oreos under my heels, feeling grim satisfaction as they crumble.

"I'm sorry, man," James says reaching a hand out as I pass.

Greta explodes, "Freaking Dr. Whiting has the loudest freaking voice ever. Why can't that man regulate his volume?" Like our principal's booming baritone is to blame.

"Yes, Gret," James says, "*He* is the root of all evil." He pats her knee.

Greta stands and delivers a quick punch to his shoulder before taking me by the hand and leading me back to my bed and coaxing me to sit down. "You doing okay in there, Charlie?"

She sits next to me, studying my face intently. When my mind broke before, Greta brought me to her mom. Dr. McCaulley taught me to look at stressful situations as triage. Scan the body and categorize the injuries: those that will heal on their own, those that will never heal regardless of the treatment, and those that treatment will immediately affect.

"I don't know, yet," I tell Greta.

We're silent while I breathe and sift through my injuries. The churning in my gut will pass. The chaos in my head will need some work to sort through. But my chest, well, I feel like a grenade has blown that wide open.

I cling to Greta's hand. "I don't know how to solve for any of this."

"So don't," she says. "Walk away. It's not your job to solve anything for the Finches. They sucked you in, and this is going to chew you up and spit you out. Charlotte should have told you. She shouldn't have pulled you into this. This is her fault. Walk away, Chuck."

She makes it sound so easy. But when I think about walking away, all I can see is the desperation in Charlotte's eyes as she sat in the rain on my front porch. Can I honestly make that better? Make things easier for her?

"I can't walk away."

Greta's sigh is a mountain shifting down to its eons old core. "Then you'll figure it out."

"That's a circular argument, Gret."

"Yes," she says, patting my knee. "And you just love circles, don't you?"

I do. Circles are my favorite.

4.1

I falter a moment before knocking on Becca's door. I finally convinced Greta and James to go, saying I was going to shower and sleep. But I couldn't sleep. I lay in my bed counting silently, holding on to the numbers like they could stitch me back together. Numbers can do many things, but they make lousy bandages. I comb my fingers through my damp hair and knock.

"Yup," Becca calls.

I open the door and peer in. Becca is reading and Charlotte is sketching. "Everyone in here feeling all right?" Jesus! That's how I open the conversation? This is not going to go well.

But the girls just smile. "Some of us can hold their liquor better than others, big bro."

"Yeah. That was rough."

We all stand there looking at each other for a minute before Charlotte asks, "Did you need something?"

"Oh, yeah. Um…I need help with something for your sister's class. Would it be cheating if I asked you?" The discomfort in my voice thuds louder than the music.

Charlotte closes her sketchbook and stands.

I study her, looking for a sign pointing to her cancer. Were there dark circles under her eyes last week? I don't remember her

MOMA T-shirt being so baggy on her. Has her hair always been so short? She looks tired and as if she needs a shopping intervention, but there's nothing screaming, "Death is coming."

Charlotte shakes her head and sighs, like I've disappointed her somehow. Did she know I was scanning her like a human MRI?

"Be right back, Bec," she calls over her shoulder. Standing in front of me she says, "Let's go get a drink, Charlie."

I can feel my pasty skin go even paler at the mention of drinks. Becca laughs. I try to smile, but I'm afraid it looks more like a facial tick, so I drop Charlotte's gaze and nod.

Once we reach the kitchen Charlotte opens the fridge and pulls out a pitcher of tea. I grab two glasses and fill them with ice, then watch her fill them with the cold, brown brew. We lean on opposite ends of the kitchen island and don't touch our drinks.

"So, listen," I start, but can't find the words to finish.

"Are you asking me out again?"

I blink, the foggy memory of my head in Charlotte's lap swirling around my mind like water in the toilet bowl. It makes me nauseated. How could I ask her out like that? She deserves better.

"That's a no?" Charlotte tries to smile, but the lines of worry between her brows make the smile look painted on. She gives up and pinches the bridge of her nose, squeezing her eyes shut. "How'd you find out?"

"Find out what?"

She opens one blue eye in a challenge. "There's only one other thing I can think you would want to ask about that would make you look this uncomfortable around me."

"Greta's mom is a shrink."

"What about the whole confidentiality thing?"

"Our principal has no volume control. He suggested your sister meet with Greta's mom to talk about—"

Charlotte heaves a giant sigh. "Awesome."

"Is it true?"

Charlotte stares at the ice in her glass. "It's complicated."

"Shouldn't be. It's either true or false."

"Maybe in your world, but not in mine."

"Jesus, Charlotte. We live in the same world. I deserve to know the truth. Answer the question." My palms are sweaty, so I press them up against the cold glass. Now the question is out there, I don't want to know the answer.

"It's true I have cancer. Brain cancer."

The words sink into the space between us.

"How long?"

"Seven years, five months, twenty days."

A spark ignites in my chest. "Seven years, five months, twenty days? How can they be so exact?"

Charlotte's brow furrows under the dark curls there. "Here I was laboring under the delusion you were smart."

"What?"

"I've *had* cancer for seven years, five months, twenty days."

The little spark flickers out.

"I meant how long until you die?"

"How long until *you* die?"

I open my mouth to snap back at her, but nothing comes out. It's a ridiculous question. How should I know? Average lifespan for a middle-class Caucasian male is 76.5 years. But I'd like to think I'm above average.

"You don't know either, do you? True: I have terminal cancer. True: I will die. False: Charles Hanson will live forever. See how true and false gets complicated?"

"But you'll die before me." The words have fallen out before I can stop them.

"Prove it." Her whole body is trembling, except her hands. They are perfect statues, squeezed into tight fists.

"You want me to do the math? Because statistically speaking, I'm right."

Charlotte leans over the counter and grabs the front of my shirt in one of her fists, like an old gangster movie. She pulls me closer to her so I'm standing on tiptoes to breach the kitchen island between us.

"Keep pushing me, Hanson, and I might kill *you* to prove my point."

I wrap one of my hands around hers. At my touch, her grip loosens.

"Charlotte, I'm worried about you," I whisper.

Fury pours through the cracks of her thick walls as her grip tightens on my collar again. Her other fist pulls back and shoots forward like a rubber band let loose.

The moment Charlotte's fist makes contact the world explodes around me. Everything goes from red to black and the only thing holding me up is Charlotte Finch's other fist wound in the fabric of my shirt.

> **Subject:** Charlotte Finch,
>
> **Method:** Try to console her after learning of her cancer,
>
> **Result:** Punched in the face.

There it is. The beating I've been expecting since the moment I laid eyes on her at the Krispy Kreme. I knew I'd end up getting hurt.

I crumple onto the counter when Charlotte lets me go. I can taste blood on my lips, but can't be sure where her punch landed because my entire head is pounding—again.

Keeping my cheek on the counter, I wrench my neck to watch for Charlotte's next attack. She's reaching into the freezer and mumbling something I can't make out through the ringing in my ears. She slams the freezer door so I know whatever she's saying isn't nice.

She advances on me with a paper towel in one hand and ice cubes in the other.

"Here," she says, thrusting them both at me. "You may want to clean up."

I take the towel and dab it on my upper lip, which is starting to feel like a hot air balloon. The towel is red in no time, so Charlotte hands me another one.

"I've got something in my purse to help," she says, stalking upstairs.

I wobble over to the mirror by the back door. My lip isn't the source of the bleeding; it's my nose. Did she break my nose? A girl punched me in the face *and* she broke my nose?

Charlotte catches me at the mirror. "It'll be fine. Your good looks are still intact."

"You punched me," I choke out, blood pooling in the back of my throat.

Charlotte's face crumbles into what looks like an apology. Before she gets it out though, she changes her mind. "Yes, I punched you," she says evenly, her hands tearing open the wrappers of whatever she retrieved from her purse.

"Why'd you punch me?"

"You were being a jerk about my cancer."

"No, I was being…"

"I don't come here for pity. I get that at home and school and pretty much everywhere else I go. Don't ruin this for me, Charlie. Your house is my cancer-free zone."

We watch each other for a moment as my nose bleeds.

Charlotte grabs my wrist and pulls me over toward the sink. "You're making a mess," she says as blood drips into the sink basin.

I silently pray Mom won't be getting back from the grocery story anytime soon. This would not go over well.

Charlotte takes a long cardboard tube from one of the wrappers. "Let me stop the bleeding."

Gently, she presses on the bridge of my nose, feeling the cartilage. "It's not broken. Just burst blood vessels. You may have some interesting bruising." She pops a white cottony thing out of the cardboard and shoves it in one nostril, then does the same with the second.

"You're a doctor now?"

"I've spent enough time with them to have earned an honorary degree." She wipes the blood away from my chin. A smile plays at the corners of her mouth. "All done. Don't take them out for at least ten minutes."

I blink back tears from the stinging in my nose, like an entire hive of yellow jackets flew up there. I turn away from Charlotte and look in the mirror again.

My reflection peers back at me with two cottony cylinders protruding from my nostrils, complete with pull-strings for easy removal. I grab one of the strings to yank, but Charlotte stops me.

"I said leave them alone."

"First, you punch me, then you shove tampons up my nose?"

"Trust me," she says, retrieving the ice from the counter and wrapping it in a paper towel. "It'll stop the bleeding."

She guides me toward the kitchen table. "This will help the swelling," she says, holding the compress to the bridge of my nose. She cups the back of my neck with her free hand to keep me from jerking away from her. The coolness of her fingers there makes me shiver.

"I'm sorry I roughed you up," she says.

"You aren't the first girl to punch me." The worried wrinkles on her forehead slide away as she smiles at me. "You won't be the last."

Her smile flickers. "I get it, okay? Cancer freaks people out. It's why I didn't tell you. I didn't want you to look at me like this." She shifts the compress, and I try not to flinch. "Everyone needs time and space to process it when they find out. *Everyone.* Some of them don't ever bridge that space to come back to me. Cancer has made me selfish. I didn't want to lose you."

"Does Becca know?"

Charlotte nods.

"Did you punch her, too?"

"No. She handled it with more grace than you."

That seems about right. It's hard to get a rise out of Becca.

She removes the ice pack and hands it to me. Standing, she leans forward and brushes my forehead with a light kiss. "Try to remember, Charlie, please. I'm more than my diagnosis."

I close my eyes to keep the room from spinning. When I feel steady enough to open them, Charlotte has disappeared.

4.2

Greta and James are impressed with my rumpled face. When I step into the kitchen where James is making a taco dinner, he drops the wooden spoon and cries out, "C-man got smacked." I think he may piss himself from laughing so hard.

Greta tries to remain cool, but it doesn't last. She pats my arm. "It's okay, sweetie. A little makeup will fix it. Maybe a paper bag, too."

"What'd you tell your parents?" James asks.

"I walked into the door while texting Greta. Dad said, 'For a genius, you can be pretty dumb.' They're both proud of me."

James laughs, but Greta says, "Wonder what everyone at school will think."

"Forget it," I say, grabbing a handful of chips and joining Melody and Ella on the couch to watch cartoons.

Melody's honey brown eyes bunch up when she smiles her gap-toothed smile. "You look like Mr. Incredible, Charlie."

"Oh yeah?"

She points at my eyes. "You're wearing a mask." She and Ella dissolve into giggles.

I don't feel like Mr. Incredible.

After dinner, James, Greta, and I go out to get some ice cream. On the way home, I can't help but turn down Charlotte's street. I slow the car across from her house. There are no lights on in the front, but Charlotte's silver Civic is in the driveway.

"You sure you're okay, man?" James asks.

I work my jaw to loosen the stiff muscles there. "No."

I drive around the corner and park the car on the side of the road.

"What're we doing here, Chuck?"

"I don't know." I open my door and get out. James and Greta follow. "I'm going to take a quick walk."

James throws a massive forearm around my shoulders. "Want some company?"

His expression is like a plate glass window, so I can see all the emotions lining up behind it. At the front of the line, friendship looks out at me.

"Thanks."

We walk up the greenway running behind Ms. Finch's house.

Once we're nearby, Greta goes street side to check the numbers painted on the mailboxes. Recognizing it from the back is tricky. I think we've passed it already.

James and I toss stones in the creek while we wait for Greta's report.

I try to judge the weight of a stone in my palm before tossing it. When I hear it hit the water, I calculate the time it will take for it to sink to the bottom.

"You really like her?" James asks, interrupting my math.

I'm not sure I want to talk about Charlotte right now. My nose aches as I wrinkle it. "Does it matter?"

"Let's do a little experiment to answer that question." James shifts his weight next to me, and I think it's to pick up another rock, but instead, his right shoulder crashes into my chest as he shoves me into the creek. I land on my butt in the murky sludge coating the bottom.

While it's not exactly cold in the south in late October, Sycamore Creek did not get the memo. The water temperature is chilly enough that my manly business shrinks to a size even the Hubble telescope couldn't pick up.

"What the hell was that for?" So much for all that friendship I thought I saw a moment ago.

James levels me with a rare look for him—gravity. "Does it matter?"

"Yes, it matters. It's cold, and I'm soaked."

"How much do you like Charlotte? I dare you to tell me it doesn't matter."

It's like the air is being squeezed from my lungs.

"See. It matters. Greta's here because she's loyal to you. I'm here for Greta. Why are you here, freezing your nuts off, for Charlotte Finch?"

And it's there. The answer is there, like it was always part of me. "Because she matters."

"Right. If I were to lose Greta, I'd never be the same. Look at my mom, for Christ's sake." He pauses, his hands opening and closing at his sides like he's trying to grasp the words right out of the air. "Without Dad, she became a shell, Chuck. And no matter what my sisters and I did, we couldn't fill her up again. It's been five years and I'm only beginning to see signs of life in her. Loss like that has a long half-life. This *matter* has a mass so heavy it could crush you if you're not careful."

I shiver from the creek, looking up at him with nothing to say. The pain in his eyes says it's true. His shoulders soften away from his ears as he takes a deep breath and blows it out.

"Look, I'm not saying you shouldn't help this girl, but you should know what you're getting into. I'm also not saying you really have a choice when it comes to your motives. I get that. No one wants to fall and get hurt." He steps closer to the creek's edge. "I'm just saying to prepare for heartache, because it's always harder to be the one still hanging around." He reaches a hand out toward me, clasping mine firmly in his and pulling me from the water.

"And know I'll be here to help pick you up," he says once we're both standing on solid ground.

I need to reevaluate. James isn't just Greta's boyfriend. James is my other best friend.

Greta reappears, her mouth falling open at the sight of me, drenched from chest to toes. "Do I even want to know why Chuck is soaking wet?" she asks James.

"He's learning," he says over his shoulder.

"He pushed me," I splutter.

But Greta looks pleased to see me soaked. "When you're done with your lesson, Chuck," she calls, walking in the direction she's pointing, "Finch's house is three down."

James chuckles as I wring creek water from the hem of my sweater. He throws an arm around me.

When we approach the back gate, Greta hisses, "Someone's outside."

We all hit the dirt, my sopping clothes squelching on impact.

Ms. Finch is pacing on a patio behind the house with her phone. "Dad, she's being ridiculous."

She stops pacing and drops the phone from her ear, looking up to the star-filled sky. Returning to the phone, she says, "We can't *make* her do anything."

She goes quiet again and picks up the pacing. "Look, I'm sorry. Can you calm down? I'm not trying to upset you." Just behind her, I make out the back door, lit by a globe light. As Ms. Finch moves away from the door, I see a flap at the bottom quiver. Suddenly, the hellhound pokes out its head, its long nose quivering as it scents the air.

Greta smacks me on the shoulder. "She has a dog?"

James mutters, "It's not a dog. It's a freaking wolf."

"In the wake of the whole cancer announcement I may have forgotten to mention it. So sue me," I snap.

Luna's supersonic hearing must be engaged because her ears stand at attention, and I swear, she stares right at me before tipping her head back and howling.

Ms. Finch jumps and growls back at the dog, "Luna, hush."

She peers out into the yard for a moment before pushing Luna back through the little door. "Hold on, Dad," she says. The door closes behind her and the light above the patio goes dark.

My brain is stretching, trying to figure out what Ms. Finch could be talking about. What is it Charlotte is refusing to do? Clean her room? Take the SAT? Go to the university next year?

How am I supposed to figure any of this out when new variables keep popping up in the problem?

James and Greta belly crawl through the brush back to the path. I stay and watch the house. One of the upstairs windows is lit, framing Charlotte's silhouette.

"Chuck," Greta calls. I wave her off.

Charlotte is sketching in her familiar sketchbook, making furious slash marks at the page with a pencil. As I watch, she throws her book across the room, her chest rising and falling like a hummingbird. She collapses in on herself like a dying star, and I watch her wipe her eyes and rock.

Charlotte is crying.

I've arrived at an event horizon and there's no turning back from the black hole sucking at all of the pieces that make me whole. Those pieces fly away from me at the speed of light. All but one. The only piece that matters. The one with Charlotte's name burned onto it.

4.3

"I'm going to tell Charlotte to clear out of her house tomorrow night," I tell Greta and James Sunday morning at Krispy Kreme. We've got our laptops and papers spread all over the table, doing homework and practicing our presentation for Ms. Finch tomorrow. "I think we've done enough ass kissing for a while."

James holds up a fist for me to pound. "What's the plan?"

I pull a scrap of paper from my back pocket and hand it to Greta.

She glances over it and pierces me with a look. "Are you serious?"

"As cancer." I scowl at the girl behind the counter who keeps gaping at my bruised face.

Greta folds and unfolds the paper. "Chuck, you know I'm not afraid of Whiting—"

"Even though you should be," James interjects, pointing his pen at her like a light saber. Greta shoots him a dirty look before continuing.

"But there's no cute explanation for this." She rattles the paper on the last word.

I rub my sweaty palms down the thighs of my pants. "It's just a stink bomb."

"Just?"

I shrug. "It's only chemistry, Gret."

James peers over Greta's shoulder. "No way, man. Finch could have us arrested."

I nod. "Only if someone gets caught." Somehow, I'm pretty sure this isn't what Mrs. Dunwitty meant when she told me to man up, but it's the best I can come up with on short notice. "Which is why I'll do it alone."

"Chuck," Greta says, her voice mournful. "This is between the Finch sisters. You shouldn't get involved. This isn't your battle."

I'm stretched out on my side of the booth, my feet up on the bench. I study my shoes, the way the laces are fraying and the fabric is worn soft after so many years. These shoes could outlast Charlotte. That's the most depressing thought I've had all day, and I've had nothing but sad-ass thoughts.

"Maybe not," I finally admit, because even I know this is insane. I knew getting involved with Charlotte would be a deviation to my arrow straight life, but this, this is like following a line in a completely different reality. "But people get caught in things they can't escape. Things like cancer. Charlotte didn't ask for that, just like I didn't ask for this. This is supposed to be a war, right? I can't cure Charlotte's cancer." These words sound so loud in my head. I'd have thought I'd shouted them if James and Greta weren't still leaning across the table to hear me. "This is all I can do for her. If I'm a casualty of war, then so be it."

"You sure you're up for the sacrifice?" James asks.

I look from him to Greta, sitting side-by-side, unaware they're so close their shoulders are touching, drawn together by the magnetic pull of emotions. I want that closeness, too.

"Well, good thing we staked out Finch's house last night," Greta says, ignoring my non-answer. She passes the paper to me over the table. "At least we know what we're up against. I, for one, am not about to get busted for this prank no matter how irresistible Charlotte Finch is."

My ears flush, but one look at the twisted smirk on Greta's face, and I know she understands. I know she's figured me out.

Becca stops me that night on my way out. Her brown hair is falling out of her ponytail in chunks just the right size for twirling around a finger.

She holds her black wool cap out for me. "You may want this," she says.

"For what?"

"For whatever you and your friends are planning tonight. I know you're up to something, and I think I want to say thanks. Thanks for helping Charlotte."

I take the cap and turn it around and around in my fingers. "You think?"

"It's complicated, isn't it?"

"I want her to be happy."

"Me too," she says, her hand brushing mine before she drifts back into her room.

We're taking James's two littlest sisters trick-or-treating as adorable decoys, so we meet at his house at dusk Sunday night. They run around the kitchen in their costumes. Ella is a black cat. Her curly hair is tied in two poufs on top of her head and Greta has drawn a cat nose and whiskers on her using eyeliner. Melody is a witch with a tall pointy hat that flops at the tip since it got crushed when the girls were wrestling.

Greta is stress eating Mrs. Thomas's Halloween candy. James grabs the Tootsie Roll she's just unwrapped and jams it in his mouth.

"Look, Gret," he says. "We aren't going to do any permanent

damage to Finch's house. We're just going to make it smell like a jock's junk." He's trying to convince himself as much as her. We're all feeling jittery.

"And we've got the cover of Halloween, a night known for hell-raising," I say as I press a mostly-frozen steak to the bridge of my nose. It still throbs like a distant drum beat. The steak is Greta's idea—a diversion for the hellhound. I'm supposed to lob it and run, but it feels awfully good pressed against my face.

Ella runs up to James and hands him his zombie mask. "Let's go. Can't we go, Jamie?" she whines, rubbing her hand across her nose and smearing the paint of her tiny black cat nose.

James looks at Greta and me. I tug on Becca's hat. I'm ready. Greta grabs another candy bar.

"Okay, kiddos." James pulls his mask on. "Let's trick-or-treat."

The little girls burst into squeals and run for the front door. They sprint from house to house, eating most of the candy before it even sees the inside of their buckets.

By the time we reach Ms. Finch's street, the girls are tired, and Ella is feeling sick to her stomach. We're two doors from Ms. Finch's house when Ella begins to cry.

"Jamie, I want to go home," she whimpers. "I'm done trick-or-treating."

Greta and I exchange wide-eyed glances. James bends down on one knee and pats Ella's shoulder. "We're almost done, El. Just a few more?" Her whimpering ceases when he hands her another piece of candy.

Anything for candy.

We steer them straight to Ms. Finch's front walk. James pulls on his mask and Greta and I disappear around the side yard. Our plan is to infiltrate the house via the doggie door. We peek into the backyard.

No sign of the dog. Still, I pull the steak out of the plastic baggie.

Greta takes it from me whispering, "We both know I've got better aim."

She's right.

She hands me the stink bomb, in a small, lidded box we nicked from the recycling bin outside Charlotte's and Becca's school this afternoon. The school's name is on an address label on the lid. I'm hoping this will make it seem more like it's one of the morons at Sandstone behind this. It's a thin veil, but I've got a lot riding on it.

A tremor runs through my hands, making the box shake. Screw Dr. Whiting getting pissed. Ms. Finch will know it's me, and she'll either bury me in poetry or just go ahead and fail me. Either way, I'm a dead man. Well, not *dead* dead. What lit term is that again? The exaggeration one? I'm all about the exaggeration one.

"We don't have to do this," Greta says, noticing my wobbly hands.

The night is cool and damp, so our breath puffs around us, making our own atmosphere—physical evidence that we are alive.

"Yes," I say, my hands calm, my jaw tense. "I do." I don't understand this war between sisters, but I've chosen my side.

I nod at Greta, and we take off running toward the lit back door. I skid to a halt in front of it and open the box. My pulse thrums in my ears.

I unscrew the lid on the jar, my eyes watering instantly. The smell is so potent Greta gags behind me. I try to shove the lid on the box, but my blurry vision makes it difficult.

"Holy stink, Batman," I mutter.

Fatal mistake.

The stench drifts into my mouth so I can taste its foulness.

Greta is backing away from me, looking pale.

I finally manage the lid and am about to shove the thing in the doggie door, when a huge gray head pokes out from inside the house, nose aquiver.

The beast eyes me. I can hear a faint growl in its throat.

"Greta," I choke. The fumes are making me lightheaded. "The meat. Throw the meat."

Greta's good arm does us no good when she's terrified. She drops the steak and covers her eyes with her hands. Peeking between fingers, she hisses, "Run, Chuck. Leave it and run."

I smile at the dog. The dog stares at me like I'm the last piece of kibble on earth. Its low growl shifts to a whimper as its left ear twists backward, listening to something I can't hear inside the house.

"Nice doggie?" I say. Effective because the nice doggie pulls its head back in the door and disappears. I look at Greta and shrug before lifting the flap to peek inside. I can see Ms. Finch's clean and empty kitchen.

Without further hesitation, I shove the putrid box through the door and I am withdrawing my head when I hear Ms. Finch's voice coming down the hallway.

"Let me get you a towel. Oh, you poor thing," she says.

I freeze.

James's voice, full of panic calls, "She's fine. Really. We've got to go."

"She's not fine. She's covered in vomit."

One of James's sisters has vomited on Ms. Finch's front porch and I've just shoved a stink bomb in her back door.

Half of me thinks, *Yesssss!*

The other half thinks, *GET OUT, FOOL.* But it's like I'm watching bad reality TV. I can't turn away until I know if the country bumpkin with questionable intelligence will shoot himself in the foot.

Ms. Finch gasps and clasps her hands over her mouth and nose as she steps into her kitchen. "The hell?" she gasps behind her hands. Luna starts to howl.

Greta decides now is the time to put her good arm to use. She snatches my collar and yanks me up, dragging me through the yard and along the greenway, coming out to the street at the end of the block.

Panting, she asks, "Did she see you?"

"No."

Greta's body thaws with relief, but mine stays taut, each muscle pulled tight with the lie I've just told.

Did Ms. Finch see me?

Yes.

4.4

At home, I flop on my bed fully dressed. Maybe I'll skip school tomorrow to job hunt. If I start working at Quick Chicken now, I could be an assistant manager by the time I'm thirty-five. There's no way I'll get into MIT with a criminal record.

MIT!

I leap from bed, ignoring the spinning sensation in my throbbing head, and open up my laptop.

"Charlie?" Becca stands at my door holding her cell phone out.

"I can't help you with your phone now. I'm busy." I pull up my application and begin skimming, but Becca's long fingers dig into my shoulder.

"I don't need your help," she says, wiggling the phone. "Charlotte wants to talk to you."

My stomach tangles with nerves and guilt.

She hates me.

This was not the help she was hoping for.

Becca hands me the phone.

"Charles Hanson, you little shit." Charlotte's voice is so light it buoys me. "That was genius. How did you get the little girl to puke simultaneously with the stink bomb?"

"You're not mad?"

"Me?" Charlotte laughs. "Jo was so pissed she went straight to bed. After she opened all the windows, of course."

"And threw out her shoes?" My stomach is still queasy, but Charlotte's enthusiasm is catching.

Charlotte laughs again, a maniacal string of notes. "Her shoes. Yes. They were disgusting."

"Glad you approved. I wasn't sure." I click to a new window in my browser, pulling up a blank search screen.

"It's like you are an angel sent to watch over me. A demented, brilliant angel."

"So everything's okay? We're okay?"

Charlotte's quiet a fraction of a second longer than I'm comfortable. But her response feels warm and settling.

"Thanks, Charlie."

She says a quick bye and I hear the *click* of her disconnecting.

I try to hold on to the sound of her voice as long as I can. She called me an angel. Demented—but brilliant.

Freshman year, my favorite science fair project was Adam March's exploration of tumors in rats. Adam's dad works at a big pharmaceutical company and had access to sick rats and chemo pills. The company sponsored Adam and he went all the way to the national science fair with the project. I remember thinking it was the coolest project. I don't remember feeling sorry for the control rat that didn't get the cancer drugs. I don't remember feeling bad when both the treated and untreated rats died. I do remember wishing I'd come up with such a badass project.

Other than Adam's rats, I've never had any experience with cancer. It's remarkable to not know anyone with cancer. This year, in the United States alone, there will be over 1.5 million new cases of cancer. How do I know? After Charlotte hung up, I did a little research.

Normally, I love research. I'm not feeling warm and fuzzy about it now.

There are as many kinds of brain cancers as there are types of brain cells. I don't know which kind Charlotte has. I touch my sore nose and think that somehow that may not be a conversation I'm ready to have with her.

But not knowing means I have no idea what's going on with her, even after three hours of research.

There are websites out there for teens with cancer. They've got bright colors and cool logos and look a little like ads for hipster clothes. There are stories of survival, but then there are these stories of loss. And I know I should be happy for the survivors, but I just found Charlotte. I don't want to lose her yet.

And I hate myself for thinking the treatments, while invasive and horrible, are also beautiful and brilliant. There's a proton treatment that's like radiation, but with pencil point accuracy. Someone made that happen. Science made that happen.

With so many types of cancer and so many ways to treat it and so many lives won and lost, I'm feeling overwhelmed. My head hurts, my eyes are blurry, and there is a kind of exhaustion stealing over me the likes of which I've never felt, all of which, I now know, are symptoms of brain tumors.

In a word, I feel hopeless.

4.5

I roll into class looking like a Goth kid with a new tube of black eyeliner thanks to Charlotte and her right jab. At least the swelling in my nose has gone down so I no longer sound like a squeaky toy.

The tardy bell sounds, and Ms. Finch closes the book she'd been reading, tucks it into her podium and examines the class like we're disembodied innards floating in jars of formaldehyde. "I trust everyone had an exciting Halloween?" Her gaze falls on me like an Iridium hammer.

My muscles twitch with the need to squirm in my seat.

"Mine was memorable, I assure you," she continues.

Greta's inhalation is as sharp as a scalpel.

"Speaking of memorable…Mr. Hanson?" Everyone turns to look at me. I try to keep breathing despite the fear squeezing my lungs. "Why doesn't your group present first today?"

I blink twice. "Y-y-yes, ma'am." She carries a stack of rubrics and a red pen to an open seat in the back of the classroom as we set up.

James begins our presentation by explaining how it's possible to create an infinite number of poems. He demonstrates some wicked math to prove his point. The class nods along. It's not hard to follow, but I catch Ms. Finch off guard when I glance at her. Her mouth is open in awe.

That's right. Math = awesome.

Next, Greta reads a few poems we found on the concept of infinity. Most of it is lame. Poets confuse infinity with heaven, which is stupid because I can prove the existence of infinity, and I can prove an "afterlife" of sorts (matter can be neither created nor destroyed), but I can't prove heaven. I don't say any of this in the presentation, but wait for my cue to begin the practical demonstration.

When Greta's done, she nods at me. "Right," I say, clearing my throat. I pass out note cards to each person. The cards have words written on them we copied from Mom's poetry magnets. "There are fifty words in the room. How many possible five-word poems can we create?"

Misty shouts out the answer first, which I write on the board (2,118,760 if you've forgotten). "How many do you estimate can be made in five minutes?" I ask, then scribble their responses on the board. Capping the marker and waving them silent, I say, "Go."

At first, everyone is competitive, trying to get the most poems and hardly paying attention to the words. But, at 2.14 minutes, I notice a shift. Things start slowing down. People aren't happy to shove any group of words together and call it a poem. They get picky about which words they pair up with, even if it means they end up with fewer poems at the end of five minutes.

I'm not the only one to notice. Ms. Finch catches my eye and smiles. Not a nice, teacher-y smile. More like a "suck it, math geek" smile.

At the end of five minutes I call time, and wrap up. "Well, we're done, I guess," I say glancing at James and Greta. They both nod. "Any questions?"

The class stays silent. Awesome. I'm about to move back to my seat when I notice one hand in the air.

Ms. Finch.

Shit.

"Yes, Ms. Finch?"

"I enjoyed your presentation, *especially* this exercise. I'm curious to hear if it went the way you planned. The class didn't get near their estimated number of poems. What happened?"

James and Greta look blankly at each other before turning to me.

"The class miscalculated. It happens to the best of us sometimes."

Ms. Finch nods, but presses on. "Was it the class's miscalculation or yours?"

James, Greta, and I all say, "The class."

Ms. Finch chuckles. When Charlotte laughs I hear music, but this sound cryogenically freezes me. Thousands of crystalline daggers stab at me from inside. Ms. Finch says, "I see."

What does she see? The lies the poets tell her about meeting our loved ones again in *the infinite*? Does she see how miserable she's making Charlotte? Can she see how hopeless any struggle to hold on to her is?

A surge of icy heat freezes my chest cavity, and I wonder, "What, exactly, do you *see*?"

"Noooo," Greta moans.

I turn and blink at her. She glares at me, a silent charge to shut up. *Did I say that out loud?* Turning back to Ms. Finch, I see I did. She's no longer smiling.

"I *see* you miscalculated the human need for poetry," Ms. Finch answers.

"Poetry is not a necessity. It's an indulgence built on lies." My voice betrays me again.

"Lies?" she asks.

"Yes, lies. It's mathematically impossible to reach infinity. Every step toward it gets us no closer. In the end, all we've done is move farther from where we began."

I finish my rant and realize my hands are tight fists.

Ms. Finch takes a deep breath and mutters to herself, "Sisyphean."

"What?" But I remember Mrs. Dunwitty and the story of the man and his rock.

"Yes," I say, "It's just like Sissy-who-sy. The top is as craptastic as the bottom. Wherever we are in the present is as far away from infinity as we can get."

I rake my fingers through my hair feeling a strange panic in my chest. "It's like being so close to the one thing you want, reaching out and almost grabbing it, but in the end, you come up empty. And that sucks."

Ms. Finch has dropped the red pen she's been holding. She's pressing her lips together so hard they've lost all color. We stare at each other for what a poet might call "an infinity," but it's only twelve seconds before she drops her eyes to the rubric and begins marking it. Without looking up she says, "Stop by my office after school, Mr. Hanson," before she calls the next group to present.

I knock on Ms. Finch's office door as quietly as I can.

"Come in, Mr. Hanson," she calls from inside.

Not quietly enough.

Ms. Finch's office is a small, windowless room. Behind her desk hangs an enormous canvas painted to look like a window. The tree outside the window is covered with fresh pink buds and leaves so green they glow yellowish in the painted sunlight. Under the tree, the shadow of a girl is reading a book. It's Charlotte.

I freeze, watching her and fighting the urge to call out and wave hello. It's the most remarkable painting I've ever seen.

Then I remember Ms. Finch sitting before me.

"How long have you two known each other?" she asks.

I steal one more glance at the painting before I focus on Ms. Finch. "Who?"

It takes a Herculean effort on her part, but she manages to smile despite her jaw being sewn together by anger. "Have a seat," she says nodding toward a puffy reading chair.

I sink into the cushions and avoid looking at the picture behind Ms. Finch.

"How long have you and my sister been planning that little Halloween stunt?"

"Your sister?" A smile slides onto my face. "Ms. Finch, I planned it myself." She asked the wrong question. I didn't have to lie.

"And I suppose you were the little girl in the witch costume that puked on my porch, too?"

"Uh, no, the puking thing wasn't part of the plan."

"Why?"

"She ate too much candy."

Ms. Finch closes her eyes and sighs. "No, Mr. Hanson. Why me? Why now?"

"Because you teach English at Brighton."

"That's all?"

"Yes, ma'am. It's nothing personal—just a Brighton thing, I guess. I can see how it'd be hard not to take it personally. The other teachers either stopped caring or outright quit after a while."

"You'd like that, wouldn't you?"

"Not exactly."

She studies me a minute, while I keep my smile glued in place and silently count prime numbers to keep calm.

She breaks the lengthening silence with a colossal sigh. "I'm not turning you in because, despite what you say, I still think my sister is somehow involved, and I don't need that kind of hassle.

However, my kitchen smells like rotten eggs. You'll serve detention with me until there isn't even the faintest whiff of unpleasantness left in my home. Understood?"

"Really?"

Ms. Finch stifles a sigh. "I've done worse."

Again. "Really?"

She taps her bottom lip considering. "When we were young, Charlotte fell behind in school. There was this one teacher—a math teacher—who made her cry. Called her stupid."

A stab of anger in my gut makes me shift in my seat.

"I *may* have stink bombed her car." She holds her hands out, shushing me before I can exclaim. "No one messes with my sister."

I school my face, trying to reign in my surprise, awe, and respect.

"Yes, ma'am. Of course." I spring from the cushy chair. Turning to go, I risk one last glance at the Charlotte in the painting. "Thanks, Ms. Finch."

"Hanson."

Damn. She saw.

I freeze, but can't seem to make myself turn around. I hear her stand from her desk.

"I don't care what you do to me, but don't mess with Charley."

When I turn around, Ms. Finch's expression is tortured.

"I'm her big sister first. I'll protect her to the grave. Do you understand?" Her jaw quivers and she clamps it shut with a snapping noise.

"Believe me, Ms. Finch. I understand."

4.6

I'm woken by a text that night.

Greta: *CHUCK! DID U HIT SEND?*

The time stamp on the message says it's 11:36 p.m. My body floods with a surge of adrenaline, pushing me from my bed.

Holy shit! The MIT early application deadline is twenty-four minutes away. My application is still open on my laptop from last night. Without much fanfare or threat of vomit, I hit send.

And then panic.

Me: *Done. Now what?*

Greta: *Congrats. Now relax.*

She and James sent off their first choice early applications a week ago. They both are hoping for schools in California. It hits me how far away that is. Ridiculously far. How am I supposed to relax when everything I thought I wanted doesn't feel right anymore?

Me: *Freaking a little.*

Greta: *You were made for MIT.*

I smile.

Greta: *Or not, but either way, you'll live.*

Me: *NOT helpful.*

Greta: *XOXO (the kisses are from James)*

4.7

On my way home on Friday, I drive by Mrs. Dunwitty's house. I want to monitor the garden's progress. If anyone asks, that's my excuse. It has nothing to do with the fact that I miss our strange conversations, and the way she never looked at me like I was a piñata about to explode. In fact, she took pleasure in poking at me.

The garden itself is filling in. The rose bushes, while only a quarter of the size of the ones I ran over, are filling out, and since we haven't had a hard frost yet to stop them from blooming, there are even a few orange flowers left amongst the glossy green leaves. The angel is grinning at me from between the plants, reminding me I still haven't gotten rid of the broken one in my trunk. I'd forgotten she was in there with everything else going on.

Mrs. Dunwitty's grass is looking shaggy though. It's too long and it looks like whoever mowed it last time didn't go in straight lines, so there are strange tufts sticking up everywhere. It's very unlike her to let her lawn get so unruly.

I park on the curb and make my way to her flamingo-ass pink door. I'm surprised to approach it without dread. When I knock, she doesn't answer. I wait a few beats and try the doorbell. Still nothing. I figure I'll come back tomorrow. She's probably at a Grouchy Granny Anonymous meeting. Step one is admitting you have a problem.

I'm chuckling to myself as I step off the porch and hear the bolt slide back. Mrs. Dunwitty is leaning heavily on her cane when I turn around to greet her, her arm trembling with the effort to hold herself upright. She's wearing this pale blue housecoat that looks three sizes too big on her instead of her normal elastic waist pants and polyester shirt.

"Hey," I say, hoping to cover my flummoxed expression with a cheerful tone. Flummox. That's a word from one of Ms. Finch's poems. I shake my head, clearing it, and motion toward the yard. "Who murdered your lawn?"

Her eyes smolder like charred coals. "There's nothing wrong with my lawn, boy. I'll have you know that took me the better part of a weekend to do on my own." She lifts her chin and peers down her hawkish nose at me. "What're you doing here anyway? Your job is done." Her voice is scratchy, perhaps from disuse. Without me around to harass lately, I bet she's bored out of her mind.

"I was just checking on the roses." I lean on the railing at the bottom of the steps, looking up at her. "I'm going to come back tomorrow and mow."

"You don't owe me that."

"I know."

We stare at each other for a moment, locked in a stubborn battle. I grin first.

Hers looks strained. "See you tomorrow, Jack."

Mrs. Dunwitty has promised me a glass of tea. She said I could even sit in one of her rocking chairs while I enjoy it. "So long as you don't get too comfortable," she'd muttered before toddling back in the house to get a glass for me.

I've just cleaned and stowed the lawn mower when a silver car comes tearing around the corner. I cup my hands against the glare of the sun as the car approaches. With a jolt, I realize it's Charlotte's Civic. I haven't seen her all week. Apparently, Ms. Finch has decided to punish Charlotte for whatever part she may or may not have played in the stink bombing by making her hang out at home and enjoy the stench.

I've missed her.

Charlotte stops her car behind mine. Both she and Becca spring from the car, leaving the doors wide open, and run toward me. My heart goes into hyper drive worrying that something is wrong, but then I notice they are both smiling. Becca's even laughing.

They each take one of my arms and haul me toward the open car, shoving and pressing until they've got me tucked into the backseat. Becca slides in after me and Charlotte runs around to her seat. She peels away from the curb, barely missing my back bumper, whooping and waving an arm out her open window.

I glance behind me to see Mrs. Dunwitty shaking her head before carrying both our drinks back into her house.

"What the hell?" I finally gasp.

Becca laughs beside me. "We're kidnapping you."

"Yeah, Hanson," Charlotte says, her eyes finding mine in the rearview mirror. "You've been working too damn hard all week, stuck in detention hell. It's supposed to be the weekend."

"Where are we going?"

Charlotte doesn't answer. Instead she turns up the music so I can feel it in the marrow of my bones, and then she melts them, each and every one, with her songbird voice.

We're somewhere near the university when Charlotte pulls into a parking lot. "We're here."

Becca shoves me out the back door, dragging her backpack behind her.

"How come Becca gets to do work while we're here?"

"It's a picnic," Becca answers, thumping me in the shoulder.

We walk, Charlotte and Becca flanking me, down a well-groomed path, over a small wooden bridge, and up a low hill. When we breach the top of the hill, the beauty before me is stunning.

It's a rose garden. One ten times the size of Mrs. Dunwitty's and the place is alive with color. The air is sweet as we descend the hill, Charlotte leading us to the shade of a small arbor overrun with climbing red roses.

"Why did you bring me here?" I ask Charlotte.

She tilts her head to one side, her lips quirking in the same direction. "I thought you'd like it. I thought you liked roses, you know, because you're always helping the old woman."

A sonic boom of a laugh explodes from within me. "You don't know me very well, do you?"

Charlotte smiles over her discouragement. "I'd like to."

"For starters, I'm not into gardening, but I *am* happy you brought me here." My stomach recoils in surprise at my candor. Charlotte wants to get to know me. That feels good, better than the first time I solved a problem using Euler's number kind of good.

We spend the rest of the day at the park. Charlotte enjoyed every last bite of the cupcake Becca packed for her. She licked the frosting off the paper liner, mumbling, "Tell Jo about this and die, Hanson." After lunch, Charlotte went off on her own to sketch the reflection of some roses in the water of a small pond.

Becca and I pack up the empty containers. We can see Charlotte from where we're sitting. I watch the way the thin sunlight plays in the eddies of her curls as she tilts her head to study the water.

"Hey, Bec, how come you didn't tell me about Charlotte's cancer?"

Becca looks up from zipping her backpack and blinks. "It wasn't my story to tell."

"That's it?"

"And Charlotte asked me not to say anything. She wanted you to decide to help her because you liked her, not because you felt crappy about her being sick."

I can't imagine weighing all my decisions on something as invasive as cancer. She may have tumors in the lining of her brain, but they metastasize throughout her life. A piece of my happiness fractures away realizing this.

"But how'd you find out?"

"It was the second week of school and Charlotte got called out of class. We were working on that group project thing, and everyone goes 'Ooooh, what'd you doooo?' when they called her name. Do they do that at your school?"

"No."

"Oh, well, they do it at mine and it's dumb. She looked so small walking out of the classroom." Becca plays with the zipper on her bag. "I waited for her by the nice picture window outside the offices. I read. When Charlotte came out, I could tell she'd been crying, and for some reason, when she saw me waiting, she burst into more tears. Turns out, Ms. Finch had set up meetings for Charlotte with the school counselor to discuss her cancer and the future, she just neglected to tell Charlotte about them."

Becca's fingers are now working through her hair, tangling long locks around a finger and then letting them loose. "Charlotte told me that afternoon. It sucked, but we weren't as close then, so it didn't suck as much. I didn't know then, you know?"

"Know what?"

"What it meant to have a friend—that having a friend would change me, make me a better person—make me more real. How was I to know?" She's watching Charlotte and her eyes fill with tears.

"I don't want to lose her," she whispers. "I think it'd be like losing myself all over again, only I didn't know I needed to be found before."

I grab Becca's hand, unwinding a piece of hair from her finger, and squeeze tightly. "I'll always look for you, Bec."

She nods with a sigh. "Good, because we can't hold on to Charlotte anymore than we can touch that cloud," she says, tipping her chin upward at a wisp of gray in the blue sky.

More clouds begin to crowd the sky, blowing in on the breath of the wind, as the afternoon draws on. We lay on our backs in the cool grass watching them soar.

"Do you think it's going to rain?" I ask, eyeing a cloud the color of an African elephant.

"It wouldn't dare," Charlotte says. She inches her fingers so they lay inside the spaces between mine, not touching, but reaching for mine. Asymptote fingers. "It'd be cruel to ruin a perfect day like this. There's only so many in a lifetime, you know."

A gust of wind plucks the petals off the rose bushes surrounding us, and suddenly we're at the heart of a storm so colorful, so chaotic, it raises goose bumps on my skin. The petals fly over us, inches from our prone faces, racing to some unseen end. They are so beautiful I have to look away.

Becca laughs from Charlotte's other side and reaches her hand in the air, but she can't catch a single petal.

Not a single one.

She tries.

And so do I.

But Charlotte only watches them float by.

By now, there's a herd of elephants in the sky, and when the first raindrop falls, I feel like it was inevitable. Becca shrieks and jogs to the safety of the covered arbor with her backpack. I roll my head in the grass to look at Charlotte. She's closed her eyes and lying still, except for a small tremor in her hand closest to mine. The rain splashes on her bare arms, the bridge of her nose, her lips. It drips down her face like tears.

I don't want her perfect day ruined. "Charlotte?"

She turns her face to mine.

"Do you want to dance?" Her eyes go wide as I stand and offer her my hand. "Like in that old movie we watched."

Charlotte laughs and raises her arm. I pull her to her feet and hope she'll think my palms are wet because of the rain and not because I'm so nervous. She begins to sing the movie song about dancing and singing in the rain and we move in a clumsy circle, slowly at first, but then faster. She tips her head back and the song spills out.

We make a ring, spinning and singing as the rain and rose petals crash down around us. When we stop, Charlotte's eyes are brighter than Sirius on a clear night, outshining every star in the Milky Way.

We're soaked, our hair stringy and pasted onto our foreheads, clothes clinging to our bodies. Logic be damned. I've never felt happier.

Charlotte smiles at me, squeezing my hand before letting go. "I guess a little rain never hurt anything."

No, the rain doesn't bother me at all.

4.8

We arrive back at my car still damp from the rain. Mrs. Dunwitty is watching the storm from her porch as we pull up. I wave at the girls and then trot up to the porch to check on Mrs. Dunwitty.

"Nice weather we're having," I say. I point to the vacant chair beside her; she *had* promised me I could sit for a while when I was done mowing. It feels like that was another lifetime ago. "May I?"

Her mouth pulls into a sour grin. "I suppose, but I already drank your tea, so don't even think about asking for that."

I chuckle as I plop down next to her. I've grown to appreciate Mrs. Dunwitty's frankness. Thunder rolls in the distance. "Sure has been a stormy fall."

Mrs. Dunwitty nods in time to her rocking, but doesn't say anything. I try a new conversation starter. "Have you ever been to the rose gardens over by the university?"

Her brows perk up. "Yes, I believe I have."

"That's where Charlotte took us today. I had no idea there were that many kinds of roses." I prop my feet on the railing and notice the peeling paint there.

"You kissed that girl yet?"

My feet slip off the railing. "I thought we were talking about roses, not girls."

"Suit yourself," Mrs. Dunwitty says, a wry smile playing at the corners of her wide mouth.

"I saw your roses there, the Harvest Moon. There's even a little plaque with your name on it. Pretty cool."

She waves a shaky hand at me. "Psshhaw. No one cares about that anymore."

"I do. And Charlotte and Becca thought it was neat. Charlotte even sketched them. You left your mark, you know. You changed the world forever. Or rose gardening, at least."

Mrs. Dunwitty works her jaw like she's chewing something for a minute. Electric fingers light up the gray sky, reaching for the tall pines along the horizon. "My son is allergic to bees."

A frown creases my brow, but I don't interrupt.

"When he was young, he was jealous of my roses, saying I spent more time with them than him. And he was right. I was a botanist. It was all I'd ever wanted to be. I didn't strive to be a mother.

"Once, when I was working in the greenhouse, he smashed all the flowers in my front garden. Got stung, too. Nearly asphyxiated before I found him."

She reaches a frail hand out, placing it on my forearm where it lies on the rocker. "I should have chosen him more often." Her fingers, with their papery skin like aged newspaper, squeeze my arm. "I should have learned to be a botanist *and* a mother."

My whole body has stilled, afraid that if I move, it'll shatter her. She seems so frail. She closes her eyes and continues to rock. I cover her hand with mine and wait for the storm to pass.

4.9

In the last few weeks, our class has hung a disco ball in Ms. Finch's classroom, rearranged the desks so they spelled Einstein's theory of general relativity, and glued the pages of her lesson planner together.

Ms. Finch is an admirable opponent, though. She's still not made a big fuss about the pranks. Perhaps because she kind of asked for it the first day of class with the whole "Bring. It. On," speech.

The planner thing got under her skin the most, but she played it off. "Guess this is someone's hint that I need to join the twenty-first century."

I expected her to retaliate with more backbreaking English stuff, but she continues to find ways to teach this crap so it relates to stuff we like. The more creative we are in torturing her, the more creative she gets teaching us. She seems to enjoy the pranks better than the silence.

As we leave class, Greta and James flank me in the hallway. Ms. Finch has flogged us with poetry.

"That was amazing," James breathes on my left. He sounds like a lovesick wuss. "I mean did you see the Fibonnacci sequence inside the poem? I had no idea you could do that."

"Well, to be fair, *you* couldn't, but it was cool," says Greta.

"Fibonnacci," I grunt.

The woman is a genius. She suckered the entire senior class. Three-fourths of class time focused on some poem about life and paths and choices, all poignancy and poem-y. Four minutes before the final bell, she switched gears and showed us a poem with stanza lengths based on dumbass mathematician Fibonnacci and his stupid numbers.

I stop walking. Greta and James are a few steps away before they realize it. Never in my life have I thought the phrase, *stupid numbers*, and Fibonnacci was no dummy.

Holy shit.

"You all right, C-man?" asks James.

Ms. Finch is using operant conditioning on us. We're getting a major dose of our own medicine, and it's working. Science is totally kicking me in the balls.

Greta and James are both giving me the underage adoptive parent look.

I change the subject. "That woman is diabolical. Fibonnacci? Seriously?"

Greta laughs. "Admit it. It was cool."

"No. Never," I say with fake bravado.

5.0

Thanksgiving break is here. Finally. I've never looked forward to a break from school, but I'm looking forward to this one. I can't look at Ms. Finch without a gaping cesspool of guilt opening up in my gut. I'm sick of classmates constantly looking toward me to gage their own reactions in English class. I'm tired of all the worries. I just want to lose myself in homework.

And Charlotte.

There's a small rap on my door before her face appears. "Hi." She steps inside and studies the piles of junk lying around. I'm not so good with putting things where they go. I do have categorized piles—dirty clothes, books, dishes and food scraps, and the broadest category, stuff.

"Becca and I made pie."

"Really?"

"Pumpkin."

My stomach purrs. "Much better than fig."

"What?"

"Pumpkin pie. It's better than fig pie."

Charlotte's mouth quirks up on one side. "I'll take your word for it. I've never had fig anything. Pumpkin is my favorite."

"Mine too," I say. My eyes flick back to the computer screen, only because I can't stand to keep staring at her, wondering what other pieces of us might fit together as perfectly as pumpkin and pie.

"I didn't meant to interr—"

"No," I say. "This isn't important. I mean, it is, but it can wait."

"Long enough for a piece of pie?"

"Definitely."

She steps further in my room. "We're having a movie marathon, too. Want to join?"

"Uh, no. No more old musicals for me."

Charlotte grins crookedly at me. "They aren't musicals, dork. They're modern remakes of Shakespeare's *Romeo and Juliet*."

My mouth drops open a bit. "Seriously? And I'm the dork?"

Charlotte crosses my room to stand between the computer and me. She leans on the edge of my desk, her butt nearly on my keyboard. "You know," she says, her face tilting toward mine. "A little literary culture won't kill you."

"Just one," I say, but my voice is malfunctioning, so it comes out as a whisper.

She whispers, too. "Good."

Midway through the second movie, Becca pauses it to use the restroom, leaving Charlotte and me sitting in the dim light of the frozen television screen. My sister sure is a sucky chaperone. Doesn't she realize how dangerous it is to leave me unsupervised around beautiful girls with infinity tattoos?

Charlotte nudges my shoulder with her own. "This is fun. Admit it."

"This is a total chick-fest," I say, motioning toward the TV. "I don't get what you guys see in these movies. That last one had a terrible ending, and I can already see this one's going down the same path."

"I admit that Romeo and Juliet are not my favorite couple. Being in love for three days is an easy gig."

"Exactly. They'd probably realize that they hate each other if they spent more time together."

"Or worse," Charlotte says, hugging a pillow, "they'd grow indifferent and their love would waste away. Nothing lasts forever."

"That's bleak. Maybe you shouldn't hang out with me so much. I think I'm rubbing off on you."

Charlotte smacks me with the pillow she was holding. "Shut up, Hanson."

"Now you sound like your sister." I chuckle and toss the pillow back at her. She retaliates by crashing two pillows around my head like cymbals.

"Game on!" I shout, grabbing as many pillows as I can and lobbing them at her one after the other.

"Uncle! Uncle," she squeals, lying buried on the couch.

Laughing, I clear away the pillows. Her dark curls are sticking up at odd angles, and I reach out to smooth them back into place. Charlotte catches my hand in hers, and I cup her cheek.

It feels as though someone has turned an electromagnet on inside of me. There is a force out of my control pulling me in. Charlotte's eyes flick to my lips, and I'm undone. I may have been able to resist before, but now I give in to the pulling and press my lips to hers. They are soft, softer than I imagined—better. Her hands are suddenly at my waist, one finger dipping under the edge of my shirt. One finger and I groan like someone is lifting a one hundred pound weight off my chest.

My tongue laps at her bottom lip, the one she bites on so much, and she parts her lips just enough for me to taste it myself. A string tightens from my chest to my groin—so taut I can barely breathe.

She tastes like sugar, so soft and warm in my mouth, I ache.

Her hands slide up my sides to my chest, where she gently pushes me back as she pulls away. "Wait. We can't do this."

Without her lips on mine, my body loosens and I catch my breath. "Sorry. Charlotte, I'm so—"

"Don't. But we can't. I can't lose—"

"What are you guys doing?" Becca calls, walking in through the kitchen. "I heard screaming from the bathroom."

Charlotte's cheeks darken in the dim light from the TV. A worry flickers across her face. Becca. She can't lose Becca.

Now you've done it, Chuck, the Greta in my head snarls. I've got to fix this.

"Help me, Bec!" I shout, jumping away from Charlotte. "Charlotte attacked me. I was just sitting here saying how much I loved this wonderful, romantic film, and WHAM. Pillow to my head."

Charlotte runs a hand through her curls and bites that lip of hers, making me want to groan all over. My expression must be a sight, because she takes one look at me and laughs before smacking me with a pillow.

"See? You gotta save me, sis."

Becca chuckles. "You guys are lame." She takes her seat on one side of Charlotte, who smacks Becca in the face with another pillow before linking their arms.

Becca turns the movie back on. And I wonder what might have happened if she'd stayed away just a little longer. The thought of kissing Charlotte again makes me feel like I'm being sucked away into the vacuum of space. Which, if you're wondering, is painful and scary and leaves me almost breathless.

Through the darkness, Charlotte's hand works its way into the crook of my arm, too. I don't move for the rest of the movie, afraid that if she lets go, I'll float away again.

Subject: Charlotte Finch,

Method: Beat her with fluffy objects until she acquiesces and kisses me,

Result: Left adrift in space with discomfort in my lower region.

5.1

Becca calls out to me from her room Saturday afternoon. I've been avoiding her since the movie ended last night. Part of me wants to come clean and tell her what happened. The other part wants to transfer to an out-of-state boarding school. This friendship she has with Charlotte is nothing shy of remarkable for Becca. She's never even tried to play nice with other kids before. I can't screw this up for her, and the probability of me screwing up is pretty damn high.

"What's up?" I ask, crossing her room to flop on her bed. Becca is sitting on the floor in the nest of blankets she usually reads in, surrounded by shredded book pages. "Aren't you like biologically incapable of destroying a book?"

"It was from the Goodwill. I read it first—boring finance stuff."

"I won't tell anyone your dirty secret if you show me what you're hiding there." I point to where she's cupping her hands around something.

"Charlotte's eighteenth birthday is coming up and I want to give her something."

"Eighteen? I thought Charlotte was your age."

Becca shakes her head. "She missed lots of school because…"

Cancer.

We don't say it out loud though.

"I'm wondering what you think of my present," Becca says, opening her hands. Inside is a small pin with a rose on it. The rose is made from the pages of a book, the petals of words delicately curving in on each other in a new story. Charlotte will love it.

"Wow, Bec." I trace the edge of a paper rose petal. "You made this?"

Becca nods. "You really think she'll like it?"

"I really do." I wonder if this will be Charlotte's last birthday, and how do you celebrate a birthday when you've got something like cancer, and how come Charlotte doesn't seem super sick right now? Or is she? I noticed at the rose garden that her left hand shakes when she's sketching.

But her personality and memory are still intact. She's verbal and her balance is fine. Maybe she's got lots more birthdays coming, and I'm just overreacting.

"Bec? What is Charlotte doing for her, uh, you know? I mean, she's in school, so she must not be so sick. Right?"

Becca seems to sink a little further in her nest of blankets. Her fingers find their way into her long hair and begin to twist. Becca knows something. Dammit, I want to be the one Charlotte shares these secrets and fears with.

I nudge her. "Right?"

Finally, she looks up at me. "Charlotte's done with all of that."

"What's that mean?"

"That she's sick of being sick."

Things reel for a second and come back into focus just as quickly. "She's just letting it kill her?"

"She's enjoying being normal for a while."

"Normal? What's normal about dying?"

"Nothing, Charlie." Becca stands up to face me, her calm features distorted into a mask of chaos and fury. "There's not one thing normal about any of this, but it's Charlotte's life. It's her decision. So what's it to you if she wants to spend a little time outside of a hospital for once?"

I blink. It's the only safe response. Becca's rare anger is about to explode.

"Exactly!" Becca is shouting now. Becca does not shout. "If Charlotte wants to spend the rest of her life as a fucking aerial-acrobat, than so fucking be it!"

Whoa. Becca definitely doesn't say *fuck*.

Her hands are shaking fists. "Bec," I murmur, reaching for her. She shrugs me off and opens her fist, holding out the beautiful rose she made for Charlotte, now crushed from her rage. She glances at it, and I think maybe she'll erupt again, but instead all the fury wilts away.

"Crap," she whispers.

I don't know what to say. This is all new for me, this friendship with my sister. I don't want to let her down. "Can you fix it?"

She looks into my eyes and shakes her head.

"I'm sorry." And I do mean the flower, but so much more, too. I reach for her hand, still clutching the flower, but she shirks away again.

Becca's voice is small in the space between us. "I'll have to start over." She tosses the flower in her trashcan and flops back into her reading nest. "There's still time."

When she's not looking, I rescue the rose from the trash.

5.2

Greta shows up Sunday afternoon without James. "Lover's spat?" I joke as I close the front door behind her.

She scoffs. "They went to visit his dad."

"Oh."

"Yeah. Oh."

James doesn't talk about his dad much. I know his dad's buried in his hometown in Eastern North Carolina, a few hours from here. I know James misses him, even if he doesn't say so.

Greta follows me up to my room, taking over my desk chair and flipping through all the open windows on my computer until she finds an online game she wants to play. She's going to screw up all my character points. I just know it. I'd get upset, except it's Greta.

I lie on my floor and read through my advanced physics notes. A silence settles between us, and it isn't exactly uncomfortable, but it's not like a pair of sweatpants either. Greta's got something to say. I can tell by the number of times she's tucked that one strand of hair behind her left ear.

Just as I'm about to bolt from the room under any pretense I can come up with, Greta turns from the screen. "When are you going to ask Charlotte out?"

I sit up so quickly all the blood whooshes in my ears. When she asked, I could taste Charlotte on my lips, like the memory was just lying in wait to attack. "Never," I manage to grunt.

Greta cocks a brow at me. "You're a terrible liar, Chuck. Your ears give you away every time."

Damn. They do feel warm.

"Besides, never is a long time."

"Depends on your perspective," I say. These feelings that I have for Charlotte will pass, but she may pass before they do. Never may be a short time to wait in this case.

Greta's face pales as she catches on. She takes a deep breath and blows it out, her freckles stretching with her rounded cheeks. "You're right. Guess I just wanted you to ask her out to assuage my guilt about going to the winter formal when you don't have a date. She's probably all wrong for you anyway."

"Wrong for me?" My nerves frazzle like sparklers in summer. "You don't even know her, so how can you say that? Her art is so beautiful, Gret. Looking at her sketches is like looking through a microscope and seeing the core of everything around us. And she's passionate, maybe not about math, but the feeling is the same, the desire to wrap your life up in something you love so you never have to be far from it. Charlotte gets that. I don't know how, but she gets me." My voice breaks at the top of a very long crescendo, and I have to catch my breath.

Greta's eyes are wide green pools. "Okay, Chuck. I didn't know."

"No—shit—I'm sorry, Greta." I slump, my spine too brittle to support me. "I'm scared," I say to the carpet. Being left behind will break me. Of this, I'm sure. "How am I supposed to fall in love with a girl when I know she's going to break my heart?"

Greta blinks, her eyes glistening in the light from my computer screen. "Maybe it's not love."

"Did you not listen to anything I just said?" The heat from my ears travels down my neck. I watch as Greta digests everything before I drop my forehead to the floor. "Plus, I kissed her," I say into the carpet.

Greta falls forward from the chair onto her knees in front of me. "You what?"

"Friday. On the couch. Watching movies."

Greta pauses long enough that I peek at her. I see the moment she swallows whatever other reservations she has and decides to be on my team, even if we're going to lose. "Well done, Professor Peacock," Greta chuckles. "How'd it go?"

I rest one cheek on the floor and look up at her. "She said we couldn't."

"Oh."

"Yeah."

Greta wrinkles her nose. "Because you suck at kissing?" Her ginger brows wag up and down, trying to lighten the mood.

I snort into the carpet. "Probably."

She nods. "I knew it. You should have practiced more."

"We can't hurt Becca."

"Have you talked to Becca?"

My horrified expression answers for me. "Right, well. You need to talk to Becca."

I move my head so I'm resting on the opposite cheek. I can't face the pity in her eyes.

"Hey," Greta says, her voice sharp enough to pull my eyes back up to hers. Maybe that wasn't pity. "You're stronger than you think. If you want to fall in love, then fall."

5.3

Since Thanksgiving, Ms. Finch has had her classroom rearranged to face the windows in the back of the room instead of the whiteboard in the front (backfire: "What a beautiful idea. Let's all write poems about the fall foliage outside our windows"), her podium wrapped in holiday paper with penguins on it ("A gift? For me? You shouldn't have"), and, my personal favorite, a full-scale cardboard cutout of Darth Vader with Ms. Finch's face and the caption, "Come to the dark side." She snapped a picture of it and texted someone immediately. Everyone's hearts were racing that day, thinking Dr. Whiting had been on the other end of that text. (It was Charlotte, and she had this to say: "That's the best you geeks can do?").

Ms. Finch's been marking off the days until winter break on the wall calendar with a fat red marker. Today she'll "X" off the last day. I think we're both relieved. It's funny because I may have started this revolution against Ms. Finch, but the longer it wages, the more sympathetic I feel toward her, and the more I want to call the whole thing off and walk away.

My lack of fight isn't because Charlotte is off-limits and my poor southern hemisphere is losing. Honestly, I feel helpless in the face of Charlotte's disease. I want to make everything else in her life as smooth as possible, since I've got no way of making the cancer better. I'm pretty sure that's what Ms. Finch is doing, too. We're fighting the same fight to protect Charlotte.

Defeating Ms. Finch is like defeating myself.

Ms. Finch has a book open on her lap at the beginning of class. The book is old and dog-eared and the pages are covered with ink illustrations and writing so there is more black than white. I've noticed she carries it around with her wherever she goes lately.

She closes the book and sets it on her podium when the bell rings. Clearing her throat she begins.

"There are many kinds of heroes in literature, and people love to argue over what makes a hero and who represents them best. I'm going to give each of you a slip of paper with a quote from a literary character on it. I'd like you to read the quote aloud and then we'll decide whether the character is a hero." She pauses to pull a large glass jar from under her podium. It's filled with colorful scraps of paper that remind me of rose petals aloft in the sky. "Oh, and why the character is heroic. Never forget *why*."

She walks up and down the aisles holding out the jar for each of us.

I pull an orange paper from the jar.

> "I wanted you to see what real courage is . . . It's when you know you're licked before you begin but you begin anyway and you see it through no matter what. You rarely win, but sometimes you do."
>
> —Atticus Finch in To Kill a Mockingbird

It's like a wave that has been pulling back from the shore, building upon itself and towering over me since I met Charlotte Finch crashes over me, and I'm choking on the salty water. I can't win, but that doesn't mean I shouldn't try. I can't hold onto Charlotte forever, but that doesn't mean I shouldn't hold her now. I can't—breathe. I fucking can't breathe.

Ms. Finch reads the slip of paper over my shoulder. She touches my desk, her fingers fluttering there like leaves in a breeze.

"It's true, you know," she says quietly beside me. I want to yell at her. Of course it's true, but I'm not that brave. I barely keep myself contained for the rest of class. All I want is Charlotte. I want to win just one more kiss and then another and…is it possible?

It's the longest class in the history of ever.

Ms. Finch doesn't linger after class. Today is Charlotte's birthday. I'm sure they have plans. No one else sticks around either. Winter formal is tonight. I wish I had asked Charlotte, but…I was afraid—of hurting Becca, but mostly of rejection. On my way out the door, I notice Ms. Finch forgot her book where she'd left it on the podium. Curious, I glance at the title: *To Kill a Mockingbird*.

It's the book—the book that will tell me more about this Atticus fellow whose words are making my insides explode.

I grab the book without further thought. I'll return it after break. She'll never even know it's missing. I just need to know. Did Atticus win?

5.4

"Charlie?" My name is whispered across the darkness of my room that night. I fell asleep with my face on my physics book like it's a pillow, so I can't see so much as feel someone in here with me. My heart stalls. Charlotte?

Becca leans over and whispers my name again.

I groan and grab my sheets to pull them over my head, but she stops me. "Charlie, I need your help."

I sit up, my eyes adjusting to the darkness and the shadowy figure of my sister. I notice she's dressed. "What's up?"

"It's Charlotte," Becca says, waving her cell phone at me. I see now the screen is lit and Charlotte is on the line. Becca foists the phone at me and starts tugging at a strand of her hair.

"'Lo?"

"CHaRliEEE!"

"Charlotte? You okay?"

"Iss my birthday! HaPPy BIRthDay to ME!"

"Oh-kay? Happy birthday, Charlotte. Whatcha doing?"

"I'm at my BirTHDay PartEEEE!"

I pull the phone away from my ear. "I don't understand. What party?"

Becca's finger is lost in a tangle of her hair. She loosens the bite on the inside of her lip. "We went to dinner earlier for her birthday. She said she had to go home and celebrate with her sister. She dropped me off here. That's all I know."

"So this isn't really her birthday party?"

Becca shakes her head.

I nod and get back to the phone. "Charlotte, where are you? Becca and I want to come to your birthday party, too."

"You do? How lovely," she says, her voice tinged with sadness.

The party isn't far from us. It's in the neighborhood. The guy who lives here goes to school with Becca and Charlotte. We park the car amongst the others on the street and head toward the house. I'm still talking to Charlotte, narrating our every move.

"Okay, we're here. Should we ring the bell?" Charlotte laughs maniacally. I decide that means no. I can hear loud music and voices. "Listen, Charlotte, once we get in here, how can we find you?"

"I'm upstairs."

"Upstairs?"

"Un-huh," her voice drifts away like she's bored or on the edge of passing out.

I take a deep breath and look at Becca. Her face is pale, a sheen of sweat on her brow. I try to smile at her, like, *No worries, I regularly crash stranger's parties to retrieve drunk, terminally ill friends. I got this.* We slip in. My plan is to get to Charlotte and get out without anyone noticing us.

"We're heading upstairs. Where are you up here?"

"Bathroom."

"Which door? There's like six."

"Ummm…"

Damn. I nod at Becca to start checking rooms. The first is unoccupied. The next is dark, but I can hear a lot of panting, so I'm guessing—occupied. Becca's is a closet. The next one we try is locked.

"Hey, Charlotte? Did you lock the door?"

"Dunno."

I chuckle. This is a pain in the ass expedition, but I have to admit, drunk Charley sounds awfully cute, from sober Charlie's perspective. "Could you check? I'm standing outside a locked door and before I kick it in and rescue you, I'd like to know I've got the right princess." I hear laughing, both on the phone and off. Yep. It's this one. "Ha. Ha. Open up, will ya?"

"I wanna see you kick it down."

I stare at the door.

"Go 'head. I'm waiting," she says.

"Charlotte, come out," I holler, pounding on the door. My hand throbs, irrefutable evidence I could never kick it down.

"All right," she says, pulling it open in my face. "Don't get your panties in a bunch. Geez."

Becca pulls Charlotte to her in a big hug.

"Let's go, ladies, before I'm spotted and someone tries to stuff me in a locker."

"But, Charlie," Becca says, looking around the dim hallway. "There aren't any."

Charlotte doubles over with a fit of laughter, slurred, but still musical. Someone else tonight must have been snared by her Siren call because a half-naked guy steps into the hall calling, "Charley, that you? Where've you been?"

Mostly-Naked stops short when he sees Becca and me propping Charlotte up between us. Beside me, Charlotte's spine stiffens and she mutters something sounding like, "not this asshole again." Which makes me smile because she isn't talking about me.

"Who the hell are you?" Mostly-Naked asks, advancing at an angle.

"Uh…I'm Charlie." *Smooth, nut sack. Maybe you should run now?* I start hauling Charlotte toward the stairs.

"Hey!" he shouts behind us. Charlotte's feet aren't working well, so he catches up, grabbing Charlotte by the shoulder and trying to wrench her from my grip.

Something snaps in my brain. "Back off, man. She's drunk. I'm taking her home."

"Who are you talking to, you little bitch?"

Becca untangles her arm and turns to face Mostly-Naked. "*To whom* are *you* talking, Derrick No-Dick?" she asks, her lips grim lines of distaste. "My brother and I are here to collect our friend. Can you wrap the only organ in your body smaller than your penis around that fact?"

My little sister. I'm so proud.

Charlotte snorts with laughter and throws her hand in the air, "Oh, yes, speak the gospel, sister-friend." Becca grins and smacks Charlotte with a high-five.

Derrick No-Dick doesn't find it funny, though. He advances on me, even though I'm the only one here not insulting him. I'm trying to figure out how to avoid being hit *and* hold Charlotte when Charlotte relieves me of my second duty. Standing on her own, she stumbles toward Derrick and places her hands on his shoulders.

"Uh, Charlotte?"

She leans close to his ear, like she's going to whisper something to him and he gives me this total *suck it, assface* grin. Charlotte knocks it off his face by ramming her knee in his groin. Big or little, that hurts like hell. My sixth grade experiment proved that, if nothing else.

Becca grabs Charlotte and takes off down the hallway. "Come on, Charlie."

Derrick crumples to the carpet.

"Keys," Becca says as we hit the curb. I toss them over and help Charlotte into the backseat. Then, I slide in beside her. Becca takes the first corner too fast, so Charlotte thumps into my shoulder. She rests her head there and looks up at me. "Thanks for coming to my party."

"It was a real killer," I deadpan.

She giggles again, which makes her hiccup. Her face, pink from the heat of the party, pales.

"You okay?"

Charlotte leans away and starts groping for the door handle even though we're going forty miles per hour through the neighborhood.

"Whoa! Hold on." I grab for her hands. "Stop, Becca."

The car's barely stopped before Charlotte bolts. She crawls behind an inflatable Santa and retches.

"Do you think puking on Santa gets you an automatic spot on the naughty list?"

"Not funny, Charlie," Becca whisper-shouts. "Go help her," she says with a shove.

"What about you?" I ask, but Becca's paler than Santa's beard. I'll have two puking girls on my hands if I send her in to help.

Charlotte's no longer puking, but she's not moving either. She's on all fours staring at the contents of her stomach. The smell is foul, the alcohol still strong enough to burn the inside of my nose. I gag. Smooth.

"Can you stand?" I offer her my hand.

Charlotte crawls away from her pile of sick to where I've retreated from the stench. She reaches up, and I grab under her arms to help her to her feet. We stumble over each other until I can prop her against the hood of my car. She leans forward into my chest and her shoulders sag forward. "I want to go home."

"What about your sister?" I ask. Charlotte moans. The vibration from her moaning is somehow both inside and outside my chest. "You can come home with me. Becca and I will take care of you."

She lifts her face up toward me, and I feel that familiar urge to kiss her, but her eyes are so glazed, and she is hiccupping, and some puke is on her chin. I clean her face with a napkin from my glove box before helping her back into the car.

At home, we sneak up the stairs, which is exponentially harder to do with Charlotte stepping in all the wrong places, and settle Charlotte in Becca's bed. Becca leaves to get aspirin and water for our patient.

Charlotte's wearing a sleeveless shirt thingy that ties behind her neck, her skin prickled with a chill. Becca's book page rose is pinned to the fabric just above her right breast. I will myself to look away and pull off my sweatshirt, so I can yank it over her head, making her glossy black curls stand up at odd, yet sexy, angles. As I'm putting her right arm through the shirt, she looks at me, her eyes more focused.

"Know what I miss the most from my old life?"

"Old life?"

"The one before I was dying."

My heart catches. "Oh."

"I miss the boredom."

Instead of saying anything, I help thread her left arm through the other sleeve.

"I miss thinking I had enough time to be bored. Nowadays, it feels like such a waste. But, I'm tired. Tired of the constant motion. Tired of running away from something so—" She fixes me with her eyes. "Consuming."

It feels like a hand is crushing my throat. "You can't give up."

"What if I'm not giving up? Nothing lasts forever. What if my number is up? Or, like, my number line thingy is simply a short line?"

"Number line thingy? Are you alluding to a math theory?"

She laughs, her small shoulders shaking inside my sweatshirt. "You said 'allude,' which is totally a literary term. We're even."

I smooth a mussed curl from her face and press my palm there. Her eyes widen, and I retract my hand.

"Sorry," I say and lean away.

Her hand reaches up to the same spot. "I don't know what to do," she says, her voice a low note on a saxophone. When her eyes overflow, I wipe the tears from her cheek with my sleeve. She catches my hand and holds it.

"Jo's making us stay with Dad for Christmas. I don't want to go. I'm nothing but a cancer patient to him anymore. It's so horrible, Charlie."

"I'm so sorry." I move closer to her.

"He's too chicken-shit to admit I'm losing this fight; the tumors are winning. We just lie to each other, like I'll live happily ever after, and I hate it. I hate the lies."

She lets go of my hand to wipe away the second round of tears coursing down her cheeks. I open my mouth, but Charlotte cuts me off. "If you apologize to me again for something out of your control, Hanson, I swear I'll make your nose bleed so badly you'll need super-size tampons to staunch the bleeding."

I need to change the subject, so I go with math. "Did you know—" My voice sounds too high, like my vocal chords are strung too tight. I clear my throat, "Did you know the number-line-thingy has a special place for imaginary numbers?"

She looks at me like maybe *my* brain is addled with tumors. "And?"

"Isn't that strange?"

"Mathematically?" Her mouth scrunches up to one side. It's kind of adorable. "I have no idea."

"The mathematical term, oddly enough, is not 'number-line-thingy.' We call it the Real line." One of her eyebrows arches. "And the imaginary line, which is part of the complex plane, intersects with the Real line."

"Complex plane? Sounds about right." Her lips pull into a smile.

"Mathematicians invented imaginary numbers to solve these ridiculously awesome problems. The real numbers weren't enough."

"What's the point, Professor Weird?"

I take a long, shaky breath. I hadn't realized how fast my heart was racing. "The point is, sometimes real problems have to be solved with imagination. Maybe the lies aren't technically lies, but imaginary numbers, and your dad needs them to cope with losing you."

"That and whiskey."

"Right."

"It's a nice fairy tale, but I'm still going to die," she says, lying back on Becca's bed and closing her eyes.

I sit on the floor next to her. "Are you afraid?"

Her eyebrows pull into a frown. It makes her look like her sister. "I'm not a coward."

"No, you are not."

She's quiet. The whole house is silent. Charlotte grabs my hand. Her fingers are frail and white in my palm, like the bare branches of the birch in the backyard. Her voice in the stillness hurts. "Yes. I am."

Becca comes back, and bustles between Charlotte and me. "Mom and Dad are still asleep," she reports, and then sits Charlotte up to administer water and aspirin like a nurse. I stand to leave, but Charlotte's grip tightens.

I sit back down next to the bed and watch as Becca strokes Charlotte's curls, untangling them so they lay neatly against her face. As Charlotte falls asleep, her fingers relax and fall away from mine. I want to grab them up and hold them again. I want to, but I don't.

5.5

Once Charlotte is sleeping, I slip off to my room. My nerves are buzzing, making me jittery. I need a good distraction. I could finish that physics chapter I was reading earlier, but for some reason it doesn't appeal to me. I pace my room a few times and notice my backpack half-slung under my bed. I drag it out and fish inside for the novel I stole today.

I collapse on my bed with Ms. Finch's copy of *To Kill A Mockingbird*. I smell the aging paper and hear the spine crackle, like it had under Ms. Finch's careful fingers, as I open the book and am transported from my world to hers.

There are inscriptions on the title page:

To Charley: You are old enough to understand real courage.

For my Jo: You need this now.

I look more closely at the ink drawings in the margins, illustrations of the story. They are beautiful and intricate and each one is overflowing with something. Some tangible feeling. This is how Charlotte sees the words.

Between the illustrations, in a cramped script, are poems, each one a snapshot of the people in the story. This is how Ms. Finch sees the words.

The book is a conversation between sisters. A love letter.

I know the right thing to do is to return the book right this instant. Drive to Ms. Finch's house and slide it in the damn doggie door. But I don't.

I read.

I read through what remains of the night, hearing the characters in my head and seeing them on the page before me in beautiful details. Scout scowling in class as the teacher instructs her to stop reading so she can learn to read = loss. But then Atticus encourages her to continue, to do what's right for her = win.

Jem wriggling out of his pants in his escape from the Radley yard = loss. Then the pants appear, patched and everything, and the kids begin to realize they have a secret ally = win. Crazy Mrs. Dubose and her Camellias. Well, that's a big win.

Atticus defends Tom in court and I'm sure he'll win. But Tom is found guilty.

Loss.

Tom Robinson's life ends as he's running to save it.

Loss.

Bob Ewell falls on his knife.

Loss.

Boo Radley saves Jem.

Win.

But goes back into hiding.

Loss.

I can't figure out how Atticus stays so strong. Why doesn't he flip the hell out? Everything is falling apart, but he's as calm as he was the day he taught Jem about courage, not by staring down a gun barrel at death, but by standing by a person he admired as she died.

I read until the sun rises and filters through the white blinds in my windows. When I finish, I am so filled with the story, I feel alive. And I want to share the feeling with Charlotte.

Becca reads in her nest beside the bed where Charlotte is still asleep. It would be cruel to wake her, so I sit next to Becca with the book in my lap and wait.

"Morning," Becca murmurs. Instead of looking at me, her eyes lock on the book in my hands. "You're reading?"

"Have you read this?" I show her the cover.

"More than a dozen times." People do that? Becca takes it from me and continues, "I've never seen one with such lovely illustrations." She squints at the margins then looks up at me with wide-eyes. "Whose is this?"

"Teacher." I shrug, but it looks more like a spasm.

"Charlie," she breathes in an exasperated huff. She flips to the front of the book and reads the inscriptions. "Did Ms. Finch let you borrow this?"

"Sure."

"Un-huh. Does Charlotte know you have it?"

I snatch it back from her.

"That's what I thought," she says, blanching at my rough treatment of the book. Her face gets a hard look about it I've never seen before. She points her finger at me like mom. "You listen to me, Charles Hanson, and you listen good. If anything happens to this book, you'll have to answer to me."

I grin. Just a tiny one because, who is she kidding? She takes the finger she's wagging at me and pokes me in the chest, hard. "I'm. No. Joke," she says, punctuating each word with another hard jab.

I nod, my grin slipping away. I flip through the pages again. "He didn't win, Bec."

"No. Atticus failed." She sighs, dropping her head onto my shoulder. "That's what makes the story so good."

I scoff. "How is it good to lose? No wonder I hate reading. Literature is weird."

Becca laughs. "Sometimes life is like that, you know. It smacks us when we're down. The brave get back up. At least, they do in the books."

"Atticus is seriously kickass."

"Duh," she says, rolling her eyes at me.

I rest my cheek on her warm, brown hair. "What are we supposed to do now?"

"Be brave," she whispers, tucking her hand in mine like when she was three and I was five and our biggest fear was thunder.

5.6

The doorbell rings that evening as I'm putting the last of the dinner dishes in the dishwasher. Mom and Dad, lounging on the couch, shout, "Not it!"

"You guys are serious slackers tonight," I say, drying my hands on a dishtowel. I snap it at them as I walk by the couch, and they both laugh.

"Some of us woke up before two in the afternoon," Dad says, tweaking his mouth to one side, his mustache following suit.

Tossing the towel over my shoulder, I open the door.

"Merry Almost Christmas," Charlotte cries. Her nose is pink from the cold and she's holding a large stack of presents, the top one threatening to fall at any second. She looks much better than this morning. I was excited to see her wake up, but she was more concerned about not puking on me than talking books. Becca cleaned her up and took her home.

"Oh, wow, uh, Merry Christmas." I step inside holding the door open. "Can I help you with those?"

"I don't know, can you?" Her face lights up.

"You have to stop," I say, catching a present as it topples.

"It's hard to resist, but I'll try."

Charlotte brought us all gifts before she leaves for her dad's.

Becca opens a handmade copy of *The Velveteen Rabbit*, one of her favorites from childhood. Charlotte illustrated the story in bright watercolors and pen and ink sketches. The brown rabbit in the illustrations has Becca's eyes. Inside, Charlotte inscribed it: *For Becca, who is indeed a Real girl.* Both Becca and Mom cry over each beautiful page.

While they are busy sharing the book, Charlotte hands me a flat package saying, "Merry Christmas, Other Charlie."

I mean to smile, but end up frowning at the present instead. "I didn't get you a gift," I say.

Charlotte's smile doesn't fade. "I have everything I need. Open this, and use it well. It'll be your present to me."

I hold her gaze for as long as I can before it hurts too much. I tear back the paper revealing a journal. The pages are blank inside, but on the cover Charlotte has drawn a complicated pattern of birds beginning with a point in the center and radiating outward. Each set of birds gets smaller as they approach the edge of a large circle.

"What is this?" I say, tracing one of the birds.

"It's a mockingbird." My head snaps up to study her, but she's still looking at her work. There are so many questions.

"Mockingbird?"

"There's one outside my window at Jo's house. Sings even in the middle of the night. Unusual birds, but I do love them."

I swallow a knot in my throat. "But what is this?" I ask trying to indicate the piece she's drawn as a whole.

Charlotte smiles, this wide glorious thing that makes my brain hum. "It's a fractal."

The humming in my head speeds to my chest; filling it with so much sound it may explode. "You know what a fractal is?"

Charlotte wrinkles her nose. "Not exactly. Becca explained it to me."

"Becca Hanson? My sister explained fractals to you?" Becca looks up at her name. Noticing the book in my hand, she smiles even more widely.

"Of course," Charlotte says. "All I remember is something about repeating patterns and infinity. Oh, and there's some geometry in there, too."

"Ya think?"

Charlotte chuckles, and tucks a curl behind her ear. "I learned to draw one by studying M.C. Escher. You've heard of him, right?"

I try to focus. I try not to pull the errant curl back out so it can curl along her cheekbone again. "Escher's the dude with the stairs."

"Yep. Pretty amazing what happens when you combine math with art."

I trace the flying mockingbirds as they soar outward in an infinite plane.

"You're the amazing one." I say it before I even think it. It's like the humming inside of me couldn't stay contained and what it sounds like on the outside is "Absolutely amazing."

Charlotte quirks an eyebrow as her cheeks flush. It makes her even more irresistible so the feeling of wanting to pull her into a kiss comes rushing back.

Unfortunately (or fortunately—I don't know anymore), Becca throws her arms around Charlotte, tackling her back into the couch pillows with a hug. "Thankyouthankyouthankyou," she's murmuring as she squeezes Charlotte. "Come on," she says, dragging Charlotte up to her room.

Studying the infinite set of mockingbirds that Charlotte has placed in my hands, I begin to understand this one simple truth: the thing I want most in this world is the thing I am most assuredly going to lose—Charlotte Finch.

I take my journal up to my room and brood over it. Charlotte said I should use it well, but I have no idea what that means. I dig in my desk drawer for a pen, but I freeze once I've found one and am poised to write in the book. For a second, I think I might write out Cantor's Infinity Proof, but the madness passes. Nothing I could ever write would be equal to Charlotte's brilliant artwork.

I close the journal and watch the mockingbirds soar on the cover. I begin counting them, but the pattern is so intricate I lose count around eighty every time. I'm not sure how long I've been counting when I hear Mom hollering for me from the foyer.

When I reach the bend in the front stairs, I see Mom and Dad and Becca all crowding around Charlotte and wishing her happy holidays and a safe trip. I can't help but notice how close she's standing to the ugly, plastic mistletoe Dad hangs up each year. She's one step away.

Everyone says good-bye and Happy New Year, and I toss in a wave before the door closes behind Charlotte.

My chest thuds with the sound of the lock clicking.

Without a real plan, I run back upstairs and grab the book I stole. I'm out the door in the freezing cold and calling, "Charlotte."

She meets me on the bottom step of the porch.

"I do have something to give you."

Charlotte stretches out her hands, and I place her book in them. Confusion flickers over her porcelain features.

"I took it."

Charlotte thumbs through the book. "Why?"

"I wondered about Atticus." Charlotte's expression masks her feelings. I hurry on, "I know now I shouldn't have taken something so special." The words pour onto the open pages of the book. I lean closer, choking on my fear and a hungry need to erase all the space between us.

Charlotte's eyebrows knit low over her eyes. I freeze. She closes the book, and her fingers linger on the spine. "You read it?"

I nod. I'm inches from Charlotte. Ensconced by her perfume. "And?"

"I liked it." I cup her face. "A lot." I can see our breath meet in the cold air. She closes her eyes, tucking an entire ocean behind her lids.

When our lips meet, it's as if all the answers I've been looking for explode and burn in hot licking flames that flare, then smolder. The ashes of those answers blow away, and I realize, I don't need them. I need this—Charlotte's warm lips moving against mine, like lines of poetry strung together on a hyperbolic plane. Her tongue caresses my bottom lip, and when I sigh, it is an invitation for her to explore more of me.

Her fingers clasp the back of my neck, pulling me closer. My heart races and my hands ache to hold her. I rest them on her shoulders, but they feel so fragile, too small. I place one on the back of her neck, slipping my fingers under her scarf, but the bones of her spine meet my fingertips and I pull them away. I cup her face again, but by now I'm concentrating on all the wrong things, and Charlotte knows it.

She sinks back on her heels to look up at me, her expression bereft. She went against her better judgment, letting me in even though we said we couldn't do this, couldn't hurt Becca, and I let my insecurities take over and ruin the moment. I swallow and try to say I'm sorry, but it comes out as a sigh. I draw my thumb across her cheek and try again, "Charlotte—"

"Charlotte!" Dad's voice echoes mine as he emerges on the porch. "You forgot—" The words die on his lips. Charlotte's keys dangle in his outstretched hand.

Charlotte pulls away, her teeth closing around her bottom lip. "Thanks, Mr. Hanson." She grabs the keys and backs toward her car, waving. "Well, I'll see you all next year, I guess."

I watch her drive away, not wanting to face Dad. When I do turn, his look, like everything else, is complicated.

5.7

hristmas break sucks. I am drowning my sorrows with cookie dough and cold milk, waiting for Dad's first batch of cookies to come out of the oven when Mom comes in from getting the mail and announces that a package has arrived. A chill wind sneaks in behind her, but she back kicks the door closed.

Tossing the mail aside, she sets the package on the island. "Cookies?"

"Almost," Dad says, opening the oven door so the kitchen fills with the aroma of sugar and goodness.

Mom turns her attention back to the package. "Open it, Charlie. Aunt Muriel said she sent you something. Maybe that's it. Her gifts are so cute."

I tear open the package without looking at the label as Dad takes the first batch out and sets them on the counter. The cookies look much better than any old package from Aunt Muriel. Last year she sent me reindeer socks.

I abandon the box for a hot cookie instead. Mom opens it for me and reads the enclosed note, her mouth tightening as she's reading, so her lips all but disappear.

"You'll want to open this, Charlie," Mom says as she finishes reading the note. "And for heaven's sake, let the cookies cool before you eat them." She removes a little brown box from the package and pushes it into the middle of the kitchen island.

I've shoved the piping hot cookie into my mouth, which means I have to chew it with my mouth open to let the gooey steam escape. It's the best way.

"Whaisit?" I garble through the molten cookie. Mom doesn't say anything, though. She just watches me. I swallow in one big, burning gulp and tug the string on the gift box.

Inside, laid upon a large, white, starched handkerchief, is the most perfect orange rose I've ever seen. Its face is huge and open and soft, and its sweet aroma wafts around me. I'm transported back to the warmth of autumn and the big harvest moon Mrs. Dunwitty loved so much. This is one of her prize-winning roses, perfectly preserved.

Mom hands me the note, which is definitely *not* from Aunt Muriel..

There, in impeccably formed letters on pristine paper, Mrs. Dunwitty rats me out for driving over her garden. The rose is a token of her gratitude for my hard work repairing it. She had it freeze-dried to preserve it for me, which is actually pretty cool. She closed the letter with, "It's not enough to be your best. You need to be someone else's best, too. And since I'm old and running short on time, I'll say it even more plainly so you don't get confused. Kiss the girl, Jack."

"You drove over her garden?" Mom asks.

I nod. Behind me, I hear my dad choke on a mouthful of cookies.

"When?" asks Mom.

"I don't know. Late August?" I say as I brush the tip of my finger along the petals.

"And you didn't tell us? And you've been driving around ever since? What else have you run over?" She's getting louder with each question.

"Nothing. Just the garden, and I fixed it."

"That's good," says my dad, licking crumbs from his finger.

My mother's look says, "Not the point."

Dad clears his throat and continues, "I mean it wouldn't do to try to sell her house with the garden a mess."

"Sell her house?" I look up from the rose.

"Haven't you seen the sign in the yard?"

I haven't mown Mrs. Dunwitty's lawn since the first frost, just after Thanksgiving. I suddenly feel horrible for not inventing some other excuse to visit her. Her porch did need repainting. Why didn't I do that? My thoughts are building to a crescendo.

"No!" Now it's my turn to shout. "I haven't seen any signs."

Dad flicks a look at Mom like my fragile mind may be slipping again. Then he places a hand on my shoulder and explains, "Charlie, Mrs. Dunwitty's son moved her to an assisted living home. She's more comfortable this way. Keeping up with her house and garden was just too much work."

That's bullshit. Dimwit doesn't need an old folks' home. She's not ready for a place to go and die.

"I've got some work to do upstairs," I say, grabbing the box.

In my room, I sit in the center of my floor with the rose in my lap, its bright moony face peering at me from the box. I feel like an ostrich that wants to stick its head in the sand, but someone's gone and filled in my head hole so I'm stuck facing all this crap.

Dimwit can't die. Yes, she's old, but it doesn't feel right. She's a permanent fixture in the neighborhood. She's always been here with her roses blooming each summer, perfuming the street while she rocks on her porch with the flamingo-ass door, looking at every kid riding by on a bike like he might be her next meal.

Of course, this explains why her yard was looking shabby. And maybe the cane was for real and not just for threatening me with blunt force trauma. And there was the way her skin felt on my arm, dry and brittle, like a breeze might crumble her to pieces and carry her away.

I struggle to remember what she said the day we planted the roses. She smelled the big orange bloom and was transported back to her youth. She said a rose would smell differently to me because my experiences are unique. Actually, what she said was, "Perception is a powerful tool."

I inhale the aroma of the rose in my lap. It smells like sadness now.

5.8

I'm driving to Greta's for our annual New Year's movie marathon. The sign in Mrs. Dunwitty's yard catches my eye, even though I try to avoid it. The garden is shrouded in frost. And her house is—

"What the hell?"

I slam on the brakes and swerve for the curb. I stamp up to her porch to stare at the offending door. How could they? Dimwit would be mad. No, pissed. Mrs. Dunwitty's once flamingo-pink door has been painted a respectable hunter green.

I fish out my cell phone as I jog back to my car.

"Where does Mrs. Dunwitty's son live?"

"What?" Dad asks.

"You said he put her in an old folks' home. I want to wish her a Happy New Year. Where is she?"

"Hold on," he says. "I just got a Christmas card from Bill. I'll find his address."

Mrs. Dunwitty's son lives two towns over. Luckily for me, it's a town even punier than mine with only one retirement joint in the whole place right on the main strip. I pull into the parking lot, all screeching wheels and nervy driving.

I haven't thought through what I'm about to do which is why my mind still hasn't caught up to my body's actions. Obviously, or

I'd be sitting at Greta's stuffing my face with popcorn instead of parking across two spots at a retirement home.

Still on autopilot, I leave the car and walk through the automatic doors that sigh *shush* as they open and close. Inside the door is a mahogany reception desk the size of Texas. My brain catches up and puts the brakes on my whole adrenaline-driven trip.

The receptionist smiles at me, a smear of pink lipstick on her left front tooth. I'm frozen on the entry mat so the automatic doors are *shush*ing like mad behind me. Open, close, open, close. Gusts of frozen wind blow in around me. The receptionist's smile fades as she waves me in.

"Well come on now, sugar. You're letting the cold air in," she says, her polished southern accent and big hair making it okay for her to call a complete stranger "sugar."

"Sorry," I mutter and step away from the doors. They come to a close with a final *shush*. I can feel my ears burning and my palms are sweaty so I wipe them on the front of my jeans and shift from one foot to the other. "Um, I'm…um."

Looking around I can see the Graceful Oaks Retirement Home is ready for a rip-roaring New Year's Eve. Paper streamers and balloons are stuck to the beige walls. I move closer to the giant desk, dwarfing myself with each step. The receptionist is wearing a glittery top hat.

The brass nameplate at the desk tells me my sparkly receptionist is Debbie. Debbie looks like she hopes the *shush*ing doors open again so a winter wind can take me away. I try once more. "I'm here to see Mrs. Dunwitty."

Debbie's eyes widen. "Is she expecting you?"

"No," I scoff and then regret it. Debbie doesn't look impressed.

"Are you family?"

"Um. No. I'm her neighbor."

Debbie looks dubious, her small eyes squinching together.

"I take care of her garden. Well, at first, I ran over her garden, then I took care of it."

"Well," she says, drawling the word out, "I'm not supposed to let unannounced guests—"

"I want to wish her a Happy New Year." The words jumble out and land flat on her gigantic desk. "Please?"

"Sign in here," she says, leaning forward like we're co-conspirators. She points toward a set of double doors. "Room 112."

Once inside, I take a huge breath to steady myself. I peek into an empty sitting room, furnished with squashy looking chairs and a television blaring some New Year's celebration to an empty room. I notice a vase of roses set on a table in the back corner of the room. I duck in and grab it, and then speed-walk to room 112. I knock before my nerves can catch up. No immediate answer.

I knock again and call out, "Mrs. Dunwitty? It's Charlie. Can I come in?"

"*May* I come in, Jack." The response is quiet, but unmistakable. Just as a nurse rounds the corner, I push open the door and step into the darkened interior room.

I can barely make out Mrs. Dunwitty lying in her bed. She has shrunk, shriveled into this strange old woman. My smile twitches as I clutch the stolen flowers like a shield.

"These are for you," I say, placing them next to her bed. She turns to look at them and her eyes, still clear and razor-sharp grow with horror.

"Those are the ugliest fucking flowers ever. Where did you steal those? You better have stolen them. Please do not tell a dying woman you paid good money for those crappy excuses for roses. Didn't I teach you anything at all? Get them out of here." Her voice, shaky at first from disuse, grows stronger and louder with each grievance. "O-U-T, OUT." She points a thin finger toward the door as her body is overrun with a spasm of coughing.

I snatch the flowers and run from the room, tossing them in a trashcan across the hallway. When I come back in, she is sitting up in her hospital bed. It makes a sluggish whirring sound, like even the beds in this joint are fixing to die. She looks me over, her eyes squinting and making me squirm. Finally, she smiles, a wide smile in a too-small face. Skeleton smile.

"It's good to see you," she says and pats the edge of her bed for me to sit.

The last thing I want to do is sit on this woman's bed, but I'm afraid another outburst like the last one will do her in. I sit.

"So what brings you here?" she asks, and I can see if I consider a lie, even a half-truth, she'll smack the back of my head.

"They painted your door," I say.

She is quiet for a moment. "What color?"

I don't want to answer. Why am I here? What was I thinking? I stare at the wide white tiled floor.

"That bad, eh?" she says with a chuckle.

I nod.

"Well, it's to be expected."

My eyes get wide. "What? What's to be expected? They painted your door boring, totally okey-dokie, covenant-approved green. How can you be so calm?"

"Charles, it isn't my door. Not technically. Who's going to buy a house with a pink door?"

"Plenty of people," I snap. Mrs. Dunwitty looks at me with a funny half smile. "Okay, fine. Nobody would want to live in a house with a flamingo-ass door. Happy? You're the only person that insane." I'm laughing now and she's laughing, too.

"That's my boy."

Our laughing quiets and her hand is sitting pale and gray on her blanket. I remember the way it looked as it dug in the fertile soil of her rose garden, holding the delicate roots of plants and coaxing them into the dirt to grow and thrive. Without thinking, I reach out and pick up her hand, so tiny and weak now, in my own.

"Everything has changed." My voice hurts as it tumbles out from my throat.

"That's how gardens grow. I thought we'd already covered that," Mrs. Dunwitty says, squeezing my hand.

"Yeah, but the changes never stop, and I can't keep up. Like I'm holding tightly to the strings of so many balloons, but they're coming untied and blowing away, and I'm left with this horrible tangle of strings. I don't know how to get free of them. You're—" I break off and look for the words.

"Dying," she offers.

The tears are beating the hell out of my eyes, working to chip away the tiniest hole in the dam. I focus on her ashen hand and the way it trembles as I hold it.

"Charles, I'm old. Surely you've noticed." She's trying to make me smile.

I close my eyes and steal a shallow breath. She called me Charles. Making light. I play along. "Mrs. Dunwitty, no offense, but I'm pretty sure you're older than Moses."

"That's my boy," she repeats. "What's going on? Why are you making my dying days such a suckfest?"

"Excuse me? Suckfest?"

Mrs. Dunwitty's eyes twinkle.

"All right. I guess I can tell you everything, seeing as how you're going to die in, like, ten minutes, which means you can't go blabbing it everywhere."

"Oh, I can get a lot done in ten minutes."

"I'm sure you can." I spill everything. I tell her about Brighton and Ms. Finch. I tell her about Charlotte and how she's dying, and I don't know what to think because shouldn't the world keep the good ones around as long as it can?

"I guess it seems like a big waste. She's young and kind and beautiful and talented and…" I stop, waiting for the words. "Unfinished," I finally say.

Her smile is sad this time. "Unfinished is ungood."

I laugh, but the sound tastes bitter. "These are your words of wisdom? Unfinished is ungood? Is ungood even a word? Thought you were brilliant—had all the answers."

"Always did say you weren't as bright as everyone claimed," she says, but then stops and inhales sharply. I look at her face, alarmed. Her eyes are closed and her face is screwed up in pain.

"Are you okay, Mrs. Dunwitty?" I don't like the way her face keeps going gray. I don't like the way her breath is rattling. "Do I need to get a nurse?"

"No, no nurses. I'm fine." She closes her eyes and rests her head back against the pillow. "So tell me more. Have you talked to Charlotte about your feelings?"

I rub my nose. "Not really. When I mentioned her cancer, she punched me."

Mrs. Dunwitty laughs so hard she starts coughing again. I get her some water and wait for her breathing to quiet. She takes a sip and says, "I like this girl."

"You're not the only one," I admit.

I tell myself it's a trick of the light when her eyes change from clear to cloudy, like heavy summer skies. "And another thing—kiss the girl, Jack. With your whole body and soul, you kiss her. Ain't nothing like it. Worth all the risks. Worth all the pain to be in that one moment. Why, my Darryl…" She slips under the spell of her memories.

I grin and fake a cough.

She squeezes my hand. "Now," she says, back to business. "If you're done crying your wussy heart out, I'm feeling tired."

I stand next to her bed, fighting down a wedge of fear in my throat. "Happy New Year, Mrs. Dunwitty," I say and kiss her on the cheek.

She smiles. "Not me, Jack," she says, touching the spot on her cheek where I kissed her. "The other one."

5.9

Driving home I make three New Year's resolutions.

Resolution 1: I pat the head of the angel Charlotte helped me place in Mrs. Dunwitty's garden as I walk around to her backyard. There's a can of flamingo-ass paint (not the official name on the can) in her old tool shed, and I know just what to do with it. I glance down the street at the dark houses, but no one is out. Mrs. Dunwitty's house is abandoned, waiting for sale with its stupid green door.

I stand under the freezing stars at Mrs. Dunwitty's and paint the door its proper color. My fingers are numb stubs, and my brush strokes are uneven, and the paint is freezing before it hits the door, but as the last seconds of this year slip away, I stand back and smile.

Now that's more like it.

I toss the paint and brush in the trash heap in my trunk, nodding at the small, broken angel statue I still haven't thrown away. But as soon as I've slammed it closed I remember Mrs. Dunwitty's lesson on properly keeping your tools, so I open it up again and pull the brush out. I trudge around to the side of the porch where the water spigot hides behind an angry bush whose branches keep scraping at my hands as I rub the brush under the freezing water, watching the pink run off into a Pepto-Bismol puddle. I use my coat to dry off the brush and put it back in my trunk.

My hands are as pink as Mrs. Dunwitty's door. Pink and cracking in the cold night air, stinging as much as the warm tears I refuse to cry. Now it's finished. Finished is good.

Resolution 2: I find Becca reading in her nest of blankets when I get home. My insides feel like an army of ants has moved in, wriggling and scurrying every which way. "We need to talk," I say, flopping down on her bed. If I thought it took balls to kiss Charlotte, it's nothing compared to the bravery I'm summoning for this conversation. "I kissed Charlotte."

Becca closes her book around a finger to save her place. "I know."

Wow. Did not see that coming. "Did Charlotte tell you?"

Becca nods. "She said you kissed her and she kissed you back, but that it was a mistake and it wouldn't happen again."

Mistake? Of course, I get my feelings all sorted out, and completely forget that Charlotte may not feel the same way. My ears, neck, face, chest—it's all on fire. Becca puts a hand on my shoulder and I'm surprised she doesn't get burned.

"Of course she was lying about the mistake thing. She just said that to make me feel better."

Relief washes over me. "The thing is, Bec, I want to kiss her again. I want to take her out on a date. I want to be her boyfriend. But I need to know it's okay with you."

She runs her thumb along the spine of the book. "Guess I'd be a pretty big bitch right now if I said it's not."

"No." I lock my eyes with hers. "I need the truth."

She twists a lock of her hair. "I do worry that you'll fuck it up."

"Becca!" Dad pops his head in her doorway, a bushy brow

raised, "Don't say that word. I nearly had a heart attack out here." He puts a basket of clean laundry on her floor before ducking back out again.

Becca claps her hands over her mouth, her cheeks flushing.

"That's what I told her, Dad," I holler after him, and then grin at Becca. "Language, missy." I *tsk* at her, shaking my head.

My sister laughs. For the first time, I notice how musical her laugh is. Not quite like Charlotte's, but alive with sound. I'm pretty sure Becca didn't laugh like that before Charlotte. Becca didn't laugh at all.

"I worry I'll fuck it up, too." I'm careful to whisper the f-word.

"Dad!" Becca shouts. "Charlie said f—"

I smack her with a pillow to shut her up and we get to laughing again.

She quiets and sets her face in an old-fashioned Becca way— serious. "Does it feel like love, Charlie?"

In the wake of her question, I struggle to draw a breath.

Becca waits.

"Love is an awfully big word. Even bigger than cancer."

She nods. "And there's no cure for it either."

I don't know if it feels like love, but what I feel seems bigger than myself, like I can't contain it no matter what I do. And the feeling seems to spill over into other areas of my life, like with that book. I fell for Atticus and all those characters. And I'm seeing all sorts of things about Becca I never took the time to notice. Things I really, really love.

I nudge her knee with mine. "I never appreciated how amazing you were before, Becca."

She blushes three shades darker, twirling her hair. "I love you, too, Charlie."

"And whatever you decide about Charlotte, I will respect."

Becca laughs. "Oh, please. Like I could say no to that sappy love-sick face of yours. You're worse than a puppy, you are."

"So I can ask her out?"

"If you don't, you might break her heart." Becca's smile is small, but pure.

I wrap an arm around her, squeezing her to my side. "Thank you, Bec." I kiss the top of her head, and she swats me away. "So, how do I do this?"

Resolution 3: Becca says the reason cheesy romance movies always have characters doing the same lame crap over and over is because it works. She rattled off at least half a dozen stories in which the man comes to the woman's window and woos her. We men have Romeo to thank for this lameness.

Becca confirms that Charlotte will be arriving home from her dad's house the next day. When I reach Charlotte's backyard that night, I crouch behind some scraggly bushes and scan the yard for the dog. There's a crystalline layer of frost covering the grass like lace.

My fingers shake as I unlatch the gate, but I tell myself it's just the coldness seeping in. Once inside, I find a few pebbles in the garden and poise myself under Charlotte's window.

The first stone I toss ricochets off the siding with a *thwack* loud enough to wake the dead. I crouch low and look behind me, expecting a swarm of vampires or cannibals or, I don't know, rabid-laser-toting squirrels on my ass at any second. When nothing happens, I toss the second rock. It lands on the roof and scuttles into the gutter. I find myself wishing Greta were here. She has better aim.

The third and fourth stones also miss. I'm out of stones. Desperate, I scan the yard and pick up a large pinecone. I give it a good heave. It arcs upward and makes a loud crunching noise as it smacks into Charlotte's window.

"Yes!" I shout, and then toss myself flat into some bushes as the patio light flicks on.

"What in the hell do you think you're doing?"

My heart flops around in my chest as I peek up from behind the bush. Charlotte is standing on the patio, a blanket pulled around her.

Jumping up, I wave. "Oh, uh, hi."

"Hi?" Charlotte says, coming at me like a tachyon. "You could have woken my sister." She grabs my elbow and pulls me back through the yard and shoves me through the open gate.

This isn't the response Romeo got from Juliet. I watched the movie. This is not how it went.

"Wait, Charlotte, I want to ask you something."

Charlotte closes the gate between us and looks at me, her jaw muscles tight. "Ask me what?"

"I'd like to take you on a proper date."

Her hard expression melts, revealing the softer Charlotte beneath it. She arches one brow. "You know what a proper date looks like?"

"No, but Becca helped me with a plan."

"Becca knows about dating?"

"Technically? No. But she reads more than me, so she says she's got it all figured out."

"I wasn't sure you'd be back after our last…whatever that was," she says, a hint of armor in her voice.

"Yeah, well, the dying thing scares the hell out of me." Her hands tense around the fence. I kick at one of the slats in the gate. How do I put this so Charlotte won't punch me, or sic her mean-ass dog on me? "I don't mean to piss you off. It's just last time, when we kissed it was so good and everything I wanted, but then I began

to wonder what my life will look like when you're dead and, well…
you were there."

"Dead chicks aren't sexy?" she asks. I roll my eyes, which
makes her snort. "Oh, but eye rolls *are* sexy."

"Not as sexy as snorting," I deadpan.

She pinches her lips together in response.

I take a deep breath and slide my fingers between hers.
"Charlotte, when you go, I'll be left here. You seem to think this
puts me at an advantage, but you're wrong because right now,
you're the most beautiful problem in my life. Compared to you,
everything seems inconsequential."

I've been staring at a fern twisting through the frosty mud at
the base of the fence. I let my eyes flick upward to gage whether
or not I need to duck or run. But Charlotte doesn't look mad. Her
eyes are big, sparkling from the porch light.

She leans over the gate between us, pressing her pink cheeks
and perfect lips close to my ear. "Impress me, then," she whispers
before brushing my lips with hers. I lean forward, as she leans
backward, a fish on a line, until the gate presses against my sternum.

"Charlotte." I inadvertently groan as my body floods with want.
When I open my eyes, she's standing a foot away from the fence
with a wicked grin. My face and ears burn despite the cold air.

"I thought you said it'd be a proper date. Shouldn't the good
night kiss come at the end?"

I nod, still flustered, and try to clear my throat. I have to take
three big breaths before I can speak again. "Charlotte, would you
go out with me this Friday?"

6.0

Charlotte hasn't been around much this week. Becca says it's to our benefit because I've had plenty of time to plan the date. Becca says I've got this one chance to impress Charlotte. Becca says don't screw it up.

Becca says an awful lot these days, but not half as much as Greta has had to say.

When I called to apologize for skipping out on New Year's Eve, I told her what'd happened.

"Are you sure this is a good idea, Chuck? I mean, this close to the end of high school, and you'll be leaving next year, plus the whole—"

"I don't know if it's a good idea, but it's what's happening. It's a risk I have to take because I can't go one more day lying to everyone about how I feel about her. She makes me happy. And most of the time I make her happy, too. Don't you want that for me?"

She was quiet before she said, "Yes. Yes, I do."

Greta was Team Charlie from that moment on, coaching me on what to say, how to listen, and randomly quizzing me throughout the week on dating dos and don'ts. Like we'd pass in the hall and she'd call out, "What do you do if she has something stuck in her teeth?"

Answer: You're screwed either way, so hope she orders something without parsley.

The only reason Greta isn't here now is because I told her the pressure would be too much. I may be strong, but no man is strong enough to deal with both Becca and Greta scheming in their love life at the same time.

Becca is studying me as I stand in the middle of her room fussing with the crease in my slacks and reviewing the details of my plans.

"After dinner, I'm taking her to the art museum's outdoor exhibit. The museum has horse-drawn carriages for the winter festival, and I've made reservations for a tour of the sculpture garden. Do you think Charlotte'll like it?"

I switch to fiddling with the cuffs of my shirt. Button. Unbutton. Roll. Unroll.

"You've asked me a million times. It's going to be perfect. Just remember—"

Button. Unbutton.

"Are you paying attention?"

"I'm listening, honest." And, I am, but I'm also listening to the crazy voices in my head shouting fifteen other things at me. Things like, *Run!* Or, *You're not good enough!* And *geek + gorgeous girl = disaster!*

I've got one sleeve rolled and the other unrolled. "Which is best, Bec?"

She cocks her head to the side, studying my "look," before coming over and unrolling and buttoning the one sleeve. "Be yourself, Charlie. Promise?"

I snort.

The doorbell rings and we both freeze. We hear Mom open the door and her warm greetings to Charlotte.

"We've missed you this week," she's saying. "How're you doing?"

Becca turns me around and shoves me hard between my shoulder blades. "Go!" She urges me out of her room. Becca says it's important I knock and pick Charlotte up properly, and Becca's door will have to do since Ms. Finch would flunk me if I showed up on her doorstep.

I duck into my room just as I hear Charlotte's footsteps on the stairs.

"**W**ho is it?" calls Becca in a sing-songy voice.

I consider bashing her door open with my forehead. It'd render me unconscious, which might make for a more successful date. But before I do anything rash, the door opens and everything tumbling and clawing around inside of me goes still.

"Hello," Charlotte says, a beautiful blush deepening the pink of her cheeks.

"Hello. I got you this," I say, thrusting out a rose corsage I picked out for her. It isn't a Harvest Moon, but it's a soft coral color. I notice it's the same color as her lipstick. Man, her lips look perfect.

Charlotte bites the bottom one as I'm watching her. Is she nervous? This possibility never occurred to me. It makes me like her even more, even though I'd have never thought that possible.

She lets go of her lip and motions me in. "Thank you. It's beautiful."

I peek in and see Becca melting into a gooey puddle beside a waist-high stack of books. She gives me a thumbs-up.

Charlotte fingers the soft petals of the rose for a moment, before slipping it on her wrist.

"Um, and Bec?" Becca looks surprised as I pull something out of my pocket for her. "It's not perfect, but I did my best to fix it," I say, opening my hand.

"Oh." An exhale. It's the storybook rose she crumpled. It's still a little bruised looking, but it doesn't look half bad.

"I wanted to say thanks for…" I shift from foot to foot. "…everything." I pat her awkwardly on the shoulder, watching her big doe eyes get glassy. Crap. I didn't mean to upset her.

Charlotte is beside me, peering into Becca's hands. "Hey, that looks just like the one you made me."

"It was supposed to be yours, but I accidentally smashed this one."

"I saved it," I admit.

Charlotte smiles. "Beaten doesn't mean the end. Not always, eh, Charlie?"

I don't know how to respond, so I don't.

Charlotte pins the rose to Becca's sweater and pulls her in for a big hug. Becca wraps her arms around Charlotte, but her eyes find mine, a silent plea to take good care of her friend. I nod. One of her hands snakes out and grabs my own. She holds tightly to me with one hand and Charlotte with the other.

When I think my chest might cave in from all the pressure building there, I clear my throat. "Well, we've got reservations to keep, so we'd better get going." I offer Charlotte my arm. She places her long fingers in the crook of my elbow, the lightest touch, but it tethers me.

I glance back at Becca on our way out. She's got a funny smile on her face, a little like Dunwitty remembering her childhood, as she peers down at the rose pinned to her chest.

I lead Charlotte out to the car, opening her door as Becca had instructed me. Charlotte arches a brow, but smiles.

We pull away in silence, but it isn't uncomfortable. This is silence filled with sound: Charlotte's breathing, her fingers tapping the center console to the time of the music, and the hum, the beautiful humming starting at my chest and radiating outward whenever she's around.

When I stop at an intersection downtown, I look over at her in the fading light. Her electric blue eyes are the exact shade of the dress she's wearing. My glance travels over her long legs, to where her ankles cross. She's wearing a familiar pair of shit-kicker boots. I chuckle and she looks over at me.

"What?" she asks.

"You're beautiful," I say, deviating from Becca's script, which called for me to remark on how much I liked Charlotte's shoes. It is supposed to show I pay attention to details. But I *don't* like her shoes. I *do*, however, like *her* in them.

Charlotte smiles, her hand flashing up to her short curls. "You look handsome, too."

"I'll pass your compliments on to Becca, as tonight I was her Barbie doll."

"Ken."

"What?"

Charlotte laughs, the song-like notes exciting the hum in my chest. "Barbie's boyfriend's name is Ken. You're a Ken doll."

"Right. I knew that."

Charlotte's brow furrows, but just as quickly it goes smooth again.

"You okay?"

She smiles, giving her head a quick shake. "Yep. Too bad about the Ken thing though."

"Why?"

"He's neutered." She flashes me a wicked grin and turns up the song on the radio to sing along.

I turn the song volume knob down. "What? You're saying I'm neutered?"

"I never said that." Charlotte's laugh fills the space in my car to overflowing. The music is turned up again and Charlotte sings, making the artist on the radio sound like a douche.

I know I should have a witty retort or something, but my brain has overheated. I'm in nuclear meltdown.

We make it to the restaurant, me avoiding any topic easily spliced with sexual innuendos. In other words, I bore Charlotte to death talking about the Higgs Boson.

I don't stop until we're seated at our table with tall, leather-bound menus in our hands. I'm hiding behind mine, trying to catch my breath. When I lay it aside on the table, Charlotte is smiling at me, the tiniest half smile.

"This is a beautiful restaurant," she says, her eyes sweeping the lush walls and upward to the hundreds of chandeliers hanging from the ceiling. Candlelight is weaving rainbow patterns through the crystals.

"It's all wrong, isn't it? Too fancy. I thought maybe you'd like fancy."

Charlotte's left brow dips like the curved top of a question mark. "What about me says fancy?"

"Your T-shirts?"

Charlotte laughs. "You don't know me that well, do you?"

"I'd like to."

"I'd like you to as well."

My ears feel like they've caught fire. The heat flashes down my cheeks and neck. The restaurant is nice, but it's got nothing on the gorgeous girl sitting across from me with a candlelight rainbow tracing the line of her cheek as a tear slides down it. Without thinking, my hand catches hers.

"Water?" The waiter interrupts, which is good, because what-ever verbal diarrhea I was about to spew would kill the mood.

Charlotte gives my hand a quick squeeze before letting it go to swipe away the tear on her cheek. The waiter pours the water and talks about specials I don't care about. I watch Charlotte's face, the way one brow dips low when she is listening, the explosion of joy when he says something about chocolate and soufflé, the nibble on the inside of her bottom lip as she considers her choices, and the smile she rewards me with when she catches me watching her.

"Thanks," I sputter at the waiter.

He tries to hide a sigh. "I'll give you a few minutes."

I don't want a few minutes. I want more time with Charlotte than I can possibly have. I want more time than an average lifespan, without cancer. I want infinity, even though I know I can't reach it.

Charlotte raises her water glass to her lips, and I catch her eyes, holding them with mine, pleading for her to see what I want without having to say it. She studies me, as she sips.

"Charlotte, I—"

I break off, watching her eyes slip into a vacant stare.

"Charlotte?"

The water glass drops from her hand, spilling on her dress, the water pooling in the fabric on her lap and changing it to a deep, dark blue before clattering to the floor and bursting into pieces.

"Charlotte!" I yell, jumping from my seat and pushing the table out of my way to get to her as she slumps to the side. I hear a gasp and someone is shouting amongst the other diners as I catch Charlotte in my arms and guide her down to the ground as far from the broken glass as possible. Her blue eyes are steely gray, locked doors, hard and unmoving. Her muscles twitch erratically.

"Charley," I choke, "What's happening? Don't go!"

Suddenly, a woman pulls me away, passing me to a man who reeks of cologne. He wraps his doughy arms around me and murmurs, "There, there," and "Dr. Michaels," and "There, there."

I try to wrestle away, but the man's solid and has a good hundred pounds on me.

The restaurant's chandeliers spill off hundreds of bright red rainbows, bleeding down the walls as the air fills with sirens.

"See?" asks my hyper-scented captor. "The ambulance is here. Everything will be fine."

I look at Charlotte, her muscles now locked into an unnatural stiffness. Her soft face composed of hard lines, her jawbone jutting out in a grimace. And, her eyes—the eyes in her face are foreign to me. Where has she gone?

6.1

In the olden days, people thought time was a constant. It could not be slowed or sped up. Time was time, and no man could move it.

Then Einstein said, *Bullshit.*

Okay, he didn't say that. What he said was $E = mc^2$.

Simply put: time is fluid. The faster your world spins out of control, the slower time crawls. The more time you need, the less you're sure to get. It's all relative.

Tonight, time has slowed to an agonizing crawl, as it did in the minutes Charlotte's seizure lasted. Dr. Michaels says those minutes totaled seven. For me, it felt like she was lost for years while we waited for her return.

Once the seizure was over, Charlotte was frantic and pissed to see she was strapped to a gurney and being led out to an ambulance. She screamed, "Get me out. Get me out, goddammit!" Time sped up then, so the EMTs could whisk her away before I could reach her.

It slowed again as Dr. Michaels and her huge, malodorous husband drove me to the university hospital. And now, it inches on as I pace between two rows of uncomfortable chairs in a waiting room, separated from Charlotte by thick metal doors with signs referring to me as UNAUTHORIZED PERSONS.

When I think it can move no slower, time stops dead in its

tracks. The emergency room doors open with a blast of cold air as Ms. Finch runs into the hospital. She freezes, glaring at me, her eyes, so like Charlotte's, wild behind her thick black hair.

Here I am, frozen in time, which I want, except I'm with the wrong Finch.

Ms. Finch is what they call "Authorized Persons." A nurse ushered her beyond the metal doors of my purgatory, leaving me behind. I don't know how long they've been gone. It feels like forever.

I collapse in a chair and start unraveling a piece of loose thread on the seat cushion. According to my previous brain tumor research, seizures are a common thing for people living with brain cancer. They result from the tumor messing up the electrical signals in the brain, like the time James and I screwed up the wiring for our robot and we ended up going to competition with a robot that danced the tango rather than smash its opponent's head. Greta was so pissed she wouldn't speak to us for a week.

The thing about seizures is they can happen any time, any place, and with little to no warning. So Charlotte could be at school, in line at Krispy Kreme, or—oh, I don't know, let's say, on a date.

I give the string I'm messing with a good yank and hear a satisfying rip. *Rip, rip, r-i-i-i-i-i-i-p!*

My phone rings. I pull it from my pocket and look at the screen. Becca.

"Hey—"

"Charlie, where are you? You guys were supposed to be back hours ago."

I start pulling foam stuffing out from the hole I've made in the cushion. "Bec, I'm at the university hospital. It all went wrong."

"What?"

"Charlotte had a seizure at the restaurant. When they put her in the ambulance, she was so mad at me." I stop and try to fill my lungs, but the panic in them is taking up too much room. "What if something happens? I let her down."

"I'm on my way."

"Bec, no."

The phone goes dead in my hands. Calling her back would do no good. Becca is even more stubborn than Charlotte.

Instead, I busy myself by pulling out larger and larger chunks of foam from my seat. The nurse pushes open the thick metal doors.

"Mr. Hanso—" she stops short, her brow creasing as I look up with a fistful of foam. She doesn't get angry though, just shakes her head like *there goes another one*. "Mr. Hanson?"

I nod and shove the foam back in place.

"You can come back now."

Standing, I ask, "I'm authorized?"

"Yes," the nurse says with a smile.

I pocket my phone and leap over the row of chairs still between the door and me, afraid that if I move too slowly, time with mess with me again and close them before I can get through.

"Charlotte is resting now, but her sister would like to speak with you."

"I can't see Charlotte?"

"When she wakes."

"But she will wake?" My heart is ramming into my ribs.

The nurse puts a warm hand on my shoulder. "Yes."

As I enter, Ms. Finch stands up from where she was sitting on Charlotte's bed. It's a big hospital bed, complete with computers and wires and wheels. Charlotte looks elfin buried under all the cords and tubes and crap they've piled all around her, each thing beeping and whirring its own tune.

For a second, I think maybe time has frozen again. I can't hear anything. I know Ms. Finch is here, but I can't see her. All I can see is Charlotte. Would I take this forever? The one in which I have Charlotte, but she's lost under medical equipment?

I shiver, and everything starts again, the humming and chirping of machines, and the rise and fall of Charlotte's chest as she sleeps. But now, I'm holding her hand. How did I get here?

For a long time there is nothing but the sound of Charlotte breathing and the gentle hum inside of me.

I guess I start crying at some point, because Ms. Finch is standing beside me with a tissue thrust out.

"I need coffee," Ms. Finch says, her voice this hoarse whisper like unfallen leaves. I look at her blankly. "You need coffee, too."

I shake my head. "I hate coffee."

"No one hates coffee," she says, wiggling the tissue in my face. I take it and wipe my wet cheeks. "The nurses have to check her vitals anyhow. Let's give her some privacy."

"Okay, but coffee still sucks."

She frowns at me. "So much to learn," she says, leading the way.

We walk to a vast cafeteria with skylights so clean you could count the stars. There are eleven people in the huge place, scattered in small groups at tables, except a man in the corner, who sits alone. Most of them stare into paper coffee cups. None of them looks happy, which makes me feel like coffee may not be the answer Ms. Finch is looking for.

I follow her to the coffee bar and watch her fill two cups with black coffee. She tears the tops off three packets of sugar and splits the contents between the two cups.

"One and a half packets of sweetener per cup is the secret," she says as she tosses away the wrappers. "It's a pain when you're making only one cup of coffee, because then you've got the half-full packet lying around. But the extra half a packet matters. The universe's way of saying you should always share coffee with a friend."

"I thought Charlotte said sugar wasn't allowed at your house."

Ms. Finch nods. "Yeah. We've been drinking crappy coffee all year."

"Why?"

"Some cancer-free diet I read about. Last ditch effort, you know?"

She's staring at the two cups, not moving, just staring. And since she said you should share with a friend, and I'm anything but a friend, I'm not sure whether to reach out and take the coffee. I'm also not sure how long we both stand there frozen by our complicated relationship.

Finally, her hand moves as she pours thick cream in the cups until they are nearly overflowing. The creamer jug makes a loud metallic thud when she sets it back on the counter. The couple sitting closest to the coffee jumps at the sound.

"Try it. Making coffee is about the only thing I can do correctly anymore," Ms. Finch says. Her chin droops as she shakes her head in defeat. I can't imagine being in her shoes, wanting to hold on to Charlotte when all Charlotte wants to do is run away. Has to suck. Ms. Finch's eyes close while she drinks, and when she opens them again, they're full of tears.

I grab my cup, sloshing a good bit of it on my hand and swearing under my breath.

"Rookie," Ms. Finch mumbles and tries to blink away the moisture in her eyes.

"You have no idea," I say as I try a sip. It's not bad. I don't know if it's great, but it feels like what I need.

We sit in silence near a bank of windows overlooking a court-yard. Around one-quarter left in my coffee cup, I work up the nerve to ask an important question.

"What's happening?"

Ms. Finch's cup is two-thirds full. She watches the tan liquid like it may have the answers. When it doesn't offer any, she says, "Charlotte is dying."

Everything inside me erupts at once. My skin is the only thing holding me together. It's not like this is a surprise, but it's the first time anyone's said it so plainly.

"There's a clinical trial for tumors similar to the newest of Charlotte's. It could help if we could get her into the trial." Ms. Finch puts her cup on the table and stuffs her shaky hands into the pockets of her sweater. "But Charlotte says, no more."

Help. One word and I'm able to pull enough pieces together to talk. "Why?"

Ms. Finch's eyes are full again. She turns her face toward the stars outside the window. "She doesn't want to die here."

Silence swallows us again.

Die? No. That's not an option right now. No one's dying here. Not when there's a chance still out there. What about Atticus Finch? This may be a losing battle, but Charlotte's got to try to fight it—we have to try to win.

"What should I do?" It slips out. I didn't mean to ask it. I instantly regret it, knowing it's a step away from what Charlotte wants—a step toward Ms. Finch.

"Tell her to do the trial."

I shrink back from the intense look Ms. Finch is giving me. I feel like I've stepped in a trap.

"She won't listen to me. But maybe you can convince her. Do this, Charlie, and I swear I'll do whatever you want. You want me to leave Brighton? Done. You want me to pull some strings at MIT? Done. You want me to drive you and Charlotte to Atlantic City to elope? Done. I'm that desperate."

"Elope?"

"Whatever it takes, get her to do the clinical trial."

"Why can't *you* make her do it?"

"She's eighteen. She took over control of her medical decisions. I'm just here to make the coffee," she says, lifting her cup in a toast. She doesn't drink any, but sets it right back in its place on the bleached linoleum table.

"What are her chances if she does it?"

Ms. Finch's whole body sags. "Slim."

"How slim?"

Ms. Finch sighs in this breathy, frustrated way. "Like a quark-sized chance."

That's the smallest damn particle of hope in the universe.

6.2

It doesn't take much hope to infect a person. Hope is worse than vampire venom. It takes hold and changes a person. Fast.

By the time we get back to Charlotte's room, I am imagining scenarios in which I casually mention a new medical breakthrough I happened to read about in a science journal. I could hold her hostage until she agrees to the clinical trial. Possibly, I'll cry until she promises to try it.

Becca is already there when Ms. Finch and I walk in. I wonder how she got "authorized" without Ms. Finch's permission, but then I notice Charlotte is awake. They've got lots of sleepy stuff coursing through her IV, but her eyes are open and the steely quality is gone. Beautiful blue eyes blink sleepily at me as I linger in the doorway.

"You must be Becca?" Ms. Finch asks, sitting at Charlotte's other side.

Becca nods, watching Charlotte for some guidance.

"Jo, this is my best friend, Becca Hanson," Charlotte says in a faraway voice.

Ms. Finch's smile freezes on her face. Poor thing must have been thinking, *finally, a friend of Charlotte's I don't hate.* Then bam! It's like the whole Hanson clan is in on it. I'm sure she's expecting Mom and Dad to parade in here any second.

Speaking of Mom and Dad… "How'd you get here, Bec?" My voice is ripe with anxiety.

"Greta and James are in the waiting room."

Ms. Finch's brow collapses as she looks from Becca to me and then at Charlotte. The three of us are a team. Plus, we've apparently got reinforcements. She's alone. I watch this new defeat sink in, pulling her further under.

Except, she isn't alone. Not with the voice of that small hope whispering to me. No, she's not alone in wanting Charlotte to fight.

Charlotte whispers to Becca, who pops up out her chair like it's been infected with the Ebola virus. "Well, Charlie, we'd better get going," she says, taking my arm and pulling me back toward the door. "Mom and Dad will be worried." She drags me into the hallway before sticking her head back in. "Nice to meet you, Ms. Finch. See you in school, Charlotte."

I allow myself to be pulled a few doors farther away from Charlotte before my senses catch up to me. "Hold on." I shake her loose. "I want to say good-bye, too."

Becca scrambles around me, her hands up, like she's going to block me if I try to get past her. "Charlie, Mom and Dad—"

"Screw 'em, Bec." I move to the right.

Becca counters. "It's sooo late." She punctuates this with a fake yawn.

"You never sleep anyway," I say, stepping toward the left, but Becca is there before me.

"Seriously, Charrrr-lieeeee," Becca whines.

My adrenaline is spiking. Becca is annoying. I scoop her up over one shoulder and start to jog back toward Charlotte's room. Becca pounds on my back a few times before she tenses each of her muscles and stretches herself out like a starfish. The toe of one of her sneakers catches on one side of a doorjamb to our right and her hand snatches the other, holding tight. The sudden change in momentum swings me sideways so we both crash into the door, which bangs open. We fall into a dark room, full of whirring and beeping.

The patient in the room screams. One of his machines starts to scream, too. Becca and I are still a tangle of limbs on the floor when a harried nurse comes running in.

"Out. Out. OUT!" she yells, yanking us to our feet.

Needless to say, our authorization is revoked. Greta and James look startled when we come barreling back through the heavy metal doors into the waiting room. I turn on my sister, my voice tight, my throat aching. "What the hell?"

Becca is rubbing an already swelling elbow from our fall. "Fine," she yells back. "Fine. I was trying to be nice, but whatever. Charlotte doesn't want to see you. Happy?"

Every bit of anger holding me up rushes out of me like a balloon deflating and flying in wild arcs, making the room spin. I sit in the nearest uncomfortable chair and hold my head between my knees.

Becca's hand brushes my back. "Don't be so dramatic, Charlie."

I peek up at her.

"She doesn't want you to remember her as sick. That's all." Becca's big brown eyes get glassy. "She wants us to remember the good stuff."

I put my head back down. I don't want to have to remember her at all.

I want her to stay.

Greta and James are both staying over for what's left of the night, James in my room and Greta with Becca. They appear to be taking turns babysitting me to be sure I don't do anything rash. I think that's funny because what could be more reckless than falling for a girl like Charlotte Finch?

Greta sits on the counter in the bathroom watching me brush my teeth. I consider stabbing myself in the ear with my toothbrush just to see what she'd do. Instead, I recite the elements of the periodic table in my head. When I reach Ununoctium, I spit and rinse.

"You still do the whole element thing?" Greta asks, a sliver of a smile on her lips.

"It's a good song. How'd you know?"

Greta points. "Tapping your fingers."

I lean over the sink, cupping the water in my hands and scrubbing my face. My eyes are burning. It's got to be well after midnight.

Greta passes me the hand towel. "You doing okay in there, Chuck?"

I pat my face dry and glance at myself in the mirror. I don't recognize myself. "I fell."

"I know."

There's a horrible pressure everywhere, on my chest, behind my eyes, squeezing my temples. I close my eyes, but it doesn't keep me from crying. Greta reaches out, grabbing the towel still in my hand, pulling it and me toward her until she can wrap her arms around my shoulders and tuck me in a hug.

"Shh," she whispers into my hair, but it does no good because my crying is evolving into this loud sobbing. It draws James and Becca toward the tiny room. Becca wraps her arms around my waist and leans against my back. James's ginormous frame barely fits, but he pulls himself up to sit next to Greta. Actually, half his ass is in the sink.

"Little better in there now?" Greta asks as soon as my sobs ebb into sniffles.

I try to suck in a full breath. It takes four tries before I can get one that doesn't sound like I'm hiccupping. Finally, I nod at Greta.

"You're strong, Chuck. You know that, right?"

I do. Struggling with my fears about losing Charlotte has put everything into perspective for me. There's only one thing that can hurt me now, and it isn't even Charlotte's death. My biggest fear now is not earning her love while she's still alive. "I know," I say with a firm nod.

Greta's smile exudes relief. "Good because you, Charles Hanson, are Charlotte's hero."

I shy away from Greta, considering this. I don't think Charlotte wants a hero. Charlotte needs someone to love every bit of her. I want to be that person for her. But I don't want to share my thoughts with everyone—they're for Charlotte. So I wipe my face with the towel and deflect by asking, "Do I get to wear a cape?"

My humor catches everyone off guard, which is good because if things don't lighten up we're all going to be crushed. Becca snorts and James slips while laughing so his entire ass is stuck in the sink. And Greta. Well, Greta starts to cry a little as she smiles at me. She never did get my sense of humor.

6.3

I beat Ms. Finch to school Monday morning by a good fifteen minutes. I wait by my locker, which used to seem too close to her office, but now seems to be in a rather convenient location. Funny how that perspective thing works. Thanks for that one, Mrs. Dunwitty.

By the time Ms. Finch arrives, there are only a few minutes before the first bell for me to find out how Charlotte is doing. I shift foot to foot, as she approaches her door, jug o' coffee in one hand, papers in the other, key ring clenched between her teeth.

"Need a hand?" I ask.

She grunts and releases her keys so they fall into my outstretched palm. "You do the honors," she says, nodding toward her office door. "Be careful for falling objects. There have been a few of those lately."

We both hold our breath as the lock releases with a *click*. I slowly open the door and brave the light switch, expecting at any moment to be electrocuted. Nothing. Everything *looks* normal, but man, what's that smell?

Ms. Finch wrinkles her nose. "God. That is rotten. What is it?" She looks at me like I should know.

"I didn't do anything. Wait here." I take a deep breath and

plunge into the small office. I open drawers, look under the desk, behind bookcases, in the trash, and behind a few of Charlotte's paintings. Nothing. My lungs feel wrung out.

I dash back out and pant a few times, doubling over to rest my hands on my knees. My eyes are watering from the stench. I look at Ms. Finch and follow her gaze up to the ceiling tiles. Her face is pinched, studying them.

"I believe the prize is hidden behind the tile over my desk chair."

She may be right. The tile is set back in place, but there is a chip in the front right corner, like maybe some jackhole was too clumsy while replacing it.

I nod at her and take one more big breath. I stand on her desk and slide the tile up and over. The hideous odor triples, making me gag. I'm going to have to stick my bare hand in there to find the source of the stink. I gag again.

I cover my mouth and nose with one hand to help block the fumes. With the other, I reach up and pat around in the ceiling until my fingers touch something smooth. It's firm as long as I'm just brushing my fingers along it. But when I grasp it, my fingers sink up to my nail beds with a horrible squelching sound. In one fast movement, I grab whatever it is and pull it from the ceiling, like a decapitated rabbit out of a demented magician's hat.

It's a rotting fetal pig. The kind we dissect in freshman biology here. Someone must have taken it from the freezer on Friday and hid it here. The sight of it pisses me off. Ms. Finch shouldn't have to put up with this. She's trying to save her sister's life. This is bullshit, and I'm stopping it here.

Ms. Finch, who had been leaning in the door to get a better view, gasps and jerks backward, stumbling into Brad Mitchell, the closest thing we have to a muscle-head at Brighton. He's standing there glaring at me with his big old arms crossed over his big old chest. It'd be intimidating except I know that he cries like a baby if he gets anything less than an A on a test.

I hold the pig by its tail and jump off Ms. Finch's desk. By some miracle of physics, I manage to stick the landing, wobbling so the pig circles like a pendulum from my grip. I march the wee piggie out into the hallway, the horrific stench of it preceding me.

"I believe I found your lab partner, Brad."

He blinks at me, his arms still crossed, but a muscle near his eye begins to twitch.

"What's all this?" Dr. Whiting's voice comes booming down the hallway. I can see his slick, dark hair weaving through the far side of the crowd.

"This," I say, waving the pig, "stops now. Got it, man?" Brad's eyes are filling up, but he nods. "Get lost," I say through clenched teeth. He hurls himself through the crowd, bowling over some girls.

I whirl around with the pig, trying to figure out what I'm going to do when a trashcan is thrust out at me. James's thick forearm muscles flex as he shakes it in my face. Where'd he come from?

"Drop the pig, Chuck," Greta's says, her voice taut like a trip wire.

I toss the rotten meat into the trash and quickly snatch up the edges of the black bag to tie it shut. Now what? I look from James to Greta, but we're out of time. Dr. Whiting strides up to us, his face puckering at the lingering odor.

"What's going on here?" He crosses his arms over his sagging chest.

I can't let anyone else go down for this. I started this revolution. I knew the risks. My mouth opens, but before I can say anything, Ms. Finch steps beside me.

"Oh, Mr. Hanson," she says, her hands flapping the air near her eyes. "Thank you so much for helping me."

Dr. Whiting's thick brow twitches. "Ms. Finch?"

"When I came in my office this morning there was a horrible—

Well, you can smell it, I'm sure. Mr. Hanson's locker is right next door," she says, pointing to my locker. "He could smell it, too." Ms. Finch looks at me and I nod. Emphatically.

"He was the one that located the poor thing." Ms. Finch breaks off, her hands flapping again, fanning away fake tears.

"What? What did you find?" he asks me, but Ms. Finch rushes to answer.

"A squirrel. A dead squirrel. It must have gotten in through a vent and couldn't get out. Oh, I do hope he didn't suffer long."

Dr. Whiting's muscles unclench. "Very well. Mr. Hanson, please deposit that trash bag in the large bin out back."

I don't say a word, afraid a full confession will fall out of my mouth instead of "yes, sir." I turn on my heel and walk as quickly as I can down the hallway to the double doors at the end.

I toss the bag in the Dumpster and step away to take a few deep breaths. Ms. Finch just saved my butt. The kindness is overwhelming.

Ms. Finch is waiting for me at the doors when I come back. The clog in the hallway has been cleared, everyone moving off to first period. James and Greta are leaning against my locker. Greta holds out my backpack for me, but I just look at my hands, gross with pig gush and Dumpster gack. Ms. Finch leads us to the private teacher's restroom down the hall.

"Wow," James says with a whistle. "This is sweet."

"It's a bathroom, J." Greta smacks his arm.

I head straight for the sinks, trying to ignore the fact that I have pork under my fingernails.

Ms. Finch leans against the wall next to me. "Thank you, Charlie."

"I'm sorry about this," I say, inspecting my sudsy hands. "These pranks have taken on a whole life of their own."

"Frankenpranksters," James whispers to Greta in his not-at-all-quiet whisper.

I'd tell him to shut up, but Greta stomps on his foot. Actions do speak louder than words.

I run hot water over the suds, scrubbing so hard my skin reddens. "It ends here. It's gone too far." I glance at Greta, who nods once. She'll get the word out to everyone. As if she's on her way to do it now, she takes James's hand and tugs him out the door.

"I wouldn't have gotten involved to begin with, but Charlotte said it would help her, and well…I'm hopeless when it comes to Charlotte."

"I knew she was behind this." I peek at Ms. Finch, expecting fury, but she's got a weird smile tugging at the corners of her mouth. "God. She's infuriating." Ms. Finch's smile hitches higher, lighting her whole face. "That girl has been driving me crazy for years, but I can't seem to stay mad. You're not the only one who'll do anything to make Charlotte happy."

I grab a wad of paper towels. "How's she doing?" I sniff experimentally at my fingers and flinch at the tinge of eau de rotten piggie still there.

"Fine. Charlotte's just fine."

"Define fine," I say, turning the water on again.

Ms. Finch sighs. "She's cantankerous, stubborn, and distant, same as she's been all year. She's fine."

I feel horrible for Ms. Finch. She moved Charlotte here to be nearer to the university hospital and the clinical trial. I can see that clearly now. Those were the great opportunities Charlotte was talking about. But I'd have done the same thing in Ms. Finch's shoes.

I rinse my hands again, watching the suds flow down the drain, swirling around the edge before they disappear.

"Can I see her?"

"I don't know. Can you?" Ms. Finch's expression is dull.

I cringe. "You sure she's not your clone? Charlotte never lets me slide either. Only her face lights up whenever she gets to correct me."

Ms. Finch's eyes look hopeful. "Really?"

I nod, drying my hands a second time.

"I should be glad the version everyone else gets isn't the same as the sullen girl I have to live with."

"Maybe you're getting the real deal because she trusts you. She knows she can be a pain in the a—uh, neck and you'll still love her. It's contractual, you know. Like with my sister, I can't get rid of her even if she brings home best friends who drive me nuts."

Ms. Finch smiles. "Let's go," she says. "I'll write you a pass to class."

I follow her back to her classroom and ignore the stares of the freshman wondering what is going on. Ms. Finch hands me two passes.

The top is my pass to class and the bottom reads, "Home resting today."

I glance up at Ms. Finch. She shrugs. "You rarely win."

My body vibrates with possibility. "But sometimes you do."

I leave the classroom and turn right instead of left to leave by the double doors at the end of the hallway.

6.4

I am skipping school to go see a girl. Charles Mortimer Hanson is voluntarily missing biochemistry. The planet is suffering a cataclysmic pole shift, and life as I know it is over.

The apocalypse is pretty amazing.

When I ring the doorbell, the hellhound breaks into a throaty wail, the sound severing my frayed nerves. There's no movement, though.

I walk around to the back and open the gate, scanning the yard for a few good pebbles to toss. Maybe I'll get lucky and hit her window this time. I'm about to launch my first missile when a burst of gray with white fangs squeezes out of the dog door. For a second, I stare and wonder how something so massive could fit through such a small space. But it can, and it does, and then it comes charging at me with hackles raised.

I'm still holding the pebble and for an insane moment I believe I can defeat the dog, David and Goliath style, but before I release it, I hear an even more frightening growl.

"Hit my dog and die, Hanson."

I freeze. Luckily, so does the dog. At the sound of Charlotte's voice, it turns 180 degrees and runs toward her, all waggling tail and wiggly butt. Charlotte puts a hand down, resting it on the dog's head as it collapses on its back haunches beside her. It grins at me like, *Ha, ha, ha. Charlotte likes me best.*

I drop my pebbles. "It was going to eat me."

Charlotte smiles. "Naw. Just maim you a little."

"Oh, well, good." I shift my weight side to side and drop my gaze to the pebbles on the ground. I'm afraid to move closer to Charlotte. With the dog at her feet and the memory of her dwarfed by all that hospital equipment, my fight-or-flight instinct is in overdrive.

"What are you doing here?" Charlotte asks.

I look up at her and know that flight is not an option. "We didn't finish our date. You said there would be a kiss at the end of it."

Charlotte's face flushes. "You still want to be with me, even after all that drama?"

I step toward her. "Yes."

She smiles and shoos the dog in the house, motioning for me to follow. "No time like the present."

We walk through the kitchen, which I've only seen through the doggie door, and into the living room. The walls are painted various shades of green and golden yellow, and every spare space is covered with bookshelves and art. The place smells nice, too. If a garden and a bakery got married, this scent would be their love child.

Covering one whole wall is an enormous canvas with a picture of a girl leaning against a barn door. The barn is old, like condemned old, so there are huge gaps in the wood and you can see straight through it. The girl's face is turned, looking through one of the holes, watching the sun slip behind the horizon.

I know her. I can't help myself, but my hand is reaching to touch the girl in the painting.

"It's Jo."

My hand falters. "What?"

"My sister. When she was younger than I am now."

"I thought it was you."

Charlotte's eyes widen. She looks at the canvas again. "No. It's Jo. I'm the barn."

I look closer. "In the barn? I can't see you."

Charlotte's light laugh seeps through my skin. "Not *in* the barn. I am. The barn."

I step away from the painting. One light summer storm would knock that barn down.

I sit on the couch consumed by my racing pulse and a deep heat radiating from my chest. Charlotte curls up next to me, pulling an afghan over her legs. Her head rests on my shoulder, glossy black curls scenting the air I'm breathing.

"Can we—"

"Make out?" Charlotte attempts to finish my sentence, looking up at me with a crooked smile.

"Uh, I was going to say talk."

Charlotte juts out her bottom lip. "Fine. I suppose you deserve some explanation." She sits up and turns to face me on the couch. "What do you want to know?"

Now that she's facing me and those blue eyes are fixed on me, the only thing I want to know is what it'd feel like to kiss her neck from her collarbone up to the soft space behind her ear.

"Seriously, I'm an open book, Charlie. Ask away." She thinks I'm stalling because I'm afraid to ask the hard questions. So wrong.

"You are not an open book, unless that book is a mystery."

She juts her chin out at me, growling in the back of her throat. I can't take it anymore. I have to be closer. I lean in, drawing my lips up her neck, devouring the smell of vanilla. By the time I reach her ear, her growl has turned into a soft moan and all my insides go nuts. I'm cupping her head in one hand, so she can open her neck more to me, and this time, as I travel downward, I flick my tongue along the hollow above her collarbone.

Charlotte's hands are in my hair, pulling my face to hers. Her lips crash into mine like a meteorite hitting Earth's atmosphere. Fire and heat explode as we fall together toward an uncertain ground. It's a long, beautiful fall.

Hearts thudding from impact, we finally pull apart, sharing the same breath. I want to live in this moment. I try not to see a spatial graph of the exact angle between our touching foreheads. I try to ignore the urge to count the exact seconds it would take to travel the distance from my personal space to hers. I try not to name the impressive variety of microorganisms living in the human mouth that we've just shared. I try to ignore the cool logic inside me that burns to ask her one question.

I must not try hard enough.

Charlotte's lips quirk to one side. "Now we talk?"

When I nod with our foreheads still touching, her face moves with mine. She leans away, wrapping her fingers through the tassels at the edge of the afghan in her lap. "You sure you want to talk?" She winks at me when she says talk.

"No."

Charlotte gives me a small smile and rests her head back on my shoulder. "There's not much to say. I have cancer."

"Are you fighting it? Can you win?"

Charlotte's shoulders tense and slide upward. "When I was first diagnosed, there was never a question in my mind I'd beat it. Like it was a cold and I could take my medicine, lay around for a few days watching cartoons while everyone else went to school, and then, ta-dah! I'm cured."

"But now?"

"The prognosis is bad, Charlie. Inoperable and metastasizing and bad. It's going to keep coming back. This cancer is going to kill me either now or next year."

"A year is a long time."

"Is it?"

"Twelve months, fifty-two weeks, three hundred sixty-five days, eight thousand seven hundred sixty hours—"

"Cute."

"I'm just getting started. Five hundred twenty-five thousand six hundred minutes, thirty-one million five hundred fifty-six thousand nine hundred twenty-six seconds…"

Charlotte is smiling up at me with a crooked grin. "That's what I love about you. Always so literal."

"Sorry."

"Don't be. I know this is hard to understand. It's hard to explain. It's not like I want to leave anyone behind." She looks over at the painting of her broken body with the sun setting through her skin. "But, if I have to die, I'd like to do it with some hair on my head. Is that so horrible?"

"But you'll be dead."

"Yep."

"It will bother you? Not having hair when you're dead?"

"Dunno. But it bothers me now, when I'm alive. Shouldn't that count for something?"

My heart does this jolting, squelching, shredding thing, and on the other side of the pain is a clear truth. "Yes. It counts," I say and brush one of the curls away from her forehead. She catches my hand and gives it a squeeze.

"But why not just try the clinical trial?"

Charlotte's body, warm and soft against me transforms into a glacier. She sits up, her face turning white, then red. The delicate lines of her jaw harden. "What did Jo tell you? It's a miracle cure I'm refusing willy-nilly?"

"Willy-what? No."

"Because it's not. It's horrible. I've done them before. Hell, one even worked for a while, which was awesome. But this one has an extremely low success rate."

"But it's a chance?"

"To be a guinea pig. I'm not a person the clinicians are trying to cure. I'm a vessel that contains what they need, cancer cells they can experiment with. I'll be injected with poisons while they chart my reactions, looking for the exact dosage at which my entire body shuts down. As an added bonus, I'll be one of the first humans ever to be injected with a man-made virus aimed at infecting and killing cancer cells."

"That's amazing." I didn't mean to speak, to say it out loud. Charlotte's face becomes foreign, sculpted by anger and betrayal.

"Amazing for a few of the animals it didn't kill." She splutters out like a snuffed flame, her anger slipping away in wisps of smoke.

"How many survived?"

Charlotte tugs on a loose string in the afghan, her eyes as sharp as scalpels dissecting me. "Sixty percent."

"That's more than half."

She scoffs. "Wow, you should go to, like, a math school or something." The sarcasm in her voice is nothing compared to the disgust. She yanks on the string, wrapping it around two fingers now. "Forty percent of those animals died, Charlie."

"But without it, your chance of dying is one hundred percent."

"Same as everyone else."

"Yeah, but Charlotte." I can feel my desperation clawing its way up from my gut. "Without the clinical trial, you'll die within a year."

"Without it, I get to keep my memories."

A jolt of adrenaline rushes out from my core, racing to my extremities and back again in less than a heartbeat. All of my senses are hyperaware. I can hear the click of the icemaker in the kitchen as it turns on. Charlotte's perfume is warm like sugar cookies. And I can see the trembling of her curls as she fights to keep her body still, to keep her shoulders from heaving under the weight of heavy sobs.

"I didn't know."

"Of course you didn't," she snaps. "Jo didn't tell you that part."

She's so angry, I know the probability of convincing her is low, but I have to keep trying. You rarely win. "But wouldn't it be worth it—to be alive—if it worked. And think of the breakthrough in medicine that would be. A virus that attacks cancer would be monumental."

Charlotte drags herself off the couch and looks down at me with her shoulders pinned back. "I am not a fucking science experiment." Her voice cracks on the last word. "Life is not an experiment." She runs from the room, wiping the tears from her face as they fall.

Subject: Charlotte Finch,

Method: Participate in super hot make out session. Follow up by suggesting girlfriend subject herself to scientific experimentation for the greater good,

Result: What do you think happened? Perhaps life should not be approached as a scientific endeavor, dumbass.

6.5

I pace the floor in front of the couch, replaying our conversation, hearing all the ways I screwed up. She was too angry to be rational, too emotional to be reasonable, too Charlotte —

Our brains rely on certain chemicals and proteins to manifest connections between different areas and tissues where memories are held. If the meds from the trial destroy those connections, the memories get either erased or stranded with no recall. Without her memories, Charlotte wouldn't know me. What if I can't get her to like me a second time? I'm still not sure how I did it this time.

Without her memories, Charlotte wouldn't even know her own self, and if there is anything in this universe I can prove to be true, it's that Charlotte Elizabeth Finch knows exactly who she is and what she wants. No one should be able to take that away.

I realize with horror that, had I won that argument, we both would have lost in the end.

The house is silent, and while I know Charlotte went to her room upstairs, I can't hear her moving around. I can't hear her crying.

My fingers ache now that my adrenaline has crashed, and as I climb the steps, my legs feel like I've just run a race. Everything about me feels worn down. There's only one door closed upstairs. I lean against it.

"Charlotte? Please, let me in."

At first there is no response, but then I hear her voice. "What's stopping you?"

I try the doorknob and find it unlocked. The door doesn't swing in like a bedroom door should. It opens out. Because it's a freaking linen closet—a very well-organized linen closet, with labels and everything.

"Charlotte?"

"Down here."

Her voice hadn't come from behind the door at all. It'd come from behind me. I'd walked right past her room, so fixated on the closed door I incorrectly deduced was hers.

The linen closet was not Charlotte's doing. Her room is messier than mine. There isn't an inch of wall space to be seen through the sketches, posters, canvases, and overflowing bookcases covering them. And the floor is littered with more papers, pencils, open pots of paints, and clothes—lots and lots of clothes. It's like all the chaos of the universe has come here to roost.

"Why is your door open?" I ask, stepping inside.

"Because I *wanted* you to find me."

We watch each other from across the room.

"I've been meaning to ask you a question about that book you love so much." I shift my weight, taking a step forward.

Charlotte's eyes are searching mine. "What's the question?"

"Do you think Atticus blamed himself for Tom?"

Charlotte's intake of breath is sharp, and it feels like a dagger in my chest.

I fight to keep my voice strong. "For not being able to save the mockingbird? Could he ever forgive himself?"

Charlotte is nodding, her dark curls bobbing around her chin. She stretches out one hand, and I cross the room and sit before she can nod again. I clasp her hand, but it isn't enough, so I pull her toward me, on top of me, curled on my lap with her head on my chest, and my arms around her.

From buried in the folds of my shirt, Charlotte says, "Things should be forgiven." Her hand reaches up and touches my cheek, coaxing my face toward hers. "Just don't forget."

"Never."

Charlotte fights to keep from crumbling. She draws her thumb back and forth over my cheekbone three times, before pulling my lips to hers.

We fell asleep, me stretched out on her bed with Charlotte curled into a ball at my side, her head resting on my shoulder. That's how Ms. Finch finds us.

She wakes me with a hand on my free arm, shaking it gently. When I startle awake, she puts her finger to her lips to shush me. "Don't wake Charley. She needs her sleep." Her eyes soften as she looks over at her sister. They are hard stones when she focuses on me. "Don't wake her, but definitely get the hell out of her bed."

I move slowly, extricating my arm from under Charlotte's head, pausing to brush back the curls that have fallen over her face. Ms. Finch pulls a blanket over her and then shoos me out the door.

I follow Ms. Finch, but am confused when she doesn't lead me straight to the front door. Instead, we end up in the kitchen, where she opens the refrigerator and stares into it for a moment before closing it again.

I'm afraid to speak first, but decide my fear of hanging out in the kitchen where there are sharp knives is greater. I mean, she did just catch me in her little sister's bed.

"I tried talking to her about the trial," I say.

She looks at me over her shoulder, her hand still on the refrigerator door. She doesn't ask how it went though. I imagine it's pretty obvious from my expression.

"The thing is…" I pause and swallow a hard ball of emotion rolling in my mouth like a marble. "I can see her point, and even though I'd do anything to keep her around longer, I'd also do anything to make her happy right now."

She nods, turning back to the pictures on the fridge. The silence fills in the spaces around us like fog. She opens the fridge door again, staring at its contents like something new will have materialized from the last time she looked. Wishful thinking—sometimes that's all we have to hold onto.

"I guess I'll be going," I say, taking a step toward the front door.

"Be sure to bring your sister back with you for dinner tonight," Ms. Finch calls after me. "I'm not comfortable letting Charlotte out of the house so soon after a seizure, but I know she'll want to be with you both." She shuts the fridge door once more. "We'll have to order pizza though because there's nothing here worth eating."

My whole face pinches as I try to understand what's happening.

Ms. Finch chuckles. "We're going to be spending a lot of time together, Mr. Hanson, if you intend to keep seeing my sister."

"Charlie."

She blinks.

"You can call me Charlie."

"No. That's my sister's name and it would be weird if I had to call her boyfriend by the same name, so I'm going to continue to call you Mr. Hanson."

"How about Jack?"

Her brows tick up with surprise.

"It's short for jackass."

Ms. Finch laughs, and I think it's the first time in a long time she's done any laughing because I can tell her face is unsure how to curve the muscles and her eyes are filled with surprise, and then tears. She blinks them away.

"That'll do."

6.6

We do homework at Ms. Finch's house most days of the week. Even Greta and James stop by. Last Friday, we all watched a movie together. Well, Ms. Finch sat at the kitchen island grading papers, but the TV can be seen from there, and we could all hear her when she'd groan, "Oh, please," during the cheesy parts.

This afternoon, Charlotte is sprawled out on the floor working on a sketch she's been trying to finish this week, an intricate spiraling fractal. She keeps smudging out the lines and huffing with frustration, so I guess it's not working the way she wants.

She grabs her phone and glances at the screen. She's got a picture of a new fern leaf there. It's the inspiration for her spiral. With a soft curse, she tosses the phone off to her side.

"Charlie, may I borrow your computer for a minute? I need to look something up online. My phone's screen—"

She breaks off. The screen is too small for her to read. Her vision is getting worse.

"No problem. I could use the break."

"I don't want to disturb your super smart science-y work." Her half grin lights up my insides. She curls up next to me and squints at my open screen. "Dear God," she says, her voice teasing. "Is your computer broken?"

"It's code."

"For broken?"

I slide the computer over to her lap and rest my head on her shoulder. I could use a break from my programming homework. It was meant to be a fun elective, but the class has turned out to be more of a pain in the neck than Finch's class. I smile to myself at that private thought.

Becca knocks once at the front door before barging in. "I come bearing gifts," she announces as she jogs into the room. Her cheeks are pink from the cold air and wind.

"Where've you been?" Charlotte asks, looking up from my laptop. She blinks a few times, her eyes adjusting.

Becca shrugs and waves her off. "The bus takes forever." A flicker of guilt for not being at school this week washes over Charlotte's face, but disappears as soon as Becca drops a large envelope on her lap. "Your missed work."

Charlotte slides my laptop onto the coffee table in front of us so she can examine the pile of assignments.

"And this," Becca says, perching on the edge of the couch beside me, "came for you." She hands me a large envelope, too. Mine has MIT emblazoned on the front and holds my future inside.

Charlotte freezes next to me. I can't seem to pull air into my lungs and have the strange sensation that if I *were* able to, they'd explode. Probably best to just stop breathing altogether right now.

Becca is the only one still moving, bouncing beside me on the couch as she pulls at a lock of hair. "Open it, Charlie," she squeals. "It's a big, fat envelope. That's a good thing."

A good thing.

For seven years, this has been my goal, this envelope in my hands right now. And suddenly all I want to do is throw it across the room and dive back into Charlotte's arms. Part of me is angry. Angry that I can't enjoy this moment. I should be screaming and punching the air and calling Greta. Right. This. Minute.

I set the envelope next to my laptop. "Will you excuse me?"

"But, Charlie?" Becca's confusion reaches out for me, trying to probe for answers I don't have. I stand and move to the other side of the coffee table.

"I need a minute," I say, looking at Charlotte—my beautiful Charlotte, an ocean of sadness behind her eyes.

She fakes a brave smile, sliding closer to Becca, patting her knee. "We're not going anywhere."

How I wish that were true. The anger and fear are choking me, making little black spots dance in my peripheral. I stride from the room, out into the backyard, pulling out my phone.

"What's up, Chuck?" Greta answers on the first ring.

"Gret." I can't seem to get anything else out. All my shallow breathing is catching up to me. I sit on a lounge chair on the patio and put my head between my knees.

"Chuck?" The worry in her voice has ratcheted up a half dozen notches.

"I got in."

There's a pause before she offers, "Congratulations."

"I feel like shit."

"I'm sorry." Another pause. "Where are you? Do you need me to come get you?"

I swallow a chunk of emotion that's choking me. "I'm at Charlotte's. How do I celebrate this with her? How do I leave her next year? How did I get into this mess, Gret? How?" I'm drowning again, tossing around in a body of feelings I can't process.

"Chuck." Greta's voice is an anchor, heavy with purpose, stilling me in the middle of my confusion. "I'm going to need you to chill the fuck out."

I'm surprised by the short bark of a laugh I cough up. I sit up straighter, suddenly able to breathe a little deeper.

"You are super smart, but you're being super dumb right now. Do you honestly think Charlotte is going to be anything other than happy for you? Do you think she expects you to sit at her feet, putting your life on hold, until she dies? Do you believe we have any say in who we fall for? And, most importantly, did MIT send a financial aid packet because you need to get started with that immediately. MIT is not cheap."

"I haven't opened the envelope yet."

"Well then this whole conversation is premature. What if it's just a really fat rejection letter? Go open your future, Chuck. And do it with your girlfriend. Girls live for that shit."

I rub my stinging eyes with my free hand. "Thanks, Gret."

"Congratulations, Chuck." She hangs up, and I stare at the phone in my hand, watching my breath puff in clouds around it.

Luna pushes herself through the doggie door and sits at my feet, resting her giant head on my knee.

"Did Charlotte send you out here to check on me?" I ask the mighty beast. She cocks one ear and thumps her tail twice.

"Do you need checking on?" Charlotte asks, standing in the open door. She's wrapped in her favorite afghan, clutching it closed at her chest like a robe. Just the sight of her makes my insides relax. I take my first deep breath in too many minutes.

I pat the space beside me on the lounge chair. Charlotte shuffles over. When she sits, she spreads the blanket over my shoulders, too. In her hands, I notice the envelope. She doesn't give it to me, but sets it on her knees.

"It occurred to me that I haven't told you about my plans."

"Plans?" I scratch behind Luna's ears.

"I told you, before. There are places I want to go, things I need to see. You didn't think I'd just be sitting around here twiddling my thumbs, did you?"

"I hadn't—twiddling?"

"I'm packing my car full of canvases and sketch pads, pencils and pens, watercolors and brushes, and then I'm heading out. Going to make a big tour of the U.S. See all the artwork I can possibly see."

I can imagine her doing that, too. Her car littered with coffee cups and sketches. "I could come with you. You know, I haven't seen the Grand Canyon either."

"No. You can't," she says, her fingers tapping a rhythm on the envelope. "Because you have important work to do at MIT."

I pull her into my lap, making Luna skitter back a few steps. Charlotte looks up at me with the saddest damn smile, and my gut hurts like a battering ram just mauled me. "Is there art around Cambridge?"

Her smile transforms, and the heavy weight in my stomach dissipates. "Assloads."

"You'll visit?"

"As often as I can, but I'll be pretty busy."

We both know this is a game, like playing superheroes with Becca when I was six. But just like then, it feels good to make our own realities.

The envelope has gotten pinned between our chests as I've been cradling Charlotte in my lap. She pulls it out and the warmth of her body floods that spot on mine.

"Open it for me?"

She nods, her fingers trembling as she opens the flap and pulls out the sheaf of papers inside. Resting her head on my shoulder, she reads, "Dear Charles, On behalf of the admissions committee, it is my pleasure to offer you admission to the MIT Class of—"

I stop her with a kiss and taste on her lips the silent tears that slipped down her cheeks as she read. And part of me is sad that when I think back on this moment, the taste of the ocean will always linger in my memories. But most of me is happy to share this with Charlotte—my beautiful Charlotte with an ocean of unlived moments behind her eyes.

6.7

Even though she's taking anti-seizure meds, no one thinks it's a good idea for Charlotte to drive long distances. When she asks to go visit their dad, I watch a flurry of panic, distaste, and resolve wash over Ms. Finch's face.

I'm getting pretty good at reading both of the Finch sisters' expressions. They are variations on a theme.

Like the expression of gratitude Ms. Finch bestowed on me the day I officially put the Brighton revolution to rest. Between me telling off Brad while flailing a dead pig in his face and Greta's big mouth, it was pretty clear the Tuesday I came back to school after skipping that a truce had been called. To be sure everyone was clear, I waited by the podium at the front of the classroom for Ms. Finch. When she arrived with her coffee, I wasted no time asking her, "Do you think you could recommend another book for me to read? I liked that Atticus character. Are there other books with heroes like him?"

Everyone waited for the punch line, but when it never came, they understood, it was truly over. I kind of like her class now that I don't have to be a dick anymore.

"I can take her," I tell Ms. Finch now. I rub Charlotte's knee. "I'll take you to see your dad." It'd be the first time since our disastrous date that we've gone anywhere, just the two of us, together.

"I can drive," Charlotte says through gritted teeth. I forgot to mention she is the only one in disagreement about the driving thing. "It's just a day trip."

"I want to help," I say, winking at her. "Would it be so bad if you let me help?"

Charlotte looks like her saliva is lemon juice. Ms. Finch presses her lips together to keep from laughing at the expression on Charlotte's face. "Let's let the boy help. I think he's earned the chance."

I lean in and kiss Charlotte's cheek. "It'll be nice to have some time alone together."

Her mood perks up after that.

Charlotte falls asleep on the drive to the small mountain town where her dad lives, a few hours from us. When she's sleeping, the shadows under her eyes lighten and the now constant crease of pain between her brows releases. When she's sleeping, she looks like the girl with the hope tattoo that I met in what is beginning to feel like another lifetime.

I can't bear to wake her.

The town I pull into looks like a backdrop from an old movie. Black and white cows dot the foothills that nestle up to the tired, crumbly Appalachian Mountains. Houses are scattered down long winding lanes, and on a distant hilltop there's a white church steeple cutting through the blue sky. I drive around town making turns at random, not wanting to stop the car for fear of waking Charlotte. I don't realize it until I've arrived, but I've been slowly making my way to the old church.

I pull into the parking lot, where the pavement buckles and entire bushes are growing up through the gaps. On closer inspection, this is not at all what I was expecting. It isn't a picturesque old church. It's an *old* old church. The double doors are hanging askew with boards over them. Half the windows are boarded over, too.

The paint is peeling and the spire on the steeple is bent. Behind the church are a handful of graves peeking out of the underbrush. An uninvited shiver runs down my spine.

"Creepy, huh?"

"Ahhaarraahheeeee!" My seat belt is the only thing keeping me in my seat.

Charlotte laughs.

"Not funny."

Between her laughter, she croaks, "Oh, but it is so, so funny."

"I thought you were asleep."

"I was until the ghosts of this place shook me awake," she says, holstering her laughter. "What are we doing here?"

"I didn't want to wake you, so I just drove around. I ended up here."

"Interesting. Everyone in town says it's haunted, you know. The church," Charlotte nods toward the sagging building. "It's one of the better ghost stories around. The preacher fell in love with a young woman in the parish, but she spurned his advances."

"Spurned?"

"Yeah, spurned. It's not as spooky if I say she thought he was lame and dissed him. So she spurned his advances, and he hung himself right there in the church. Legend has it that if you peek in the stained glass windows on a full moon night, you can see him dangling from the center beam."

"Have you ever seen him?"

"I don't believe in ghosts."

"But if you don't believe in ghosts, how will you come back to haunt me?"

A wisp of a smile crosses her face. "Damn, you're smart. Okay. I'm the only ghost I believe in."

"And my haunting?"

She grabs my hand. "I'd be honored to scare the bejesus out of you. Maybe you'll wake one morning to find all your science books have been replaced with the complete works of Shakespeare. Or all the precious formulas on your white board have been replaced with quotes from Jane Austen's *Sense and Sensibility*."

"How will I know it's you and not some random science-hating specter?"

"Well, we've already established I'll be keeping my hair," she says, tugging my hand closer to her. She opens my fingers and presses her soft lips to my palm before looking up at me. "You'll know."

Would it be wrong to ravage my girlfriend in the parking lot of a haunted church? I swallow back my want as Charlotte opens her door. A wisp of cool air curls around my ankles. The weather may be warming up where we've come from, but the mountain air still clings to winter like the Kudzu strangling the trees back home.

"Come on," Charlotte says, motioning for me to follow. "I want to introduce you to some friends."

Friends? In a cemetery? Dementia is an advanced symptom of brain tumors. But the devilish grin she gives me says she knows exactly what she's doing. I reach in the backseat for our coats. Meeting her at the edge of the parking lot, I help her into hers.

Charlotte high steps her way through the underbrush. "As you've probably surmised, there isn't a lot to do in this town. Kids have to be creative. Finding spooky places and daring each other to see who can stay the longest without freaking out is a popular pastime."

"Oh-kay." I pick my way through the graves, fighting the urge to keep saying, *Sorry. Pardon me. Doh, my bad.* I'd hate to think I was stepping on anyone's hand or leg or face.

"I hold the record for every haunt in town." Charlotte pulls a vine off the face of a tombstone to read the inscription. "Here they are." She brushes pine needles from the top of a long, low stone and sits down. "Charlie, meet the Montgomerys."

I peer around at the stones surrounding us—beloved mother, devoted father, dearest daughter, cherished son, even some teeny tiny stones—all Montgomerys. I shift from foot to foot, uncomfortable around their silence.

"I once spent the whole night out here."

"Why?"

"Someone told me I couldn't." She motions for me to sit next to her, then leans back, closing her eyes and letting the sun wash over her. I sit, silently apologizing if my ass is in someone's face, and try to relax, too. I'm not as brave as Charlotte, though, so I keep fidgeting. Her hand, colder than the stone we're sitting on, sneaks between my elbow and side. I press it there, warming her slender fingers. When she rests her head on my shoulder, I kiss her hair. She smells like sugary gardens blooming in this mountain sunshine. I don't mean to, but my chest feels full of lead, and my eyes sting as they fight to hold back tears.

I hate this place. I hate its stillness. I hate the loneliness of it. I hate the ghosts Charlotte isn't afraid of. The hate is choking me. I jump up, knocking Charlotte off balance, and walk a few paces away from her. I stare up at the sun, willing it to burn away the tears before I cry them in front of Charlotte.

"Charlie?"

I shake my head and wave her away.

"I'm sorry."

I whirl around and kneel before her. "You have nothing to be sorry for," I say, wiping my face with the back of one hand and blindly reaching with the other for her. Her fingers tangle with mine, and I can breathe again. "Nothing."

She leans forward, brushing her lips against mine.

"I'm fine," I whisper into the breath between us. "I was just startled when Mrs. Montgomery's ghost reached out and pinched my butt." I give her a smile. I try to take away the worry in her eyes. "I've never been felt up by a ghost before."

Her eyes smile first, the most beautiful kind of smile. "Strange, since we were sitting on *Mr.* Montgomery." She punctuates the joke with her laughter, which kind of makes me want to cry all over again, but I figure there will be a time for that. It just isn't right now.

6.8

There's nothing special about Charlotte's dad. He's a drunk. He wept from the moment she stepped into the dim, dingy house she used to call home. Like the old church, I can see it was once warm and inviting, but now it's full of shadows, and it smells like old cheese. Charlotte says her dad started drinking after her mom died. She says he's like Juliet without the balls to use the knife. He's slowly poisoning himself instead.

"Baby," he moans into her shoulder as he's hugging her good-bye. "Please, please do the trial. Please." He breaks off sobbing. This is the fifth time in forty-five minutes he's begged.

Charlotte's already explained (four times) why the trial isn't the miracle he's looking for. It's like he's deliberately trying not to hear her so he can keep up his melodrama. It makes me wonder, if she were doing the trial, would he be begging her not to take such a big risk with her life?

Charlotte pulls away from Mr. Finch. He drops his head into his hands and continues to wail. "Let's talk about something else, okay? You're coming to visit for my spring break, right? There's an art show at school I'm entering a few pieces in."

"About that," he says with a sniffle. He stares at a point over her shoulder. "I think I'm going to be too busy here to get away."

Charlotte's face falls, and I wonder why she cares. Why she still tries. "Oh, okay," she murmurs. Clearing her throat, she stands up straighter. "Well, then I'll see you this summer."

Mr. Finch's eyes get full again and he grabs Charlotte up in his arms once more.

"Dad, can't we just say good-bye without the tears? Can't you just give me a big hug and say 'love ya, Charley' and give me a smile?"

It's like she's talking to a toddler. Mr. Finch snuffs out his big tears with the heels of his hands. His bleary eyes lock on mine. "What are you looking at?"

I step back from his anger. "Nothing, sir."

"Think you're better than me? You're nothing. You're just the son of a bitch nothing that's going to let her die." I'm sure he'd come after me if he could stand up straight.

"I'm not going to let her die." I wanted it to come out all macho and loud and shit, but my voice has shrunk. Being around him scares me because I can't hate him like I know I should. Part of me would love to join him, wailing on Charlotte's other shoulder, begging her to stay with me a little longer.

"Don't lie. You're all in this together. You all want me to be miserable."

Charlotte crosses her arms over her chest. "Now you listen to me." Her body trembles as she waits for him to look at her. "You leave him out of this. And Jo, too. This is my choice. This is my life."

He understands. For a picosecond, I saw the understanding wash over him, but Mr. Finch pushes it away, reaching for his glass. He takes a big swig, standing there in a Leaning Tower of Pisa sort of way, and says, "Well don't let me get in the way." He stumbles off with his glass in tow. "Love ya, Charley," I hear him mumble as he rounds the dark corner.

Charlotte makes it to the car before everything falls apart.

This horrible scream tears itself from her lungs, startling the birds around the house so they explode from the trees like machine-gun fire. She beats her purse on top of the car until the strap breaks and then she just uses her fists. Afraid she'll hurt herself, I jump between her and her car, absorbing her fury as best I can, wishing I could draw the pain, like snake venom, from her body.

Eventually, she stops beating on my chest, and I scoop her up in my arms, holding her together as best I can, while sobs rack her body. I press my lips to her forehead, her cheeks, her neck, her hair, her eyelids—infusing her body with as much love as I've got to give. And then a little more.

It takes me 22.41 minutes to pick up all the pieces of Charlotte and patch her back together.

6.9

There comes a point when crying doesn't make you feel better anymore—but never underestimate the power of the donut. There's no Krispy Kreme in this little town, but Charlotte has assured me the ones at Miss Rose's bakery are better.

"That's blasphemy, you know."

Charlotte doesn't argue, but arches a brow at me in a *we'll see* sort of way.

I smile when we reach the bakery. The door is not any old pink— it's flamingo-ass pink.

As soon as we step inside, a large woman wearing a tiny pink apron descends on Charlotte like the Joker in baking gear. She's got flour in her black hair and a big white smile framed by bright pink lips. My instinct is to grab Charlotte and run, but one of the woman's meaty arms reaches out traps me in her crazy bear hug, too.

"Charlotte! Oh, my sweet girl." The woman pulls back, keeping one hand on my shoulder and the other on Charlotte's. "And you've brought me your beau."

She drops Charlotte and takes me in both of her paws to examine me. "He's tall." She turns me this way and that. "And clean."

Charlotte stands next to the woman, admiring me. "He's smart, too, Miss Rose."

"Of course he's smart. He's with you, isn't he?"

"Yes. Yes, he is."

Miss Rose pulls us in for another smothering hug before breaking away and dusting off her hands. "So, what can I get you?" She steps behind her counter, her cheeks flushed.

"As if you have to ask?"

Miss Rose smiles and busies herself putting together a pink cardboard box. "Charlotte, be a dear and get me some fresh cream from the back for your coffee."

Miss Rose watches her go. "Jo tells me things," she says, taking the box to the case and beginning to fill it with donuts.

"Oh, well." My ears are on red alert.

"I'm glad Charlotte has you." She shrugs a shoulder to wipe her cheek. "It's not often we find people that can see through our shortcomings."

"Cancer isn't a shortcoming."

Miss Rose's hand falters and a glazed donut falls to the floor. Her brow wrinkles as she studies it where it has landed. "No, you're right. It's a damn curse," she says, looking up at me. "But maybe I wasn't talking about Charlotte." Her pink lips curl into a wry smile. "As far as I know, Charlotte doesn't have any flaws. Now you, on the other hand…"

A sharp laugh escapes me. "You *have* been talking with Ms. Finch."

Charlotte comes out from the back with a jug of cream and a fresh pastry she snagged. "Talking to Jo about what?"

Miss Rose and I share a look. She smiles at me before pulling Charlotte into another big hug. "How much I've missed you, child," she whispers into Charlotte's hair.

Miss Rose joins us around a small bistro table half her size. She tells me stories about the Finch girls, until Charlotte and I are crying with laughter.

"She was so stubborn," Miss Rose says. "Jo was learning to ride a two-wheeled bike, and Marcus—that's Charley's daddy—said she wasn't big enough. Well, Charley wasn't having any of it."

Charlotte's face takes on a determined light as she remembers. "I didn't want to get left behind."

"That's right," says Miss Rose. "Charley followed Jo around everywhere. So there's Marcus running alongside Jo, encouraging her as she wobbled along, and the next thing we know little Charley comes zooming by on her bike, blood running down her legs and arms like she'd just gotten into a scrabble with a bobcat."

"I stole Daddy's tools and took off my training wheels."

"And taught yourself to ride?"

"It wasn't hard. I only fell twice." Charlotte pulls up her sleeve to show me a scar on her elbow. "It healed up nice."

"How old were you?"

Charley looks to Miss Rose for confirmation. "About four? Not too little at all. Daddy was just overprotective. Guess that's where Jo gets it from."

Miss Rose nods. "After that, we'd see the Finch girls riding all over town together. Inseparable."

Charlotte's eyes get glassy. "I just didn't want to get left behind," she says again, more to herself than to us. She looks up at Miss Rose. "Guess I don't have to worry about that anymore."

"No, child, I guess you won't."

Charlotte gives me a shaky smile, and I pull her chair closer to mine. Miss Rose excuses herself, saying, "We need another round of donuts."

Charlotte and I sit in the bakery window with the afternoon sun glancing off her black curls, my hand touching the small of her back, and the sound of her breathing soft in my ear. I kiss her neck and whisper, "You aren't leaving us behind—not really."

She pulls my face to hers, kissing me fiercely, like if we never come up for air, never move from this moment in space and time, then cancer and the past won't matter because this is all there will ever be from here until forever.

Or from here until Miss Rose comes back with fresh donuts, which she does. She drops the tray on the table with a clang. We pull apart, my ears aflame, Charlotte's cheeks flamingo-ass pink, and try to compose ourselves, but Miss Rose laughs, a loud booming laugh like a church bell. "Oh, excuse me. Did I interrupt something?"

Charlotte growls and throws a donut at Miss Rose, who chuckles and walks to the counter. "Let me get y'all a box so you can be going."

On our way out of town, Charlotte points out the landmarks of her childhood—the playground where she broke her arm, the brightly painted cottage where she took her first art lesson, the junior high basketball court where her friends would meet late at night to play truth or dare.

"What kinds of dares?"

"The usual."

"For the sake of argument, let's say, someone isn't familiar with 'the usual.' Examples?"

Charlotte arches a brow. "Stupid stuff like daring each other to jump off bleachers, sit in the Dumpster for two minutes, or kiss someone everyone knows you have a crush on." She rests her head back, appraising me. "You never played?"

"No one ever asked me to."

"Truth or dare?"

My fingers tingle. I'm not sure I want to play this game. "Uh… truth?"

"When did you first know you wanted to ask me out?"

"The moment you didn't punch me for touching your tattoo at the Krispy Kreme."

She laughs. "For real?"

I nod.

"Do me."

"Excuse me?"

Charlotte rolls her eyes. "Say, 'truth or dare,' Charlie."

"Oh." I grin. "Truth or dare."

"Dare."

Crap. Now what? I drum my fingers on the steering wheel, considering. "Are there limits?"

A smile slithers across Charlotte's face. "What do I have to lose?"

My stomach clenches and I crack my window open to let in a cool breeze. Fast food joints and gas stations begin to dot the landscape as we near another small town. "I think you're feeling hungry, Charlotte," I say, my dare taking shape in my mind.

I slow and pull into the drive-through at a Burger King. Charlotte's wicked smile spreads in anticipation.

"When they ask for your order, you're going to tell them your name and that I'm the best boyfriend in the world."

"That's my dare?" Charlotte leans over me to get closer to the order board. "Rookie," she whispers in my ear.

"Welcome to Burger King. May I take your order, please?"

"Yes, please. My name is Charlotte Elizabeth Finch and my boyfriend Charles Mortimer Hanson has the prettiest penis in all the land."

"Charlotte!"

She dissolves in puddle of laughter.

"Uh…w-well, yes…congratulations, but…would you like fries with that?"

"N-n-no thanks," I splutter before Charlotte's contagious laughter infects me. I peel out of there like a madman, my window still open, and the cool air whipping Charlotte's curls into my face. My body is humming. I've never felt so alive.

Charlotte grazes my jaw with a kiss. "I kind of cheated," she says, peppering my neck with kisses. I'm finding it hard to stay in my lane. "Now I owe you a truth."

It's my turn to arch a brow at her.

"If I thought there was a chance it'd save me, I'd do that trial just to have more time with you." She kisses my neck once more before sitting back in her seat and turning up the radio to sing along. Her voice fills the car and rises through the open window. I imagine it reaching all the way to the great infinite those poets write about.

7.0

Lately I get texts from Charlotte in the middle of the night.

Can't sleep.

The part of me that knows insomnia is a symptom brought on by her growing tumors has a tiny anxiety attack. The rest of me is thankful for the extra time those long nights give us.

On the sleepless nights, we meet on the greenway halfway between our homes and walk for hours, her thumb tracing circles on the back of my hand and making me have to stop every so often and wrap her in my arms. She looks up at me with those eyes of hers, and it takes all my strength to keep standing under their weight. When we kiss, I feel like gravity releases me.

But tonight is different. Tonight is special. Tonight Charlotte is sleeping over. It's the first time in two months. It's the first time since the seizure.

Technically, Charlotte's spending the night with Becca.

I've been in my room for eons, waiting for Charlotte. Mom and Dad went to bed hours ago. And the girls turned off the music 17.54 minutes ago. I slip into bed and pull my pillow over my head to drown out the silence. Maybe I misinterpreted. Maybe this is just another sleepover night, like all the others. Becca and Charlotte holed up together—me alone.

"Charlie, you awake?" Charlotte whispers into the darkness.

I don't see how I'll ever sleep again now that I'll forever hold the memory of Charlotte leaning into my bedroom with my name on her lips, wearing short shorts, and an MIT T-shirt I'd given Becca for Christmas this year.

I can hear her footsteps padding across the carpet. I sit up and make room for her on the bed. She weighs so little the bed barely moves under her as she tucks her body beside mine.

Her fingers drum a rhythm on my chest as she hums a familiar tune. Eventually her fingers slow and the tune drifts away. I bury my face in her curls and listen to her steady breathing, feeling the pulse in her carotid artery as it thrums against my shoulder. It feels strong.

I whisper into her hair, "You asleep?"

Her pulse flies. "Difficult to sleep with something so *stiff* in bed with you," she says.

I can feel my ears flame up.

She giggles. "I didn't realize my being here would make it so *hard* for you to relax."

"You're an idiot," I say, but I'm laughing now, too.

"True, but at least I don't need to *bone up* on my bedroom etiquette like someone else I know." She points toward me and dissolves into laughter. Listening to her laugh is like hearing my favorite song playing on the radio as I drive home on Friday afternoon with the windows open. Down-in-your-soul goodness.

Maybe it's because she's getting too loud or I'm loopy from the sleep deprivation of late or maybe it's the song of her laughter in my head, but I let the words fall from my mouth. "I love you."

She tips her face to mine and I kiss her. Not one of those long, deep, end-of-the-movie type kisses. Just long enough to know I like doing it, and deep enough to know she does, too. So, pretty much, the perfect kiss. When I pull away, I have a goofy just-been-kissed grin on my face, which makes Charlotte start laughing all over. So, I kiss her again. And again.

I get the feeling Charlotte wants to do *more*—that feeling being her hand working its way into my boxers. The thrill of it makes me do this gasp-groan thing in a not-very-sexy kind of way. Charlotte snickers. I kiss her neck to shut her up, working my way to the top of her collarbone just below the neck her T-shirt. As much as I love seeing her in MIT colors, as soon as she lifts her arms above her head, I lose no time dragging the hem of the shirt up along her stomach, exposing her chest, and finally tossing the shirt off to the side.

This is the first set of breasts I've seen in real life. The best part is that they're Charlotte's. My breath catches in my stomach. They are beautiful.

A patch of tight, angry, pink skin just under her right collarbone distracts me. My finger caresses the scar. Charlotte's smile tightens. "What's this?"

"It's from my port." I must look confused because she continues. "Where the chemo drugs go? Or, where they went anyway."

The scar is all I can see. Everything else becomes a blur. Cancer. It is inside of her, eating her, killing her even as her fingers are brushing against my groin. A better man could ignore the panic and give Charlotte what she wants. All I can think is she can't be my first while I'm her last.

"We have to slow down," I say and move away from her enticing fingers. Hands down, hardest thing ever (har har, Charlotte). She looks bewildered. "I mean, Becca is right down the hall. And my parents."

"Right. Of course." Charlotte's whole body has gone rigid.

I try to laugh, but it sounds wrong. "I don't know if I can be quiet." Which seems kinder than saying, *I can't have sex with you because you'll soon be a corpse, which depresses me to the point of flaccidity.*

Charlotte doesn't let me pull too far from her grip. "Charlie, look at me," she says, catching my face in her hands. "It's okay. I love you. It's okay."

My eyes feel heavy with tears and I don't want to cry now. Charlotte's breasts are right there in front of me, and I'm going to have a sobfest? I take a few deep breaths, Charlotte breathing along with me, her hands still holding my face.

"We don't have to do anything you don't want—"

I groan. "I want, Charlotte." Her thumb traces my bottom lip. "I want all of you, but I feel like we're sprinting through this relationship, racing the clock, and no matter how fast we go, there will never be enough time."

I pull her close, our skin melding together, and goddamn it feels so good, but it also hurts so much to know it won't stay like this. I can't make any of it stay.

"What if I'd like to marry you someday? We'll never get that chance."

"Marry me?"

"I know. It's crazy. This is Charles Mortimer Hanson talking crazy here."

"Charlie most couples in high school don't actually get married."

"Are you trying to be logical with me right now? Did you want to talk statistics?" My voice is verging on cracking as it jumps in octaves.

"No," Charlotte says, she brushes my hair from my forehead with her fingertips. Holding her this way, lying on our sides with our chests breathing in and out together, her lips are very close to mine. She brushes a kiss over my lips and whispers, "I'd probably marry you, if given the choice."

I swallow. She's just said what I was thinking. I don't know if I'd want to marry her in a few years, but I do know that this stupid, fucking disease is taking that choice away from me. Away from us. And there are so many other choices being stolen. The choice to move in together. The choice to have children together. Big choices, but little ones, too. Like what color should we paint our bedroom? And do we get a dog or a cat?

Charlotte's face is so…despondent, sorrowful, forlorn…all those words the poets in Ms. Finch's books like to use. They all mean the same damn thing.

Sad.

I sigh and burrow my face in the crook of her neck. Her fingers trail along my shoulder blades.

Damn it. I want *happy*. I choose happy.

"There are so many things we're never going to get to do with each other," I say and kiss the spot I love behind her ear.

Her breath catches. She slides her hands down my spine.

"We get now," I murmur in her ear. She shivers beside me. "We get *this*." I lift my head and kiss her tattoo. "I like this."

I drown myself in the endless sweetness of her mouth.

7.1

Light filters through my blinds as the sun rises in the morning. Charlotte is next to me, one arm flung over my chest and a leg hooked in mine. The first thing I notice is how beautiful she looks, even with her mouth slightly parted and her hair matted. She looks real, so real.

The second thing I notice is my full bladder. I manage to slide like a boneless squid off the edge of my bed without waking her. She shifts onto her belly, her breathing soft and slow.

When I slip back into the room, I take time to notice the way the light plays along her spine. I lie down beside her and let my fingers drift from the small of her back to her neck. She murmurs and stirs, just as everything inside of me stirs to life as well. I trace the lines of her tattoo over and over.

I smile at the memory of our first meeting. So much has changed. I lean in and kiss her neck. She turns her face and catches my mouth with hers, her hands pulling me closer, her leg wrapping around me again.

"Good morning," she sighs when the kiss ends. She flattens her right hand over the center of my chest, studying her fingers there.

"Tell me about your tattoo, Charlotte."

She looks up at me, a playful quirk in one eyebrow. "Which one?"

"You've got more than one?" My eyes scan her body, looking

for something I missed last night. She's wearing shorts that show most of her legs and nothing else. I can't find any other tattoos, which means…holy crap—I try to angle my hips away from her.

Charlotte grabs my hips and pulls me back. "Oh, no you don't," she says as she laughs. The sound is victorious. She's got me right where she wants me. "Got my first tat when I was fifteen." She slides her hands from my hips to cup my butt.

"What did your sister say?" I squeak.

She pulls away, her eyebrows high. "Seriously? You're thinking of my sister right now?" I groan and she smiles before nipping at my chin. "Jo was thrilled. It's where they zapped me with the radiation therapy."

I try not to flinch, but I feel like I've been slapped. "Oh."

She places my hand on the side of her head. "It's here," she says, pressing our fingers together over the spot. "I thought I was seriously badass, but when my hair grew back, you couldn't see it anymore. I figured since the doctors got to pick my first one, I should get to pick one, too."

I slide my fingers out of her hair to the nape of her neck. "And you chose hope."

She nods, tears magnifying her eyes.

"What do you hope for, Charlotte?"

She takes a shaky breath and kisses me, like she can press her lips to mine and regain her strength. "I hope Jo learns to relax and take care of herself for a change. I hope Becca continues to have adventures that aren't confined by the margins of a book." She tightens her grip around my neck and looks up at me. "And I hope that your life gives you everything you truly need."

My throat feels bloated, and I have to clear it before I can speak. "What about you? What do you hope for yourself?"

She bites the corner of her bottom lip, her eyes darting up like she's considering. "I'm kind of hoping that you'll shut up and kiss me."

0.0

My phone rings. Bleary-eyed, I look at the screen and see it's Charlotte. It's also 4:38 a.m., but that's not unusual. Charlotte's insomnia has been out of control the past few weeks. She's living on catnaps and coffee.

"Hey," I say, clearing the sleep from my throat. "You okay?"

She doesn't answer. Not really. All I hear is sobbing.

"Charlotte?"

The sobs build on each other, until they've formed a giant wall of sadness. Without thinking, I'm up and pulling on a T-shirt and shoes. "I'm coming."

I grab my keys from the counter and make it to my car before she's quieted down enough to speak, but her voice is so raw from all the crying that I can barely make out what she's saying. I put the keys in the ignition and switch the phone to my other hand. "Charlotte, just breathe. It'll be okay."

"Hanson…"

Not Charlotte.

"Charlotte is—" The rest is washed away with a wave of fresh sobs.

I hang up the phone.

This is my absolute zero.

I. Am. Nothing.

I am without Charlotte.

0.1

I now understand the expression, *That's when the bottom drops out*. As a general rule, idioms are stupid, but this one, *the bottom drops out*, this one I totally get.

Gravity is a constant force in all of our lives, pulling us at 9.80665 m/s^2 to be exact. But, I swear, when the bottom drops out, gravity pulls at me much faster than is physically possible. There's no hope. The force of my landing will annihilate me.

I drive to Charlotte's house. Every muscle in my body feels like lead, so I'm driving fast, the wheels screeching as my heavy arms struggle to make the turns.

Be there. Be okay. Be there. Be okay. Be there. Be okay. My mind can't move beyond these two phrases. They are the parachute I pull during free fall.

Ms. Finch is waiting for me. Her long hair is pulled into a messy ponytail that makes her look younger than she is. But the redness around her eyes and the emptiness within them give the impression of too many years.

"She's gone," Ms. Finch says. These words, too, are made of the heaviest elements. They clatter at our feet.

I push past her, taking the stairs two at a time, Luna loping after me, beating me to the top. Ms. Finch calls out, "She's not here.

She's gone."

Be there. Be okay. Be there. Be okay. Be there. Be okay. I will get to Charlotte's room and she will be there. She will be okay. It's the only reality that makes sense. When I lift the lid, the cat will be alive. The cat has to be alive.

I'm about to charge into Charlotte's room when I suddenly panic. What if she's sleeping? I'd feel like a shit if I woke her. I whisper for Luna to stay. She sits on her haunches and whines. "Shh," I say, holding a finger to my lips. Luna's ears flick backward.

The blinds are open so moonlight pools into the room. I creep toward her bed, stepping carefully to avoid tripping over the debris on her floor. I place my hand on the end of her bed, sliding myself forward, lowering my face. My eyes adjust to the empty darkness.

Fucking cat.

I can't be here. I can't be in this room. I can't be where she was. I want to be where she is.

Luna follows me to the kitchen where we find Ms. Finch sitting at the counter staring at an empty coffee mug. Her hands are wrapped around it in a stranglehold. Tears follow the canyons carved down her face from earlier tears.

I envy her. I envy her sadness. I feel nothing right now, which some might think is a blessing, except I can't even feel the good stuff, like the love I know I have for Charlotte. It's buried, too. I can't reach it, so I sit like a stone and watch Ms. Finch grieve instead.

Those websites I found for teens with cancer also had sections for parents and friends. The stages of grief were outlined very clearly: Denial and isolation, anger, bargaining, depression, and acceptance. According to the testimonies I read from grieving parents, the stages don't always happen in order and often you move from one to another only to cycle right back where you started. It sounds horrible, unpredictable, and completely unavoidable.

Ms. Finch is currently at stage two.

"She's gone. She left us." She spits the words. "She's somewhere else and we're left here. Alone." She stands, her arms shaky as she braces them on the counter. Then her right arm is a blur, and she's hurling the coffee mug as hard as she can at the refrigerator. It hits the metal, a loud crack piercing the air, and shatters as it falls to the floor. Luna skitters back, watching Ms. Finch intently.

"They took her away in the ambulance," she hiccups, trying to regain control. "When we got to the hospital, a doctor told me she'd had a stroke—bleeding from the tumors." She's yelling and her voice has gone all raspy. It makes my whole body ache to hear her. "He said it was quick. She wouldn't have felt any pain. He said it like it matters. Like *anything* matters now."

I'm not sure why I'm here. I knew from the moment I heard Ms. Finch say, "Hanson," that Charlotte was gone. Why did I come? But now that I'm sitting here, looking at the couch where I held Charlotte's head in my lap as we watched her favorite movies, I can't leave. Except Charlotte isn't on the couch.

Once again, I'm left with the wrong Finch.

"It should have been me."

I'm brought back from my thoughts—scared I may have said that last bit out loud.

"From the moment she was diagnosed, I believed someone had made a grave mistake," Ms. Finch says. "If one of us had to go, it should have been me."

I should tell her she's wrong. But I can't. If it could have been anyone else, I wish it had been me.

Welcome to phase three.

0.2

I don't remember driving home, but sure enough, here I am. Mom and Dad have already left for school. Hearing the car pull up, Becca bounds out the front door. Too late, I glance at the clock in the dashboard and realize this is when Charlotte should be picking Becca up for school.

Becca freezes mid-step when she sees me. She knows. Before I can say anything, she charges back through the front door. I race inside after her, but I hear her bedroom door slam as I hit the bottom step.

"Becca?" I knock.

No response. Becca has chosen to dive right into stage one. Isolation.

"Becca, please don't make me do this from the other side of a door." I try the knob, but it's locked. I slide down, making a puddle of myself on the carpet in the hall.

Melting this way makes it easier to ignore the feeling that my chest is caving in. I feel like my whole body will become a black hole of pain. For the life of me, I cannot imagine why people want to fall in love when it will inevitably end like this. If I can survive this, I swear, I'll never do anything so stupid again.

I hear movement behind the door. "Bec?" A muffled thud and

the breeze-like sound of pages being fanned is her only reply. Is she reading? Now? I'll never be able to drag her out from her stories.

"I'm so sorry, Bec." There's more I need to say, but the silence buries me.

0.3

"Chuck?" Greta's voice calls from downstairs.

I hear two sets of feet. I consider counting the footfalls, but fuck it.

"Chuck!" Greta rushes over, pulling me up into a hug before holding me at arm's length to examine me. "There's a substitute in English. What happened?"

"Charlotte—" Nope. I can't say it. How did I think I could tell Becca when I can't even tell Greta? *Hello, Denial. Why don't you go fuck yourself and your little friend Anger?*

"Oh, Chuck, I'm so sorry." Greta's face crumples. Somehow, I feel like slapping her. Like her grief takes away from mine. And I want all of mine. I want it to crush me into oblivion.

When I speak, the words taste like nails in my mouth. "Don't. Please."

James stoops beside Greta. "How's Becca?"

I look away from the two of them. "Dunno. She won't open the door."

James nods. "I can fix that," he says, reaching into Greta's hair and extracting a bobby pin. He straightens it and pokes it into the little hole in the knob, and then jiggles it until we hear a click.

Greta looks impressed and outraged.

"I live with a house full of drama queens," he says, shrugging.

I open the door, calling, "Bec?" I expect to see her in her nest with a book, but what I find is unbearable.

She's taken every book in her room and laid them like bricks in a circle around her. Crazy part is the books aren't all closed, most are open to random pages then stacked, like she was looking for something in them and the resulting wall was an accident as she tossed them aside and grabbed a new book.

My throat feels full. My hands fall away from where I'd been gripping the doorframe and rest limply at my sides.

"Oh, Bec." I circle the wall. "Don't disappear on me, too." It's only a whisper.

I drag the wooden desk chair across the carpet toward the book wall and hop up so I can look down to see Becca inside. She looks so small, buried under all those stories. "Hey."

She flinches and burrows deeper in her nest at the heart of the fortress.

"Bec—" But I stop myself. I was about to tell her about the stroke and how Charlotte died so quickly she didn't even know it. How in the hell is that supposed to make anyone feel better? I'd like to drive to the hospital and slug a doctor—any doctor will do.

Becca's shoulders slump forward even further, like she's a mountain caving in under the weight of my stare. I sit down in the chair, and all I can see are the books. I sigh. "Dammit, Bec."

No response.

From my seat, I notice a chink in the wall. It's a space in which there is an absence of a book more than anything else. I whisper into the space, "I'm sorry. I know it's not enough, but I love you."

I stand to put the chair away, managing to knock its legs into the desk and tip over a picture frame. I pick it up and am blinded by instant tears that refuse to fall. Smiling back at me is Charlotte, one arm wrapped around Becca and the other around me. The picture is from Becca's sixteenth birthday dinner, the first and only one to which she invited a friend.

Bringing it back to the wall, I nudge it into the place that is not a book. "When you're ready to come out, I'm here. I can wait."

Greta shifts next to me. I'd forgotten she and James were here. I stub out my tears with the backs of my wrists and offer a weak smile. It feels awful, so I let it slide away. "I need to get out of here."

"Where do you want to go?" James asks.

"No. By myself."

"That's maybe not a good idea, Chuck."

"I'm not asking for permission." Greta flinches, and I feel like a schmuck for being so angry, but I don't want any part of either of them right now. It's like I'm pissed at them for having heartbeats and brain waves and circulatory systems that are still up and running.

And while I know this is normal, this is the way the human psyche has evolved over the ages to survive loss, the knowing doesn't make it feel any better, which is a first. Knowing is always better than not knowing. Or at least, it was.

I push past them and take the stairs in great leaps to get away faster. I climb in my car, hoping to drive away from the large crater in my chest where goodness and hope and Charlotte used to be.

0.4

I drive without knowing where I'm going. I'm out in the farmland that surrounds the suburbs. My phone rings, but I don't answer. James texts me once.

Dude?

Greta sends three.

Where are you?

Are you ok in there?

Don't be stupid.

Oh, I'm well past stupid. I left stupid in the dust when I thought I could handle a serious relationship with a terminally ill girl. A gorgeous, talented, funny, and most awesomest girl in the world. But still, a girl destined to leave me.

I scan the horizon. Soybeans and tobacco as far as the eye can see. The road curves and I follow it. On the horizon is a dilapidated structure practically falling in on itself. The physics involved in holding its shape are beyond my scope. It's the ghost of a barn.

I'm reminded of Charlotte's painting. *I am. The barn.* Part of me wants to pull a fast U-turn and haul balls home. The part in control of the car slows down and pulls onto the dusty shoulder.

I march through high grass, crickets rising like popcorn kernels in hot oil with each step. The early spring sun is still hot even though it is sinking lower in the sky.

When I reach the barn, I place a hand on the worn wood, feeling the sun's heat there. I let myself remember Charlotte and the warm smell of her skin. Charlotte always smelled like vanilla, like sugar cookies just out of the oven.

I think of the Harvest Moon and how it reminded Mrs. Dunwitty of her youth, even when she was so far away from it. But the memory of Charlotte is painful. Whenever I get a whiff of a bakery, will I feel like shit? Even when I'm eighty? I need to tell Becca no cookies can be served in whatever old folks' home she dumps me in. The more sterile the better. I can't think of any memories involving industrial cleaning products.

I don't know when the madness slips in, but I start talking to the barn like it's Charlotte. At first, I'm moaning stuff like, "How am I supposed to go on without you?" Melodramatic crap. Soon though, I'm telling her all the things I should have said, but never did. Things like, "I love the way your nose wrinkles when you smile."

I wonder if I can stay here. The thought of going back and facing my friends and family and Ms. Finch and school and all the dumb expectations I had for my life feels overwhelming. Definitely unappealing. I could hide in this barn, this falling down wreck of a barn, until everyone forgets about me. I could hide here with nothing but Charlotte in my mind.

I don't want to go back because as soon as I do, everyone will try to help me forget her. I promised I wouldn't forget, and if that means hanging on to this pain until I die, then that's what I will do.

I lie down on the warm earth and shut my eyes, willing Charlotte to me. She's tilting her head back and closing her eyes, too. Our fingers are tangled together, so it's hard to tell which are mine and which are hers. She's so beautiful and so alive—if only for that one moment.

I don't know what step on the whole grieving process this is, but man does it hurt. Tears leak out in streams that run down the sides of my face, dripping along my ears, and pooling in the dry dirt.

0.5

I walk into a maelstrom of activity when I get back. Dad is staring into a huge pot of soup on the stove even though it's one of those classic southern spring-is-for-wussies-so-how's-about-we-jump-straight-to-90-degrees days. Mom is upstairs, and I can hear her pleading with Becca to come down. Greta is pacing the kitchen, gnawing on her fingernails, as James plows through the last of the chips in a jumbo-sized bag.

I freeze in the entryway enjoying the last few seconds of anonymity before they notice me. Then I'll be the guy with the dead girlfriend and everyone will examine me like I'm a time bomb. I understand now how Charlotte must have felt trapped inside her cancer with no way to escape it while we stood around watching her like she was a caged bird.

I drop my keys on the counter and everyone turns to look at me. Somehow, even Mom heard it over her own voice. She comes barreling down the back staircase, eyes wild, and hair sticking out in odd places. She reaches the bottom step and freezes. No one speaks.

"I'm sorry," I say to them all. "I needed some time."

They still don't move. Dad asks, "But you're okay?"

"No. Not really." I try a smile, but it's like it doesn't fit on my face anymore. "But I'm not the Romeo type, so everyone can relax."

Dad's mouth pulls up on one side, and he turns away to stir his soup. James grabs Greta's hand from where she's biting at her cuticles. Mom approaches me like I'm a wounded animal she's not sure about. She reaches out and runs her fingers through my hair, then hugs me and smothers me all at the same time. I give in to the comfort of it for a second before I pull away.

"I've got to talk to Becca." I squeeze mom's arm before going up to Becca's room.

I pull the chair back over to the wall and climb up. "Hey!"

Her eyes flit up to mine.

"Good," I say. "Eye contact is good. Now, how about coming out of there?"

Becca looks back down at the book in her lap. I can just make out one page. A brown rabbit pokes out of a garbage sack as a fairy with electric blue eyes flits above its head. It's the copy of *The Velveteen Rabbit* that Charlotte illustrated for her.

"Oh, Bec."

The silence from within her wall shatters into big, hiccupping sobs.

"Please, come out, Bec. Please?"

She nods, the barest of movements, but it's all I need to start chucking books off the top of the wall. Inside, she stands and starts to push them away from her. Open books cascade like an avalanche of snowy paper. I hurdle over the books between us and grab her in a big hug.

She disintegrates, and it's all I can do to catch her and hold her while she sobs and melts through my fingers. I realize I'm not alone. Becca won't forget either.

0.6

The funeral is the worst thing I've ever endured. I've decided I hate funeral flowers more than I hate poetry. I leave the rose Mrs. Dunwitty gave me on Charlotte's coffin. I think it'd make both of them happy. I don't want to talk about it anymore. Possibly ever.

Charlotte's buried in a cemetery next to her mother. There's space for Mr. Finch and Ms. Finch. It's a family plot. There's no room for me.

We stop at a gas station on our way out of town. Greta and Becca go inside to use the restroom. I pump the gas.

"It's getting cold," James says as he climbs out from the back-seat. "You got a sweatshirt or something?"

I nod toward the trunk and toss him the keys. He unlocks it and swears. "Jesus, Charlie. This trunk is disgusting. How do you find anything?"

"I don't. It's where I put things to forget about them."

"Wait, I see a sweatshirt trapped under all this crap. I'll save you." He dives in, his feet kicking in the air. I shake my head as I walk around to help him.

"You can relax," says James, as he scrambles back out of the trunk with the hoodie. "You're safe now." He pulls it on, and even though it's big on me, it looks like he went shopping at the baby gap.

I smirk.

"Little tight," James grimaces. "You need to clean this trunk, man. I may have even seen a body back there."

I chuckle and peer further into the depths of my trunk. My heart misses a step as I recognize a face. Mrs. Dunwitty's angel. The angel I smashed in a time and place far from this reality. She is lying on her side, broken wing lost somewhere in the clutter, neglected.

"Get me that trash can," I say, pointing toward the pumps.

"Man, I didn't mean clean it now."

"Trash can," I plead and start pulling out crap as fast as I can. As James returns, dragging the heavy canister, I emerge from my trunk, arms full of papers, fast food wrappers, and a single shoe. I shove it all in the can and dive back for more. My hands shake and I feel like I'm moving through Jell-O. I can't get the stuff out fast enough.

I look at James. Behind him, Becca and Greta are walking toward us from the station.

"Help me."

James nods and starts to pull out papers and soda bottles. He holds a few questionable things up, dangling each over the trash can in turn and asking, "Trash?" Things like gym shorts, an old duffle bag, and a science journal stolen from my dad's office at school. For each of these I grunt and nod. Trash, trash, trash. It's all trash.

But then James is holding a can of flamingo-ass paint over the can and jiggling it, saying, "Trash?"

"No!" I rescue the paint can and dig around to find the brush, setting them to one side.

After a few more armloads, the trunk is empty except for the angel, her wing, the paint, and paintbrush. I'm frozen in the angel's concrete stare until James clears his throat beside me.

"It looks much better, but we should get on the road. Don't you think?" He places one hand on my shoulder and the other on the trunk lid, ready to close it. I nod, still watching the angel watch me. "Okay, good," he says as he begins to close the trunk.

"Wait!" I shout and brace the lid. I reach in and pull the angel out. She's heavy. My body strains against her weight. But I lift her out and hug her to my chest.

James looks at me as if he's wondering what size straightjacket to get me for my birthday. He screws up his mouth into a twisted half-grimace. I can't meet his eyes, so I look down at the angel in my arms and say, "Okay, now I'm good."

Greta recognizes the angel. "Oh," she says, like she's been holding her breath for too long. She helps me place the angel on the bench seat in the back. She slides in on one side and braces it with her arm. I do the same with mine.

From the front seat, I can hear Becca sniffle. I pull Mrs. Dunwitty's handkerchief from my suit coat pocket and hand it to her.

"Where to?" James asks from the driver's seat.

"I need to see Charlotte one more time."

James nods and puts the car in gear.

Becca wipes her tears on Mrs. Dunwitty's starched white handkerchief that still smells a little like the Harvest Moon it cradled. She looks from me to the angel and back again. "Charlotte will love her, Charlie."

I nod and hold more tightly to my angel.

"You make a good hero." Becca's voice is a whisper of wings. "Atticus would be proud."

0.7

The cemetery sits in a valley, surrounded by rolling green hills, ringed by woods. The funeral home has taken away the tent and chairs, but from the parking lot I can still see the huge bouquets of flowers surrounding the place where Charlotte lies.

I heft my angel out from the backseat. James hops out and pops the trunk lid. I feel good now that I have a plan, like I'm in charge of at least one small thing in this world.

"Bec, could you grab that paint and brush?"

Becca peers into the clean trunk. "Is this her wing?" she asks, holding up my angel's broken wing. I nod. She takes the wing and the paint supplies.

Greta comes around to the back, too, and asks with definite mom-ness in her tone, "Whatcha doing with the paint, Chuck?"

James touches Greta's shoulder to keep her from following. "Let him go."

"What's he going to do?"

"Whatever he has to do." He closes the trunk, and as I walk away, I hear him saying something about trusting me for once and haven't I grown this year and Greta isn't the boss of me.

She punches him in the shoulder saying, "I'm the boss of everyone." And he laughs and pulls her close, kissing her on the top of her head.

Becca and I walk through the maze of graves. The angel is pretty small (as angels go), but she feels heavier the closer I get to Charlotte. There's a layer of sod covering her grave, bits of black earth visible in the seams. I place the angel at Charlotte's head.

"I hate that she's broken," I say, straightening the statue so she can watch over Charlotte.

Becca takes Mrs. Dunwitty's handkerchief from her pocket, saying, "Hold her steady."

I kneel beside the angel and watch as Becca ties the handkerchief like a sling, fastening the wing back on the statue.

"How'd you do that?" I ask.

"It's not like I fixed it, really. I just made it more bearable." She leans across the angel and kisses me on the cheek like she did when she was a little girl. Her eyes are calm.

She dips her head toward the earth where Charlotte lies. "Best friends forever," she whispers. She only glances back once as she returns to the car.

As I paint the angel pink, I think about the Finches, and all I've learned from them. The more I think, the more confused I become. There's no way to sort it out right now, and in the end, there's no reason to. I have plenty of time. Perhaps I'll be an old curmudgeon like Dimwit one day. Imagine how genius I could be with so much time to sort through this mess.

Or not.

What I do know is that the world looks different crouching here on Charlotte Finch's grave, a paintbrush in hand, the smell of flowers in my nose. From here, the world looks less like the orderly line of concrete numbers I had always relied on and more like chaos.

I am so involved in painting the broken wing that I don't hear the footsteps. I feel a change in the air around me and smell a certain familiar perfume—Charlotte, but not quite.

"Hanson, what are you doing?" Ms. Finch asks.

"She shouldn't be alone."

There's silence behind me. I keep painting. Luna sits beside me, watching my every move, like she's still protecting Charlotte somehow.

I finish the wings before I face Ms. Finch. She's changed out of her funeral clothes. Her blue eyes are ringed with red and her skin is as pale as the bleached stones in the oldest section of the cemetery. She looks like hell.

I hold out the paint can and brush and nod at the angel. "Want a turn?"

Ms Finch stares at the angel. "She's broken," she mumbles.

"It happens," I say. "But, see? She's on the mend."

"How did she break?"

"I ran her over with my car." I smile at the memory of my time with Mrs. Dunwitty.

Ms. Finch laughs, a short, hard sound. She runs a finger over the handkerchief holding on the broken wing. "Hand over that brush."

I watch her in the failing light. Her eyes focus on each molecule of paint adhering to the rough stone of the angel's body. And I have to know.

"Are you coming back to school?"

"No." She paints a few more strokes and lets the brush fall across her lap.

"For what it's worth, you were a good teacher."

She smiles crookedly and something that should have been a laugh gurgles in her throat.

Ms. Finch finishes painting. She sets the brush down and wipes her fingers on her jeans, leaving pink smudges along her thighs. "I have something for you." She reaches into the purse behind her. "I wasn't going to give it back. I'm sorry about that."

A familiar paperback novel is in her hands.

"No," I say, an electric current coursing through my spine, "I gave that back to Charlotte. It belongs to you."

Ms. Finch opens the book to the page with the inscriptions. "Not anymore," she says as she leans across Charlotte's grave to hand me the book. Inscribed in Charlotte's looping script I see my own name.

> To other Charlie, who may need reminding
> he's the reason the mockingbird sings.

I choke back a sob and flip through the pages, running my finger along the lines of the drawings as if they were the lines of Charlotte's face. I love this book.

0.8

When Ms. Finch leaves, I notice she's in Charlotte's silver Civic with the dented fender. For a moment, I pretend it's Charlotte pulling away. I tell myself that she'll be back. She's just going out for donuts.

It's a nice dream, and short-lived.

"Charlotte, did I ever tell you about time travel?" I pluck a few blades of grass and shred them, my fingers turning green from the chlorophyll. "If you plot your life along the real line, it will encompass a finite space. We begin, move steadily in a positive direction, and end. The bodies we're given aren't meant to last forever." I lie back in the grass beside her. In my mind's eye, our fingertips are touching.

"Here's the bit I never told you. The real line, and I mean the whole line—the line all of our lives and the life of the Universe itself can be plotted along—begins and ends in infinity. If you take that line and make infinity one point, the straight line becomes a circle. It's never ending. Boundless. Infinite. Any two points in the circle can be connected.

"Scientists believe time travel is something like that, in its simplest sense, the leaping across from one part of the circle to another. If it's true, everything lasts forever.

"Which sucks, because it means I will miss you forever. But it's cool, too, because it means in my own stupid way, I get to love you forever."

I don't want to cry anymore right now, so I focus on my infinite circle and pull up a memory that has nothing to do with crying.

In the memory, the afternoon sun is sliced into parallel lines by the blinds in Charlotte's window. We're stretched out on her bed, Charlotte quiet, almost asleep, but she looks up at me, resting her chin on my chest, a question in her eyes, and I'm suddenly terrified I won't know the right answer.

"Are you here because I'm dying?"

"No," I say, my voice cracking, nerves exploding. I feel larger than every infinite set in the infinite universe, because I know the answer. "I'm here because I'm alive."

"Good answer, Charlie Hanson. Good answer," Charlotte says, stretching up to meet my lips. Our fingers tangle in infinite knots.

We kiss, forever.

0.9

I'd like to say my story ends with the kiss, but it has no real end.

A beautiful girl once gave me an extraordinary journal. The infinite possibilities of the blank pages were so intimidating I almost left them blank.

But then, I didn't.

1.0

Beginnings are tricky things. I've been staring at this blank page for forty-seven minutes. It is infinite with possibilities. Once I begin, they diminish.

Scientifically, I know beginnings don't exist. The world is made of energy, which is neither created nor destroyed. Everything she is was here before me. Everything she was will remain. Her existence touches both my past and my future at one point—infinity.

Lifelines aren't lines at all. They're more like circles.

It's safe to start anywhere and the story will curve its way back to the starting point. Eventually.

In other words, it doesn't matter where I begin. It doesn't change the end.

hope

Dear Reader,

Years ago, I sat in a hospital lab with wide windows that let the sun shine in, overlooking a green courtyard bursting with flowers. I joked with my friend, Em, as a nurse in full Hazmat gear hooked her up to a bag full of toxins. There was a small moment, tinier than a breath, where I saw fear flit across Em's face, but then she smiled and the fear was gone, replaced with a joke to keep us laughing and the hope that one day, one of these bags of poison would hold the cure for cancer.

That moment defines bravery for me. And since then, I have tried to face my fears with laughter and a hell of a lot of hope.

My hope for you, readers, is that you find what you are passionate about—be it math like Charlie, drawing like Charlotte, writing, cancer advocacy, animal rescue, or unicorn needlepoint—find it and hold onto it despite any fears you may have. Fill your life with what you love. That's my hope for you.

Yours with heart, humor, and hope. Always hope,

Shannon lee Alexander

Acknowledgments

This story began with encouragement from my friend Emily Bright. Her beautiful life, laugh, and infinite hope inspired me to become a *Real* writer. Thanks, Em, for showing me how to be brave. I'm hopelessly devoted to you!

I want to thank everyone at Entangled who had a hand in bringing Charlie and Charlotte's story to readers. Thank you, Heather Howland, for your enthusiasm, patience, and insight—and for understanding the importance of reaching 1.0. Thanks to Liz Pelletier, Stacy Cantor Abrams, Kari Olson, the entire Entangled Teen team, and the amazing Entangled authors who've been so helpful along this path to publication.

Huge hugs and bouquets of thanks go out to my wonderful agent, Jessica Sinsheimer. Our first phone conversation is plotted on my life's number line thingy as one of my happiest moments. I can't imagine doing any of this without you. Thanks to everyone at Sarah Jane Freymann Literary Agency for your continued support.

Every writer needs an amazing critique group like the YA Cannibals. Mike and Margaret Mullin, Jody Sparks, Robert and Sharmin Kent, Lisa Fipps, and Virginia Vasquez Vought, your critiques, support, and shoulders to cry on were instrumental in helping me tell Charlie's story properly. Thanks for ripping my heart out, Cannibals!

Josh Prokopy and Julia Karr, I'm so glad you've joined us for the fun and bloodshed.

For my friends that have been with me throughout this journey, the coffee is on me! I'd be lost if it weren't for you (and the candy you gave me). Avery, Lisa, Ann, Devee, Tabbatha, and my Gwen, you are all irreplaceable. Cheers!

I have an amazing, insane family that I love to pieces. Thanks to each and every one of you. Special thanks go to Beth Weibust and John Kelley for reading a very early version of this story. Wait until you guys see what I've done with it! Bethann Wilkie, I'm the luckiest big sister in the history of ever to have such an inspiring little sister. Thank you, Mom, for teaching me the art of kindness. And Dad. Well, Atticus has nothing on you.

Finally, without the unflagging love and support of my kids and husband, I would never have had the courage to see this through. Thanks for being my own personal cheering section. I love you all more than anything in this infinite universe.

And to my husband, my heart, my Drew—I'm so glad I wore those hand-me-down jeans on that night long, long ago. You are the center of my circle.

OPPOSITION

by Jennifer L. Armentrout

Katy knows the world changed the night the Luxen came. The lines between good and bad have blurred, and love has become an emotion that could destroy her—could destroy them all. Daemon will do anything to save those he loves, even if it means betrayal. When he and Katy team with an unlikely enemy, it quickly becomes impossible to tell friend from foe. With the world is crumbling around them, they may lose everything—even what they cherish most—to ensure the survival of their friends...and mankind.

THE BOOK OF IVY

by Amy Engel

After a brutal nuclear war, the United States was left decimated. A small group of survivors eventually banded together, but fifty years later, peace and control are only maintained by marrying the daughters of the losing side to the sons of the winning group in a yearly ritual. This year, it is Ivy Westfall's turn. Only her bridegroom is no average boy. He is Bishop Lattimer, the president's son. And Ivy's mission is not simply to marry him. Her mission, one she's been preparing for all her life, is to restore the Westfall family to power...by killing him.

PERFECTED

by Kate Jarvik Birch

Ever since the government passed legislation allowing people to be genetically engineered and raised as pets, the rich and powerful can own beautiful girls like sixteen-year-old Ella as companions. But when Ella moves in with her new masters and discovers the glamorous life she's been promised isn't at all what it seems, she's forced to choose between a pampered existence full of gorgeous gowns and veiled threats, or seizing her chance at freedom with the boy she's come to love, risking both of their lives in a daring escape no one will ever forget.

ANOMALY

by Tonya Kuper

What if the world isn't what we think?

What if reality is only an illusion?

What if you were one of the few who could control it?

Yeah, Josie Harper didn't believe it, either, until strange things started happening. And when this hot guy tried to kidnap her… Well, that's when things got real. Now Josie's got it bad for a boy who weakens her every time he's near and a world of enemies want to control her gift. She's going to need more than just her wits if she hopes to survive much longer.

THE WINTER PEOPLE

by Rebekah L. Purdy

Salome Montgomery is a key player in a world she's tried for years to avoid. At the center of it is the strange and beautiful Nevin. Cursed with dark secrets and knowledge of the creatures in the woods, his interactions with Salome take her life in a new direction. A direction where she'll have to decide between her longtime crush Colton, who could cure her fear of winter. Or Nevin who, along with an appointed bodyguard, Gareth, protects her from the darkness that swirls in the snowy backdrop. An evil that, given the chance, will kill her.

SCINTILLATE

by Tracy Clark

Cora Sandoval sees colorful light around everyone—except herself. Instead, she glows a brilliant, sparkling silver. As she realizes the danger associated with these strange auras, she is inexplicably drawn to Finn, a gorgeous Irish exchange student who makes her feel safe. Their attraction is instant, magnetic, and primal—but her father disapproves. After Finn is forced to return home to Ireland, Cora follows him. There she meets another silver-haloed person and discovers the meaning of her newfound powers and their role in a conspiracy spanning centuries—one that could change mankind forever…and end her life.

WHATEVER LIFE THROWS AT YOU

by Julie Cross

When seventeen-year-old track star Annie Lucas's dad starts mentoring nineteen-year-old baseball rookie phenom, Jason Brody, Annie's convinced she knows his type—arrogant, bossy, and most likely not into high school girls. But as Brody and her father grow closer, Annie starts to see through his façade to the lonely boy in over his head. When opening day comes around and her dad—and Brody's—job is on the line, she's reminded why he's off-limits. But Brody needs her, and staying away isn't an option.